A Taste for Death

MODESTY BLAISE

A TASTE FOR DEATH

Peter O'Donnell

SOUVENIR PRESS

FOR
KATIE AND BERNIE

I

As a cautious man, Willie Garvin felt he had a right to be annoyed.

He had checked that his scuba gear was in perfect condition. He had rubbed a cigarette butt over the outside of the wrap-round mask, to keep the water flowing smoothly over the lens and prevent distortion. He had rubbed the inside with kelp, to prevent misting. He had made frequent adjustments to the air demand regulator, knowing that a depth variation of only a few inches called for compensation to give easy breathing.

He also knew, from the stainless steel Rolex on his wrist, that he had been at a depth of forty feet for seventeen minutes on this dive, his sixth of the day. That made a total of over two hours, which meant that on the ascent he must take a two minute pause at ten feet below the surface, for decompression.

In short, he had observed all the rules with great care; and then, on a bed of sand and coral, he had kicked back with the bare heel of his rubber-finned foot against the needle-sharp spines of a sea star.

Impossible to speak his feelings aloud under water. Difficult even to curse mentally, for there was a tendency to hold the breath, and to do this while scuba diving was to invite trouble.

Patiently, breathing evenly, Willie Garvin set down the big rope basket and eased the flipper from his foot. With his prying-iron he carefully detached the sea star from the rock to which it clung. Scarlet spines rippled around a huge leathery body that measured two feet across. The tips of some of those spines, with their own unpleasant poison, were broken off in the flesh of his heel.

Using the iron, he turned the quivering body over and thrust

7

his heel against the vent on its soft underside. At once he felt the fierce suction.

'You could've cut out the middleman, Dorah girl,' he thought. 'Go on, keep at it.'

After two minutes the sharp pain had ebbed. He prised the clinging mass of the sea star away with the iron and put on his flipper again, wondering vaguely why he should have thought of the creature as 'Dorah'. For the next ten minutes he moved quietly about his work, pausing every twenty seconds to scan the clear still waters for any sign of sharks or moray eels.

Spotting the big oyster shells called for an experienced eye, especially when they were partly embedded in the sand. But he had long ago learned to watch for the slight movement as they closed on his approach, or the tell-tale air bubble rising. Working easily, economically, he dug them from sand or broke the byssus threads that anchored them to rock. The boat forty feet above threw a huge shadow across the sea bed.

When the basket was full he moved to where the weighted rope hung down, and knotted the end to the basket's thick plaited handle. During the leisurely ascent, watching his small air bubbles to make sure he did not rise faster than they did, it occurred to him that the memory stirred by the vacuum action of the sea urchin concerned a remarkable girl called Dorah he had once known for a while in Portsmouth.

Three minutes later he broke surface and climbed the short wooden steps lashed to the side of the fishing boat. His body was burned to a deep umber by long days in the sun, and the once blue denim trunks he wore had faded almost to white. He slipped off the mask and fins, and turned for Luco to help with the 70 cubic inch lung on his back.

'Sea star,' Willie said, and sat down, lifting his foot. Luco took the broken-stemmed pipe from his mouth and spat over the side, then peered at Willie's heel and pinched the flesh with sinewy fingers.

'Is okay,' he said. Putting the pipe back in his mouth he resumed work on the pile of oysters in the well of the boat, opening each one with a quick movement of his short, broad-bladed knife, probing and squeezing the slippery mantle with his fingers, then studying the glistening interior of the shell closely before tossing it on to a pile of shells behind him.

Luco was an Indian who had only once in his life made the enormous forty-mile journey from Paloto, in the Archipiélago de las Perlas, to the mainland of Panama. He was fifty, looked seventy, and had forgotten his age. His body was twisted from the long years of pearl-diving in the past. His wife had died diving, ten years ago, and he had married a younger woman who nagged him.

Twenty generations past, the great Balboa had led a handful of Spaniards in an incredible conquest across the isthmus of Panama. His were the first European eyes ever to see the Pacific. He had taken as his mistress a Cuna Indian girl, daughter of the cacique, Careta, and been faithful to her for the rest of his life. It was from the Pearl Islands that he had been lured to the mainland, to stand trial and to meet death by strangling. It was on the Pearl Islands that he had sired upon his mistress the line which led to Luco.

Luco did not know this, and would never know it. To him, Balboa was money, the coin of Panama, unminted but equal to an American dollar. With luck, he earned perhaps two hundred balboa in a year. But this year would be different. The strange Americano, who was not an Americano, was paying a full year's money for each week of work.

It was amazing, thought Luco, as his hands moved skilfully in their automatic task, prising a shell open, cutting the retaining muscle, probing amid the stringy mass, feeling the glossy interior of the shell for the blister which might hide a pearl, and finally tossing the shell aside. Truly amazing.

The way in which the Americano . . . what was his name? *Hweelee?* The way he worked was amazing, also. For a month now he had never failed to bring up at least two hundred shells in a day. They had found two very fine round pearls, four button pearls, two drop pearls, and perhaps a dozen

9

baroque and seed pearls of little worth. But, and this surely was madness, all but the two fine round pearls were of no interest to the Americano. The rest he had given to Luco together with all the shell, which itself was of no small value.

'Seed pearl,' said Willie Garvin, and withdrew his fingers from the slippery mantle of a mussel. Carefully he put the tiny nacreous bead into Luco's palm. Luco examined it, gave a grunt which might have meant anything, then folded the pearl in a scrap of cloth and tucked it away in the small pouch that hung from a thong round his neck.

Willy grinned. He knew that Luco thought he was mad.

'They're too good to waste just selling 'em, Luco,' he said. 'What you want to do is dissolve 'em in vinegar and drink 'em. Like Cleopatra. You'll go off like a bomb on the old jig-a-jig. It'll stop your old woman nagging for a bit. You might even cheer yourself up, too, you miserable old sod.'

Luco shrugged with bare comprehension and picked up another shell.

Together they worked on under the hot sun. Four miles to the east lay the Isla del Rey, to the west a heat mist shrouded the coast of San José. Between, the south passage was dotted with small wooded islands rising steeply from the sea. The sun, edging down now, was still strong.

Willie Garvin threw the last shell aside and started to haul in the little anchor. He said, 'We'll call it a day, Luco. Early start tomorrow.'

Luco ran up the sail and brought the ancient boat round before the wind. His home village was on Paloto, two miles north. Four hundred yards to port stood a small brown and green island with a long promontory shaped like a hand with fingers spread.

'Girls go there,' Luco said, jerking the pipe between his teeth towards the peak of land. 'Two Americano girls in nice boat.'

'Americano girls?' Willie stared. 'You ought to be joking, only you don't know 'ow. We're right off the tourist track 'ere.'

Luco shrugged. What the Americano said was true enough. All the same, he had seen the two girls in the blue and white motorboat pass a few hundred yards away an hour ago, while the Americano was down gathering shells. They had waved to him. Perhaps they were among the few people who made the trip from Panama City to Isla del Rey. There they might have taken the motorboat to explore some of the surrounding islands.

'Two girls,' he repeated. 'I see them.'

'Let's take a look then,' said Willie. 'We might chat 'em up a bit.' He relaxed hopefully, listening to the chuckle of water under the bows as Luco ran before the warm gentle wind.

After a little while Luco said, 'Hey, Americano.' It was his way of addressing Willie, who had long since given up the problem of explaining that there existed people of his colouring, language and incomprehensible ways who were not in fact Americanos.

Luco was leaning forward, holding out a half shell. 'You want keep?'

Willie took the shell. From the slippery surface near the hinge projected a thin stalk of nacre terminating in a nobbly blister the size of a small walnut—a freak growth. He broke off the grey-black protuberance and eyed it casually. It was worthless, but might be useful for scraping practice. The art of improving a pearl, of eliminating a small blemish by scraping, was subtle, delicate and important. You could increase a pearl's value five-fold or reduce it to nothing. A knob of nacre like this was suitable for practice and experiment. He slipped it into the fob pocket of his shorts and closed the plastic zip.

Luco ran the bows of the clumsy boat gently up on to the soft sand of the shallows. The pulleys groaned as he dropped the big gaff mainsail. Willie pulled on his sandals and picked up the rucksack beside him. Together the two men splashed thigh-deep through the water to the hot yellow beach.

A belt of palms lay beyond the half-circle of the little bay. Behind them the ground sloped up to a high ridge, the root of the first finger of the hand.

'It'll be the thrill of a lifetime for 'em,' Willie said. 'A strange, golden man like a Greek god, walking out of the sea. Well, along the beach, anyway.' He took a pair of 8 × 50 Zeiss binoculars from the rucksack. 'You got a wife and eight kids, Luco, so you'd better just sit 'ere and try to figure out what causes it.'

Luco nodded, settled down in the shade of the palms, put away his pipe and lit one of the cigarettes with which the Americano kept him well supplied. Willie Garvin moved on through the trees and started up the steep broken slope of the ridge.

In all the scores of islands which made up the archipelago there were no more than fifteen hundred souls. Luco's village held sixty-two. After a month there, Willie Garvin now found himself with a sudden longing for an English voice. Or an Americano voice. But especially a girl's voice.

The sand gave way to rock and thin soil where trees and bushes laboured for life under the fierce sun. In five minutes he reached the top of the ridge. Leaning against a tree, he put the binoculars to his eyes. The inlet below him was empty, but the ridge formed by the finger of land on the far side was low, and he could see across it to the next beach, a quarter of a mile away. There something moved against the background of the sand. He sharpened the focus, then stood very still, muscles suddenly locked with tension.

Sick, raging and helpless, he watched as murder was done.

The powerful binoculars spared no detail. There were two men, and they were not islanders. One stood holding a girl with honey-coloured hair and a white swimsuit, her arms twisted up her back. Twenty yards away, near the water's edge, the other man was kneeling. Beneath him two slim bare legs kicked feebly. Willie could see no more of the second girl, for she was face down and the man was kneeling on her back, hands pressing down on her head, holding her face rammed into the wet sand.

Willie Garvin let out a shaky breath. Given a rifle he could have killed both men in seconds. But nobody was going to give him a rifle. To reach the men would take ten minutes if he cut across inland; probably longer by the direct route across the inlet and the ridge beyond, for the slopes were of badly broken rock and he would spend more time clambering than running.

Ten minutes . . .

The long slim legs were still. He watched the man rise. The girl did not move. Willie could see her more clearly now. She wore a bikini, and her hair was darker than that of her friend. For a moment he saw the man's face, and instantly recognised it—not the face itself, but the type. He had seen it a hundred times all over the world. It was the cold, curiously dull face of the professional; the professional killer, whose gun or knife or hands were for hire. He was a big, thick-chested man, in black slacks and a white shirt with short sleeves. Face and forearms were red from sunburn, marking him as a city dweller. The harness of his shoulder holster stood out clearly.

Willie Garvin swore softly, venomously. He saw the killer drag the girl's body into shallow water and bend to hold her head beneath the surface.

So it was to be an accident. A drowning accident. The blue and white boat would be found, eventually, where it now lay, moored in the shallows. If the girl's body was found at all there would be water in the lungs and no sign of violence.

But where had the two men come from? *Two* men——

He moved the binoculars quickly. For a moment he had forgotten the other girl and her captor in the horror of watching the cold, methodical murder. He thought of shouting. If the killers knew they were watched, it might save the second girl. Even as the thought came he knew it was hopeless. The

13

wind was blowing steadily in his face, and no shout would carry the distance.

She was still held in that painful grip. Did they mean to kill her too? If so, why one at a time? Never mind why. Perhaps it gave him a chance to reach the scene, a bare thread of a chance.

He was about to drop the glasses when a sudden movement held him. The girl with honey-coloured hair had done something, kicked backwards perhaps, and made lucky contact. She was free, and running, while her captor stood for a moment half crouched with a hand to his crotch. Then he began to plunge after her. Like his companion, he wore a gun in a shoulder rig. And he had the same face, the same kind of face.

Willie held the girl in focus.

'Come on, love,' he muttered desperately. 'Come *on!*' He could see her face now, a young face, twisted with fear. Her mouth seemed to be pursed, almost as if she were whistling. Stranger still, both arms were held at full stretch before her as she ran. She was bearing slightly away from the sea. A low rock jutted from the sand ahead of her. For a moment Willie thought she meant to jump it, but she seemed not even to see it until she was upon it. There was an instant when she tried to swerve, but too late. Her leg caught the rock as she twisted aside, and she fell.

In a moment she was up and running again.

'Oh, Christ!' Willie breathed incredulously. Her back was towards him now, and she was running straight at her pursuer, her arms outstretched as before. The man stopped and waited, arms spread. Willie could see the beginning of a grin on the broad fleshy face.

Again the girl seemed unaware of his presence until the last moment, and again came that hopeless attempt to twist aside. The man caught her by the shoulder and she went down. He held her fast as she fought wildly. His companion had let go of the body in the shallows and was moving up the beach, calling something.

14

A heavy hand chopped down edgewise and the girl lay still.

Understanding came to Willie Garvin. *'God Almighty, the kid's blind!'* he whispered. His hands were slippery with sweat. If the men were going to kill her now, he could do nothing to save her. But if not . . .

They were kneeling over the girl, doing something to one of her arms. He caught a bright glint of metal. A hypodermic perhaps. He prayed that it was. The two men stood up. One of them had the girl's limp body across his shoulders. They turned and began to trudge slowly towards the slope leading up out of the bay.

Willie Garvin lowered the glasses and wiped a forearm across his brow. 'She's *blind*, Princess!' he croaked.

He was talking to Modesty Blaise. She was half a world away, but in moments of stress Willie often spoke as if she were beside him in the flesh. There had been times when this helped him to think more clearly, to make a decision, to devise a plan. But this was not such a time. Willie Garvin knew exactly what he was going to do.

He was already on the move, running deeper inland, climbing a little. The binoculars were tucked under one arm. The big Bowie knife that he used for pearling rested in its sheath at the back of his belt.

As he ran his mind worked coldly, weighing chances and making deductions. The killers must have come from a boat, a biggish boat, since it had not entered the shallow waters of the bay. They had come over the hump of the promontory on foot. They were going back the same way, burdened with the unconscious girl.

Willie Garvin wanted to see the boat. More important, he wanted to be up there on the hump ahead of the two men, to meet them. He came to the thinly wooded crest and worked his way forward through scanty cover, keeping low.

There was the boat, standing two hundred yards offshore, a forty foot twin diesel yacht with raised saloon and fly bridge.

In the shallows, a man in a blue and white striped shirt stood by a big inflatable dinghy. A glance to the right told Willie that the killers had not yet reached the top of the slope leading up from the bay.

He crouched beside a scrubby bush and lifted the binoculars. Three men were in view on the foredeck of the yacht. One, dressed like the man by the dinghy, was standing by the gangway. Willie focused his glasses on the other two, and froze. His lips rounded in a silent whistle of shock.

One man was lean and thin-faced, fair of hair, with an odd springy walk and a clownish manner of gesturing and wagging his head. Willie knew him. But it was the second man who held his attention, the man who stood quite still, gazing towards the shore.

There was no mistaking the putty-coloured face and the pointed ears. Impossible to see any detail of the eyes, but they would be the same; empty, untenanted, the irises so pale and bleached as to be almost invisible. Only the hair was different. Two years ago it had been sleek and dark. Now it was heavily flecked with grey.

Willie Garvin had good reason to believe that he and Modesty Blaise were responsible for that change. Take ten million pound's-worth of stolen diamonds from a man and come within a touch of killing him, and you were more than likely to put grey in his hair. Especially if the man was Gabriel, who had never before known failure.

Gabriel. And McWhirter.

Five seconds had passed since Willie raised the glasses. He lowered them and edged back until a fold of ground hid the yacht from view. Now he knew that behind the killing, behind the kidnapping, there was something big. He did not begin to speculate on what it might be. That could come later, if Modesty Blaise so decided. For the moment Willie Garvin's objective was quite clear, simple, and limited. He was going to kill the two men he had seen on the beach.

He moved north, along a natural path leading to the lip

of the slope that the killers would now be ascending. There was no solid cover, only a tall spindly tree that stood some twenty paces from where they would breast the rise. The sun was low now, and the thin trunk threw a long shadow obliquely across the path. He stood with his back against the tree, drew the Bowie knife from its sheath, and waited.

There was no expectancy in his waiting. His mind was empty, and as still as his body. Apart from the unblinking focus of his eyes, he did not exist. He was the tree, the ground, the air around him.

This was one of the elements of *ninjutsu*, the art of being in full view yet not drawing the eye of an observer. It was said that the great *ninja* adepts of old time could pass invisible through a crowd. Willie Garvin would be well content if he could remain unseen by the killers while they covered ten paces. He would need that much grace. If one of them got a shot off it would be heard on the yacht, and . . .

A man came into view at the top of the slope. It was the man who had held the blind girl. He was panting a little and his face was wet. The other, in the white shirt and black slacks, came a few steps behind. He was a bigger man, and moved slightly crouched under the burden of the girl across his shoulders. He halted and said, 'Gimme a spell, Eddie,' in a deep, wheezing voice.

Willie Garvin watched remotely, uninvolved, as the girl was transferred. Each man wore the same rig, a George Lawrence shoulder holster with spring clip, holding a .38 Special Bodyguard, a five-shot hammerless revolver.

The bigger man took the lead, trudging on up the sandy gradient. Twice his gaze had passed across Willie Garvin without focusing. He was eight paces away when the shock of realisation hit him and he stopped dead, a hand flashing to the gun.

Willie Garvin's wrist flickered in a hard underarm throw, and he launched himself after the heavy knife. Its eleven-inch blade drove home just below the sternum, angling upwards with the line of the throw, up into the heart. The man died as his hand snapped the gun down from the spring clip of the Lawrence. It was a quicker death than the girl on the beach had died.

Willie Garvin cleared the crumpling body as if taking a hurdle. To the second man it must have seemed that the brown, half-naked creature with chilling blue eyes had dropped from the sky. A long arm flashed out; a finger and thumb like iron hooks closed on the flesh of his upper lip just below the nose, and a muffled squeal of pain broke from him as he was jerked forward.

Because he fell face down, his body cushioned the fall of the girl. And because he fell face down, his gun-hand, gripping the butt now, was crushed against the ground by his own weight.

Willie Garvin thrust his fingers into the thick, oiled hair and held the struggling man's face down hard for a second while he rolled the girl aside. Then he jerked the head up sharply and at the same moment chopped down with a hand like a spade to the nape of the neck.

There was a faint but audible crack.

Willie Garvin straightened up and went to retrieve his knife. He cleaned it in the sand, slipped it into the sheath, then picked up the girl and began to move steadily back up the path, bearing left towards the slope down to the bay where Luco's boat lay.

His mind ticked smoothly, assessing probabilities. Twenty minutes minimum before Gabriel would begin to wonder about the delay and send somebody to check. Another fifteen before he would know enough to get the yacht under way and start looking for a boat, any boat which might hold the girl and whoever had killed the two hoods.

That wasn't time enough for Luco's old tub to get clear.

The grotto. It lay under the northern point of the island, hidden by a curving arm of rock. Only the islanders in the immediate locality knew of it. The entrance was big enough for Luco's boat with the mast down. They could wait there in safety for a couple of hours. After dark, Gabriel wouldn't have a hope.

For a moment he glanced down at the girl in his arms. She was light, perhaps 110 pounds, small-boned with firmly fleshed limbs. In her early twenties, he guessed. The face was neither pretty nor beautiful, but something between, at the same time tough yet vulnerable; the face of a fighter accustomed to taking a beating but always coming back for more, never giving up. It touched a deep chord in Willie Garvin.

Now she had taken another beating. When she came round, when the lids of her sightless eyes opened, he would have to tell her that her friend had been murdered.

He felt a sick apprehension in his stomach, and wished again that Modesty Blaise was with him.

An hour had gone by, and there were two men on the sandy path where the spindly palm grew; two living men.

McWhirter straightened up from the corpse, wiping damp hands on his shirt. 'Eddie has a broken neck,' he said, and moved back to where the other body lay.

Gabriel stood with his hands in the pockets of the light cream jacket he wore, staring at nothing. 'A broken neck,' he repeated flatly. 'And this was a knife?' He touched the supine body with his foot.

'Aye. What else?'

'What kind of knife?'

'A big one.' McWhirter gazed down at the savage wound. 'You'd not fix that wi' a styptic pencil.' He glanced about him shrewdly, eyes narrowed in the bony face. 'I'd say it was thrown. Margello was too good to let anyone walk up close.'

Gabriel stared with dead eyes towards the west, where the setting sun made the sea a glossy shield of burnished red steel. 'Garvin,' he said softly, positively.

'Not one o' his regular knives.' McWhirter rubbed his chin doubtfully. 'They're toothpicks compared wi' this.'

'Garvin,' repeated Gabriel without emphasis. 'I don't know how or why.' His eyes focused and moved from one body to the other. 'But Garvin was here.'

'Wi'out Blaise?'

'That only means it was by chance.'

'Och, it's a hell of a chance!'

Gabriel shook his head, and for a moment something flared in the dull eyes. 'No. It had to happen.'

McWhirter watched his master thoughtfully. Something had gone out of Gabriel since the day two years ago, when he had held every card in the pack and still gone down to defeat. The power, the intelligence, the ice-cold calculation were still there; but the element of total confidence had been marginally diminished. McWhirter, who had served him for many years, believed that Gabriel on his own might no longer be a match for Blaise and Garvin now. He was profoundly thankful, in view of what had happened in the past hour or so, that there was somebody who was very much more than a match for them.

'The big feller won't like this,' he said tentatively.

'He'll laugh.' Gabriel's voice held an edge of fury.

He would laugh. It was true, McWhirter thought with sour relief. The big feller would enjoy Gabriel's failure more than he would care about the fact of that failure. He would laugh, and take over the job of getting the girl himself. But it might not come to that . . .

'Is he in London now?' McWhirter asked.

'He should be. There's Aaronson to kill.'

'Aye, wee Doctor Aaronson.' McWhirter pondered. 'Well, he'll not be pressing us for a few days, then. And the girl can't be far.' He shaded his eyes to gaze at two fishing boats beating slowly south.

Gabriel nodded. 'We'll look till it's dark. Then we head back to Panama. I want every eye we can hire on this job, so get the word out fast. Set up intercepts at the airports and on the highway, then get the local organisations busy combing the ports and the towns. Give them a description of Garvin.'

'Garvin? That's still a guess.'

Gabriel looked down upon the body at his feet and kicked it without passion, then turned away. 'It's not a guess,' he said.

2

THE long blades slithered one upon the other in a swift flurry of movement.

'No, no, *no!*' Professor Giulio Barbi screamed softly, and stepped back, lowering the point of his épée to the asphalt surface of the flat roof. 'I have *told* you, signorina—never attempt an envelopment in the low line against a fencer of quality! In sixte, certainly. Even in quarte it is difficult to hold the opponent's blade. But in the low line it is *stupid!*'

'But it worked,' Modesty Blaise said mildly from behind her mask. 'I got the hit.'

'Got the hit! Got the *hit?*' The voice of the fencing master rose shrilly and he lifted his mask. 'We are making tuition, are we not? I do not come here to fight *duels* with you, signorina! I come to instruct you in the art of the sword—the tactics, the manipulation, the style, the *art!* For tuition, we fence to make hits in the *correct way,* signorina!'

'I'm sorry,' Modesty Blaise said meekly. 'I forgot.' Professor Barbi glared, pulled on his mask and snapped, 'En garde!'

The blades engaged.

Sir Gerald Tarrant, sitting on a swing lounger to one side of the penthouse roof, watched the moving white-clad figures with quiet amusement. It was not the first time he had sat here early on a pleasant spring morning for half an hour before going on to his office in Whitehall.

Weng, the houseboy, appeared in the doorway which opened on to the roof from the penthouse below. Behind him was a man of tall spare build, with a pleasant face and gently humorous eyes.

Tarrant lifted a hand in greeting, and beckoned. He had met Stephen Collier twice before, once at dinner here in

Modesty's penthouse and once with her at Wimbledon. Collier smiled and moved round the area of the piste marked out on the roof. He shook hands with Tarrant and sat down.

'Coffee?' said Tarrant, picking up the percolator from the table at his elbow. 'Modesty said she was expecting you.'

'Yes, I rang from the airport an hour ago.' Collier's eyes were on the fencers. 'Black, please.'

'You were over in the States?'

'Just for six weeks, at Duke University. Helping with a long statistical run.'

Collier's hobby was investigating the phenomena of extra-sensory perception. He could afford to indulge his hobby. Some years earlier, as a mathematician, he had written a primer for schools which brought in a regular and ample income. Tarrant liked the man. He also envied him, because not long ago, and for several weeks, Collier had been caught up in a bizarre adventure with Modesty Blaise and Willie Garvin. With them he had known a peculiarly horrifying captivity, had dwelt among killers and faced seemingly inevitable death. And with them he had taken part in an extraordinary battle of destruction that ended it all.

Collier, to the extent that he ever talked about it, claimed that his part in the affair had consisted exclusively of being a burden and a handicap. He also claimed to have been in a state of terror from start to finish. He would only admit that, having survived, he was glad not to have missed the caper.

There came a soft quick stamp of feet from the piste, and the sound of steel on steel.

'No!' cried Professor Barbi in anguish. 'Where is your intelligence, signorina? Are you an imbecile? I give you the opportunity to make the stop-hit, yes? I make a one-two with a step forward on the first feint, then disengage to lunge. But do you make the stop-hit? No! You defend with a simple parry. I waste my time!'

'Your lunge would still have hit me,' Modesty said appeasingly.

23

'But *your* hit would arrive *first!*' screamed Professor Barbi. 'What does it matter if my own hit follows?'

'Well, it would matter if——' Modesty stopped. She lifted her mask for a moment and gave Barbi a dazzling smile of apology. 'Let's try it again.'

Tarrant chuckled as the blades engaged. Collier said, 'I'm surprised. I thought she'd be very good at this.'

'Don't be misled by Barbi's recriminations. The thing is, she can't make herself fence on the basis that it doesn't matter if you get hit as long as you hit your adversary first.'

Collier thought about it, then nodded. 'I can see it wouldn't be desirable in a real duel.'

'That's the point. And that's why she favours the épée, of course. Most women prefer the foil. Lighter, and a limited target—the trunk. But the épée is the nearest thing to the old rapier or duelling sword, so she prefers it.'

Collier nodded again. If you knew Modesty, it made sense. He said, 'I believe you're well up in this?'

'I've done a little.'

'Like fencing for England before the war. Modesty told me.'

'I'm rather less supple now,' Tarrant said wryly. 'You thought Modesty would be good at this. She is. I've tried her more than once. She has astonishing co-ordination, as you'd expect. Any amount of stamina. A very fine sense of point——'

'What's that?'

'Knowing where your point is, exactly, in relation to your adversary and his blade, by feel alone. Not so easy. Try it with your eyes closed, and you'll find you're anything up to a foot wrong.'

'I'll take your word for it. What else?'

Tarrant smiled. 'She hasn't any habits. No favourite line of engagement, thrusts or parries. You can never guess what she's going to do.'

'I know what you mean, quite apart from the fencing,'

24

Collier said, remembering. 'She has a gift for the unexpected. It can be disconcerting, but it makes life interesting.'

'For her friends. It's made life impossible for one or two others,' Tarrant said drily.

'So I've seen. I weep no tears for them.' Collier set down his cup.

'*The fingers! The fingers!*' cried Professor Barbi angrily. 'Only a *cretin* directs the blade with the wrist! That is an épée in your hand, signorina, not a tennis bat!'

'Racket,' Modesty said helpfully.

'I beg your pardon. It is not a tennis racket. So control it with the *fingers*! Now again, please.'

'This isn't like on the movies,' said Collier, watching. 'When I used to go and see Errol Flynn, you got a fight lasting five minutes with the swords whirling like windmills. All I can see here is a little bit of tip-tap with the blades, a quick flurry, then this chap steps back and shrieks at her.'

Tarrant laughed. 'It's not a spectator sport, I'm afraid. Or rather it's only for the initiated. That flurry just now consisted of a feint of disengagement, a bind into octave, an evasion by disengagement and thrust into the low line, parry, compound riposte, circular parry—and return to guard with absence of blade. Nobody hit anyone.'

'It took about one second,' said Collier. 'Give me Errol Flynn. And he used to take them on four at a time. Up and down staircases.'

'The script-writer was on his side—oh, my God.' Tarrant put a hand to his mouth, struggling to keep a straight face. A phrase had just ended. Modesty and Barbi stood looking at each other for a moment, then the fencing master turned, walked to a low table near the piste, and laid down his épée and mask. Modesty said, 'I'm sorry.'

Barbi ignored her, wiping his face and neck with a handkerchief.

'What's that all about?' Collier asked quietly.

'She attacked en flèche,' said Tarrant. 'A running lunge.

He parry-riposted in quarte. An almost certain hit by all the laws of logic. But she parried prime, still en flèche, which is unlikely, and riposted by cut-over, which is absurd. Except that it worked.'

Modesty came towards them, épée in her right hand, mask under the same arm. Both men rose to their feet.

'Now you've done it,' said Tarrant.

She pulled a face. 'I hope not. But I couldn't just give up because the flèche failed, could I? Hallo Steve.'

She offered her cheek. He kissed it lightly, then said, 'Your face is all sweaty. Ladies are only supposed to glow.'

'You try jumping about wearing a plastron and a fencing jacket with a couple of breast protectors in it.'

'Breast protectors?' He prodded her experimentally. 'So there are. I won't try it on, though. Misunderstandings could arise——'

He broke off. Professor Barbi was striding towards them, carrying his mask and épée. His eyes were fixed sternly on Modesty Blaise and he had a tight-lipped air of finality.

Tarrant lifted his voice a little and said to Modesty, 'There's Professor Forrester, of course. Or better still, Lebrun. He's very good.'

'*Lebrun?*' Professor Barbi cried with incredulous fury. He glared at Tarrant, then turned to Modesty. Abruptly the thin, aristocratic face melted in a sad smile. He extended his left hand to take hers in the formal salute that follows a bout.

'Forgive my discourtesy, signorina, but you are really most exasperating.'

'I know. I'll make a real effort next week.' She smiled warmly. 'You will come?'

'I cannot help myself.' Barbi looked at Tarrant and sighed. 'One hour each week, and with the épée, signore. It is absurd, no? Give her to me for three hours each day, with the foil, and in six months I will show you a fencer to make your Forresters and your Lebruns look like—like *plumbers!*'

When Professor Barbi had gone Modesty smiled at Tarrant.

26

'Thanks. The Lebrun touch was very cunning.'

'I am indeed a very cunning old gentleman,' Tarrant agreed, looking at his watch. 'And I must go and exercise that talent.'

'Your desk can wait five minutes. Do sit down. I don't know why you haven't been drummed out of the Civil Service, starting work at eight.'

'I like to make all the unpleasant decisions before ten. Perhaps just another half cup of coffee . . . ?' Tarrant sat beside Modesty on the swing lounger with the awning. Collier took the striped canvas garden chair.

'I wonder if you could dine with me on Thursday,' Tarrant said after a little silence. 'You too, Collier, if you're going to be in London.'

'I haven't any definite plans.' Collier looked at Modesty with an amiable smile. 'But I might be around, and I'd be delighted.'

'We both would,' said Modesty. 'Is it purely social? Or something to do with one of your unpleasant decisions?'

'Mainly social,' said Tarrant. 'And nothing to do with any unpleasantness.' He sounded relieved. 'After we've dined I'd like you to meet an old friend of mine. A personal friend. Dr. Aaronson.'

'Aaronson . . . ?' She thought for a moment. 'Oh yes, the historian. He did the work on those Roman scrolls they found near In Salah.'

Collier remembered reading about it now, though he recalled only the bare details. Some scrolls had been found, and these had led to the discovery of a small half-buried city tucked away on the edge of . . . what was the place?

'The Tademait plateau,' Tarrant was saying. 'You might give thought to how you'd feel about paying a visit to the dig that's going on there, Modesty. Very small archaeological team, with Tangye in charge. I only mention it now so that you can think about it before Thursday.'

'And this isn't business? I mean Civil Service business.'

'No.' Tarrant's brows contracted. 'I thought I'd made it

clear that I'm not inviting your interest or participation in any future business.'

'You said that last bit . . . how did he say that last bit, Steve?'

'Darkly?'

'Yes. You said that last bit darkly, Sir Gerald.'

'And well I might. The fact that you're still alive is no thanks to me. But that's all over. So this isn't a caper. Are you disappointed?'

She laughed. 'Not really. Why do I visit a bunch of lonely men in the middle of the Sahara? Do they want a cook or a comforter?'

'With Mrs. Tangye there, I imagine the cooking is taken care of and a comforter would be frowned upon,' said Tarrant absently. 'Aaronson's at a convention in Stockholm. He rang me, and was rather guarded and anxious and enigmatic. I gather he thinks there's something wrong at the dig. I don't know what, and I can't imagine. But he begged me to send somebody out there, just to take a look at things.'

Collier said, 'It sounds a bit vague, doesn't it?'

'I know.' Tarrant shrugged. 'But he's a very old friend and I'd like to humour him.' He looked at Modesty. 'I can't send anyone out officially, of course. Maybe Aaronson will be more specific when we see him on Thursday.'

She nodded. 'Let's talk to him, anyway. It's a long time since I was in the desert, and it always had something for me. Who's financing the dig?'

Tarrant hesitated. Then—'Presteign. But that's hush. He makes a great point of keeping his philanthropy dark.'

'He's listed as a patron on half the charity circulars I get,' said Modesty. 'Sir Howard Presteign. Will he get a peerage?'

'Don't be cynical. He's refused twice.' Tarrant rose, took her hand and touched her fingers to his lips. 'I'll ring you about time and place for Thursday, my dear.'

'Fine.'

Collier went down with her to see Tarrant off. When the

doors of the private lift in the penthouse foyer had closed, he turned and looked at the huge living-room with the floor to ceiling window at the far end, noting the changes. A Braque still life had gone from the golden cedar strip walls and been replaced by a vivid Franz Marc abstract. The Tompion had given way to an ormolu and blue enamel automata clock. He was not sure that he liked it. But the François Boucher tapestry was still there, and——

His eye fell on the glass paperweights, and he sighed with pleasure, moving to the small niche with concealed lighting where they stood, touching one of them gently. They were old French, and in a class of their own.

'That's a St. Louis,' Modesty said behind him. 'The other two are Baccarat and Clichy-la-Garenne. Aren't they beautiful?'

'Yes.' He turned. 'But I'll look at them later.' He took her face gently between his hands and kissed her on the lips. 'Ah . . . you taste good.'

'And you look tired.'

'It's rushing about in these heavier-than-air machines. My mental clock says it's two a.m.'

She took his hand and moved to one of the teak veneer sliding doors that led from the living-room. It opened on to a room of pale green and silver-grey, with panelled walls in ivory. Her bedroom.

She said, 'Go on, get some sleep,' and went on through to the bathroom.

Collier heard the sound of a shower. Through the half open door he could glimpse pale pink walls and a black tiled floor. After a moment he followed her and stood leaning in the doorway. She had taken off the fencing jacket, plastron and breeches.

'Hallo again,' he said vaguely. 'I was just wondering . . .'

She slipped off the plain black briefs, unhooked the bra, and pulled on a shower-cap. 'Hallo, darling. What were you wondering?' She stepped under the shower and picked up soap and sponge. Collier's eyes dwelt on her splendid body with deep pleasure, remembering. He had never known a woman so unconscious of her body. She had a way of wearing nakedness as if it were clothes.

'I was just wondering about Weng,' he said, and saw sudden laughter in her face through the needle jets of the shower.

'Weng's an Asiatic.' She tilted her head back and let the water flow down over her body. 'Try telling him that I ought to consult him about who can use my bed. He'll think you're out of your mind.'

'All the same. Since there's Willie's room, and another spare room, he's bound to think——'

'He'll know. And he'll be right, won't he? After you've had some sleep.' She turned off the shower, stepped out and pulled a big bath towel round her, looking at Collier with affectionate amusement. 'Or rather he would know if he was here, and it still wouldn't matter a damn.'

'He's gone?' Collier was surprised.

'Down to Benildon for me. I'm having a few things done to the cottage.' She took off the shower-cap and towelled her face. 'Go on Steve, get some sleep now and I'll wake you before lunch.'

Collier began to take off his tie. He said, 'No. I don't feel tired any more.'

His body remembered hers with the poignant joy of a longed-for homecoming, and he dwelt upon its loveliness with absorbed wonderment.

When he saw her smiling at him he said lightly, 'I must read the Song of Solomon again.'

'There's a bit about *"Thy hair is as a flock of goats."* Was that what you meant? Those fencing masks wreck a hair-do.'

'No. Something about honey is under her tongue. And *"Thou art all fair, my love; there is no spot in thee."* '

'You can't have looked carefully.'

30

'I did. Eight scars. But you can hardly see any of them now, and they don't count anyway.'

A little later Collier said suddenly, 'Look, for God's sake why don't we regularise this?'

'Us?'

'Yes.'

'Well, this is a fine position for a man to start making a proposal.' She began to shake with laughter. Collier felt no touch of wounded pride. There was always a strong element of exuberant happiness in her love-making.

'It's highly recommended in the Kama Sutra,' he said.

'Theorist.'

'Stop shaking about. It has a . . . discomposing effect.'

'That's what I'm here for. Maybe you should have read on.'

Then there were no more words, but only the almost unbearable sweetness of mounting the long hill of joy and soaring into the world of sunlight beyond.

A long while later, as she lay with her head on his shoulder, Collier put the cigarette they were sharing to her lips and said sleepily. 'How's my old mate Willie Garvin?'

She exhaled a lazy coil of smoke. 'I expect he's all right.'

'Not around?'

'The States or Mexico, I think. I haven't heard for a while.'

'What's he doing there?'

She wrinkled her brow. 'I don't know. It's just about the only thing I don't know about Willie.'

'What do you mean?'

'It happens once a year, going back . . . oh, six or seven years now, back to the days when he was working for me in The Network. Every year he goes off on his own for five or six weeks. Australia, Japan, India, all over. And he never tells me what he's been doing.'

'Girls, most likely.'

'No. He tells me about his girls, and anything he does on an ordinary trip. But these annual jaunts are something different.'

'Have you asked him?'

'I don't own him, darling. He'll tell me if he ever wants to.'

'He'll tell you if you ask. There's not a goddam thing Willie wouldn't do for you at the lift of a finger.'

'I know it. So I always have to think hard before I lift a finger. And I'm not entitled to know his secrets.'

'Does it worry you, this Willie mystery?' Collier said curiously.

'Oh, no.' He felt her shrug in the crook of his arm. 'I'm just a bit puzzled. But he always comes back looking cheerful and full of beans, so why worry?'

'I'm not worried,' Collier murmured absently. 'I'm just nosey. I wonder what he's up to right now?'

Modesty took his wrist and turned it so that she could see the watch. 'It's anything between one and four a.m. in the States,' she said. 'He's probably in bed.'

3

THE moon was high and clear.

Willie Garvin looked down at the girl's face in the cool metallic light. She lay at his feet in the well of Luco's boat on an old mattress and with a blanket wrapped about her. They had picked up Willie's bags from Luco's house, and for the last hour the creaking boat had been running with wind and current through the shoal patches of the North Passage.

Now at last the girl was stirring. Her eyelids flickered and opened. They closed again, and she lay quite still for a moment. Her face became increasingly alert and puzzled, then twisted in sudden fear as memory returned. She cried out, struggling to throw off the blanket.

'It's all right, love. Take it nice and slow.' Willie spoke very gently, a hand resting on her shoulder. She froze. Her sightless eyes were open again and seemed to be staring straight at him. He saw her nostrils widen for a moment, and she sniffed quickly.

'You're safe now,' Willie said. 'I'm not one of the blokes that grabbed you on the beach.'

'I know.' Her voice was hoarse, and very low, but he could detect the North American accent. 'I know. You smell different.'

'Well, I'm glad about that,' Willie said soberly.

Her head turned a little. 'There's someone else in the boat.'

Willie looked towards the dark shape that was Luco in the stern. 'Yes, that's Luco. But you needn't worry about 'im. You're safe now, love. Honest.'

'Please, I—I'm going to be sick.'

He scooped her up in the blanket and held her half across

his lap with her head over the side until the spasms had passed, then lifted her so that she could rest with her head on his shoulder while he wiped her face clean with a handkerchief soaked in salt water.

'I'm sorry,' she panted, shuddering.

'Don't worry. It's just the dope they shoved into you.'

Her breathing grew quieter, and he could almost see her mind tracking back. Abruptly she stiffened in his arms and said, 'Judy?'

One bare arm was free of the blanket now. Willie took the hand and held it. He said, 'The girl that was with you?'

'Yes. My sister. Where is she? Please——?' Her voice broke with anxiety.

'It's bad news. Try to 'ang on tight,' Willie said. 'I turned up too late. She's . . . well, she's dead.'

Her face puckered and bunched. After a long while he saw tears squeezing from beneath her tight-shut eyelids. At last, in a voice shaken by pain and anger—'They *killed* her?'

'Yes. I saw it through glasses. Too far off to do anything.'

'Tell me.'

'Don't make things worse for yourself, love.'

'*Tell me.*'

Quietly he told her all that he had seen on the beach. When he had finished she turned her face against his shoulder. For ten minutes, as she fought her solitary battle, there was silence but for the creak of the stays and the steady lapping of water along the clinker-built hull.

When she lifted her face again it was gaunt with hatred, and her voice was a bitter cry. '*Why Judy?* It's crazy! She was the gentlest creature. Oh God, *why?*'

'I don't know, love. And why not you? I thought we might talk about that later, when you feel up to it.'

She seemed not to hear him. After a moment she said in a low voice, looking up blindly at the sky, 'The law won't catch up with them. Not here. I'd like to kill them. Yes. More than anything in the world, I'd like to kill them.'

'That's been done,' Willie said.

Her head came round sharply. 'You?'

He nodded, remembered her blindness, and said, 'Yes.'

'But they had guns. I felt one on the man who caught me.'

'I know. They didn't get a chance to use 'em.'

Luco spoke for the first time. 'The Americano has a knife.'

'Americano?'

'Luco can't tell the difference, love.'

'How did it happen? Tell me.'

He hesitated, decided that she would brook no protest, and told her briefly what had passed on the ridge. When he had finished she eased her fingers from his grasp and felt his forearm, then ran her hand quickly and with practised perception up his arm to the shoulder and across the chest.

She gave a little nod and said with a touch of wonder, 'Did you mean to kill them?'

'Like you said, they'd have got away with it. So I reckoned I'd better see 'em off meself. They can't do it again now.'

A tired, twisted smile. 'You must be a very unusual person. I'm glad. But doesn't it put you in a spot?'

'No. Not from the law, anyway. The man on the yacht won't squawk. Look, we're heading for the mainland south of Panama City, and we won't be there till dawn. I've got to talk to you before we get there, but you say when you're ready, eh?'

'I'm ready now.'

'Good girl. Want to lie down?'

'It's better like this, as long as I'm not too heavy.'

He could feel the sense of loss and loneliness in her, and knew that she found some measure of comfort even in a stranger's arms. He said, 'You're not heavy. Now first thing, do you know a man called Gabriel?'

She frowned and shook her head. 'Should I?'

'Well, he's the one who was standing off on the yacht and sent those two hoods to get you.'

'And to kill Judy.' She bit her lip hard, struggling against

35

a new wave of grief. 'Sorry. It just caught up with me for a moment. No, I don't know anyone called Gabriel. Why should he want to get hold of me?'

'That was my next question. Gabriel's a big operator and bad medicine. I can't see him going for ransom, but . . . you're not an heiress or anything like that?'

'I've got eight hundred dollars in the bank, and no expectations.'

'Do you work for a Government department? Anything like that?'

'No. Like what?'

'Intelligence.'

She would have laughed if there had been any laughter in her. 'You think they take on blind people?'

'I've known stranger things. Never mind. A big firm? Industrial secrets?'

'What makes you think I can work at all?' she asked curiously.

'You'd find a way. You've got that sort of face.' His voice was casual but certain, and through her aching grief she felt a quick spark of pleasure at his implied approval of her. Before she could say anything he spoke again. 'Look, suppose you tell me about everything, then I can pick the bones out of it and see if there's anything that might interest Gabriel.'

'All right.' She began to speak slowly, sometimes with long pauses. He did not hurry her.

Her name was Dinah Pilgrim and her parents were dead. She came from Toronto and she had gone blind when she was eleven years old, after a near fatal onset of meningitis. She was now twenty-two, and knew that she would never see again. Her sister Judy, two years older, had looked after her. She had worried about this, because Judy would rarely go out with a boyfriend and Dinah felt responsible for perhaps spoiling her chances.

'I tried to help by getting a boyfriend myself,' Dinah said. 'I didn't want to. It's a queer feeling.' Willie felt her shrug.

'Like a permanent blind date. There were only two. I never knew what they looked like. I don't even know what *I* look like. I think I was just a novelty for the first one. He didn't stay around long once he'd had me. Judy was so mad. It was the only time I ever heard her sound vicious. I liked the second one, but he was really only sorry for me. He was pretty nice, though—too nice to walk out on me. I had to break it up myself. It wouldn't have worked out. I'm sorry, this isn't the stuff you want to hear, is it?'

Willie had felt her grow gradually more relaxed, and knew that the telling of her story was a therapy for her. 'I want to hear it all, Dinah,' he said truthfully. 'You just carry on.'

There was little more to tell. Judy was a first-class secretary, the truly efficient kind that top executives yearned for. Dinah had made herself an efficient dictaphone typist . . .

Willie saw the slight turn of her head and wondered why she was lying at this point. Whatever it was, he felt certain that it rose from some personal inhibition. This was no cover story she was giving him. He did not challenge the single lie.

The two girls worked together, freelance, travelling around Canada and the States. Mainly they had worked for big public utility companies supplying electricity, water, gas. They had also worked for one or two oil and mining companies. But Dinah knew no secrets, knew nothing that might be remotely of value to any criminal organisation. Neither, she was sure, did Judy.

'We took a vacation,' she said. 'We'd been working pretty hard. Judy hired a car and drove us down through Mexico. It was great. She was my eyes, she really had a way of describing everything so I could almost see it. We thought since we'd got so far we'd push on to Panama. We were going to turn the car in there and take a boat back to New York or maybe San Francisco.'

It was Dinah who had wanted to make the trip out to the Pearl Islands, because she and Judy had always lived on a slab of land three thousand miles wide and had never set foot on an island—except Long Island, and you couldn't count that.

So they had taken the little steamer from Panama City to San Miguel. And the same afternoon they had hired the motorboat so that they could run around the many small islets, and find a place where they could be alone and lie in the sun and bathe.

'I know it sounds a little crazy,' Dinah said, 'but we'd been doing things on impulse all through the vacation, and somehow it had been real good. So Judy found this beach. She saw a small yacht passing while we were landing, and I remember we said something about it, because you don't see many folks around here. We'd only been on the beach an hour I guess, and then . . .'

Her voice wavered a little, and she swallowed hard. 'Then suddenly Judy said two men were coming. I think they must have got right down to the beach before she saw them. She sounded kind of jumpy and started hustling me to the boat. But they were too quick.'

She lay silent with her eyes closed for a few seconds, then said, 'The rest was all confused. I guess you know more about it than I do. Have I told you anything that helps?'

'Nothing I can figure,' Willie said slowly. 'The way I see it they wanted you alive but they couldn't leave your sister around. So she's found drowned and it looks like you're drowned too, only you've been washed out to sea. That way Gabriel's got you with no come-backs.'

'That's how. Not why.'

'I know. The main thing is, it's not finished. I know Gabriel's form. If he wants you, he won't give up.' She shivered, and he reached down for the flask of brandy in his pack. 'Here, 'ave a swig of this.'

He helped her hold the flask to her lips. She sipped gratefully, and the spirit seemed to steady her. She said, 'Sorry. I'm not really afraid of him. I don't care enough to be scared. I just wish you'd killed him too.'

'It'll come to that before we're through.'

38

She grew tense in his arms, and he went on, 'Look, I wouldn't say this now except I reckon you can take it, Dinah. Wherever you run to, this thing goes on till Gabriel's got you. Or till he's dead. So we've got to play it very carefully.'

She relaxed slowly. 'Are we going to the police when we get to Panama City?'

'If that's what you want. But it's dodgy. Gabriel's got more contacts than a telephone exchange. He'll 'ave every small-time crook in Panama looking for you by dawn. And I'd sooner bet on a three-legged 'orse than police protection.'

'Even in the Canal Zone? The Americans control that.'

'Anywhere. Besides, I just signed off a couple of U.S. citizens.'

She did not speak for quite a long time. Her head was cocked a little as if listening to his breathing. He saw her nostrils flare and felt her fingers ripple gently over his forearm. He realised that in some strange way she was sensing him, assessing him.

At last she said, 'You sound very experienced. You haven't said who you are yet.'

'Sorry. Garvin. Willie Garvin. From London and elsewhere. Occupation, retired. Purpose of visit, vacation.'

After another long silence she said, 'Well, thank you for everything, Willie Garvin. I think you've decided what you want to do, so you'd better tell me.'

'I've got a crummy little cottage near the road be'ind Puerto de Chorrera. Can you walk a couple of miles?'

'Yes. In a blanket?'

'I brought along some clothes and sandals I borrowed from one of Luco's daughters. They'll do till I can get you some more. I've got a car in the garage at the cottage, but I don't want to use it. We'll just lie low.'

'Why?'

'Because there aren't many ways out of Panama and they're all easy to watch. There'll be Gabriel eyes at the airports and the ports. And on the highway border crossings.'

'He has that much organisation?'

'It's cheap 'ere.'

'So we lie low until when?'

'Until I've been in touch with a friend of mine in England. Two or three days, maybe.'

Dinah Pilgrim wondered who the friend was, and what he could do that Willie Garvin couldn't, but she was suddenly too tired to ask. A grey drowsiness was stealing over her. She felt him tuck the blanket more closely about her.

'That's right,' he said softly. 'You 'ave a nice sleep, love.'

The mellow luxury of the Coq d'Or enfolded the late diners.

'It is the considered opinion of the stars in their courses,' said Stephen Collier, 'that today being Thursday, I am to receive an unexpected gift from someone in a high position.'

He lit Modesty's cigarette for her, leaned back and looked at his watch. 'The day is on its last knockings. Only ninety minutes left. Yet consider the astrological predictions in the *Evening Standard*. Vast suns, whirling through space at unimaginable distances from us, and a number of planets somewhat closer to home, have apparently combined their movements and subtle energies to this intent—that I should receive an unexpected gift from one in a high position. An event as yet unfulfilled.'

The waiter set down three brandies and went away.

'I'm not in a high position,' Modesty said.

'But Tarrant is,' said Collier hopefully. 'And he carries splendid cigars.'

Tarrant laughed, took out his case and offered it. He felt very content. They had dined well. He always enjoyed being with Modesty. And Collier was excellent company.

They made a good couple, Tarrant thought, holding a match to his cigar. It would be nice if Modesty settled down . . . for one thing it would remove the last lingering fear that he might, just might, be tempted to use her again.

Tonight she wore a vivid green silk dress, sleeveless, with

a mandarin collar. Her only jewellery was a brooch worn just below the collar, a splendid dark amethyst, step-cut and set in white gold. Her eyes, darker than the amethyst, were bright. She was not talking a lot, but listening well and acting as a foil for Collier's droll humour.

'I can't see why you should hate flying,' she was saying now.

'Because it's for the birds,' Collier answered lazily. 'Ah, now that's a double-entendre. In case you missed it, I should explain that in the first place, or probably in the second place, it's an Americanism which means——'

'Yes. We saw the movie. But flying is statistically very safe. You know that.'

'I'm a statistician. Of course I know the comparative safety factor. I spent the whole trip from New York computing it to six hundred decimal points. But when we got over Heathrow and were told to fasten our safety-belts, I didn't have to. Mine was still fastened from the take-off at Kennedy.'

Modesty laughed and looked at Tarrant. 'What time do you want us to meet your friend Aaronson?'

'If his plane was on time he should just about be home by now,' said Tarrant. 'Let's give him twenty minutes. I'll ring through before we leave.'

'I'm still not clear about what he thinks may be wrong at—where is it?'

'According to the scrolls, the place was called Mus, after a Roman tribune in Numidia soon after the Third Punic War. The writer of the scrolls, in fact, Domitian Mus.'

'Surely the Romans didn't get down as far as In Salah?'

'Not by occupation,' Tarrant agreed. 'But they made pacts with a number of Berber chieftains, so there must have been a certain amount of coming and going by Roman officials. This chap Mus actually married a Berber princess. And the city itself was built, or rather carved out, by Berbers under Roman direction. The Berbers assimilated quite a lot of Roman customs and culture, it seems.'

'You can still see it,' said Modesty. 'It's there in Moroccan architecture. And the oasis *ksar* is like pictures I've seen of Roman camps.

'*Castra*,' said Collier. 'The words are similar, too.'

'It's a very small place, of course.' Tarrant eased the ash from his cigar. 'Rather like Petra in Jordan, I imagine, but smaller.'

'I don't see what can be wrong there,' Collier said pensively. 'What *kind* of wrong does Aaronson mean?'

'I wish I knew, but at least he'll tell us shortly. On the phone he just kept saying there was something amiss, he was sure of it. The letters from Professor Tangye aren't right, they're concealing something. When I asked what he suspected about Tangye he was very cross. Insisted that they were lifetime friends and that he'd trust Tangye as he'd trust himself.' Tarrant shrugged helplessly. 'Mus is in the middle of nowhere, and there's just Tangye's team, no local workers, so he can't have any labour trouble.'

'You mentioned letters,' Modesty said after a moment.

'Yes. Presteign has backed the dig very handsomely. They have the best of equipment. And an aircraft takes out supplies once a week from Algiers. It also carries mail.'

'Why doesn't Aaronson go out himself?' Collier asked.

Tarrant tapped a thumb to his chest. 'Heart. It's pretty hot out there.' He looked at Modesty. 'I'm sorry.'

She smiled. 'I don't mind the trip. I'd rather like to see a dig. Do I make my own way there?'

'Good Lord, no. If you agree, Aaronson will fix with Presteign that you can go from Algiers with the supply aircraft.'

'Has he told Presteign of his worries?'

'Yes. Presteign listens politely and makes reassuring noises. He's almost certainly right. Poor old Aaronson's developed an obsession, I'm afraid.'

'Never mind. I'll go out and talk nicely to Tangye, then come back and make reassuring noises myself.'

'I shall be pathetically grateful.'

42

'Would two heads be better than one?' asked Collier. 'I mean, could I go along for the ride? I feel my presence would add a touch of academic distinction to the whole thing. Better than just having a female hoodlum rolling up out of the blue.'

Tarrant exhaled thoughtfully. 'You have a point——'

Modesty said, 'Thank you.'

'I mean he has a point to the extent that he might help if Tangye is difficult. He's said to be tetchy.'

'All right.' Modesty looked at Collier. 'I'll hold your hand and quote statistics during the flight.'

'You may do so,' Collier agreed, 'whenever you have a moment to spare from carrying advice, exhortations and urgent technical questions from me to the pilot. Just don't try to unfasten my safety-belt, that's all.'

4

It was five minutes to eleven when Modesty eased the Jensen FF through the traffic at Hyde Park Corner and into the park. She wore a matching wild silk coat now. Tarrant sat beside her, Collier in the back.

She flicked a switch on the dash and said, 'Willie hasn't surfaced for the last month, but you never know.'

'I love it when you're cryptic,' Collier said. 'What for God's sake was that supposed to mean?'

'We have a casual listening-out sked for twenty-three hundred hours daily, our time. Willie hasn't answered for quite a while, but if it's convenient I like to give him a call.'

'Are you talking about radio?' asked Collier. 'Is that what all that gubbins under the dash is about?'

'That gubbins under the dash is a KW 2000A transceiver, powered from the battery through transistorised circuits. Willie has one at The Treadmill and one mobile to take around with him on long trips.'

'I didn't know you were a ham operator,' said Tarrant.

'Licensed radio amateur. Ham isn't a popular word among hams.' She drew up at the traffic lights at Grosvenor Gate and clipped on a small, lightweight attachment which presented a mike close to her mouth.

'Say some more cryptic things,' Collier encouraged.

'All right. This is vox-operated transmission, which means the set automatically switches to send when you start speaking, and to receive when you stop. No hands. Our sked is on the 20-metre band—spot frequency fourteen one-o-three megs.'

'You're joking of course,' said Collier. 'Willie's in the States or beyond. You can't have a chat with him from a car driving

44

through Hyde Park. They only do that in television spy-thrillers.'

'I've driven through London talking to Willie and other amateurs in Hong Kong, India, Brazil, New Zealand—you name it.'

'And I spent ten minutes this morning trying to make a phone-call to Harrods,' said Collier. He leaned forward. 'I don't believe you, of course. But if he does come on the air can I say something rude to him?'

'No. You can't even say hallo without a licence. As a matter of fact we're not supposed to operate while in a Royal Park, but we'll be out in a minute and it's an archaic rule anyway.' The lights changed, and the Jensen flowed forward.

'The amateur bands are monitored,' Tarrant said over his shoulder to Collier, 'and I understand the rules are tough. No religion, no politics, no third-party messages, and no sex.'

'I don't think sex by shortwave would interest me enormously,' said Collier. 'Still, if it's illegal it should attract Modesty——' He broke off, startled. The faint mush of sound from the speaker on the dash had suddenly taken on a hollow, businesslike note. Then Willie Garvin's voice spoke clearly.

'G3QRO, G3QRO, here is G3QRM stroke HP calling on sked. How copy?'

Before Collier could fully take in the extraordinary simplicity of it all, Modesty was replying. 'G3QRM stroke HP, here is G3QRO mobile replying. You're coming in fine. My QTH is—well, call it the Bayswater Road. I've got Sir Gerald and Steve with me. Steve doesn't believe it. How copy?'

Willie's voice said, 'Good and clear. I've got Jacqueline here.'

In the mirror Collier saw Modesty's face change. She said, 'Hold it,' and turned into the big roundabout at Marble Arch. Instead of continuing she pulled left into the lay-by and cut the engine. She said into the mike, 'Will she be there for long?'

Willie's voice said, 'Well, it depends on our old friend Uncle Gabby.'

This time Collier saw Tarrant stiffen in his seat and turn to

45

stare at Modesty. His face was no longer relaxed and amiable, and Collier suddenly remembered the kind of world in which Tarrant performed his grim and hidden tasks.

'. . . we both feel it's a bit claustrophobic 'ere,' Willie was saying. 'Still, I'm keeping meself busy.'

'What are you busy at?' Modesty asked. Her face was intent, and Collier felt she was listening for a cue of some kind.

'The old Arabic,' said Willie. 'Coming on a treat, too. I reckon I'll be as good as you by the time I get 'ome.'

Modesty relaxed. 'That's fine. I seem to remember you were having a lot of trouble with that long poem by Sa'ad.'

'I've got if off by 'eart now.' There was pride in Willie's voice. 'Listen . . .' He began to speak another language, rhythmically but with occasional hesitations.

Modesty pulled a small pad from under the dash and flicked her hand at Tarrant, who put a gold propelling pencil in it.

Willie spoke for perhaps two minutes, and during that time Modesty wrote only once—a number. Collier sat very still. This was business. He did not know what shape it took, but his stomach fluttered with unease.

'How was that, then?' Willie ended.

'Not bad. You've been practising your accent. But that second stanza wasn't quite right. It should go——' She broke into Arabic for a few seconds, then added, 'Got it?'

'Ah, yes. Fine. Thanks a lot.'

'Always glad to help,' said Modesty. 'Look, the traffic's getting a little tangled so I'd better sign off. On sked again as soon as I can make it. This is G3QRO mobile, off and clear with eighty-eight.'

She waited for Willie's formal reply, then switched off and unclipped the mike. Collier said, 'Well . . . that was all a bit rum. What's eighty-eight?'

Modesty said briefly, 'Standard code for love and kisses.' She was looking at Tarrant.

'Gabriel.' Tarrant's voice was tired.

'Yes. He's climbed to the top of the heap again.'

'And now?'

'Willie's in trouble. I knew it when he didn't give his QTH right away and when he spoke about Jacqueline. That's our danger-word.' She pulled out a World Airways Guide from under her seat and began to thumb through the pages.

'It can't be bad trouble if he's able to transmit?' Tarrant made it a question.

'Not bad. But tricky. Willie was careful, even in Arabic. Used a lot of argot. But he's got a blind girl with him. Two of Gabriel's hatchetmen killed her sister and were trying to take the girl alive. Willie doesn't know why. He's got her in a cottage about an hour from Panama City, and they're lying low.'

'They'd better,' Tarrant said bleakly. 'Gabriel doesn't stop.'

'Willie knows that. So they're pinned down. He's afraid to try getting this girl out on his own. He thinks it needs someone to run an interference play, and someone who's not blown to take the girl out.'

'I wouldn't try anything less against Gabriel. Not in Panama. Is Willie uncovered?'

'He doesn't know. Gabriel may have guessed.'

'How?'

'Willie signed the hoods off.'

'Knife?'

'I imagine so. He didn't give details.'

'Quite.' Tarrant sighed and rubbed his eyes. 'We'll give Aaronson a miss.'

'Half an hour won't make any difference. Leave Heathrow for New York at 1830 tomorrow, and a DC8 from there gets me to Panama City at 1930 Saturday.' She closed the thick book and switched on the engine. 'At least I can hear what Aaronson has to say—and offer to go later if you can't find anyone else.'

'You'll come straight back to England with the girl?' Tarrant asked.

'I think so. She'll be safer here. Then we can get a few of our old contacts busy to find what Gabriel's up to.'

'And then?'

'Take Gabriel out.' She eased down the accelerator. 'It's the only way to end it.'

'Oh, my God,' Collier said quietly. 'I thought we'd finished with all that.'

'Don't be silly, Steve. You're not involved.'

'I meant you.' Collier was silent for a few seconds, fighting against a sudden stupid compulsion that slid obscenely into his mind. It made his palms sweat and his heart thump with fright. He went on, 'But come to think of it, you need somebody in Panama who's not blown, don't you?'

Tarrant turned in his seat and lifted an eyebrow. 'There won't be any safety-belt,' he said mildly.

'I know that!' Collier snapped. 'I bloody well know that as well as you do. What's more, I scare easily and I'm no good at sticking knives in hatchetmen. But if Modesty just wants somebody who can grab this girl and run like the clappers while all the frolic is going on elsewhere, I'm well up on the short-list.'

Modesty glanced at Tarrant, 'He may be right. And he's had a bit of experience.'

'Don't remind me,' Collier said resentfully. 'I'm going to sleep badly tonight as it is. Oh, and I haven't a visa for Panama. But no doubt you have some gruesome friend who'll forge one for me at short notice.'

'You don't need one for Panama. All the same, I must ring Dimple Haigh tonight and get hold of a blank for this girl.'

'Dimple Haigh,' echoed Collier, and wiped his brow. 'I knew it. God help me, I'll *look* like my passport photograph before this is over.'

Modesty flicked a smile at him in the mirror. 'You said that darkly.'

Five minutes later the car drew up outside a small terraced house off the Bayswater Road. As Collier handed Modesty out he saw a figure by the white-painted front door at the end of the short tiled path leading up to it.

For a moment he doubted his eyes. The figure seemed impossibly huge for a man, and wrongly proportioned. Then it moved, as a hand was raised to press the door-bell, and Collier saw that neither his eyes nor the darkness had misled him.

The man stood over six and a half feet tall. His shoulders were almost as wide as the door, and very square, with a huge round head perched upon them. There seemed to be no neck. His massive trunk was an unnaturally long oblong from which short legs projected, so short that it was hard to imagine any articulation at the knee. But despite the length of body, the hands hung almost to the knees.

Collier felt distaste, and was immediately ashamed.

'Shall I lead the way?' Tarrant said quietly, and moved up the path. Collier took Modesty's arm and followed. The man at the door turned. He wore a dark suit that in some way encompassed his great bulk without hanging badly. His hair was thick and auburn above the pale moon of the face, a face so big that the features seemed to have no unity.

The man inclined his head courteously and said to Tarrant, 'Are you Dr. Aaronson?' The voice was deep and cultured, with the quiet ease of a man completely unembarrassed by a physical appearance verging on the grotesque.

'No, I'm afraid not,' said Tarrant. 'I'm calling on him.'

'So was I,' said the big man. 'He doesn't seem to be at home.' His eyes moved past Tarrant to take in Modesty and Collier without interest. 'I've rung four times, and I can see no lights.'

'He was here when I phoned a quarter of an hour ago,' Tarrant said, frowning. 'And he's expecting us.'

'I understood that he was expecting me, too.' There was a shadow of annoyance in the big man's voice.

'Perhaps he slipped out to borrow a cup of sugar or something,' said Collier with forced cheerfulness.

The big man looked at him, and suddenly grinned. 'You

may be right. I prefer not to wait, though. If you'll excuse me . . .'

They had to move aside to allow his bulk to pass. Tarrant said, 'Shall we say who called?'

'Armitage. Of the British Museum. If you'd tell him I'll ring tomorrow, that would be very kind. Goodnight.' He moved down the path, his short legs carrying him with incredible lightness, and turned through the gate towards the main road.

'Your friend Aaronson has big friends,' said Collier, and moved to the door. 'Now, one always feels very furtive doing this, but I think it's called for.' He bent down, pushed open the flap of the letter-box and peered through. 'Ah! Would anyone like to see this magnificent view of the inside of a mail box?' He straightened up, and saw that Modesty had moved down the path to the gate. She was looking along the road after Armitage.

When she returned she said to Tarrant, 'You don't know him—by description, I mean?'

'No.' Tarrant looked hard at her. 'Why do you ask?'

She gave a little shrug. 'I'm not sure. Try the bell, Steve.'

'Our friend from the British Museum tried it four times.'

'So he said. Don't let's have a debate about it, darling.'

Collier pressed the button. With his ear close to the door he could hear a bell ringing faintly at the rear of the house. 'I think he must live at the back,' he said. 'That would account for no lights showing.'

'He does,' said Tarrant. 'Is the bell ringing?'

'Yes.'

'Just a minute, Steve.' Modesty reached past him. 'It's only a Yale lock,' she said, and her hand moved up and down against the jamb of the door for a few seconds. 'All right, give it a push.'

Collier pushed and the door swung open. He stared as Modesty returned a thin strip of celluloid to her handbag. 'You can't do that!'

'It's not even a misdemeanour yet, let alone a felony.' She looked at Tarrant. 'Would Dr. Aaronson mind if we waited inside?'

Tarrant said calmly, 'Since the door's open, I'll invite you to do so.' He led the way in. There was light coming from somewhere above, towards the back of the house, and a bright line of it showing under a door at the end of a long passage. Collier closed the front door as Tarrant found a switch. The twin lamps of a wrought iron chandelier lit up the close-carpeted hall.

'That's his study.' Tarrant indicated a door to the right. 'I think we'd better go through to the living-room.' He moved forward. As he reached the end of the passage he stopped abruptly.

Here the staircase ran up on the right, doubling back from the passage. At the foot of the stairs, his legs sprawled limply up the first three, lay a small man in a rather baggy grey suit. He was face down, his head bent acutely under one arm. A pair of broken spectacles jutted out between his shoulder and the floor.

Collier's stomach heaved and he said, 'Oh, Christ . . .'

Tarrant bent and lifted one arm carefully so that he could see the face, then lowered the arm again. 'It's Aaronson,' he said.

Modesty was kneeling, resting two fingers against the side of the neck. After ten seconds she looked up at Tarrant with a wry grimace.

Collier felt a sudden unreasoning anger against her. An hour ago everything had been so good. But she was just bloody trouble-prone. Tomorrow they would be off on some lunatic jaunt to Panama. And as if that wasn't enough, she was now busy feeling the carotid artery of a man who had fallen downstairs and killed himself.

'You didn't expect him to be alive with his neck broken, did you?' he said savagely.

'Just making sure.' Her voice was gentle, almost soothing,

and his irritation rose. With an effort he took control of himself and said, 'Sorry. A bit jumpy.'

Tarrant was standing still, hands in the pockets of his jacket, not quite masking his grief as he stared down. 'I know his heart had been bad for a long time,' he said, and glanced up the stairs. 'Or he could simply have fallen. He was always one of those unco-ordinated people.'

'I'm sorry.' Modesty stood up as she spoke, and touched Tarrant's arm. Collier remembered with a pang of shame that the dead man and Tarrant had been old friends. Tarrant, many years a widower, with two sons killed in the war, and holding the dirty, lonely, but necessary job that was his, probably had few enough friends.

'Who should we phone?' Collier asked quietly.

Tarrant looked up. 'Nobody yet. I'll see to all that when you've gone.' He turned back to Modesty and took her hand. 'You have things to do in a hurry. Just get in the car and drive quietly away. I'll deal with everything here.'

She nodded, then said again, 'I'm sorry.'

Tarrant lifted her hand and kissed the fingers briefly. 'Forget about it now. And take care. Please.'

'I always do.' She took Collier's arm. When they had moved only two paces she halted and looked back at Tarrant. 'Just as a long shot, try ringing the British Museum tomorrow. Ask if they have a Mr. Armitage.'

5

DINAH PILGRIM lay awake in bed with only a sheet over her, wearing the nightdress Willie Garvin had bought for her. It felt pretty, and he said it was very pale pink. All the clothes he had bought felt good and fitted surprisingly well; she thought he was probably quite experienced in buying for girls.

After three days she knew the little cottage and the placing of the furniture in every detail. The shock, if not the grief, of Judy's death had passed. Willie Garvin had helped in that, not by words of comfort but simply by his presence and his manner, which in themselves were strangely healing.

If he pitied her blindness he had never said so. If he admired the way she overcame it, he had never said so. He did not avoid speaking of the fact that she was blind. For all this she was glad. And he never forgot her blindness even in idle conversation; when she had spoken of Balboa he did not ask if she had seen the orchid gardens there, he asked if she had smelt them.

The cottage, a single-storey building with a gabled roof and thick adobe walls, lay a few miles from the Pan-American Highway, set back from a minor road and screened by trees. It belonged to an Englishman who was the local man for a London importer of turtle shell and mother-of-pearl. He and his wife had gone home on three months' leave. There was one bedroom, a big living-room, a kitchen and a small room for an office. Willie had set up a camp bed in the office for himself.

He had been out only once, the first morning, and then he had not used the old Pontiac which stood in the asbestos frame garage behind the cottage, but had worn peasant clothes and borrowed a battered van from a boat repairer in

Puerto de Chorrera. He had returned after four hours, with clothes, toiletry and make-up for her, and provisions for at least ten days. He had also bought a Polaroid camera. Those four hours were the only time that she had felt afraid.

The cottage had electricity, a fridge, and a telephone. He had not used the phone to call London because the details of all international calls would be logged at the exchange in Panama City. And, in Willie's words, '. . . with the right contacts you could buy a sight of that log for ten bucks'.

But there was some kind of radio in the Pontiac. Twice, at six in the afternoon, he had driven the car out of the garage and made a call. Today when he returned she had sensed the contentment in him even before he told her that Modesty Blaise would reach Panama City in the next two or three days.

Modesty Blaise. He had told Dinah a little about her, but not much. She still found it extraordinary that Willie's friend in London, the friend who would come and help to get her out, was a woman; and even more extraordinary that he seemed to regard this woman as being in command. When she had asked Willie about it he had said simply, 'She's better at it than I am. Better than anyone.'

It was past midnight now, but Willie was still up, doing something in the living-room. Her sensitive ears could pick up an occasional movement, and sometimes he whistled softly and rather tunelessly to himself, as if he were concentrating.

Dinah Pilgrim threw back the sheet and sat up, reaching for the house-coat she had hung over the chair beside the bed. A few moments later she opened the door and went into the living-room.

Willie Garvin looked up and saw her standing in the now familiar position, her eyes looking a little to one side of him and her head cocked to listen. He saw that she had put on a touch of lipstick and that it was slightly askew.

'You ought to be asleep,' he said. 'Did you want something, love?'

'No. I just felt a bit restless.'

'It's a muggy sort of heat.'

'Oh, sure. But that doesn't worry me. Would you like a cup of coffee, Willie?'

'Love it.' He did not offer to make the coffee for her, or to help, but only looked quickly round to see that the furniture was in its proper place. She smiled in his direction and went across the room towards the kitchen.

When they first came to the cottage she had moved about with lips slightly pursed, making a series of short, barely audible whistles. Her ears were tuned to pick up the reflection of the sound, and so give her warning of any object in her way. This ability had fascinated Willie. Watching her now as she went into the kitchen he felt a wave of pity for her. To imagine being in darkness for ever was as impossible as imagining the light-year distances of astronomy. He closed his eyes and tried to think that he would never be able to open them again.

He could hear her in the kitchen, opening the fridge, putting a saucepan on the stove. Her touch was always deft and sure as long as everything was in its proper place, and he was very careful about that.

'What have you stopped for?' she called from the kitchen. 'You've been scraping at something for the last hour.'

'Just 'aving a think,' he said, and opened his eyes to look at the muddy knob of nacre in his fingers. 'You've got ears like radar trackers.'

'As big?'

'You miniaturised 'em somehow.' He blinked once or twice, looking at the table. On it lay several goldsmith's files, flat and triangular, coarse and smooth, a Stanley knife, emery paper, ruby powder, a chamois leather and a Zeiss lens.

He picked up the knife and resumed his gentle scraping to make the nacreous lump spherical. Dinah came in carrying two cups of coffee. She put them down on the table and sat in the chair opposite him.

'Thanks, love.'

'What are you scraping, Willie?'

'A pearl. Not really a pearl, a sort of freak blister. All right for practice, though.'

'Practising what?'

'Well, most pearls need a beauty specialist, whether they're round, drop-shape or baroque. They've often got a little dimple, or a bump, or maybe a coloration blemish. But a pearl's like an onion, with lots of skins. You can sometimes take a poor 45-grain pearl and scrape it down till you've got a 30-grain that's a little beauty. But it's tricky. If you slip up you can start with a thousand quid and end up with a pile of chalk-dust.'

She giggled. 'Say "thahsand quid" again.'

'Why?'

'It's cute. Quid means a pound, doesn't it?'

'M'mm. But I'm not going to say a thousand quid again. Not if it's cute.'

'Okay.' She sipped her coffee. 'You like pearls, Willie?'

'Better than gemstones. There's something about 'em. They're sort of living things.'

'And you collect them?'

'Just a pastime. I was looking for two or three specials over in Paloto. Lucky, too. But I still need a nice 40-grain.'

She was silent for a while, listening to him work. Idly she wondered why it did not worry her that officially she would be thought dead by now. Only Willie Garvin and Modesty Blaise knew she was alive. And Luco, who would keep his silence. And Gabriel.

Gabriel was a strangely unreal figure to her, but still frightening. The fact that Willie Garvin would take not the smallest chance with Gabriel held a significance that was a little terrifying. She had stopped wondering why Gabriel wanted her. Surprisingly, she found herself reluctant to wonder about it now. Her life had contracted suddenly to the very small world of the cottage and Willie Garvin, and for the moment she was strangely content. After the shock and horror and grief it was a relief to have this breathing space when time stood still for a while.

Modesty Blaise would come, and take her to London. She had agreed to go because Willie thought it best. Her own passport was lost. But Willie had told her not to worry about that.

She heard him move his chair, and he said, 'Cigarette?'

'Please.'

She held out her hand and he put a lighted cigarette between her fingers, then resumed his scraping. She said, 'Is Modesty your girl-friend, Willie?'

She could tell when he smiled by the slight difference in his voice. He said, 'Girl and friend, yes. Girl-friend, no. I used to work for her.'

'As what?'

'That's a bit of a story. I'll tell you another time.'

'Tonight.'

'It's too late tonight.'

She said firmly, 'Tomorrow, then. And make it a promise.'

'All right. Tomorrow.'

Willie Garvin paused in his scraping and watched with a touch of amusement as the frown of determination left her face. She was small, and young, and blind, and in many ways defenceless, but she had resilience and a lot of strength in her.

He picked up one of the files and began to use it with a light touch, turning the little sphere in his fingers.

'Do you have a girl-friend—a regular one?' Dinah asked.

'No. I only 'ave irregular ones.' He put down his cigarette and peered closely at the nacre. ''Allo . . .'

'What is it?'

'Not sure. This blister's cracked, I think.' He picked up the lens and screwed it into his eye. Under the magnification a hairline crack showed in the muddy surface of the sphere. He drew the file across lightly and the crack widened. Picking

57

up the knife, he probed delicately with the point of the blade. The nacre split suddenly like the shell of a walnut, and he was barely quick enough to catch what fell from within.

Dinah sat listening, hearing the clatter of the knife as it dropped to the table and his sudden intake of breath. When he spoke there was a world of wonder and delight in his voice.

'God, it's a pearl, Dinah! A beauty. There's not a flaw in it!'

'But how——?'

'It was *inside* the chunk I was working on.' She heard him get up and move round the table. 'Here, feel it.' He took her hand and put the pearl on her palm. She felt it with the fingertips of her other hand.

'I don't know about pearls, but it seems a fair size, Willie.'

'About forty to forty-five grains. Honest to God, it's the very thing I was after.'

'Valuable?'

'Not a fortune. Seven-fifty to a thousand quid. But it's exactly what I wanted.' His voice was shot with excitement, and her own pleasure rose at his delight.

'I'm so glad for you, Willie. Here.' She held the pearl for him to take. 'You said a thousand quid again.'

'I'll say it as often as you like now, love. You've brought me luck.'

'Well, that's something. I hope it makes up for the trouble I brought.'

His hand touched her shoulder for a moment and his voice was cheerful. 'I find trouble like the sparks fly upwards, Dinah. I'm just glad it was dumped in me lap by a pretty girl this time.'

'You mean that? Pretty?' She turned her head in the direction of his voice.

'No. You're a lot better than pretty. You're a looker, Dinah. Now get your beauty sleep so you stay that way. Go on, off you go.'

She got up and moved towards the open bedroom door. 'What about your own beauty sleep?'

'I'll just wash the cups and clear up 'ere first.'

When he returned from the kitchen she was still standing in the bedroom doorway and seemed to be lost in thought. She said, 'Willie, come here a minute.'

'What's up?'

'Nothing. Come here. You haven't got a face yet.'

'I *what*?' He moved across the room.

'I know you're big and I know what you're like inside, but I haven't let myself make a picture of your face yet because I want it to be right when I do. Stand still a minute.'

Her hands touched his chest, then slid quickly up. He said nothing, but felt at once moved and embarrassed as her slim fingers moved with butterfly lightness over his face, dwelling on the line of his jaw and brow, the set of his ears, and the shape of his mouth. Her own eyes were closed, her face absorbed as she concentrated.

'You reckon beauty sleep can 'elp?' he said with an awkward laugh.

She lowered her hands. 'Blue eyes and fair hair?'

'That's right. How d'you know?'

'I've got good at guessing.' She opened her eyes and lifted her head a little, then put up her hands again and linked them behind his neck. She said quietly, firmly, 'Love me, Willie.'

It was many years since Willie Garvin had been thrown completely off balance by a girl. Confused, he stared down into the sightless eyes and felt ashamed that his pulse raced. He said hurriedly, 'Have you gone round the twist or something? I can't do that!'

'Why not? There won't be any strings.'

'It's not that——'

'Then why not? I'm not stealing anything from another girl. You said so.'

'No, but——'

'You think I won't be much good at it. I guess you could be

59

right. Or maybe you were only being kind just now when you said I was a looker.'

He swore. 'I wasn't!'

'Then what?'

'I . . . for Pete's sake, I don't know!'

A smile warmed her face and she gave him a little shake. 'Is it because you feel you'd be taking an advantage? Like stealing pennies from a blind girl's cup?'

After a long moment Willie Garvin said helplessly, 'I suppose so. Yes. Christ, I feel *exactly* that! So stop it, Dinah, please.'

'No. I'm offering my pennies, for what they're worth. Not as a thank-you. Not because I owe them. Just because I want to. I'll only stop if you say flat out that you don't feel anything and don't want to love me. It'll hurt a bit, but not nearly as much as if you just took me out of pity. If you did that, I'd know. And I'd hate you for it.'

Willie Garvin swore again. Then he let out a long slow breath. She felt the tension go from his shoulders. He took her wrists and drew her hands gently from behind his neck.

'You won't need to 'ate me, Dinah,' he said slowly. 'I've spent three days being careful not to look at you or think about you this way. Now you've bloody well wrecked it.'

'Good,' she said in a low voice. 'So do something about it, Willie.' He bent and picked her up easily in his arms. She felt warm and light as he carried her into the bedroom.

Some time later she said, 'Why did you put the light on?'

'Because you're a looker. All over. You look like a million dollars.'

He saw laughter touch her face as she said, 'Make it a thousand quid. You know something? I'm getting a better picture of you all the time. You've got too many scars on your body . . . do they show much?'

'Not much. I heal pretty good. Don't make a picture of me with seams all over, like a football.'

She smiled and touched his face. 'I won't. Which scars did you get in bed?'

Indignantly—'Only one!'

She laughed again, and held him fiercely.

Later she said, 'Am I . . . you know, not very good?'

'You're fine, Dinah. Fine.'

'Then do something for me, Willie. Try to remember I'm not made of spun glass. I won't break.'

Later still she cried out with happiness as the tempest of release swept through her and merged with his own.

McWhirter put down the phone and went through to the living-room of the suite on the fourth floor of the Hotel Cadiz, a glossy new pillar of chrome and black glass on the eastern edge of Panama City.

Gabriel sat in an armchair, chin resting on the linked fingers of his hands. He said in a flat voice. 'Situation.'

McWhirter took a thick notebook with a limp black leather cover from his pocket and flicked it open. 'Finding of the boat and the girl's body by a fisherman was reported in the press yesterday morning. Since her blind sister's not been found, she's presumed drowned. We had all outlets from Panama covered as from o-one-hundred hours next day, and every available contact is looking for the girl now. We've enough heavies on immediate call for any action required once we have a lead to the girl. Costs to date, eight thousand six hundred and forty-five dollars, wi' a contingency of two thousand.'

'The eyes have descriptions of Garvin as well as the girl?'

'Aye. You still think it was him?'

'I know it.' Gabriel turned lifeless eyes on McWhirter. 'And Garvin knows it was us. He must have seen us on the yacht. He wouldn't just lie low with the girl for anyone less.'

McWhirter nodded gloomily. 'D'ye think he followed us there?'

'I think it was chance,' said Gabriel, and got up. 'But it doesn't matter. It was bound to happen.'

McWhirter watched him curiously, wondering at the depth of hatred which had marred some small component in that cold, logical mind. Gabriel did not believe in the workings of fate, yet he believed with fanatic certainty that somehow, sometime, there would come a return match against Blaise and Garvin.

McWhirter had never shared this obsession, but now he felt the growing conviction that it was to be fulfilled. From his own hatred sprang a sudden longing; he had a vivid mental picture of Garvin lying broken and dead. And Blaise, too. Broken and dead . . .

That reminded him. McWhirter moistened his lips before he said warily, watching Gabriel, 'That call just now. It was from London. The big feller. He's seen to Aaronson.'

Gabriel was at the window, staring down over the parking lot and the rich green swathe of tropical trees beyond. He did not turn as he spoke. 'You told him we missed getting the girl?'

'Aye.'

'And?'

McWhirter hesitated. 'He laughed.'

'That's right.' Now Gabriel turned, and his pale eyes came briefly alive with sudden bitterness. 'He's mad. He plays it all like a game, and it always works for him. Mad, but lucky.'

McWhirter made a noncommittal sound in his throat. 'He said perhaps he ought to come and do the job himself. I told him no.'

Gabriel nodded bleakly. 'Anything else?'

'You reckoned that Garvin turning up here was chance. Here's another. The big feller was much amused that when he came out of Aaronson's house he ran into Tarrant and Modesty Blaise paying a call.'

'*What?*'

'Aye, it made me jump, too. But then I checked . . .' McWhirter flicked back to an early page in the black notebook, a page headed *Aaronson*. 'He was an old friend of Tarrant's.

We know he was worried, that's why he had to go. If Presteign didn't want to listen, Tarrant might.'

'And Blaise?'

McWhirter shrugged. 'Second opinion. But they were too late. They can't *know* anything. And if they're making guesses it's the big feller's worry, not ours.'

'Yes.' The monosyllable held a note of satisfaction. 'You're still checking on international calls?'

'We have a running check. I don't say Garvin hasn't got a call out, but there's been nothing o' significance to us on the log.'

'Never mind.' Gabriel grinned suddenly, a grimace without humour. 'You're a fool McWhirter, and so am I. Garvin's pinned down with the blind girl. He'll yell for Blaise somehow, and she'll come fast. And she'll lead us to Garvin. So warn all your eyes at the airport.'

McWhirter chuckled, and his bright cruel eyes began to twinkle. He put the notebook away and moved to the door.

6

STEPHEN COLLIER came out of the Customs Hall into a red and purple sunset. He felt sticky. The day's heat still lingered, coming up from the baked ground now. The porter carrying his two cases said, 'Que hotel quiere usted, señor?'

'Hotel Santa Rosa, Calle Torrella.'

'Bueno.'

A cab drew up and Collier watched as the bags were put inside. Modesty Blaise was somewhere behind him, he did not know where. They had travelled separately to London Airport. On the seven and a half hour flight of the Boeing 707, he had travelled tourist and she first class.

He felt neither elated nor apprehensive, only slightly unreal. Twenty paces from where he stood a police car was parked with two uniformed men in it. Everything was safe and civilised and normal. It was hard to accept that somewhere nearby were men who had been watching for Willie Garvin and a blind girl for the past four days.

He gave the porter a dollar and got into the cab, wondering how long it would be before he saw the airport again. A day? A week?

'It shouldn't be long,' Modesty had said. 'But don't start counting hours. You're there to talk to the education authorities with a view to marketing a translation of your book. But you're going to be more or less confined to your hotel with stomach trouble as soon as you arrive, maybe for a few hours, maybe longer.'

As the cab drew away Collier practised making a brave grimace and pointing to his stomach.

It was five minutes later when Modesty Blaise came out of the airport building followed by a porter with a trolley. She wore a light Crimplene dress in navy with white edging, and carried only a large handbag. As she reached the kerb, the door of the police car opened and a tall slender man got out. He wore a lightweight olive green uniform with a Sam Browne and a flap holster. His face was very lean, with large cool eyes and a moustache like two thin pencil-strokes.

He stood in front of Modesty and saluted languidly. 'Miss Blaise?'

'Yes.'

'I would like you to accompany me, if you please.' His English was good. 'I am Captain Sagasta, of the Panama City police.'

She stared, a little hostile. 'I don't understand.'

'You have been in Panama before, I believe?'

'Yes. Four or five years ago.'

'That is what our records say, Miss Blaise. There are certain irregularities which occurred during that visit, and we wish to inquire into them now that you are available.'

'I see.' She stood very still for a few moments. 'Can't it wait until I've booked into my hotel? I'll be at the Hilton——'

'I am afraid not, Miss Blaise. As for booking in . . .' A shrug. 'The inquiry may take some time.'

After another pause she said, 'I'd like to make a phone-call.'

'Later, perhaps. Please enter the car.'

When McWhirter went through to Gabriel's bedroom to report, he was frowning. Gabriel had taken off his jacket and lay on the bed, hands behind his head, eyes hooded.

'She's here,' said McWhirter. 'But the police picked her up at the airport an' took her in to help wi' inquiries. Unfinished business from a few years ago.' He shrugged. 'They might keep her a couple of hours or God knows how long. I've a man watching police headquarters.'

Gabriel propped himself on an elbow. He said balefully, 'We need her for the lead. Use some oil and get her sprung.'

'It's Sagasta,' said McWhirter. His voice held disgust. 'He'll not be bought. We can go higher, but Sagasta's stubborn and it'll take time.'

The extension phone beside the bed rang. Gabriel nodded and McWhirter picked it up. The voice was American. McWhirter said, 'Aye, go ahead, Reilly.' After a few seconds he said, 'Hold it,' then put his hand over the mouthpiece and looked at Gabriel with a gleam of excitement lighting his long face. 'Reilly's stumbled on a lead. He took the yacht to a wee boat-yard along the coast, wanting the keel checked after we scraped bottom in the shallows that night. Talked to a feller there who said an Englishman was living in a house somewhere up behind Puerto de Chorrera.'

'There could be a thousand Englishmen living in Panama,' Gabriel said coldly.

'This one's big and fair . . . wi' a great scar on the back of his hand, shaped like an S.' Gabriel sat up slowly as McWhirter went on. 'And he's lying low. He has a car, but he borrowed their van, the boat-yard van, to drive into Panama City an' back a few days ago, dressed like a local.'

For a moment there were strange flecks of colour in Gabriel's eyes. Then he said, 'Tell Reilly to check it through, pin-point the house and cover it—but not too close. Garvin can smell trouble a long way off.'

McWhirter spoke concisely into the phone. When he rang off Gabriel said, 'Lay on a party for after dusk, and make it watertight, McWhirter.' He drew in a long breath. 'Watertight.'

The police car moved smoothly down the Avenida Central, past the cathedral with its twin mother-of-pearl domes gleaming under the frayed red disc of the dying sun. To the west rose the laval peak of Ancon Hill, sitting above the blend of modern and Spanish colonial buildings, above the busy new roads and the ancient maze of alleys and bazaars, above the living pot-pourri of Mestizos and Negroes, Chinese, Hindus and Europeans.

The car turned down beside the police station and into the courtyard at the back. Captain Sagasta got out and held the door open for Modesty. They had not spoken a word during the journey from the airport.

When they were in Captain Sagasta's office he closed the door, hung his cap on a peg, and held a tubular-legged chair for Modesty to be seated. In silence he offered her a cigarette and lit it with a cheap lighter. Moving to his swivel chair behind the desk he lit a cigarette for himself, leaned back and surveyed Modesty with quiet appraisal.

She smiled suddenly, inclined her head in a little gesture of acknowledgment and said, 'That was very kind of you. And congratulations. From sergeant to captain in five years is very good going for an honest cop.'

The teeth showed in his handsome but masculine face. 'You said very little when you rang from London. Now tell me. And remember please, I am still an honest cop.'

Modesty nodded. Five years ago she had visited one of her Network stringers in Panama. During that visit she had tried to secure a useful contact in the police force by bribing an intelligent young sergeant of considerable personality called Miguel Sagasta. He had not been indignant, but he had smiled into her eyes and told her that he was an honest cop. The movie cliché had amused them both, and she had felt glad that her business in Panama was almost legitimate—trading at a world cross-roads where ten thousand ships a year passed by. The fact that her goods for trade were mainly stolen was a minor matter. They had not been stolen in Panama, which was the only thing to concern Sagasta.

Her presence in the area at that time caused concern to someone else, however; to Marroc, the Chigro who controlled the thriving vice rackets in Panama. Marroc sent out orders that Modesty Blaise was to have an accident. It was five days later that Sagasta received a phone-call from her and went to a warehouse where he found Marroc unconscious, wounded in one arm, and with a bundle of files from his safe. The files provided enough evidence to put Marroc away for fifteen years, but he had died after four.

The Marroc affair had been the beginning of Sergeant Sagasta's rapid promotion.

Watching Modesty Blaise now across the desk, he drew on his cigarette unhurriedly, waiting for her answer.

She smiled at him and said, 'I wanted you to pick me up at the airport and take me in, because there are people watching for me there. I want them to think I'm out of action for the time being.'

'Who is watching for you?'

'Gabriel's men. You know him?'

'By reputation only.' Sagasta's eyes had become a little more alert. 'I heard through the grapevine that you had put him out of business a little while ago.'

'Not completely, it seems. He's managed to build a new organisation.'

'And he is here in Panama?'

'Yes. I don't know what name he's using, and you won't be able to touch him of course. He usually manages to keep his own hands clean.'

'Then what do you wish me to do?'

'Very little. Let me stay here till after dark. Hire a car for me and have it parked in the Plaza Bolivar. Take me out after dark, hidden in the back of a police car, and drop me at the Plaza. And stall if anyone inquires whether I'm still detained. That's all. Oh, and first let me make a phone-call to Willie Garvin.'

'Garvin. Another I know only by reputation. I was interested to see his name on the list of visitors.' He paused, then gestured with a slim, powerful hand. 'There has been a curious ripple through the underworld here over the past few days. This disturbs me.'

'Don't worry that you may have trouble building up. It just means that Gabriel has hired every mob and every small time hoodlum in Panama to look for Willie Garvin and a girl who's with him. I've come to take them out. When we've gone, Gabriel will go.'

Sagasta smoked in silence for a while. At last he looked at his watch, registered mild surprise, and said, 'I am officially off duty now.' His manner changed. He leaned back, unbuttoned the top of his jacket, and grinned at her engagingly.

'Very well, Miss Blaise. And if I do as you ask, what is my return for this assistance?'

'Your return?' She was puzzled. 'I thought——'

'There is a difference between a bribe and a return for services rendered—services which in no way conflict with my duty.' He continued to gaze at her steadily, amusement and a challenge in his eyes, and she remembered his reputation. Captain Sagasta was an athlete with women. It was a purely private hobby which had no effect whatever on his work. As she remembered, he smoked rarely and drank not at all. He had no family. He was single-minded in his work, and had only one relaxation. He was single-minded in that, too.

'You have lost a little of your hardness since we last met,' he mused. 'Certainly you are more beautiful, and there is perhaps a greater capacity for warmth.' He shrugged. 'Dinner at The Antigua one evening, the floor show at El Sombrero, a stroll along the Malecon, and . . . etcetera.'

With a quick urchin grin she said, 'Honest cop and honest lecher, too.'

'Lecher? I do not know this word.'

She explained, and he nodded grave agreement. 'That describes me admirably.'

She put out the cigarette and said without a shred of resentment, 'All right. You've got a deal.'

He gazed at her curiously, half smiling. After a long moment he gave a little shake of his head. 'No, we will not make a deal. I wanted to know if you had changed. To go against one like Gabriel calls for much firmness of purpose. There must be a force here,' he touched a hand to his temple, 'and here.' A long finger tapped at his heart. 'I wished to be sure.'

He leaned forward, resting a hand on one of the three telephones ranged neatly on his desk, and smiled. 'If you had hesitated to pay for what you want, I would not let you begin this.' He pushed the instrument towards her. 'Make your call.'

When the telephone rang, and Willie Garvin said 'Ah!', Dinah felt a little stab of sorrow. This was the end of a time when she had known more happiness than ever before in her life; a very brief time, little more than forty-eight hours, but holding a richness she would never know again in quite the same way, because the circumstances could never again be the same.

The circumstances. Terror and grief, then safety and trust. The haven of the cottage, a world outside time. Willie Garvin and security. Willie Garvin and gentleness and humour and making love in a way that opened wonderful new dimensions in her darkened world . . .

Willie lifted the phone and waited for the caller to speak. Then Dinah heard him say warmly, 'Princess.' A pause, then, 'Sure. No sweat so far.' A much longer pause. Once he chuckled. At last he said, 'Okay, we'll be ready.'

He put down the phone, moved to where Dinah sat on the long couch, and took her hands. 'We're off, love. Tonight.'

She made herself smile up at him. 'That was Modesty?'

'Sure.' He sat down and slipped an arm about her shoulders. She could feel the exhilaration in him and knew a sharp twinge of jealousy. He said, 'She'll be along with a car at nine-thirty sharp. That's only a couple of hours.'

'What about your own car?'

'Gabriel might 'ave checked the garages and found where I bought it. If he's got the make, model and number, he'll 'ave blokes looking out for it.' He chuckled again. 'I was a bit worried they might pick Modesty up at the airport. They did. But she'd fixed for some police captain she knows to take 'er straight in for questioning. That'll throw 'em.'

'What happens when she comes?'

'We'll take you to a little hotel in Calle Torrella. A bloke called Steve Collier's booked two rooms there, one for 'imself and one for 'is sister, Ellen Collier, arriving later. That's you.'

'I'll need a passport for signing in.'

'Modesty's brought along a used blank and a stamp. All we need is a photo, that's why I bought the camera. We'll take a few shots when I've made you look a bit different. Can you sign in without giving away that you can't see?'

'With just a little help. An arm to hold walking through the lobby and a finger resting on the register to guide me. Will you be there?'

'No. Steve'll meet the car outside and take you in.'

She frowned anxiously. 'You take me in, Willie, you're tuned in to me. He'll overdo it. People always help too much.'

'I can't show meself, Dinah. But you'll be okay with Steve. He's clever—a lot cleverer than he thinks. And sensitive as a radar antenna.'

She gave a little sigh. 'All right. What happens then?'

'You both stay in your rooms. Take meals there. The rooms communicate, so you can 'ave a chat.'

'I meant what happens to *you* then. And Modesty.'

'Then we get busy.' She sensed that he was smiling, and put up a hand to make sure. Willie let her fingers play quickly over his lips. He was used to this now, used to the idea that her impressions were audio-tactile and that because of this her patterns of thought were in many ways different from those of sighted people.

He said, 'I start showing meself a bit in town. Gabriel's boys tail me, maybe try to grab me. But Modesty's covering. That's easy because they reckon she's still in the nick. We play countertime——'

'What's that?'

'Sorry. Fencing term. You invite a hit so you can parry and get in yourself. We'll 'ave Gabriel's lot going round the bend in twenty-four hours, and a few of 'em out of action. When it's all humming nicely we'll call Steve. Mr. Collier books out with his sister, they go to the airport and catch the next plane. There's two seats booked on every plane for the next four days. You'll look different, you'll be with someone the eyes don't know, and if you act sighted they'll never spot you. Once you're clear, we'll pack in the interference play and follow. They'll see us go, but it won't matter by then.'

'It'll matter to me if they shoot you or something.'

'We'll be careful.' He got up and drew her to her feet. 'Come in the bathroom and let's 'ave a go at your hair.'

'What are you going to do with it?'

'Darken it with a spray rinse and fix it in another style.'

'You?' Her head tilted to one side in surprise. 'Where did you learn to do a girl's hair?'

'I got all kinds of talents.'

'I know.' She pulled his head down and kissed him. 'Where did you learn this one?'

'Looking after Modesty a couple of times when she'd been hurt pretty bad. I can put make-up on, too.'

She thought for a while, then said slowly, 'Willie . . . don't be mad. I know I ought to be grateful to Modesty, and I am. But I think maybe I'm not going to like her too much.'

'You don't 'ave to,' he said amiably, without resentment. 'You make up your own mind. Now let's get you altered a bit.'

Half an hour later she sat in an upright chair with her eyes open while Willie took flash pictures. Her hair was darker now, back-combed and smoothly domed. Two small pieces of foam rubber pushed up high inside her cheeks had changed the shape of her face. The third print was a good one. He trimmed it carefully and put it in an envelope.

'You can take the pads out now till you get to the hotel, Dinah,' he said.

For the next forty-five minutes Willie Garvin was busy clearing up and packing. It was as he fastened the strap of the case he had bought for Dinah that his ears began suddenly to prickle. He went into the small office, put out the light and stood looking through the slats of the blinds. He could see no movement in the darkness that swallowed the drive running between the trees.

He went through to the kitchen and looked out. There was nothing to be seen at the back of the house. When he returned to the living-room Dinah was standing up, facing him. She said a little tensely, 'What is it, Willie?'

'Trouble I think,' His voice was thoughtful. 'Can you 'ear anything?'

She listened with her whole being. At last—'No. Only natural sounds. But I think there are people near. I get feelings.'

'So do I.'

'It's not Modesty?'

'Too early. I think they've found us. Now don't worry.' For ten seconds he stood thinking, weighing chances. 'Just sit tight. I'm going to get the car out and bring it round to the front.'

'No, Willie! They'll shoot you!'

'Not yet, love. They know I'm 'ere. They can't know for sure that *you* are. They need to be certain of that before they kill me.'

'Then they—they'll rush you.'

'No. Not if they're Gabriel's boys.' He unbuttoned his shirt.

'Why not?'

'Because they know me,' he said simply, without vanity. Beneath the shirt, two small and beautifully-made throwing-knives lay sheathed against the left side of his chest. Dinah had followed the infinitesimal sound of his fingers unbuttoning the shirt. She knew about the knives, and fear expanded within her. 'Besides,' he went on, 'I'm going to offer 'em an easier way. Now listen while I tell you what to do.'

Two minutes later she waited with hammering heart while he brought the car round and came in by the front door, whistling quietly but cheerfully to himself. He took his own

73

two bags, went out again and put them in the back of the car. It was parked with its off-side towards the house and close to the small porch. The headlights were on, the engine was ticking over, and he had left both front doors of the car standing wide. A yellow porch light illuminated the area.

He returned to the house, put out the lights, took her hand and moved into the hall. Before going out he switched off the porch light, and the darkness was suddenly heavier by contrast. He closed the door behind them and said in a normal voice, 'Right, let's go.'

She was shivering as he moved with her round to the other side of the car. He whispered softly, 'Relax. Last thing they want is to get you damaged.'

As soon as she was in the passenger seat he closed the door, then moved very quickly round to the open off-side door. She came snaking face-down along the seat and slid out on to the ground. Looking into the car he said, 'All set?' She crawled past his legs and across the short space between the car and the house.

She was in the darkness of the porch, huddled on the tiled floor, when he got into the car and slammed the door.

Willie took the Pontiac away fast, the wheels spinning for a moment on the gravel. Along the drive a dark figure stepped out from the trees and shone a flashlamp on the ground, waving it up and down in an order to halt. Willie put his foot down and heard a yell as the man hurled himself clear. Three seconds later the Pontiac was out on the road.

In the porch Dinah still lay huddled, her face hidden in the crook of her arm, as Willie had told her, the front door key in her hand. She heard the fierce acceleration of the Pontiac, then other noises from different directions, feet moving on dry grass and crunching on gravel. Somebody ran past within a few yards of her. She heard a voice curse. Another voice, American, laughed and said, '. . . bottled up in a goddam car is no place for making with the knives.' The sound of feet and voices faded. Somewhere she heard

74

another car start up. With a throb of confident power that made her shiver anew, it snarled away in pursuit of the Pontiac.

Slowly she got to her feet and fumbled to put the key in the door.

7

'I DON'T like it very much,' Tarrant said moodily, and looked again at the Identikit picture on his desk, a likeness of the enormous man who had been at Aaronson's door on the night Aaronson had died.

London was asleep, as far as London ever slept. Tarrant had played bridge at his club until one, then called in at his Whitehall office before going home. His assistant, Fraser, was the night duty officer.

'I don't like it, Jack,' Tarrant repeated.

'You think this chap Armitage did him in?' Fraser said without much concern.

'There's no Armitage at the British Museum.'

Fraser sniffed, settled his spectacles more firmly on his long thin nose, and glanced again at the picture of the huge face. 'Maybe he was just flogging encyclopaedias. They'll give you any kind of spiel to get a foot in, day or night. My sister got talked into buying a set for her thirteen-year-old, Malcolm. The chap must have bloody well hypnotised her. It makes Malcolm's nose bleed trying to read Korky the Cat. Big sod, isn't he?'

'Malcolm?'

'No. He's a little sod. Man mountain there.'

'Yes. He's big all right. Big enough.'

'You mean did Aaronson fall downstairs and break his neck or did he have it wrung for him?'

'Our colleagues of the Metropolitan Police say accidental death.' Tarrant moved to the window and looked down on Whitehall. 'Frobisher let me compose the Identikit picture and said he'd try to trace the fellow, but I don't think he was very interested.'

'So what now?'

'That's what I don't like very much. I've got to decide about asking Modesty to take a look at the dig in Mus when she gets back from Panama.'

'She said she'd do it.'

'I know.' Irritation crept into Tarrant's voice. 'I don't know whether to drop the idea. I've done this kind of thing before —asked her to take a look at something innocuous that turned out to be a Red One job.'

'She's never complained.' Fraser put his feet up on the desk and rocked back in his chair. 'I don't see what's worrying you. We sit here knowing we can't do this job without getting a few people killed, so we go ahead and get them killed. I think you've gone soft on that girl.'

Tarrant looked round. 'Modesty's not one of our people. And even if she were, this Aaronson thing isn't one of our jobs.' He turned again, frowning, to look out upon the mild spring night, and said absently, 'Besides, it's late autumn, and she warms the chill from my bones.'

Fraser sighed. 'She'll go and have a look at that dig if she wants to, whether you like it or not. And anyway, there's Gabriel first and she's not back from Panama yet.'

Tarrant nodded, only half his attention on Fraser. He was thinking about a man, a kind of man; the kind, if he existed, who could kill, and walk out of a house and close the door just as a car drew up with visitors; who could coolly pretend that he had just arrived, and at the same time be genuinely amused by the moment of unexpected danger. It was abnormal, rather horribly abnormal.

'I don't like it very much,' Tarrant said again. 'But as you point out, she's not back from Panama yet.' He looked at his watch and deducted five hours. 'In fact it's not very long since she landed.'

Modesty Blaise stood in the shadows of the trees at the back of the house. The hired Plymouth was parked out of sight off

77

the road. No light showed from any of the windows, and she knew that something was wrong.

She took the MAB automatic from her black shoulder bag and moved forward. She had changed in Sagasta's office and now wore a button-through black crêpe shirt tucked into a dark flared skirt, and moccasins. The skirt was held by a Velcro fastener down one side and could be ripped off with a single movement to give more freedom of action.

At the back door she waited for a while, her senses and instinct probing for hidden watchers. She found nothing. Pursing her lips she gave a short, two-note whistle in a minor key. Almost at once from somewhere in the house she heard the whistle repeated. She waited. Ten seconds later somebody tapped on the inside of the back door, three knocks followed by two.

Modesty rapped gently with the butt of the small automatic, a single knock followed by two.

A key turned and the door opened. It was the girl, not Willie, and the tension that emanated from her was almost tangible.

Modesty said, 'It's all right. I'm Modesty Blaise.' The girl stepped back and Modesty went into the kitchen, closing the door behind her. It was almost completely dark. She could see only the blurred shape of the girl.

'Some men came . . .' The voice would have been shaky but for the determination that held it steady. 'Willie led them away.'

No confused babble. The essentials first. This girl was uncommon. Modesty said, 'They won't be watching the house now.' With a pencil torch she found the light switch and put it on. 'Willie didn't give me your name on the radio.'

'Dinah. Dinah Pilgrim.'

She was small and attractive, and would be even more attractive with her hair done in its natural style and the face relieved of its fear. Her eyes were open, and for anyone not knowing that she was blind it would have been easy to miss the fact, for there was life in the eyes and it was only the lack of focus in their gaze that betrayed her.

Modesty put a hand on her arm and said, 'All right, Dinah. You've had a bad time, but try not to be scared any more. We'll soon have you out.'

'It's Willie I'm worried about.' There was a core of anger in her voice, and again Modesty found herself approving of the girl.

'So am I. But he's handled trouble before, so we'll worry about him later. Have you got a photograph?'

'Yes. Willie took it after he'd made me look a bit different.' She fumbled for the envelope in her bag. 'Here.'

'Good. We'll fix this now.' Modesty put her shoulder bag on the kitchen unit and took out a passport, a pen, a metal stamp and a little tube of adhesive. 'It won't take more than a few minutes. Fill me in, Dinah.'

The pleasant, cool voice that came to Dinah out of the darkness was unaccountably reassuring. It was utterly different from Willie's voice, and yet this one quality seemed to be the same. Dinah felt herself relaxing, as she had relaxed with Willie from the first moment of knowing that she was in his care.

'After you rang, Willie did things with my hair and took the photo,' she said. 'He packed our cases, and then he felt something was wrong. So did I. We knew they'd found us . . .' Quietly she told how Willie had worked the deception to make it seem that they had driven off together. 'I heard them go after him in another car,' she ended. 'It sounded faster than Willie's.'

Modesty said, 'They'll need more than that. Willie's quite a driver. Can you sign this thing now? I've filled in the description. Sign as Ellen Collier.'

'Just put your finger where I start.' Dinah took the pen and signed. 'Is it all right?'

'Fine. So they all chased off after Willie. Then what?'

'When everything was quiet I came in and waited for you.

Willie had left my case here, the one he bought me, and said you'd come at nine-thirty and take me to a man called Steve Collier. He told me to leave the lights out, so you'd know something was wrong, and he told me how you'd whistle in a special way and then knock in a special way.'

'How long have you been waiting, Dinah?'

'About half an hour.'

'That's quite a wait. Don't jump, I'm just going to make a bang with this stamp. There.'

'Thanks. Most people wouldn't think to warn me.'

'Willie would.'

'Yes.' A shaky breath. 'God, I'm scared for him.'

Willie Garvin relaxed. He was sure he had lost them now. On the highway, the Pan-Americana, the other car had the legs of his Pontiac, but after he turned off on to the minor roads it had been easier. He was on a section of the old road now, cruising at fifty, heading for Panama City. There was a car behind, some way off, but it was not the pursuit car. The headlights were set differently.

Willie decided that he would stop on the outskirts of the town and call Captain Sagasta at the police station. That was where Modesty would expect him to make contact, not at the Santa Rosa. She would get well clear of the hotel the moment she had delivered Dinah safely.

Fumbling in his pocket to check that he had a five centavo piece for the phone call, he glanced in the mirror. The following car was closer, and now beyond the glare of headlights he could see the revolving light on top. It was a police car of the *patrulla-de-camino*. He eased up gently on the accelerator, glad that his speed was little more than ten m.p.h. over the limit for this stretch of road.

The police car moved alongside fast, then hovered. It was a Dodge utility truck, grey, with a big yellow number painted on the door. He saw two figures in high-crowned peaked caps in the front. An arm emerged from the nearside window, waving him down. With a sigh Willie slowed and eased the car on to the verge. The Dodge pulled in behind him. He killed the engine, wound down the window and waited. His Spanish was good, but he began to compose a few stumbling phrases of tourist-Spanish in his mind. With luck he would get away with a stern warning.

In the mirror he saw the two policemen get out and move with leisured tread towards the Pontiac, one on either side. He looked out of the open window with the polite and anxious expression of the stranger wondering what he has done wrong, and saw a big hand holding an automatic less than twelve inches from his face.

Willie Garvin felt very unhappy. The Smith & Wesson double-action 9mm. automatic was just about the fastest holster automatic to get into action, because it could be carried safely with the chamber loaded and the hammer down. It was a very unlikely side-arm for a Panamanian cop. He lifted his gaze and saw a heavy face with the same unmistakable look of the professional that he had recognised in the two killers on the island.

The door behind him opened and a voice said without emphasis, 'Freeze.' The car rocked slightly on its springs as the man behind him knelt on the seat to peer into the back. The police cap and jacket of the man in front of him had been made for somebody smaller; the trousers were not uniform, but were part of a dark grey suit.

Willie Garvin looked into the black eye of the automatic and knew that there was nothing he could do. The voice behind said angrily, 'The broad ain't here!'

The man in front bent lower, flicked his eyes past Willie, then nodded. Willie's last thought, before the searing flash of light in his mind expunged everything, was the hope that it would be a cosh, not a gun-butt. With a gun-butt it took fine judgment to avoid cracking the skull.

Captain Sagasta picked up the telephone and said, 'Sagasta.'

He was off-duty and had expected by this hour to be well advanced in the project of allowing himself to be seduced by the dissatisfied young wife of a middle-aged and temporarily absent French diplomat. But he had postponed that pleasure.

Modesty Blaise's voice said, 'I'm calling from a booth on the corner of Calle 46 and Arosemena. Has Willie Garvin rung you?'

'Here? No. I understood he would be with you.'

'They found him and he had to draw them off. I've got the girl settled, but Willie won't call there. He'll call you.'

'He has not done so yet.' Sagasta glanced at his watch and frowned. 'It looks bad. I do not want any killings in my area.'

'Neither do I,' her voice said bleakly. 'I'd better come in. Can you have me collected?'

'There is no need. There were two men watching the station. I had them detained ten minutes ago. You can drive in yourself.'

Fifteen minutes later she came into his office. Sagasta was eating from a plate of tamales wrapped in banana leaves. He pushed the plate towards her. She sat down, hung her shoulder-bag over the chair, and took one of the spicy squares of crushed maize and meat. Sagasta poured her a cup of *café tinto*, then studied with appreciation the increased area of dark nylon tights revealed by the crossing of her legs.

'What are you going to do?' he asked.

'Wait. Wait here, if you'll let me, Miguel.'

'I prefer it. But will waiting help Garvin?'

'I don't know yet that he needs help. If they've got him, they've either killed him or they're trying to make him tell where the girl is.'

'It could be unpleasant for him. You do not seem concerned.'

'I'm concerned.' Her voice was quiet, yet there was something in it that startled Sagasta. He was, he knew without conceit, a man not lacking in courage, and he bore the scars of his long fight to make the city clean. But he felt very glad at this moment that it was not he who had killed Willie Garvin or who was now trying to make him talk.

He said, 'I think they have got him, Modesty.'

'Why?'

'An hour ago on the highway between here and Chorrera a police car was stolen. The driver and his companion were knocked out. They believe the men who flagged them down were Americans, but I have few details. Our men were severely hurt.'

'A police car,' she repeated, and he could almost see her mind calculating the varieties of possible significance. 'There's more?'

'Yes. A little later the police car was found. And a mile away, on the old road, an empty Pontiac was also found abandoned. There was nothing to identify the owner, but we are checking garages. The car was fitted with an amateur radio transceiver under the dash.'

Modesty finished the tamale, wiped her fingers and took cigarettes from her bag. 'That was Willie's car,' she said. 'They used the police car to get him.'

There was a long silence.

Sagasta said, 'I am bloody angry. We are trying to find Gabriel. But my men have orders not to take action, only to report.'

She nodded. 'Thanks, Miguel. I can't help with any short cuts. I've no reliable contacts of my own here any longer.'

'My men have started to check the hotels.'

'And the ports. Gabriel has a yacht.'

'The ports also. It is difficult. We do not know what name he is using and we do not have a photograph, only the description you gave me. But I am working on two lines. First, that he will have a small entourage of Americans, among them a Scottish man. This was what you told me. Second, that some of our own Panamanian hoodlums must have contact with him since he is using them. The two we have detained, who were watching this police station, are small people, very far

83

down the chain of command, but they have given us a beginning.'

She reflected that Miguel Sagasta deserved his promotion. He had immediately found the only two lines that could be followed. She said, 'Thanks again, Miguel. I'm very grateful.'

He smiled. 'I am sure you are. But we will not explore that subject again. Do you play chess?'

She nodded. He opened a drawer and took out a board and a box of chessmen. He said, 'I think we shall find Gabriel by dawn. Earlier, if we have good fortune. But not soon.' He held out two closed hands towards her. She tapped the right hand and he opened it to reveal a white pawn. He turned the board round and she began to set up the white pieces as he arranged the black. Her movements were very precise, very controlled.

McWhirter said brightly, 'Och, you're an awful liar, Garvin.'

'Yeah, I know,' Willie agreed, and tried to forget the throbbing in his head. 'I could flog you a half-share in the Panama Canal, McWhirter, because you're a stupid gitt. I could give you a story now that you'd lap up. But Modesty Blaise won't 'ave it.'

'What d'ye mean, laddie?'

'We work on a principle,' Willie said patiently. 'If you get nailed, like I am now, an' someone wants you to sing, then you sing straight. You're bound to do it sooner or later. I mean, nobody lasts long with a candle under their toes. Except in movies.'

'A candle,' McWhirter echoed blithely. 'Now that's a thought.'

'Two minutes, I reckon,' Willie said with a nod. 'Then you spill the lot. So why get 'ot toes anyway?'

'To give an old friend a little fun, maybe?'

'Bit tricky in an 'otel,' Willie said doubtfully. 'I'd yell me 'ead off.'

'It's a point. But the hotel's half empty, d'ye see. We could

84

put sticky tape over your mouth, and then you nod when you're ready to talk. Och, I'm sure we could iron out the little details.'

'I've already talked.'

'Aye. But we might try wi' the candle to see if the story's the same,' McWhirter said tentatively, with the manner of one offering a suggestion for approval.

'It won't be the same story,' Willie said with a note of apology in his voice. 'You toast my toes to get a different story and I'll give you one bloody quick. Then you'll 'ave to check it out, and you'll end up finding it's wrong. Christ, you can check what I've told you in about fifteen minutes, you dumb bastard.'

McWhirter chuckled and paced thoughtfully away with a slow, bouncy stride, his hands clasped behind his back.

It was an hour since Willie had opened his eyes and found himself lying on the floor with a hatchet beating a tattoo inside his head. One arm was free, the other wrist was handcuffed to a pipe running into the top of a radiator.

They were barrel lock handcuffs. He could open them easily if he were left alone; and if he could get out the probes hidden in the sole of his right shoe; if he could get at his shoes, which had been taken off and tossed in the far corner of the room together with his jacket and shirt.

McWhirter had only hit him three times so far, as he was coming round and before he got to his feet. The blows had not been very hard, for McWhirter was not particularly muscular. The signet ring he wore had cut Willie's cheek and the whole thing had failed to improve his aching head, but that was all.

Willie thought he had been lucky till now, and knew he would be a lot less lucky soon. Stalling for time was likely to be a long and very painful business, serving little purpose in the end. But it was the only hope he had. Modesty would be looking for Gabriel now. She might find him in time. Twenty to one against would be about the right odds.

There were two men in the bedroom apart from Willie Garvin and McWhirter. One was called Reilly. He leaned against the wall, a narrow man of sallow face and possessing a mouth apparently without lips. The other was Gabriel. He sat in an armchair, slumped low, not looking up, idly toying with the slender leather harness that bore Willie Garvin's throwing knives.

McWhirter said, 'Let's take it again. You knew Blaise would arrive on a flight this evening, heh?'

'That's right.'

'And how did you know that?'

'If my Pontiac's where you left it,' Willie said patiently, 'send someone to take a look under the dash. There's a KW 2000A radio.'

'So there is,' McWhirter grinned. 'They checked when they picked you up. So Blaise was going to collect you an' the girl from the cottage at Chorrera and take you—where?'

'Panama Hilton. Two rooms booked for one night only. Double for her and the Pilgrim girl. Single for me.'

McWhirter glanced at Reilly, who nodded fractionally.

'We're all right so far then,' McWhirter said. 'The porter at the airport said she'd booked for the Hilton, and Reilly's checked wi' the hotel. Go on, laddie.'

'I told you. She was late getting to the cottage. I don't know why. Anyway, about nine I spotted your apes—they may be great in San Francisco or Chicago, but I don't reckon they've ever seen a bloody tree before.'

'So?'

'So I drew 'em off. Worked a dodge with the girl getting into the car and out again. Then I pulled out, and they followed.'

'The girl went back into the house?'

'That was the idea. She went back and waited for Modesty.' Willie grinned. 'But they won't use the Hilton now, not with me gone missing.'

McWhirter surveyed him, fingering a long chin. 'Blaise didn't pick Dinah Pilgrim up,' he said slowly.

Willie Garvin laughed. 'Okay. Then you can pick 'er up yourself.'

'I said Blaise didn't pick her up,' McWhirter repeated. 'The police took Blaise in as soon as she landed at the airport. Unfinished business. She's still with them. She never got to the cottage.'

The grin faded from Willie Garvin's face. He gazed at McWhirter for a long time, and allowed the knowledge of defeat to dawn slowly in his eyes. 'Then you've got Dinah,' he said roughly at last. 'You went back and took 'er. So why all the comedy now?'

'We didn't get her. The house was empty.'

Willie Garvin stared incredulously. He shook his head. 'She was scared,' he said slowly, 'dead scared about being left. Maybe she——' He broke off.

'What small thought occurred to you then, Garvin?' McWhirter asked softly, 'Tell us, laddie. You said yourself it's only two minutes wi' the candle.'

Willie hesitated for a long moment. Then he said in a tired voice, 'It was dark. She can move better in the dark than anyone with eyes. She got panicky when Modesty didn't turn up, so she went out. Through the woods, I reckon.'

'Where to?'

'Nowhere, you bloody stupid scut. Just *out*. She was scared spitless an' she knew the people who killed 'er sister would be coming back for 'er. So when Modesty didn't show, she skipped. What d'you want 'er for, anyway?'

Gabriel said, 'For research. Archaeological research.' He slid a knife into its sheath and grinned suddenly, then switched his gaze to McWhirter. 'Get every available man searching the country around that cottage. All the local men. She won't be far, not in that kind of terrain. They ought to have her within an hour of first light. And check that the yacht's ready.'

McWhirter plucked at his lower lip. 'It might attract a wee

bit of attention around Chorrera,' he said, 'You'll not want the police asking questions.'

'They'll have something else to keep them busy. Maybe two things.' Gabriel looked at Reilly. 'How would you like a chance to cut Blaise in half with your chopper?' The slit of flesh that hid Reilly's big white teeth opened. 'Blaise, anyone boss,' he said with pleasure. He picked up a small black case and opened it, holding it low to show the contents.

A moment earlier Willie Garvin had looked unhappy but felt reasonably satisfied. His story had held, and the bulk of the opposition would soon be out looking vainly for Dinah in the woods behind the cottage until well after dawn. But now he both looked and felt unhappy.

The Czech M61 submachine gun in the case showed that Reilly had come a long way since the days of the old tommy-gun. It was similar to the Russian Stechkin machine pistol or the M1932 Mauser. A hinged stock, like a great hairpin of steel, could be folded forward so that the gun could be fired from one hand, or unfolded for firing from shoulder or hip. He saw that it carried the longer magazine, which held twenty rounds of 7.65 mm. Browning short cartridges.

With the stock folded, the gun's overall length was less than eleven inches. It could fire automatic or semi-automatic. On automatic, the M61 would empty its twenty rounds into the target in less than two seconds. And because the muzzle velocity was little more than a thousand f.p.s., the gun could take a silencer. There was a silencer in the case.

It was a weapon perfectly suited to Reilly. He was one of the old-style killers. A blaster. A chopper-man.

'What d'ye have in mind?' McWhirter said, looking at Gabriel.

'We've as good as got the Pilgrim girl.' Gabriel stood up and tossed the harness and knives into the far corner of the room. 'So we don't need Blaise and Garvin any more. I want Garvin to die sweating . . . and I want Blaise to die fast and ugly.'

'She's still wi' the police.'

'So far.' Gabriel looked at his watch. 'If she can't talk or bribe her way out in the next few hours she must be slipping.' He walked towards the door leading into the living-room. 'Get hold of Rosita. I want her to fix up a parcel. Then she can call the station and ask about Modesty Blaise.'

8

COLLIER said, 'It's getting very late. Shouldn't you go to bed?'

Dinah shook her head. 'I wouldn't sleep. But don't sit up if you're tired.'

'I'm not supposed to sleep,' Collier explained. 'Modesty left me a gun and a bottle of tranquillisers. The gun's to guard you with, and the tranquillisers are to make sure I don't shoot my foot off. Or yours.'

He saw her face lose its tension for a moment and crease in a quick smile. She said, 'Self depreciation. You're very English.'

'That's a myth. Anyway, we have plenty to be modest about these days. Do you fancy a tranquilliser?'

'Not just now, thanks.'

'I feel the same. The idea of some damn chemical telling me to keep calm when I've got good reason to gnaw my nails is a personal affront. I know best. Cigarette?'

'Please.'

They were in Collier's room. It was two hours since a waiter had brought a cold meal and a bottle of wine. Dinah had stayed in her own room until the waiter had left. The hotel was small and rather old and very quiet. Collier was in his shirt-sleeves. Dinah wore a simple cotton frock in fine grey and white check.

'The way you got me through signing-in and up to the room was real smooth,' she said. 'Willie told me you were cleverer than you think.'

Collier sighed. 'It's just that you simply have to pull out a few stops when they're running a show,' he said with vague resentment. 'They tell you to do something, and take it for granted that only a drunken idiot could slip up. So you manage somehow.'

'I'm not sure they take anything for granted,' Dinah said slowly. 'They seem to know what you can manage. But I'm sorry—I guess you didn't want to come on this trip.'

'No, I didn't. I was a very reluctant participant. But I'm glad now.' Collier meant it. He had once, and not long ago, known the unutterable fear and horror that comes from being the victim of men without scruple or pity, men completely evil, who kill as lightly as other men might crush a beetle. Dinah Pilgrim had known that fear. His first sight of her had roused in him a storm of hatred towards the men who had brought savagery and violence into her life, a hatred so raw that it shocked him.

She said, 'Have you been on anything like this with Willie and Modesty before?'

'Only once, thank God. And that was by accident.'

'But you know them well?'

'Pretty well. You get to know people quickly under those kind of conditions. Under these kind.'

'Yes, you do. I got to know Willie well these past few days.' She hesitated. 'I mean really well. No holds barred.' The silence told her that Collier was startled, and she went on quickly with a smile. 'Oh, don't be shocked. He didn't seduce a blind girl. I had to damn near break his arm.'

'That's something new for Willie.' Collier sounded relieved and amused.

'It was something pretty new for me.'

'Oh lord, I didn't mean——'

'I know you didn't. Don't worry. Are you and Modesty close? Just tell a brash Canadian girl to shut up if you want to.'

'That's all right. Yes, we're close. We have what she amusingly calls a loose relationship. I wish it were something more.'

'Doesn't it feel a little odd? I mean . . . well, having a girl who's more at home with a gun than a make-up box?'

Collier said amiably, 'Oh, I know what you mean. But she's quite deft with a make-up box. And she doesn't spend all her time kicking crooks in the teeth. Mostly she just lives an ordinary life—no, not ordinary. She enjoys it, and how many people do that? But she really enjoys it. You go to the ballet with her, or walk down Portobello Road——'

'What's that?'

'A street market for antiques and junk. You take a boat trip up the river, or sit in the smithy at Benildon while one of her horses is shod. Anything. It somehow has an extra zing because she's enjoying it so much.'

'All the same, she can shoot your ears off or throw you over the bed-head if she wants to. Isn't that a little . . . depressing?'

'No,' said Collier, and she could tell that he was smiling. 'It was at first, but I've stopped having any male resentment. Modesty put me straight on that. She's an expert in a particular field because it's what she's done all her life; and I mean all her life, without any choice at the start. There's nothing clever about it. There really isn't.'

'And Willie thinks the same way?'

'I don't imagine he feels that anyone should stand up and cheer because he's good at throwing a knife or breaking a neck.'

'I wanted to stand up and cheer,' she said. Her face crumpled suddenly and she pressed the palms of her hands to her eyes for a moment. 'I'm sorry.' Her voice was shaky and a little desperate. 'Couldn't we ring the police station and see if Modesty's there and what's happening?'

'No, Dinah.' He got up, knelt beside her and took her hand. His manner was gentle but quite positive. 'I'm worried, too. About them both. We just have to sweat it out. Modesty will let us know the moment there's any good news. Until then, the one unforgivable thing would be to get under her feet with phone calls.'

'So . . . there can't have been any good news yet?'

'Not yet. But listen. You know I'm not an optimist. I haven't tried to pretend, or brush your worries aside, or kid you that everything's going to work out just fine. Right?'

She nodded, and he went on. 'Right. So just hang on to this. I've seen them at work against pretty horrid odds, and they're quite unbelievably good. If Willie's in trouble he'll get out of it, or she'll get him out. I believe that. It doesn't stop me worrying, but I believe it.'

She pressed his hand and drew a deep breath. 'All right. I'll believe it too. But it's hard when you can only sit and wait.'

'The hardest bit of all. Modesty says that herself.' Collier straightened up. 'Can you play gin rummy with Braille cards?'

Her head turned sharply in surprise. 'Why, sure. Judy used to play with me a lot. But I haven't any. I lost all my baggage.'

'I managed to get a couple of packs in London a few hours before we took off,' said Collier. 'They're in my case.' He moved away.

Dinah listened to the sounds as he opened his case. There was a curious look on her face. After a moment she said, 'For a reluctant participant, that's not bad.'

Willie Garvin had never seen a woman like Rosita before. She was rather tall and lumpy, with a blotchy yellow face. Her black hair was parted in the middle and drawn tightly back in a wispy knot behind her head. She wore a drab grey coat and old shoes. But it was not her appearance that Willie found unique.

A small cheap suitcase lay open on the bed. Rosita sat with a grenade in her lap, a pair of wire-cutters in her hand. The grenade was not yet primed. She drew out the pin and cut the ring away from it, then took a small file from the case and began to stroke the pin gently to make it a loose fit.

It was only five minutes since she had arrived. There had

been a muffled conversation in the living-room with Gabriel, and then Rosita had entered with her case. She had said *Buenos dias* to Reilly and to Willie, with frigid dignity, then settled down to her work.

Satisfied with the pin now, she took one end of a reel of thin wire and ran it through a short length of half-inch copper tube. With pliers, she twisted the end of the wire tightly about the butt of the pin.

Willie watched with uneasy fascination. Rosita worked with a look of prim distaste on her unhealthy face, but her movements were deft and practised. She took a large cylindrical tin with a screw cap from the case, then opened a packet of what looked like yellow putty wrapped in oilskin. Plastic explosive.

Reilly looked unhappy as she casually pulled off chunks of the P.E. and wadded them down into the bottom of the tin. She glanced at him, and her thin nose twitched with contempt or indignation, then she resumed her work, frowning and muttering, turning over the tools and oddments in her case like a handyman sorting through a junk box for the item he wants.

With a metal punch she made a hole in the lid of the tin and jammed the piece of tubing through it. The door opened and Gabriel came in with McWhirter behind him. Rosita looked up and said in accented English, 'It is necessary to have a screw eye placed there.' She pointed to the ceiling about six feet from the wall where Willie Garvin stood handcuffed to the radiator. 'Perhaps your man will attend to it.'

Gabriel nodded at Reilly, who pulled a small table forward and set a chair on top of it. Rosita gave him a gimlet and a one-inch screw eye, and he clambered up on to the chair.

Gabriel said, 'Find a joist for it, Reilly.'

Rosita said coldly, 'Of course,' and slipped a primer into the grenade. Five minutes later she put her tools away, closed her case and said, 'It is finished.'

94

Gabriel nodded. 'Right. Now the phone call.'

The first two games had been drawn. They were setting up the chess pieces anew when the telephone rang. Sagasta picked it up and listened, then said in Spanish, 'Put her through.'

He cupped a hand over the mouthpiece and looked across the table at Modesty. 'A woman is inquiring if we are still holding you.'

Modesty stared at a rook in her hand. 'Tell her I'm being released now, Miguel, and ask what she wants.'

He spoke in Spanish into the phone. After a brief exchange of question and answer he covered the mouthpiece again and said, 'She has a message for you. She has been calling the Hilton, and has only just learned that you were brought here. She will give the message only if she speaks to you.'

A little spark showed in Modesty's eyes. 'Stall for a few moments and act officious. Then agree.'

Sagasta smiled, and turned to the phone again. Two minutes later he passed it across the desk to Modesty. A woman's voice said, 'You are Modesty Blaise?'

'Yes. Who's that?'

'It does not matter. An Englishman came to the bar where I work. He gave me twenty dollars to say a message to you. Then he went quickly. Some men were following.'

'What was the message?'

'Hotel Cadiz. The lobby. He will be there at two o'clock . . . and something else I did not understand.'

Modesty glanced down at her watch. It was one-thirty. She said, 'What was the something else?'

'If he can shake them. That is what he said. He will be there at two o'clock, if he can shake them.'

'And that was all?'

'Yes.'

'Thank you very much.'

There was a click at the other end. Modesty passed the

phone back to Sagasta and repeated the conversation. He began to put the chessmen into their box and said, 'It is a trap, of course.'

'Yes. Willie wouldn't get a girl to ring me at the Hilton. He knows I never went there anyway.'

'So Gabriel is at the Cadiz.'

She shrugged and got up, unfastening the top three buttons of her shirt. The button-hole hem was stiffened with buckram and stood away from her chest. She said, 'I don't know about Gabriel. But somebody's waiting for me. I'll get along there. Where does it lie?'

'A little way out of town. But we know this is a trap.'

'I have to spring it. I think Willie's there.'

Sagasta nodded. 'That could well be so. The Cadiz is conveniently placed and very good for Gabriel. It is too expensive, unsuccessful, and less than half booked.' He got to his feet. 'I will come with you.'

'Not police cars and a raid, Miguel,' she said quickly.

'Why not?'

'I'm hoping Willie Garvin is still alive, and I want him to stay that way.'

'A small hope.'

'No. They caught him, they wanted him to talk, he talked. But Willie's very devious.' She turned towards the door.

Sagasta shrugged and picked up his gunbelt. 'As you wish,' he said wryly. 'But I do not like traps. They are bloody nasty.'

Gabriel looked at his watch and said, 'She'll be here in another fifteen minutes. We'll go.'

'I'd like to see it,' McWhirter said wistfully.

'Reilly can tell us later.' Gabriel grinned at Reilly. 'Get yourself set up. Whichever way she comes in, she has to pass through the lobby to reach the stairs or the lift. The moment you see her, blast her. Walk out the side door and into the car. Monson will be waiting with the engine running. You switch cars at Bella Vista, and you're clear.'

'Sure.' Reilly put the M61 under his coat and moved to the door. He looked back for a moment at Willie Garvin, whose mouth was now covered by a broad strip of adhesive plaster, and said, 'Hope you hear her go before you book out, pal. I won't be using the silencer.' He went through the doorway and across the living-room.

McWhirter chuckled. 'I've a fancy you'll just about hear Reilly kill her laddie.'

'She'll die ugly,' Gabriel said with slow, bitter satisfaction. 'And you'll die sweating, Garvin.' He looked at Rosita. 'Explain it to him, then fix him up.'

Rosita inclined her head graciously and took a small Browning .25 automatic from the pocket of her coat. Gabriel and McWhirter went out. Willie heard the outer door of the living-room close after them. All the luggage had been taken down. Now he was alone with Rosita, and her automatic, and the round yellow tin standing on the floor with the thin wire running up from the hole in the top. The wire passed through the screw eye in the ceiling, then trailed slackly and obliquely down towards the door.

Rosita said with disapproval, 'The device is clumsy. I do not like to work in haste like this. But it will operate.'

Willie nodded his head vigorously and lifted his free hand towards the plaster on his mouth. The gun moved and she said sharply, 'No!'

Willie lowered his hand. He had had some experience in judging whether people with guns meant what they said. Rosita meant it.

She said, 'The grenade is packed round with plastic explosive, except that there is space for the lever to operate when the pin is drawn. There is a one second fuse. When the wire is pulled it will draw the pin free. The tubing allows the wire to run freely, you understand?'

Willie Garvin nodded his head again, staring at her. He felt a little dazed. The bomb was the most diabolically jury-rigged device he had ever seen put together. But it would

97

work all right; and when it did, nothing in the room could live with it.

Rosita stepped back towards the door. She picked up the end of the wire, threaded it through another screw eye set in the jamb of the door, then through the key-hole. Lifting her case from the bed she put it outside in the living-room. Willie debated the idea of ripping off the plaster and making a feverish attempt to bribe Rosita. It was not a long debate. She would probably use the automatic if he moved, and she would certainly bridle indignantly at the suggestion of a bribe. He had seen enough of her to know that she was of the old school, loyal to her employer. Besides, the bomb was her handiwork; its function must be fulfilled.

She ran her muddy eyes over the scene once more, checking carefully, then said in a frosty tone, like a woman long used to the discourtesy of man, 'I do not suppose you will be able to hold the device for very long, but I hope you will try to do so at least until I have left the hotel. A loud noise disturbs me very much.'

She backed out of the room and closed the door to a gap of six inches, then drew the wire through the key-hole until it was almost taut. '*Buenas noches, señor.* It will be better if you pick up the device now.'

Willie leaned down hastily and got his fingers round the tin as the door closed. A second later the wire was drawn slowly through the key-hole. Willie straightened up, his arm extended, holding the bomb. Sweat broke on his brow and he thought, '*Christ, I 'ope she marked where to stop!*'

The pull on the wire ceased when his right arm was just horizontal. He stood with the other arm stretched out and down towards the radiator, the wrist held by the handcuffs. His right hand, holding the bomb, was extended to a point directly below the screw eye in the ceiling; if he lowered his arm by only a few inches the pin of the grenade would be pulled out. The resulting explosion might blow the door out and damage Rosita. It would certainly damage Willie Garvin.

Outside the door, Rosita clipped the wire off short, wound an inch of it tightly round a small screw, then pushed the screw at an angle into the key-hole so that it lodged there out of sight. Picking up her case she marched briskly to the door of the suite with the tight-lipped air of one who has deserved some measure of appreciation but failed to receive it.

Willie Garvin heard the light-switch in the outer room click off, the door close. He stared at the bomb in his out-stretched hand, and killed the flutter of panic that stirred in him. Ten minutes. Then Modesty would arrive, and Reilly would be waiting to cut her down.

Gently now . . . the arm was beginning to tighten up. Deliberately he relaxed his whole body, maintaining just enough power in the arm to hold the bomb steady. Ten minutes. Now think . . .

If he could twist the bomb so that the wire caught round the inch of tube jutting from the tin . . . no. There wasn't enough play. Impossible to shout with his mouth plastered, but he could make a noise, a muffled bellow, and stamp his feet. And if anyone came they would open the bedroom door —which would drag the wire and pull the pin from the grenade. Three inches would do it.

If he could . . . ? No. That wouldn't work. What else? Jerk hard on the bomb, break the wire, pitch the bomb out of the window before it could explode.

On a one second fuse? With the shutters closed? Very likely. Just as well send for Superman.

And . . . if Modesty got past Reilly it would be the same. She would reach the suite, open the bedroom door. That would be the last thing she ever did.

The handcuffs. No hope of opening a cuff, but . . .

He lifted his left foot carefully, braced it against the radiator and began to pull steadily, twisting his wrist in the metal hoop of the cuff. Two minutes later, his wrist slippery with blood, he gave up. Flesh could give, but not bone. His hand was too big to slip the cuff.

Jesus! His right arm had sagged a little. The wire was taut. He eased the bomb up an inch, then once again made a steady, deliberate effort to relax the crawling nerves of both body and mind.

There must be some way. He stared at the bomb, unable to credit that he held it in his hand and yet was helpless. The arm was beginning to ache now.

So. Think of something, and if you can't think of something at least stop them getting Modesty. Let go. The room blows apart. Uproar and confusion in the hotel. Police called. But they wouldn't get here before Modesty now. And Reilly wouldn't be confused; he'd wondered if Willie would hold out until she got here. Reilly would just sit in a corner of the lobby with his submachine gun under the table, waiting. Confusion would not stop Reilly. It might make his getaway that much easier.

Sweat ran down Willie's brow and into his eyes, warm and stinging. He was afraid.

Down in the lobby it was very quiet, deserted except for Reilly and the night porter who manned the reception desk. The night porter lay at Reilly's feet behind the long counter, blood oozing from the back of his head. Reilly wore the porter's jacket. It fitted well enough. A newspaper was spread untidily in front of him, partly propped against a small nest of drawers. It hid the M61 submachine gun resting on the counter.

Reilly's right hand was curved round the grip. He was feeling very happy. It was a long time since he had chopped anyone down, seen the stitching of little black holes race across the living target, the black turning to red. And this would be the first woman. Pleasure expanded within him.

She would come through the swing doors and make for the stairs, or the lift beside them. Or she would come from the other corridor leading through from the side entrance. It did not matter. She would have to come obliquely towards him to reach the stairs or lift. He would get a good look at her before he pulled the trigger. That was the moment, when you knew that in two seconds they would be dead; and they didn't know. That was when you felt real good.

He hoped Garvin would last out. If the bomb went off it meant switching the set-up a little. That wouldn't matter. But he wanted Garvin to hear this Blaise dame go. With the getaway car standing ready there was no need for silence. A silencer spoiled things somehow. The noise was all a part of it, and good.

Not long now.

Two hundred yards from the hotel Captain Sagasta glanced at the mirror to make sure that the following police car with four men had halted. Satisfied, he drove on, then slowed and turned into the hotel forecourt. 'Do you wish me to take the front while you take the side entrance?' he asked.

Modesty Blaise said, 'No. This is my trap and I'll spring it, Miguel. What they'll expect is for me to pussyfoot around with a certain amount of caution. So I'm going straight in and fast.'

'But——' He had no time to say more. Already they were at the foot of the three broad steps leading up to the hotel entrance. She was out of the car before it stopped, and running up the steps.

Sagasta swore, cut the engine, dragged on the handbrake and scrambled out after her.

Standing behind the reception desk, Reilly heard the thump of the slow-closing mechanism on the swing door. Two seconds later she came into view round the angle of the wall where the lobby widened out.

She wore a black male-style shirt with pockets, and a short skirt to match. Dark nylons, moccasin shoes. Her legs were beautiful. So was her face. Her hands were empty. The shirt was unbuttoned almost to the waist.

She slowed as she entered the lobby, sweeping it with one quick turn of her head in an instant appreciation.

Reilly's finger curved lovingly round the trigger. This was the moment. Her eyes were on him now, and she had halted.

Dark eyes, dark midnight blue. They stabbed him, cold and sure and with no shred of warmth. Reilly's pleasure was wiped out by sudden and unaccountable fear. His left hand slid forward to steady the barrel, and the newspaper slipped, uncovering the gun. He snatched at the trigger.

There is a mystery in the higher grades of combat. The movements of a judoka seem unhurried, his victim will appear to co-operate submissively in the performance of the throw. It is a strange illusion. By the same strange illusion the movement of Modesty's right hand seemed unhurried, yet suddenly it held a small black object which yapped viciously, once, and she was falling sideways, and Reilly was standing up dead, with a round black spot just above the bridge of his nose as the M61 chattered a roaring burst of six rounds in less than half a second and then stopped.

Sagasta came into the lobby fast, a .45 revolver in his hand. He saw Modesty Blaise first, coming to her feet, a wisp of smoke rising from the small French MAB .25 automatic. Then he saw Reilly with the black spot on his brow beginning to show a dark glint of red as he folded forward over the sub-machine gun on the counter. The plaster high on the wall behind Modesty was cracked and pitted. Reilly's gun had ridden up as he fired, because he was dead.

Modesty said sharply, 'Must be a getaway car waiting by the sideway. Put his jacket on, Miguel.'

Ten seconds later Sagasta went out of the side door at a crouching run, capless and with the porter's jacket flapping unbuttoned about him. The car was there, a black Chevrolet. One man in it.

Sagasta wrenched open the door, smashed at the man's hand on the wheel with the barrel of his gun, then thrust it close to the heavy, startled face.

'Where is Garvin?' Sagasta said coldly as Modesty came

up behind him. The man was in pain, but his lips tightened stubbornly. Then they loosened again as Sagasta jabbed the barrel brutally at his mouth.

'Answer,' said Sagasta.

The man whimpered and shrank back. Shrilly, indistinctly through mashed lips and broken teeth, he said, 'Four one five. Room four one five.'

Sagasta nodded, hit the man hard on the head with his revolver, and backed out of the car. Together they ran back into the hotel. Sixty seconds had passed since Modesty first entered it. A frightened man in a dressing gown emerged from a door marked private in the passage which ran from the side entrance. Somewhere a switchboard was buzzing.

Sagasta snapped. 'Manager?'

The man nodded. 'There was shooting——'

'Yes. Tell your guests to stay in their rooms. On police orders.'

They moved on. Modesty said, 'The stairs. Lifts can stick.' Sagasta glanced at her. Her face was smooth and hard, like polished stone, and there was a ring of pallor round her mouth.

He said, 'You think they——? You think it is too late for Garvin?'

She started up the stairs, taking them three at a time. 'I don't know. I just know this isn't all.'

When the brief distant chatter of the submachine gun sounded, Willie Garvin was standing quite still, fighting the waves of pain that engulfed his tortured mind and quivering arm.

But with the sound, the sweat grew suddenly cold on his body and the pain receded until it no longer seemed a part of his being. He stopped working his lips against the plaster that covered them, and looked without emotion at the bomb, then at his handcuffed wrist. One part of his mind was dead, the rest was extraordinarily clear.

There were six links in the chain that joined the two cuffs. Speculatively he bent his wrist and twisted it round, down and up again. The cuff slid round his wrist, and now there was a twist in the chain.

The arm holding the bomb was shaking a little. He concentrated on it. Mustn't slip up now. There was too much to be done, too many people to seek out and destroy. When he was satisfied that the arm was fixed in obedience, he turned his attention to the handcuffs once again, gently circling his hand round the chain.

In a little while the chain had shortened by an inch or two and the links were twisted and locked one against another, so that the flexible chain had become a rigid bar. He could turn his hand no further, could only move it fractionally to take the last millimetre of play.

Now.

He let his head droop, allowed all his muscles to go slack except for those in the distant arm holding the bomb, an arm that no longer belonged to him. His breathing slowed. His open eyes saw nothing. He was suspended in velvet darkness and nothing existed except the sleeping energies slowly concentrating in another limb that was no longer his.

Two minutes passed.

His head came up and he inhaled through his nose one long, deep breath. Then a fury of power exploded in his left shoulder and arm; a total concentration of force, twisting against the locked links.

Pain, somewhere far away. Coming closer now, stabbing into his wrist. His eyes focused and he looked down. His left arm hung by his side. Two links of chain dangled from the cuff round the radiator. The third had snapped.

He lifted his left hand. The metal cuff had bitten deep into the already torn flesh, but his fingers still worked. Moving very carefully he edged sideways, coaxing his numbed right arm to bend. Now he had two shaky hands on the bomb and it was resting on his shoulder. Sweat ran down his face, soaking the plaster over his mouth.

Not far to go. Steady now. No hurry. Nobody would be coming to open the door . . .

He lifted one leg and reached down with his left hand to work the sock from his shoeless foot. No point in getting fingers cut to the bone as well. He rose up on his toes to make enough slack in the wire, and took a turn of it about his hand, using the sock as a pad. Gently at first, holding the bomb steady, he dragged down on the wire. Harder, harder . . .

The wire snapped where it ran through the screw eye in the ceiling. With both hands on the bomb again he sank slowly to his knees, then eased the bomb to the floor. He was kneeling over it, nursing his wrist and trying to stop his body shaking, when the window shattered.

He turned his head and saw one shutter standing open. Modesty Blaise was crouched on the sill four floors above the ground. Her gun probed the room, then her eyes came back to Willie. He felt sudden wild laughter rising inside him; the wrong kind of laughter. He held it back, shook his head in what was meant to be a reassuring movement, and lifted a feeble hand with the thumb pointing up.

She was beside him, an arm about his shoulders. There came a sharp, good pain as she ripped the plaster from his mouth. He knelt with hands resting on his knees, dragging long gulps of air into his lungs, then croaked, 'Reilly?'

'The chopper-man?' She lifted the MAB automatic.

Willie said, 'Christ.' Then, 'You were still supposed to get it when you opened the door.'

She slipped the gun into the Bucheimer Semi-shoulder holster that lay beneath her shirt, strapped flat at an angle under her left breast. Willie Garvin had adapted that holster for her. 'There had to be something else, Willie. So I came down from the room above. Those big recessed stone blocks, they're the next best thing to a ladder.'

He nodded, and the beginnings of a grin showed against

the pallor of pain in his face. 'I could've saved me wrist,' he said. His voice was husky, but stronger now.

She took the wrist gently in her hands. It was turning dark purple around the cut flesh under the broken cuff. Her eyes searched the room, found the other cuff locked round the radiator pipe, moved to the trailing wire, the screw eyes in the ceiling and door jamb, then came at last to rest on the yellow tin with the broken wire protruding from it on the floor in front of her.

She said slowly, 'I can only half figure it, Willie love.'

'That's pretty good going.' He drew a shaky arm across his forehead. 'It's something you don't run into every day.'

Fifteen minutes had gone by. Modesty Blaise had dismantled the bomb, removed the primer from the grenade, and picked the lock of the cuff on Willie's wrist. He lay on the bed, smoking a cigarette. There were two stiff whiskies inside him and he was feeling pleasantly relaxed.

His wrist was not broken. Modesty was bandaging it now, sitting on the edge of the bed. Captain Sagasta had called in a doctor and Modesty Blaise had sent him away. She had phoned Steve Collier, and Collier had sworn at her in the violence of his relief.

Sagasta was using the room as a temporary headquarters. He was on the phone now and was very angry. He did not like American gangsters and their methods; he most especially did not like attempts at gangster-style killings in his territory.

Modesty secured the bandage, took the cigarette from Willie's mouth, dropped a kiss on his cheek and put the cigarette back again. It was something she had done only two or three times over the years, and he knew it was a measure of her relief. She had thought him dead, and been wrong.

Willie Garvin closed his eyes, feeling very happy. He had been certain she was dead. He wondered if he could have broken free otherwise. The thought that it had been unnecessary anyway was suddenly amusing. The Bucheimer Semi was a little beauty, now that he had adapted it for her. He wished he could have seen her take Reilly. That must have been one for the book.

Sagasta put down the phone and stood up.

'Nothing so far,' he said tightly. 'But I have switched every available man to this one thing. I am afraid we shall annoy a lot of innocent Americans with a lot of questions during the next twenty-four hours.'

Modesty said, 'When can you let us go, Miguel?'

He spread his hands. 'As soon as you wish. There will be no trouble from Gabriel. He is on the run now and will be lucky to save his own skin.'

'I think he'll be lucky,' Modesty said. 'It's not far to the three-mile limit. But at least he's too busy to worry us. What about the man I killed in the lobby?'

'What man? The man with the submachine gun who threatened me? I killed him myself.'

'With a point two-five bullet fired from a point four-five gun?'

Sagasta smiled. 'I do not think the police doctor will argue with me.'

'You're bending the rules, Miguel.'

'Certainly. I am interested in justice, not the law. There is an unfortunate difference.'

She got up and stood facing him, smiling a little. 'I like you, you honest cop,' she said softly. 'Soon I'll come back and say thank you. Not just sometime, but soon.'

Sagasta's dark bold eyes sparkled, and he inclined his head politely. 'There is no obligation,' he said. 'But it would be bloody nice.'

9

THE big man put down the headset and switched off the radio. He laughed without making a sound, and the folding chair creaked under his bulk.

He wore a khaki drill shirt and slacks of the same material, tailored to encase his short massive legs.

'Oh dear, oh dear,' he said. 'Poor Gabriel.'

The other man was doing a long series of knees-bend exercises. He wore dark, beautifully creased lightweight slacks, and a white gym vest. His face was handsome and arrogant, his black hair cropped short. When he stood or walked his sinewy body was held in a military posture, very erect. He would have looked at home in the uniform of an old-time Hungarian cavalry officer. His name was Wenczel, and he spoke good English with a marked accent.

Outside, beyond the rock confines of the deep valley, the desert lay silent and burning under the patient ferocity of the sun. The valley itself, protected by towering walls of rock, was hot but not unbearably so. In the rooms and passages carved from the living rock by hands long dead, the temperature was little more than pleasantly comfortable.

Wenczel straightened up for the last time. He bounced springily up and down on his toes once or twice, then moved to the table where the radio stood.

'They have the girl?' he asked.

'They have not the girl,' said the big man, his face creasing in a smile. 'Garvin fooled them. They caught him and laid a trap for Modesty Blaise. She sprang it, and apparently blasted the hood who was supposed to blast her. Poor Gabriel had to scuttle with most of the Panama police force on his heels.'

'I do not think it is amusing,' Wenczel said stiffly.

'No.' The wide blue eyes rested genially on Wenczel for a moment. 'No, you wouldn't. I suppose lack of humour goes hand in hand with stupidity.' The big man watched with enjoyment as Wenczel mentally construed the phrase, saw him flush with anger but control it. Wenczel was a little afraid of him, he thought idly, but only a little; he might do something about that when the situation was convenient.

Wenczel said, 'Time is passing, and we need the girl. What is to happen now?'

'She's probably on her way to England,' said the big man. 'Care of Blaise and Garvin. It looks as if I'll have to slip over and get her.' Again his shoulders shook with silent laughter.

'And Gabriel?'

'Algiers in four days. I'll meet him there before I go on to England. Oh dear, he'll be so cross.'

'Time is passing,' Wenczel repeated.

'You said that before.' The big man still smiled. 'If you say it again I might be tempted to break a bone somewhere, Major Wenczel. In that important right arm of yours, perhaps.'

Wenczel's lips drew tight. 'I do not like such threats.'

'Then don't invite them. Has our labour force behaved itself while I've been away?'

'Professor Tangye's wife had a bout of hysterics. A spell of treatment in the rest-room cured her.'

'Hysterics? In the mem-sahib herself?' The big man was both surprised and entertained by the thought. 'I'd never have believed it. Oh dear, what a pity I missed the occasion. But perhaps she'll do it again. What about the others?'

Wenczel shrugged. 'I have had no trouble.' He sounded a shade regretful. 'They have cleared more of the tomb area, as you saw. They are a little sluggish in their work, but obedient. Severe treatment will not make them work harder. It will only exhaust them. I have struck the best balance, I think.'

'And our minions, the Children of Allah?'

Wenczel took time to work it out. Then, 'The Algerian guards have given no trouble.'

There was silence in the big, rock-walled chamber. Overhead an electric lamp burned, and from somewhere nearby came the smooth purr of a generator.

The big man took a thin metal box from his shirt pocket and opened it. Inside lay a white crystalline powder. There was no clumsiness in his great finger and thumb as he took a pinch of the powder. He held it to each nostril in turn and sniffed vigorously, as if taking snuff.

Wenczel watched with a blend of awe and disgust.

'Our hosts have been writing letters for the supply plane to take out?' said the big man, putting the box away.

'Yes. I have vetted the letters thoroughly, of course.'

'Of course. Everything must appear normal.' The big man's right eye began to water heavily and he mopped it with a handkerchief. 'How long do you estimate this job will take under the present system, Major Wenczel?'

'Anything from one month to five years. We can hardly maintain an appearance of normality for so long.'

'Quite. And with the girl?'

'If she can do what Gabriel claims she can do, then we should be finished in a few days.'

'Gabriel doesn't make mistakes about that kind of thing. A few days.' He sighed. 'What a pity. I've found all this very entertaining. Still, what's left should be of some interest.'

Wenczel drew up another folding chair and sat down, leaning forward a little. 'You are not worried about Blaise and Garvin?'

For a moment the features beneath the incongruous thatch of auburn hair took on some relation with each other as the big man smiled brilliantly. 'Worried? I wish you could explain that to me, Major Wenczel. I've always wondered what it meant.'

Wenczel sat back. He knew that the words were true, but to find an answer baffled him. At last he said, 'I mean that from what I have heard they are dangerous. They shattered the biggest operation Gabriel ever launched, and all but destroyed him. Can they do the same again?'

'Oh no. Oh dear, no,' the big man said mildly. 'I'm here this time.' He dabbed his moist eye again. 'We can only hope they'll try, Wenczel. I want to deal with Garvin myself.' He paused, a reminiscent smile in his eyes. 'And I believe Modesty Blaise has a useful right arm. Perhaps you'll be able to put her through her paces.'

Eagerness shone in Wenczel's smooth, hard face; more than eagerness, it was a swift and avid craving. 'I should like that,' he said. 'I should like that very much.'

'It would certainly be amusing.'

Wenczel got up and moved to the rough-hewn stone arch from which a passage wound out into the valley. The big man did not look round. He seemed to be daydreaming; if so, the daydream was pleasant.

Wenczel paused in the archway and said, 'Garvin uses a knife, I believe?'

'On occasion.' The mellow voice was remote, uncaring. 'And very capably by all accounts. He used a knife to remove one of Gabriel's minions, it seems. That's how Gabriel first suspected Garvin was involved.'

'A knife,' Wenczel repeated, and in his voice there was untold disgust. 'That is not a weapon. It is a tool for butchers.' He went out.

'Purist,' said the big man softly, and again the massive body was shaken by a tremor of silent laughter.

'For God's sake don't *do* that!' Collier said breathlessly, and urged his horse alongside Dinah's as she slowed to a trot. Her head turned towards him and she grinned. 'Stop fussing. There aren't any trees to duck on this stretch, and Jonathan never puts a foot wrong.'

'I'm not thinking about you. You ride like a blasted centaur,' Collier said resentfully. 'I'm thinking about me. When *you* gallop, Kitty gallops. And it just so happens that I ride like a sack of turnips.'

They were moving at a walk now down the western side of the long pasture which rose from the sprawl of stables and outbuildings where Modesty's cottage lay, two miles from the village of Benildon.

'You have to use your knees,' Dinah said. 'Really grip with them.'

'Grip? Don't be sadistic. Another pound of pressure and I'll either crush this poor beast to a paste or split all the way up to my neck. But I still keep going down when she's coming up. Kitty's got no sense of rhythm, that's the trouble. Bear left now if you want a spell on the range.'

There was a pistol, clay pigeon and archery range in the small field at the foot of the slope. In the three days that she had been here Dinah had learned to use a bow at short range, aiming by sound. Modesty had fixed a simple buzzer to the target, operated by a button at the firing end.

'We'd better get on home,' Dinah said. 'Tea-time. Boy, I really love English tea-time. Scones and butter and jam and honey, and that clink-clink of bone china and spoons. I bet you can practically see through those cups.'

'They have quality,' Collier agreed. Since being with Dinah he had found himself looking at things much more closely and with far deeper appreciation. It was six days since the return from Panama. The first three had been spent at Modesty's penthouse, and it had fallen to Collier to take Dinah under his wing. Modesty had been out and about on unspecified business and had made a number of phone-calls abroad. Willie Garvin had departed for Europe after only twenty-four hours.

So it was Collier who took Dinah Pilgrim round London and learned to think in terms of sound and smell rather than sight. She loved the fruit and vegetable smells of Covent Garden; the blend of foreign cooking smells in Soho. She enjoyed the river and the parks, and a concert one evening at Festival Hall. Collier had read to her, played cards with her, and started to teach her chess.

The move to Benildon delighted her. Collier smiled to himself as he remembered her standing by a manure heap and sniffing with great content. When he had laughed, she tried to explain to him about the world of smells; made him close his eyes and told him to forget what he knew about manure heaps and savour the strong rich smell anew. Modesty had found them at it, and her bewilderment had brought the experiment to an end in laughter.

To Collier, the task of looking after Dinah Pilgrim was a source of fascination rather than a burden. There was, Modesty said, no danger from Gabriel to worry about. Not yet. It would come, but in the meantime they would try to locate him and find out what kind of caper he was engaged in. That was why Willie had gone to Europe, to set old and trusted contacts on the alert for whispers along the underworld grapevine, while Modesty cast a net further afield by telephone.

Looking at Dinah now as she rode beside him with wisps of honey-coloured hair escaping beneath the headscarf, her cheeks showing a healthy glow under the tan, her face so much younger than when he had first seen her, Collier felt unashamedly glad that Modesty and Willie intended to kill Gabriel. His only reservation rose from the certainty that it would be an appallingly high-risk undertaking.

'Do you think he'll get here today?' Dinah asked as they came up the grassy track to the stables.

'Sure to,' Collier said confidently. He knew she meant Willie, knew that Willie Garvin was the one thing lacking in Dinah's world at this moment. 'He was back from Amsterdam yesterday. Modesty said he had to sort out a few things at that pub of his, The Treadmill, but he'll be here soon.'

'Good. I miss him a lot. Damn! That sounded real mean. I'd miss you too, if you weren't here, Steve.'

Collier grinned. 'It's too late. You've said it now.'

'Pig.' She made a face at him. 'I heard a car when we were passing the range. Maybe that was Willie.'

They dismounted at the stables and handed their horses over to the Benildon villager Modesty employed as a groom. When they walked round to the front of the cottage Collier saw an old Rover three litre parked in the drive to one side of the small garden, dusty from the mile-long track that wound down from the main road.

'It's not Willie,' he said. 'It's Tarrant.'

'Tarrant?'

'Sir Gerald Tarrant. Another friend of Modesty's.'

'A sir! Is he nice?'

'Sort of. He's quiet-spoken—you always like that—and has a lot of olde worlde charm, and I rather think Modesty is a daughter-substitute for him. Except that he bloody well gets her to go out and do things where she's likely to get killed.'

'Huh?'

'Don't say "huh". And don't ask me questions about Tarrant, there's a good girl.'

They walked towards the open door of the cottage. Dinah said, 'Can I have a quick wash and change before I'm introduced?'

'Of course. I'm going to do the same.' He took her arm and guided her round to the back, where a door opened into the kitchen. It was a rambling and beautifully converted cottage with an inglenook fireplace set in one rough white wall of the big hall. On the upper floor a mazy passage wound between five bedrooms and two bathrooms. Collier said, 'Do you want help with anything?'

'No, I've got settled and I know where everything is now.'

'Right. I'll wait for you in the hall.'

'Ten minutes.'

In the big comfortable living-room Tarrant leaned back in a corner of the deep couch and stretched his legs.

'I rather thought we'd forget about the Aaronson thing,' he said.

'Why? It looks like murder to me.' Modesty Blaise sat in an enormous armchair with her feet tucked up. She wore a short-sleeved jumper in yellow cashmere and an oatmeal skirt, with sandals on her bare feet.

'Murder is a police matter,' said Tarrant. He nodded towards the Identikit picture she held in her hands. 'I gave them that. They haven't found him. I rather doubt that he's still in the country. I may be wrong. Frobisher's had nothing from the ports or airports, and God knows it would be hard for anyone to miss a freak like that.'

'Only if he went out through departure control. He may have other ways.' When Tarrant shrugged she looked at him curiously and went on, 'I don't understand you.'

'This isn't my business, Modesty. Because Aaronson was a friend, I asked you to have a look round the dig at Mus. Now he's dead, so it doesn't arise.'

'I'd have thought you'd be all the more anxious for me to look around, if Aaronson was murdered.'

'If. We don't know.' Tarrant looked out of the window and said absently. 'I want you to forget it, Modesty. You've enough to think about with Gabriel.'

'For the moment, yes. But we're hoping to get that settled fast.' She paused, then added a little sombrely, 'We'd better, for Dinah's sake. I'll have a look at Mus for you when it's over.'

'No,' Tarrant said flatly. 'I'm hungry and dry. Aren't you going to offer me any tea?'

She looked at him steadily for several seconds, then smiled suddenly and stood up. 'Five minutes. I was just waiting for the others. Dinah loves English tea-time. It'll be a bonus for her with a courtly old English gentleman like you.'

'Let her keep her illusions,' Tarrant said gloomily. 'Don't tell her what a bastard I am.'

When Modesty wheeled in the laden tea trolley Collier was making introductions and Tarrant was holding Dinah's hand, bowing over it.

'Count your fingers, Dinah,' she said. 'Then help me hand round, if you've got enough left.'

'Slander,' said Tarrant gravely. As he spoke he looked a surprised query at Modesty, who shook her head reassuringly and gestured for him to watch the girl.

Tarrant looked on with fascination as Dinah ran her fingers lightly over the cups and plates on the trolley, sniffing gently. 'Scones, and that strawberry jam,' she said contentedly. 'Who's going to pour?'

Conversation ran easily, casually.

'Is Willie going to be here today?' Tarrant inquired as Dinah handed him his second cup of tea.

'Any time now,' Modesty said. 'I'm not sure I'm speaking to Willie.'

'Why not?' Collier asked.

'He forgot my present. Whenever he goes away he brings me back a present. He didn't bring me one from Panama.'

'Mercenary baggage,' Collier said amiably. 'He was a bit busy in Panama. What kind of thing were you expecting?'

'I'm not mercenary. I just love Willie's presents. And I've no idea what to expect. They're never all that expensive, but they're always something special.'

'That matched pair of ivory stocked Williamson derringers were little gems,' said Tarrant.

Collier made a grimace. 'Guns.'

'Antiques.' Modesty put down her cup. 'They're beautiful. He brought me back a zip-fastener last year.'

Collier looked blank. 'Also antique?'

'No.' She smiled. 'But unique. He'd had it hand made in ivory by a man in Bangkok. The teeth are big chunky things an inch long and a quarter deep, but perfect. There's a huge silver ring on the runner. I had an evening dress made round it, with the zip running down the front from top to bottom.'

'I haven't seen you wear it,' said Collier.

'You haven't been around. When I wore it to the ballet at

Covent Garden it fairly knocked people's eyes out. I'll wear it if you'll take me——'

She broke off. Collier had groaned suddenly and was pressing the palm of one hand to his brow. He said, 'Oh, God. I put it on the shelf over the fridge. Didn't you see it?'

'See what?'

'Small parcel, addressed in Willie's writing. The postman brought it this morning while you were down in the village.' His tone became indignant. 'That Canadian girl should have reminded me.'

Dinah jumped. '*Me?* You didn't tell me!'

'Let us not bicker about it, pray.' Collier got up and went into the kitchen. He returned with a parcel about the size of a large cigar box and handed it to Modesty. 'It was unstamped.'

'Safest way to make sure it arrives.'

'I paid the postage.'

'That doesn't let you out.'

'Sorry, darling. I'll muck out the stables.'

'No. That means you loll around instructing Dinah.' Modesty looked at the parcel and began to open it. 'I'm going to tell Willie.'

'That's the idea,' Tarrant approved. 'Willie goes in for early morning roadwork. Maybe he'll take Collier along for company——' He stopped, looking at Modesty.

She had opened the tin box inside the wrapping and was staring down with an expression Tarrant had never seen on her face before.

Nobody spoke. After what seemed a very long time Modesty got to her feet, moved to the Pugin oak sidetable by the window, then carefully lifted something from the box and spread it on the table.

Tarrant stood up, Collier took Dinah's arm, and they gathered round. On a square of black velvet lay huddled a necklace of pearls. Modesty straightened it, then stood gazing down with the same strange look on her face.

Collier said quietly to Dinah, 'Pearls. A necklace. Magnificent.' Then, to Modesty, 'Well, it's certainly something special, but if that wasn't expensive then I'm the Queen of Bulgaria.'

Tarrant caught his breath. There were thirty-seven pearls. The centre pearl was at least a hundred grains, and the rest were superbly graduated to twenty-five grains at the clasp, which was of silver set with seed pearls. The necklace glowed with the living lustre that is unique to the natural pearl. It was, quite simply, beautiful; and the pearls were matched in a way he had never seen before. From the huge centre pearl, the colouring ran smoothly from the delicate pink of an imprisoned spark, through seventy-grainers with the lustre of flame reflected on translucent steel, then on through glowing shades of cream to the camphor white of the smaller pearls. The two smallest, on each side of the silver clasp, were black pearls.

Tarrant said softly, 'This is an unmannerly remark, but I'm going to make it. You could expect no change out of twenty-five thousand pounds for that little bauble.'

Collier caught Modesty's eye, made a quick gesture towards Dinah and said, 'May I?' She nodded absently. He picked up the necklace and put it into the girl's hands. 'Feel, Dinah.'

Tarrant said, 'I can't imagine he bought that in Panama. Rue de la Paix more likely.'

Modesty shook her head, her eyes on the pearls as Dinah ran them slowly through sensitive fingers.

'This one,' Dinah said with a quick smile. 'I think so. Yes. This is the one he found the day he got me away from those men. It was in a lump of—what did he call it? Nacre. It was just the one he wanted, and he was so pleased.'

'*Found* it?' Collier said blankly.

Modesty Blaise spoke for the first time, her tone uncertain. 'Yes . . . now I know what he's been doing on those mystery trips for the last seven years. Remember, Steve? You've never seen pearls matched like this before, with the colours graded. That's because they come from different pearl-beds all over the world.' She looked at Collier, then at Tarrant, and shook her head wonderingly. 'He didn't buy them. He dived for them.'

Tarrant said quietly, 'God Almighty.' Then, after an awed silence, 'And they must be a selection. You'd have to get far more to make a graded and matched necklace.'

'Yes.' Modesty's voice seemed a little forced. 'Far more. And there's not even a seed pearl in every oyster, or every hundred oysters.'

She reached out, took the necklace gently from Dinah and spread it on the velvet again. 'It's something I know about, so let me tell you. A good diver might bring up as many as two hundred oysters in a day. A very good diver, working hard. To make this necklace, you'd need . . . well, with a lot of luck you might make it up from the yield of fifty thousand oysters. That's if you were a skilled improver. And if you stayed undamaged. There's always a good chance you might get the bends or miss spotting a shark until it was too late.'

She ran a finger across the pearls on each side of the magnificent centre pearl. 'These are Orientals, from the Persian Gulf; these, with the touch of fiery steel, are Madras; then Ceylon, Panama, Shark Bay I think, and the Philippines, with a few in between that I couldn't be sure of. The two small blacks by the clasp are from Tahiti.'

There was a long silence.

'About nine months' work spread over seven years,' Collier said, and gave an incredulous laugh. 'Hasn't he put in a note to say who they're from?'

Modesty gave him a lopsided smile and did not answer.

Dinah jabbed him with her elbow and said, 'Could it be anyone else, dopey?' She turned to Modesty. 'You'll *have* to wear them for when he arrives. What have you got on?'

Collier said, 'A yellow jumper that will kill them. Go and put on that little black dress with the round neck.'

'Yes . . . yes, all right.'

'And for God's sake cheer up a bit,' Collier went on. 'It's fair enough being stupefied. I'm stupefied myself. But a girl who can wear twenty-five thousand quid's worth of pearls from all parts of the oyster world ought to grin like a cat. It's better than stickers on your windscreen, isn't it?'

Modesty rubbed a hand across her brow. 'I know. I know, Steve. But how in the world do I say thank you to Willie for a thing like this?'

It was the first time Collier had ever seen her discountenanced, unsure of herself. He found it pleasantly gratifying. A flicker of Tarrant's eyelid told Collier that this feeling was shared.

He grinned, and said cheerfully, 'Don't be damn silly. The pleasure's all Willie's. Pearls for his Princess. Christ, what an achievement! He won't want a thank-you. If you really want to please him, tick him off for taking unnecessary risks, like you usually do. He'll enjoy that. Now go and put your black dress on.'

TARRANT sat on a bench in the unfenced garden with Collier. They were both enjoying cigars. It was a day off for the village girl who came daily. Modesty and Dinah were in the kitchen dealing with the aftermath of tea-time. Willie Garvin had still not arrived.

'We should have offered our help in the kitchen,' said Tarrant. 'But I break things.'

Collier nodded agreement. 'So do I. It's a splendid failing, particularly if you get down to it right away. Future offers are flatly rejected.'

Modesty and Dinah came out into the garden. Modesty wore the fine woollen dress Collier had called black, and which was charcoal grey. Tarrant looked at the pearls and the slender column of her throat, and sighed with pleasure.

'We want to have the pool on that patch of ground between the trees and the house,' Modesty was saying, 'but there are problems.' She took the swing seat with Dinah. 'I don't suppose many bombs fell around here during the war, but one fell on the local council offices and destroyed all their records. We don't know the run of the gas pipes, electricity cables, water and sewers—at least, not in enough detail.'

'What are you doing about it?' Collier asked.

'I don't know. We can't just start digging. I'm hoping Willie might come up with some sort of detector.'

Collier was aware of a momentary tension in Dinah. He looked at her, puzzled, and saw her come to some decision. She relaxed and said a little ruefully, 'I'll check it for you now, Modesty. Is there any wire in the garage? Galvanised steel wire for preference.'

Modesty had started to open a packet of cigarettes. She

stopped, shot a querying glance at Collier, then said, 'How d'you mean, Dinah?'

'It's what I do. Find pipes and things.'

Modesty put the cigarettes and a lighter into Dinah's hands. 'Have a smoke and talk to Sir Gerald,' she said. 'Steve, come and see what we can find.'

In the big barn that accepted three cars and still had space for a workshop, Modesty looked at Collier and lifted an eyebrow. 'Some kind of dowsing? Water divining?'

He nodded. 'A very practical kind. My God, I wish I'd known about this before. It's a phenomenon that's hardly been researched at all, and I've kept promising myself I'd make a study of it.'

'Dinah's psychic?'

He gave a wry laugh. 'She doesn't have to be, that's what makes it difficult for us nosey folk. The funny thing is that plenty of people with no apparent psychic abilities can get varying degrees of success with pipe-locators. You might well get a response yourself.'

'Anybody?'

'Yes.' Collier looked round the garage, then moved to lift a coil of 5 gauge galvanised steel wire from a nail in the wall. 'There's a company in Michigan that actually manufactures pipe-locators. And ordinary, no-nonsense engineers use them. But I think Dinah must be something pretty special in this line. Find me some pliers, darling.'

She brought him a pair of pliers from the bench and watched as he cut two lengths of wire a little more than a foot long.

'You spoke about water divining,' he said, 'but the rum thing is that it doesn't matter whether or not the pipes have water in them. The Division of Water Supply in Michigan have used these damn things to locate cast-iron pipes, clay-tile drains, and brick intakes. Wet or dry. Other companies use them for gas pipes or electric cables.'

'I thought you hadn't studied this subject.'

'I haven't, under controlled conditions. A lot of scientists say it can't be explained and therefore it doesn't work. But a lot of engineers in the States just go right ahead and find pipes. And the Scottish Electricity Board over here are trying them out.'

He had straightened the two pieces of wire, and now he bent each length to a right-angle, with one arm longer than the other.

Modesty said, 'What percentage success do these engineers get?'

'I've no statistics,' Collier answered regretfully. 'But I know they've used them at the Milford Water Works, Connecticut, for fifteen years. And these are everyday down-to-earth technicians who just want results. Do you want that bit of copper tubing?'

'No. Why?'

'We'll give the girl a treat. And a surprise. Can you find a hacksaw?'

Modesty watched in silence as Collier clamped a length of half-inch copper tubing in the vice and cut off two pieces, each four inches long.

He wiped the small tubes clean and said, 'I've heard of people doing this with a bit of wire from a coat-hanger, and I've heard of them doing it on a map, not on the actual terrain.'

'A map?'

'Just a little old map. That really would be psychic.' He sighed. 'I must get down to a controlled study of this. Maybe Dinah would run a series of experiments for me.' He wrinkled his brow. 'It's funny she's never mentioned this talent.'

'No it's not.' Modesty looked at him with amusement. 'She didn't mention it for the same reason *you* never mention to anyone that you investigate psychic phenomena. You'd been sleeping with me for three weeks before you told me. You said you were a metallurgist, you liar.'

'Oh, well . . .' He grinned and shrugged, then slipped the

short arm of each piece of angled wire into the lengths of copper tubing. 'If you tell people you study psychic phenomena they think you're a screwball.'

'Yes. So Dinah's reluctant to tell people she locates pipes and cables by a screwball method.'

'I suppose so.' He gripped one piece of tubing in each hand so that the horizontal arms of the two thick wires pointed at her like guns. 'Get going, babe. I've got you covered.'

Dinah stood up as they came round the cottage and into the garden. 'If you can't find any wire I could manage with a coat-hanger,' she said.

Collier glanced at Modesty with a smile. 'So I was just saying, Dinah. But we've done better than that. Here.'

He went to her and put the tubing grips in her hands. Her eyes widened. 'But these are proper locators. How did you know?'

'He's just about the top psychic investigator in this country,' Modesty said. 'That's how he knows.'

'Steve! You didn't tell me.'

'You didn't tell *me*. And we both know why. But you're in sympathetic company here. Nobody's going to think you've escaped from the laughing academy.'

'Well, that's fine.' The last shadow of uneasiness vanished from Dinah and she smiled. 'Bring some pegs and a ball of string, Steve. It shouldn't take long.'

Two minutes later they stood at one end of the patch of grassy ground which lay on the west side of the cottage.

'I should have left half-an-hour ago,' Tarrant murmured to Modesty. 'But I'd like to see Willie and I certainly don't intend missing this little bit of magic. Do you think it will work?'

Modesty nodded. 'Dinah doesn't seem to have any doubts.'

'Head me across the ground at right-angles to a line between the village and the house, Steve,' Dinah said. 'We'll cross check the other way later.'

She stood with the two locators like guns in her hands, the

wires pointing forward, then began to move slowly across the stretch of grass.

She had moved six paces when the two wires swivelled smoothly in the tubing to point away from each other. She must have heard the tiny sound, for she said, 'Line up on that with two pegs, Steve, then I'll check the run at each end of the patch. Mark this as sewer crock. Depth, six feet.'

He moved round to gaze along the line of the pointing wires, and pushed a peg into the ground. 'How do you know it's sewer crock?'

'Because that's what I'm looking for this time. I'll do gas, main water and electricity later.'

'How do you know the depth?'

'I know. Shut up and get the pegs in.'

He moved to her other side, drove in a second peg and said, 'Right.' She tilted the locators so that the wires swung loosely forward again, then moved on.

During the next fifteen minutes the wires swivelled a number of times as she checked the run of pipes and cables, first at the centre and then at each end of the patch. There was the sewer; a water pipe angling across one corner of the area; a gas pipe striking across its width at one end; no electric cables.

Dinah gave the locators to Collier as if glad to be rid of them, and rubbed her bare arms.

'How do you know the depth?' he repeated.

'I feel it. My arms tingle more when the pipe or whatever I'm looking for is nearer the surface. You get so you can tell to inches.'

'And this is what you do for a living?'

'Yes. I'm no typist, and this pays more. Judy came round on surveys to look after me. Have you got those lines strung out?'

'All done.'

Modesty and Tarrant were moving up from thirty yards away, but Dinah heard them. She looked in their direction and called, 'Could I have a drink, Modesty? It always leaves me a little jittery.'

'You can have a magnum of champagne if you fancy it.' Modesty's voice was warm, and there was a touch of excitement in it that surprised Collier. 'I'm really grateful, Dinah. If we sink the pool a few yards farther from the trees, we'll miss the sewer and gas pipe. That means we just have to get the water pipe re-routed. It has to come up anyway, to run a proper feed for the pool.'

Dinah cocked her head a little to one side and said, 'There's a car coming.'

A minute later they saw it breast the ridge and begin to move down the track to the cottage. Modesty said, 'It's Willie.' Dinah's face puckered for a moment as if she might be about to cry; then it cleared and was alight with open happiness.

Modesty looked at Collier and said, 'Will you go ahead with Dinah? Give her time to say hallo, then take her in for that drink. We want a quick word with Willie before Sir Gerald goes.'

'Glad to be absent.' Collier took Dinah's arm. 'Very glad, by God. Your business conferences turn my bowels to water.'

Modesty said, 'Don't tell us about your bowels. It's disgusting.'

'That may well be. All the same, I trust you'll remember them in your deliberations. Come on, Dinah. I'll give you thirty seconds to chew Willie's ear.'

When they were out of earshot Tarrant said, 'That girl's rather bowled over by Willie. I hope she doesn't get hurt.'

It was some moments before Modesty replied. She was in what Tarrant had learned to recognise as one of her quiet moods, a mood that came upon her when future action was confused and uncertain. It was, he suspected, a mood she deliberately created as a defence against waste of mental energy.

At last she said quietly, 'Yes, Dinah may get hurt. But she's different from Willie's list of runners. It wouldn't astound me if he threw away his address book for Dinah.'

Tarrant stared. 'Would you mind very much?' he asked after a little silence.

She laughed and shrugged. 'I don't own Willie. If he was happy I'd be glad for him. But I'd hate it for me.'

'I can't quite imagine him settling down.'

'Why not? It only needs the right girl.'

Tarrant fingered his chin. 'You might settle down yourself, of course,' he reflected, a question in his voice. 'I think I'd be relieved.'

'All things are possible,' she said with gentle mockery, and looked towards the cottage. Tarrant followed her gaze.

They saw the Lotus Elan convertible halt and Willie uncoil himself lazily from the driving seat. Dinah ran to him. Collier hung back. Willie picked her up, lifted her high in the air, then set her down and kissed her at length, without embarrassment. An arm about her, he turned to Collier. They spoke briefly. Willie glanced across to where Modesty and Tarrant had begun to walk slowly down the grassy slope towards the garden. He waved, spoke to Dinah, patted her bottom and handed her over to Collier, then began moving across the unfenced garden.

Modesty halted, fingering the pearls. Tarrant moved a little to one side as Willie approached, curious to observe this meeting. Willie's carved mahogany face held a huge grin. Modesty waited for him gravely. There was the familiar greeting that Tarrant knew of old. Willie took her right hand in his left, bent a little to touch her fingers briefly to his cheek, and said, ' 'Allo, Princess.'

'Hallo, Willie love.' Modesty kept hold of his hand and pushed back the jacket sleeve, turning his wrist to look at it carefully. Fading blue marks were all that remained of the cuts made by the handcuffs, and the heavy bruising had become no more than a faint discoloration. Satisfied, she let go of his hand and stood back a little, looking at him, touching her fingers to the pearls for a moment. 'How do they look, Willie?'

He studied her with a judicial air, then gave a pleased nod of his head. 'Fine. I was worried about grading the colours, but you make 'em look marvellous.'

'My God, they *are* marvellous,' she said, almost fiercely. 'And I've been trying to think of words for the last hour. I want to know all about it, the story of every pearl.' She stepped closer, put her hands on his arms and rested her head against his shoulder for a moment before looking up. 'Leave a girl something to say another time, Willie love.'

'I enjoyed it,' Willie said simply. 'Honest, Princess.'

Modesty slipped an arm through his and they began to stroll. Tarrant fell in on her other side. 'Kept me out of mischief, too,' Willie added, then grinned suddenly. 'Except in Papeete. Met a girl called Lala who took a shine to me. After three weeks I could 'ardly stand up. Then I found she was the local witch-woman an' was priming me with love potions. Lucky I was only after a couple of small black pearls there.'

'Love potions?' said Tarrant with disbelief. 'I thought primitive aphrodisiacs of rhinoceros horn and the like had been disproven.'

'Try a week with Lala sometime,' Willie said. 'She uses some kind of crushed ant, I think. Anyway, it works.'

'There's something else that works too, Willie.' Modesty pointed to the strings Collier had laid, and in a few brief sentences told of Dinah's strange faculty.

Willie rubbed his chin. 'Right up Steve's street. I knew there was something she 'adn't told me. You reckon this is why Gabriel wants her?'

Tarrant grunted. 'Why should Gabriel want to locate pipes?'

'It's not just pipes,' Modesty said. 'Somebody must get Dinah to open up about what she can do. Steve thinks this talent could extend to locating other things.'

'Like what, Princess?'

'I don't know yet. It doesn't seem to have dawned on Dinah that this could be why Gabriel wants her.'

'Jesus, you'd think she'd wonder.'

'Yes. But she doesn't like talking about her ability in this line, and maybe she doesn't like thinking about it, or even doing it. She was jittery after that session just now. Anyway, getting her to talk might give us some kind of clue. So would finding out where Gabriel's operating. Did you get anything, Willie?'

They had reached the stables and were turning to stroll back now. Willie said, 'I got all the old contacts with their ears to the ground. Some we can trust, some we can't. There's nothing so far.'

Tarrant said, 'I have my own people trying to pick up Gabriel's trail. If I get any positive reports I'll call you at once, Modesty.'

'Thank you, Sir Gerald.'

'Perhaps you'll keep me posted on any progress. Oh, and forget about the Aaronson business. You've told Willie about that?'

'Not yet. There hasn't been much time. We'll forget it for the moment. But I still don't like it.'

'My dear,' Tarrant said with a sigh, 'I have so many things on my plate that I don't like. But one adjusts.'

Dinah moved her bishop and said, 'Check.'

Collier said, 'Sorry, it's not check. You forgot your own pawn on king's knight four.'

'Damn.' She scowled and moved the bishop back, then ran her fingers quickly over the pocket chess set on her knee, which duplicated the game and allowed her to check the position by feel when her memory lapsed.

Night had fallen, Willie Garvin was upstairs completing his check of the ultrasonic and infra-red alarm systems. Modesty Blaise sat in an armchair, the radiogram turned low, absently listening to the pianistics of Earl Hines in a running fight against drums and bass in *Satin Doll*. When she heard Willie coming downstairs she got up and poured him a beer.

'You know what I fancy?' he said as he came into the room. 'Ah—that's it. Thanks Princess.' He took the glass, lifted it to her, and looked at the chess players. 'What's Steve smell like, Dinah?'

Collier said bitterly, 'I don't know what's got into the lower classes these days. There's no respect left.'

'He smells like suede feels,' said Dinah. 'Kind of soft but not smooth, stretchy but tough.'

Collier considered. 'It doesn't sound too bad as smells go,' he admitted.

'There aren't any bad smells. Well, not many.'

'What about Willie? Like walking through a nice rich compost heap?'

'No.' She grinned and then thought for a moment. 'Willie smells like when you hear a muted trumpet, kind of brassy but mellow.'

'And Modesty? Is she a feel-smell or a sound-smell?'

'Neither. Brandy-taste. Smooth and warm but with a bite to it.'

Collier laughed and said, 'I go along with that.' Then he stiffened. Modesty and Willie had stopped listening. Willie stood by the brick fireplace, an elbow on the mantelpiece. In one hand he held the Identikit picture Tarrant had left, and he was staring at it rigidly, unbelievingly, and with something close to sick alarm in his eyes. Modesty was watching him, puzzled, waiting.

In the silence Dinah said, 'What's wrong?' Collier reached out, rested a hand on hers with gentle warning pressure, and murmured, 'Wait.'

Willie Garvin looked up at Modesty and said in a strained voice. 'Where'd this come from, Princess?'

'From Tarrant. It's to do with the Aaronson business. Do you know him?'

Willie put down the picture carefully and drew a deep breath. 'Yes. I know 'im. But it's over ten years ago now. I thought he was dead.'

Modesty took two cigarettes from a carved ebony box, lit them, and put one in Willie's hand. 'He's not dead,' she said. 'I saw him. So did Steve and Tarrant. It was that evening just after you came on the air from Panama. What do you know about him, Willie?'

He inhaled on the cigarette, then stared at the glowing tip. 'I was gun-running off Uruguay,' he said slowly. 'Just one of the crew.' His eyes flickered towards the picture. 'He was the boss. Christ, he's bad, Princess. Bad, and lucky. He'd do mad things and get away with 'em. And it didn't worry 'im, he never cared.'

'Would he kill?' Modesty asked, and Collier knew from her gaze that the question was not an idle one.

Willie nodded. 'He's a freak. Not just to look at, but inside.' He gestured vaguely. 'I can't describe the bastard, he doesn't add up. I can only tell you things about 'im. He can drink a bottle of whisky a day, every day for a month, and stay cold sober. Then he can stop, just like that. He can take a shot of heroin that would kill you——'

'*Heroin?*' Modesty stared incredulously.

'That's right, Princess. But he's no junkie. He can use 'ard drugs, an' not get addicted. Total control. He's built like a rhino and moves like a cat.' Willie half closed his eyes, remembering, and it was as if he had to compel a reluctant memory. 'Strong . . .' he went on softly. 'They reckon a gorilla's about fifteen times stronger than a man. Well, I'd put this one halfway between. Freak strong.'

He was silent for a moment, then looked at Modesty. 'I've seen 'im kill, Princess. It wasn't for anything much, not even for kicks. But he was always prodding, needling, trying to get blokes narked. That's what he enjoyed most. He could cut you to ribbons in that public school voice, smooth an' grinning all the time. I saw a bloke round on 'im once, and there was a fight.' Willie shrugged and ground out the half smoked cigarette. 'No. Not a fight. Just a killing.'

Modesty said, 'How?' And again Collier sensed that there was some purpose in her question.

Willie Garvin drew a hand down his face and looked at the palm as if to see if it was damp. He said, 'Ever seen a terrier with a rat? It gets the rat by the neck, then flicks its 'ead up sharp. Breaks the rat's neck. That's what it was like. He took this bloke by the back of the neck with one bloody great paw . . . and just shook 'im. Once. We were at sea, and I 'elped to wrap the bloke up in a blanket and slip 'im over. There wasn't a mark on 'im. Just 'is neck was broken.'

Modesty turned her head slowly to look at Collier, and he felt his flesh crawl as he remembered little Dr. Aaronson lying in a huddle at the foot of the stairs, his neck broken, without a mark on him.

Dinah got up, moved across the room and groped for Willie's hand. Her face was anxious and puzzled. She said, 'For God's sake, what is it, Willie? You sound so strange.'

He made an effort and grinned, putting her hand up to his cheek. 'I got a stinking past, Dinah. I told you. Always gives me the dry 'eaves when I remember the way things were before Modesty came along.'

'It's more than that,' Dinah said with a touch of anger. 'I'm already scared to hell about you and Modesty going after Gabriel. I don't want you to do it for me, but you won't listen. Now I'm more scared, because this other thing is worse somehow. I can feel it. I've heard the way you talk about Gabriel, but it was a lot different from the way you talked about this man just now. I don't like it. I *hate* it, Willie.'

'So do I,' Collier said, and stood up. 'I have a statement to make. It will no doubt be ignored, but I'm going to make it anyway. Quaint though it seems, I don't like being shot at or having a knife stuck in me or even having my neck broken. I'm just not cut out for that sort of pursuit. Unlike Willie, I can say that my past has been reasonably untroubled. It's my present that gives me the shudders. Oh yes, and my possible future. I've never seen a terrier kill a rat, and don't wish to. I particularly don't wish to know about this man and his canine impersonations. We're stuck with Gabriel because he's after Dinah. We didn't ask for it but we're stuck with him. All right. But for Christ's sake, isn't that enough to worry about for now? For bloody *ever*, as far as I'm concerned.'

He looked at Modesty with exasperation on his lean face. 'Go and shuffle off Gabriel's mortal coil for him by all means. I'll hold your handbag for you and even send a greetings telegram when you've done it. But if you're going to have a bash at Big Daddy contemporaneously, or even subsequently, then turn down an empty glass for me, because I'll be on the list of absent friends.'

He ended rather breathlessly, and there was a silence. Modesty moved to him, linked her hands behind his neck, and kissed him on the chin. 'I love it when you get mad,' she said. 'The tip of your nose twitches. What's contemporaneously?'

Collier gave a strangled laugh. 'Look it up. As for my nasal powers, I practise daily. But will you *please* tear your attention away from my nose for a moment and concentrate on the general content of my recent statement?'

'I did, darling, and it was masterly. Don't worry. We're just going to concern ourselves with Gabriel. You and Dinah can forget about Big Daddy.' She turned and looked across the room at Willie. 'Does he have a name?'

Willie's lips twisted in a smile without humour. 'Delicata,' he said, 'Simon Delicata.'

II

Dinah lay in bed wishing she could sleep. It was half an hour since Willie Garvin had looked in, talked to her for a little while, then kissed her goodnight. She had hoped he would stay, but something told her that the moment was not right, and she had done nothing to keep him.

She sighed, and groped for the packet of cigarettes on her bedside table.

In a room at the far end of a twisting passage Collier lifted his head from the pillow and looked at Modesty as she sat brushing her hair. A flame-coloured silk dressing gown rustled with the movement of her arm. She wore no nightdress beneath it.

Collier said, 'Come to bed. I'm not going to pounce on you, by the way. It's occurred to me that Gabriel can find you much more easily than you can find him. So I'm just going to wrap myself round you and hang on tight, leaving your gun arm free of course. Don't fire too close to my ear if you have to shoot anybody.'

Modesty smiled. 'I don't think Gabriel will be busy just yet. But anyway we'll have plenty of warning. Willie fixed an infra-red modification on the ultrasonic system when he rigged the alarms. If anyone gets within two hundred yards of the cottage they'll break a beam and trigger the buzzers.'

'And I'll get under the bed,' said Collier. 'What about a stray fox?'

'No effect. Too close to the ground.'

'Gabriel might do a hundred yard dash on his belly.'

'It won't be Gabriel. He'll hire the labour. And if they come in on their bellies they'll find the steel mesh screens.'

The screens she spoke of slid out from recesses beside windows and doors, and were normally hidden. Collier had been surprised and relieved to see them. He knew now that the screen alarms were connected through telephone lines to the village police station. The system was basically for use when the cottage was untenanted.

'I like Willie. He's thorough,' Collier said. 'Come to bed, dammit. I require warmth, comfort and protection.'

Modesty stood up. 'Later. Go to sleep, Steve. I want to talk to Willie.'

'What about, for God's sake?'

'If I tell you, you'll only start saying I've afflicted your bowels again.'

'Consideration at last.' Collier propped himself on one elbow. 'But don't you think it's likely that Willie's with Dinah now?'

'No. Not under my roof. I wouldn't give a damn, but Willie has his own rules.' She moved to the bed, leaned down, and kissed him. 'Don't stay awake for me.'

'Dear Hetty Heart-throb: My girl-friend sometimes spends half the night in another man's room. Mum says this is un-usual and I ought to say something, but I'm afraid if I ask her about it she might break my arms, because she is the Northern Counties mud-wrestling champion——'

Modesty went out, smiling a little as she heard his muffled voice beyond the closed door continuing the monologue.

There was a light under Willie's door when she tapped on it. He did not answer, but a moment later the door opened and he stood back for her to enter. He had taken off his jacket and tie, but was otherwise still dressed. When he had closed the door she took his arm and moved to the bed. They sat down side by side. Still holding his arm she said, 'Steve and Dinah aren't here now. Tell me about it Willie.'

He sat gazing at the floor, and ran a hand slowly through his hair. 'I was going to tell you, soon as we got a chance, Princess.' He looked at her. 'Delicata's got a hex on me.'

Her eyes revealed no hint of shock as she nodded soberly.

Fear, of a kind, was no stranger to them; they knew its shape and power well, and had long since learned the mental chemistry whereby that power could be transformed and harnessed to serve as energy for the will. But this was something different.

'Where does it start?' she asked quietly.

'On that same trip I told you about. But later, in some little port. I was pretty young then, and you know what a mean bastard I was before you took me on. Cocky, too. I reckoned I could take Delicata, reckoned I'd got the speed and know-how to offset brute strength. I was wrong.'

She had felt his muscles growing taut as he spoke. Now he relaxed with a conscious effort and went on. 'It was like tangling with a gorilla. But he's not just strong. He's fast with it. I got to 'im all right. Enough to cripple a normal man. But it just didn't seem to worry the bastard. He never stopped grinning an' needling. Then 'e managed to catch me with one 'and. He clubbed me with the other. Just once. When I went down I was like jelly.'

He was silent for a while, and Modesty waited without impatience for him to go on.

'He's got short stubby legs, thick as your body,' Willie said absently, his mind far away in the past. 'No good for a fight. But the fight was over. Delicata started to kick me ribs in. No hurry. A kick like a sledge-'ammer, then he'd walk off a bit an' take a pull at 'is drink—did I say we were in a dockside bar?'

Modesty shook her head.

'Well, there was just the barman and three of the crew. The barman was scared green round the gills an' the others weren't going to get in the middle. So after Delicata put the boot in, he'd take a pull at 'is drink, laugh a bit an' make some smooth crack in that nice cultured voice, then stroll back to where I was lying and slam another kick in.'

Willie rubbed a hand slowly down his side. 'I've taken a few bashings before an' since, but never like that one, Princess.

I could feel the ribs going, and I knew Delicata wasn't going to stop when they'd gone. So I was finished. Then I'm not sure what 'appened. I think a bloke looked in and said a couple of cops were coming. But anyway, something 'appened, because Delicata and the rest scarpered. I passed out and came round in the Seaman's Hospital. They said it was like I'd been in a car smash. Five ribs bust, and bruising like I was wearing black corsets. It was eight weeks before I came out, and a year before I was right again.'

He stopped speaking and looked about him vaguely. Modesty took cigarettes from the pocket of her dressing gown and gave him one.

'You never told me about this,' she said, curiously but without reproach.

'I know.' He lit the cigarette and she saw that his hand was steady. 'It was a couple of years before you took me on. By then I'd 'eard Delicata played one of 'is mad tricks once too often, in Jakarta. The story was he'd died in some Indonesian clink.' He shrugged. 'I s'pose I believed it because I wanted to. And I forgot what Delicata did to me because I wanted to.'

'It didn't knock your confidence.' Modesty's tone was thoughtful, objective. 'And I'd say it would be different if you met him again. It's ten years. You know a lot more, you're stronger, more experienced, and you haven't lost any speed.'

'It wouldn't be different, Princess,' Willie said, and his own voice was objective now, as if they were talking of someone else. 'That rib-busting in slow-time went too deep.' He tapped a finger to his temple. 'The old p.d.'

Modesty nodded. He was speaking shorthand for psychological domination, a vital element in any form of close combat. With relief she realised that Willie was not all mixed up about this. He had analysed the matter, assessed his weakness, and concluded that it was too deep-rooted in his subconscious to be removed by any amount of logical reassurance.

It was an unpleasant conclusion, but he had faced it, accepted it, and revealed it to her without wraps.

'You were going to tell me about how you ran into Delicata,' Willie said.

'Yes.' She gave him the story in spare phrases. He made no comment, but nodded once when she spoke of Delicata's seeming amusement at the encounter, and again as she told of finding Aaronson with his neck broken.

When the story ended he said, 'We going to follow it up, Princess?'

'We?' It was a serious question.

He grinned crookedly. 'I couldn't stay out. And you needn't worry about the hex. I'm not even interested in trying to bust it, so I wouldn't take 'im on like before. If it comes to a rumble I'll settle for a knife at fifty feet. There's no p.d. going to stop that.'

Again Modesty felt a surge of relief. She knew, and was glad, that he sensed it in her. 'We'll decide about that later, Willie love,' she said quietly. 'Steve was right when he took the floor and said we had trouble enough for now. It's Gabriel we have to think about, not Delicata.'

'Sure.' Willie frowned for a moment as if trying to capture a thought that eluded him. Then he shrugged. 'I just wanted you to know about that hex, but it doesn't affect the Gabriel job. Want to try me with a workout tomorrow?'

'All right. In the small barn. Oh—I don't know though.' She turned towards him and smiled as she pulled open the neck of her dressing gown a little, to show the row of pearls round her neck. 'Look, I can't bring myself to take them off.'

He looked pleased, then amused. 'You'll 'ave Steve complaining they dig in.'

'Steve's enjoying other worries just now. He says he's getting under the bed if the alarms go off. Oh, did you speak to Dinah about finding things apart from pipes?'

'Yes. She's done silver in Mexico and gold in Alaska, both for the Laresco Mining Corporation.' Willie scratched his nose speculatively. 'Dinah didn't say so, but I've got a hunch she can show a hell of a talent in this field.'

'Silver and gold,' Modesty said, and leaned her head thoughtfully against his shoulder. 'That sounds more like Gabriel. Except he's not the mining type. Would Dinah have taken on a metal-locating job if they'd made a normal business offer?'

'She says not. She only went after precious metals twice. You know she gets a bit jittery locating pipes? Well, metals are ten times worse. There's some kind of nervous effect that nearly drives 'er bonkers.'

'So if Gabriel knew that——' She broke off as there came the faint sound of the extension telephone ringing in her bedroom. 'That just might be what we're waiting for, Willie.'

The ringing stopped as they went along the passage. Collier was sitting up in bed and speaking into the telephone when Modesty entered with Willie behind her. '. . . No, I'm not in bonne santé at all, René. My bowels are in a hideous condition. It's Modesty. She's at it again, as you no doubt know.' He favoured them with a sour glare.

Modesty and Willie exchanged a glance. René Vaubois was head of the Deuxième Bureau and a good friend. It was not long since they had saved him from assassination in Paris by five professional killers. Steve Collier had been present that night in Montmartre and naturally claimed that the occasion had left him mentally scarred for life.

There were contacts and contacts. Only some could be fully trusted. Vaubois came first of these.

Collier was saying, 'Yes, I know, but try telling that to my ulcers.'

Modesty took the phone from him. 'Hallo, René. He hasn't really got ulcers, he eats like a horse. Have you got anything for me?'

Vaubois spoke English that was close to perfect. He said, 'Your friend and his colleague are in Beauvais. Hotel Cosmos in Rue St. Nicolas. One of my men spotted them at Orly and followed them.'

'Are you picking them up?'

139

'I have nothing to hold them on. Neither have the police unless your friends ignore a *défense de cracher* notice. I could of course arrange something, but from what Willie told me I think it would only be an obstacle to your intention.'

'Yes, it would. We want to clear this up for good.'

'My man is keeping an eye on your friends in Beauvais. If you need to contact him, go to the Bar Louis in Boulevard de l'Assaut. The concierge there is your link. Tell him you have a message for Madame Bobin, and he will arrange contact.'

'Thank you, René.'

'How soon will you be there?'

'By dawn. We'll travel unofficially.'

'Good. I will not keep you now. Au'voir, chère amie.'

'Au'voir, René. And thank you again.' She put down the telephone.

'How do you travel unofficially?' asked Collier.

Her answer was directed to Willie. 'I've got Dave Craythorpe on twenty-four hour standby with his Beagle. We ought to be airborne in ninety minutes. Ring Dave, then start getting our gear together, Willie.'

'Right.' Willie went out. Modesty took off her dressing gown, looked in the mirror, sighed, and unclasped the row of pearls. As she turned to the wardrobe Collier said, 'You can't enter France illegally by air. You'll be shot down or something.'

'Dave Craythorpe flies in and out with smuggled goods a dozen times a year. There's plenty of the coast unscreened by radar on both sides of the Channel.' She pulled on a pair of black stretch briefs and fastened a black bra. 'It's different in the States. You have to keep at about zero feet to get under the screens there.'

'Oh God,' said Collier heavily, 'what a mine of appalling knowledge you are.' He got out of bed and began to dress.

'We'll probably be back tomorrow night,' Modesty said.

And that, thought Collier, would be when Gabriel was dead. He wondered briefly how they intended to go about the grim task, then decided he would rather not know.

Modesty had put on a shirt and slacks. She said, 'Why are you getting dressed?'

'Because I'll be left here to look after Dinah. And I feel vulnerable in pyjamas. I mean even more vulnerable.'

'There won't be any trouble, darling.'

'No. But just supposing. What do I do if the alarms go off?'

'If they do, there'll be a couple of policemen along in about fifteen minutes. Nobody can get through the mesh screens in a hurry. And if they try, you blaze off with the shotgun.'

'You can bet on that,' Collier said fervently. Her shotgun was a light Churchill 25-inch Première model, and superb to handle. 'I'll be sleeping with it beside the bed,' he added. 'Staying awake would probably be more accurate.'

Dinah appeared in the open doorway wearing a dark green housecoat. She said uncertainly, 'I can hear things happening.'

'It's the last lap,' Collier said cheerfully. 'Gabriel's been spotted, so Modesty and Willie are just hopping over to France to do him in. You'll be left in my clutches without a chaperon, you poor child.'

Modesty went to the girl and took her hands. 'That's just about all you have to worry about, Dinah. Fight him off till tomorrow night, and we'll be back by then.'

Dinah said slowly, 'Your hands are cold. You wouldn't mind if these men came here and you killed them in a fight. But this is different. An execution. And you don't like it. I can tell.'

'You make up for not being able to see, don't you? Yes, it's different. But it doesn't *make* any difference. I've learned what can happen if you duck the issue and give people like Gabriel a chance.'

Collier said with sudden violence, 'I hate their guts. I hate these bloody swine who kill and brutalise and do any goddam filthy thing to anybody, just to get what they want. I've seen it, and I hate them so much it hurts.' He looked at Modesty, and his lean face was drawn. 'Don't give them a chance. An execution before they do any more damage suits me fine. Just fine. I don't have the guts or ability to do it myself, but just give me a button to press and tell me it'll blow Gabriel apart, and I'll bloody nearly break my thumb on it.'

Dinah's head was turned in his direction and there was surprise in her sightless eyes. 'I didn't know you felt so fierce,' she said.

'I didn't once.' Collier sat down on the bed to lace his shoes. 'That was before I got in the middle of something. Modesty once spoke to me about evil people, and I was embarrassed. It's an old-fashioned word and you feel self-conscious saying it. But then I had them all round me. Saw them at their scummy work. That's when you find out what evil means.'

Dinah nodded. 'I found out on the beach that day. It has an awful, awful smell.'

Willie came upstairs and along the passage. He said, 'Dave'll be at the airfield in an hour. I've put some gear together, Princess. What do we take to wear?'

'Better make it a small selection for all occasions, Willie. We don't know how or when we're going to play it.'

'Right.' Willie took Dinah's hand. 'Come and help me pack, love.'

Collier lay back on the bed with his hands behind his head. 'For all occasions,' he echoed broodingly, watching Modesty pull a pigskin travelling case from her wardrobe. 'You know, I've made up my mind, and I'm going to brook no argument. When this lot's over I'm going to make an honest woman of you.'

Beyond the fields and the low ridge, a black car stood thirty yards off the road, shielded by trees. It was a little down on its rear springs from the weight of the huge man who sat in the back.

He watched the dancing intermittence of the Lotus Elan's

lights through the trees as it turned from the track on to the road and accelerated smoothly. The sound of the engine faded and was gone.

Delicata quivered with laughter, and the car swayed a little, rousing the man who dozed at the wheel.

'Off to Beauvais,' Delicata murmured. 'Excellent.'

The man at the wheel said, 'Eh?'

Delicata said, 'Be quiet, Casey.' He took out a cigar and looked at it with relish, then decided that he would not smoke. It was amusing to feel the steel cogs of his mind engage irresistibly with the decision. He broke the cigar in two and tossed it out of the open window.

Leaning back comfortably he said, 'Be quiet while I think aloud. Our hero and heroine have left the cottage. The blind girl remains with a male companion as yet unidentified. Are they accessible now? Perhaps. But one thinks not. Miss Blaise and young Garvin are ingenious and cautious. In parentheses, we must note that young Garvin's ribs should be dealt with more thoroughly next time. Don't go to sleep while I'm talking you bastard, or I'll smack your face till it swells like a pumpkin.'

The man at the wheel sat up very straight and did not answer.

'Now,' Delicata went on musingly, 'have you ever observed that in the less experienced portion of the human race, the fears that loom by night are swept away by the rising sun? Don't answer, Casey, I dislike interruptions. Yes, the happy dawn is our time, I think. Meanwhile we must telephone Beauvais. A call-box? No. Putting quantities of coin in a slot is a tedious matter.'

He leaned forward and gripped the back of the seat in an enormous hand. Casey shivered slightly.

'A private phone, or shall we say semi private?' There was rich amusement in Delicata's voice. 'The police station is not too far. I'm sure I can persuade them to let me make a call when the matter is so urgent. An A.D. and C. call of course.

The rate-payers' pockets mustn't suffer.' He settled back again. 'Yes, let us drive to the police station.'

Casey wiped his face and said *'Gawd!'* under his breath, then reached for the starter.

Collier woke from an uneasy doze with a sour taste in his mouth. He looked at his watch and found that he had slept for just over an hour. It was seven-thirty, and the sun was up.

He splashed water in his face and ran a hand through his hair, then went along to Dinah's room. The door stood open but she was not there. He listened, and heard the chink of crockery in the kitchen below, then the whirr of the electric grinder as she ground coffee beans.

He switched off the infra-red circuit and looked out of the window. One or two tradesmen might call during the morning, and he did not want them to trigger the alarms. The sky was blue, the earth green, and his spirits lifted. During the night he had decided to keep the steel mesh screens in place and their alarm circuits switched on, even by day. He and Dinah would stay safely encaged, and if the milkman didn't like it he could pour the milk under the door.

But now the idea seemed vaguely ludicrous. The daily girl and the stableman would come at nine. Undecided, he toyed with the second switch, which controlled the screen alarms, then left it. Might as well make up his mind when the two from the village arrived. Send the girl home for the day and tell the stableman to get on with things? He shrugged and postponed the decision.

As he turned from the window he saw the small red shape of the post van appear over the ridge and begin to wind its way down the track. He grinned with relief, glad that he had woken in time to kill the infra-red beams.

When he hurried downstairs and entered the kitchen he saw that Dinah had started cooking breakfast. She was dressed, and looked fresh and attractive. Her smile as she turned to him almost hid the underlying shadow of strain.

144

'Hi, Steve.'

'Hallo, Dinah.' He put his arm round her shoulders for a moment. 'Why don't you look terrible? I'd feel much better if you did.'

'Is that how you look?'

'Yes. Have I got time for a shave before that's ready?'

'If you're quick.'

'Four minutes. Oh, don't worry if you hear something coming——'

'I already heard it, but it's only the post van. I know the engine.'

Collier sighed. 'And I nearly broke my neck getting downstairs to clutch you to my bosom and quiet your girlish fears.' He could hear the engine himself now. It grew louder, then cut suddenly to a tick-over as the van halted. He turned away. 'I hope it's just letters. If it's another unstamped packet of pearls he'll want postage money; and I'll have to decide whether to open the door.'

He went out and walked along the passage to the hall. The letterbox flap opened and two letters fluttered down on to the mat. As Collier bent to pick them up a great crash of glass jangled every nerve in his body.

He jerked upright and for a moment his whirling thoughts snatched at the idea that the post van had crashed into something. But the crash had come from the back of the cottage. Then he heard Dinah cry out, and as he flung himself along the passage he heard another sound. It was the rending, groaning sound of tortured metal.

He collided with Dinah as he swung through the open door of the kitchen, and caught her to steady her. Then, looking beyond her, he saw the whole screen of steel mesh fold and crumple, torn bodily away from outside. A few spears of glass were all that remained of the window.

As the screen disappeared he saw beyond the high sill the head and torso of the man who had ripped it away, and his stomach shrank to a tiny ball of cold terror. The big man

145

smiled, put his hands on the inner ledge and pushed himself up with astonishing lightness. One hand bore a smear of blood.

Collier said very quietly to Dinah in a voice he did not recognise. 'Out the front way. The screen opens with the door. Run for the woods. Police here soon now.'

She was trying to speak, and her whole body was shaking as he pushed her gently behind him into the passage and closed the door after her.

Delicata was kneeling in the shattered window. Collier looked round for a knife, a weapon, anything. He thought with sick self-hatred of the shotgun still lying beside his bed.

There was nothing in reach but crockery and a copper-bottomed saucepan. Delicata had dropped lightly to the floor, cutting him off from the kitchen units and the hot pan on the stove. Collier gripped the saucepan. He was quite sure that he was going to die, but it was suddenly unimportant as long as he could keep those monstrous hands off Dinah. New hatred welled up in him and he felt his face twist in an involuntary snarl, felt the lips actually curling back from his teeth.

There was no pause. Delicata came at him fast, smoothly, irresistibly. Collier lashed out at the great face, and felt the blow brushed aside by an arm like the branch of a tree.

He kicked for the shins, felt his toecap strike bone, heard the big man laugh. Light exploded before his eyes and he felt himself to be flying. There came a jarring pain. Through red mists of agony he heard, as if from a thousand miles away, the sound of Delicata flinging the kitchen door open; and still more distant, from the front door at the end of the passage, a wordless and despairing cry from Dinah.

The red mists became black and heavy, closing about him. His last thought as they engulfed him was to hope bitterly that this was death.

Modesty Blaise came out of the phone cubicle in the Bar Louis. It was eight-thirty in the morning. She did not look like

Modesty Blaise. In a corner of the bar, Willie Garvin sat at a table with two black coffees. Wearing blue overalls and a beret, with soft charcoal rubbed into his eyebrows and hair, and into the thirty-six hour stubble on his chin, he did not look like Willie Garvin.

She sat down and began to stir her coffee. Her manner was natural, casual, but Willie knew that something had gone badly wrong. She said very quietly, 'That was René Vaubois. They've got Dinah.'

Willie stubbed his cigarette with slow movements. He kept jabbing it in the ashtray after it was out. At last he said, 'This was a feint to draw us off?'

'Yes. Gabriel and McWhirter left for Orly at two this morning, and caught a plane for Barcelona.'

'Who got Dinah?'

'René didn't have details. Tarrant rang him half an hour ago.'

'Steve?'

'Must be alive. He'd rung Tarrant from the cottage. Stop it, Willie.' He was still mashing the stub of cigarette and his lips were pale.

'Sorry.' He looked at her with stunned eyes. 'She'll go out of 'er mind.'

'No she won't. Dinah's gutsy, and she'll hang on to one sure thing—that we'll go after her and get her back.'

'Go after her where?'

'I'm hoping Steve can give us the answer.' She stood up. 'If not, we do it the long way. Go after Gabriel and rip it out of him.'

12

TARRANT stood by the big window of the penthouse, gazing absently down upon Hyde Park and the lunchtime strollers.

'The post van was found abandoned only two miles away,' he said. 'The local police don't know about Dinah. I thought it better to avoid headlines. They're simply looking for the person or persons who clubbed the driver and stole the van. But Frobisher has all official outlets looking for Delicata and the girl.' He shrugged. 'It's my own view that they're out of the country by now. Unofficially, by air. If you can do it, they can do it.'

Modesty paced slowly across the room, arms crossed, hands holding her elbows. Willie Garvin sat in one of the big armchairs, his brown face a little ugly in its hardness. They had arrived only ten minutes earlier and were still grubby from travelling.

Stephen Collier sat upright in the middle of the long couch, a strip of plaster across the side of his face just below the hairline. He was staring at nothing, his fingers busily tearing a piece of card from a cigarette packet into tiny pieces. Every scruple of his habitual dry humour had drained from him. He looked like a ghost.

'Can you stop any leaks to the press?' Modesty said.

'Yes. Frobisher will see to that.' Tarrant turned from the window. 'I got on to him as soon as Collier phoned. It seemed best to keep things hush until I'd had a chance to talk with you.'

Modesty nodded. 'This is about as far from good as things can get.' She looked at Collier. 'But at least you're alive, Steve. I can't think why Delicata didn't kill you.'

'I wish he had,' Collier said emptily and with simple truth.

'I believe he thought he had. When I came round I was lying in a heap against the gas-stove with blood all over my face and my neck twisted up against the wall. I thought it was broken at first. Maybe Delicata thought the same.'

'Yes. Go on, darling.'

'I've told you.' He did not look at her as he spoke.

'Tell us again.'

He closed his eyes. 'I came round. I got up. I threw up. I couldn't think. I got to the phone and rang the number you'd given me for Tarrant. I told him. He said to leave Dinah out of it when the police came; that he'd handle that side of it, and that he'd contact you. He said he'd send a car down for me with somebody who'd see the local police didn't keep me for a lot of questions and statements. He rang off. About two minutes later a couple of police arrived from Benildon. The alarm in the station there had been triggered. I don't suppose what I told them made much sense, but they didn't seem to expect much. I must have looked pretty well out of my mind. That's how I felt. Then there's a bit I don't remember, and then I was at the station being looked over by a doctor. Tarrant's man arrived and drove me here.'

He had finished tearing the piece of card to bits. His hands began to shake and he folded them under his armpits.

'I'm sorry.' He looked at Willie with drained eyes. 'It just sounds pathetic, but I'm desperately, desperately sorry.'

For a moment Willie's bleak face relaxed. 'Don't beat yourself into the ground,' he said a little wearily. 'When I rigged those screens I didn't cater for anyone like Delicata.'

'No,' Tarrant said quietly. 'One doesn't normally cater for a man who can rip away a steel mesh screen with his bare hands. I suggest everybody stops feeling guilty. What we couldn't possibly know was that between us we'd run into two ends of the same caper; Willie with Gabriel in Panama, and us with an unknown man here who turned out to be Delicata.'

'The pipes,' said Willie Garvin, and pressed the heel of one hand against his forehead. 'Oh Christ, the pipes.'

Tarrant stared. Collier roused from his apathy to look dully uncomprehending. Modesty said, 'Go on, Willie.'

He looked at her, and when he spoke his voice was harsh with self contempt. 'I'm the dumbest bastard breathing. I knew there was something when you said last night we'd got to fix Gabriel first and we could decide about Delicata later. I knew something didn't fit right.'

He got up with sudden energy, as if unable to sit still under the lash of his own anger. 'I forgot something, Princess. When Gabriel and McWhirter 'ad me trussed for cooking in Panama there was a bit of chit-chat and I slipped in a quick one, asking why they wanted Dinah. Gabriel said, for archaeological research. I thought he was just being funny.'

Collier said slowly, 'I don't quite see . . .'

'It sticks out a mile.' Willie's voice was taut with impatience. 'Dinah can find things. Not just pipes. Precious metals. I knew yesterday that Gabriel wanted Dinah *because* she can find things. Buried things. He'd bloody well *said* he wanted her for archaeological research, and I forgot—even when the Princess told me about Aaronson being worried over the excavations at Mus. Aaronson smelt something fishy, and Delicata killed him. I knew all that last night, knew both ends of it . . . and didn't connect 'em. There's something at Mus that Gabriel and Delicata want. And only Dinah can find it.'

There was a little silence. Tarrant said, 'It was a very tenuous link, Willie. Certainly it adds up after a fashion, but only with the benefit of hindsight, I think.'

'You stay in business with foresight,' Willie said savagely. 'I *knew* there was something, but I couldn't get 'old of it. God Almighty, I ought to be shot.'

Modesty said, 'That's enough, Willie.' She did not raise her voice but it held a whiplash of command. Slowly he put his hands in his trouser pockets: slowly he relaxed, the anger and contempt draining out of him. He leaned with one shoulder against the mantelpiece and said in a quite different voice, 'Sorry, Princess.'

She gave him a quick smile, then looked at Tarrant. 'How quickly can you fix for us to see Presteign?'

For a moment Collier wondered who she was talking about. With an effort he recalled that Sir Howard Presteign was financing the excavations at Mus. He still did not understand.

Tarrant, too, seemed uncertain. He said, 'What have you in mind?'

'Mus is in Algerian territory. You'll get nowhere on an official level with the Algerian government. Willie and I can get to Mus under our own steam by the caravan routes, but it'll take too long. Presteign has an aircraft at Algiers with official permission to fly back and forth with supplies. So we have to see him.'

Collier was only vaguely conscious of the conversation during the next minute or two. A little spark had come to life inside him, and it was growing to a fierce flame of determination.

He said suddenly. 'I want to come with you.'

Modesty broke off in the middle of something she was saying to Willie, and looked at Collier with a curious blend of impatience and compassion. She said, 'You're not very fit just now, darling. I don't think——'

'Never mind what you think!' His thin, sensitive face held sudden fury. 'I'm coming with you. I can't, I *can't* sit here for days and nights wondering.' His voice shook. 'I heard Dinah cry out when Delicata caught her. I can still hear it.'

He pressed his hands to his eyes for a long moment. 'This is what it's like for her,' he said in a muffled voice. 'Dark. Always dark. I know about being scared, but God alone knows what it must be like for her.'

He lowered his hands, and when he looked up all emotion had been washed away and his pallid face held a ghostly replica of his old mournful smile. 'I'm coming with you,' he said apologetically. 'You needn't worry that I'll throw any faints. I'm past being scared now. I don't care. I don't even

151

care if Delicata does his terrier trick on me. It might give you a chance to shoot him while he's doing it.'

It had taken all Tarrant's considerable influence to arrange the meeting with Presteign at six o'clock in the magnificent tower suite of offices that crowned the square white column of Presteign House.

Sir Howard Presteign not only controlled a massive group of companies; he was also patron of a score of charities and on the governing board of a dozen hospitals. In no instance was his function nominal. He performed each one of his various duties with meticulous care. It was therefore hardly surprising that he was more charitable in answering sudden calls on his money than on his time.

He had made his mark in the City before he was thirty, and a million before he was thirty-five. It had all been done without flamboyance. Presteign was a quiet tycoon. He did not give interviews to the press or appear on television. He subscribed to no party, and was considered politically neutral.

Now, at fifty-five, he had been a widower for fifteen years. There was no issue of the marriage. He belonged to one old-established club, drank little, played bridge occasionally, and had no mistress as far as was known. His only hobby was cultivating orchids. He had a villa on the Riviera where he spent several weeks in the early summer, but he did not entertain there. He played no golf. For exercise, he walked and swam.

The big desk held a small memo-pad, a large desk diary, two telephones and an intercom. Presteign sat in a deep swivel chair, leaning back, his arms folded. He was a big man, with thick straight greying hair brushed back neatly. His face was smooth and remarkably unlined.

Tarrant had been speaking for almost five minutes now, and Presteign had not once interrupted.

Beside Tarrant sat Modesty Blaise. She wore a fine wool dress, creamy beige, with a high rib-knit jersey collar in maroon and black, and a slender belt striped in the same colours; her shoes and handbag were of black suede.

She looked calm and effortlessly elegant. Occasionally Presteign's eyes moved to her, but most of the time they rested on Tarrant. They were the quiet eyes of a man who has lived through a hundred crises in the tortuous jungle paths of industry and commerce. If he was incredulous at Tarrant's story he gave no hint of it. He listened as if to a report by one of his executives, absorbing every detail, analysing, assessing.

When Tarrant finished speaking Presteign had his first question ready. Modesty was certain that every question he might ask was already listed in the mind behind those quiet eyes.

'How valid do you believe this theory to be, Tarrant?' The voice was cultured but not affected, the manner pleasant and courteous.

'I have no doubt at all that it's substantially correct,' Tarrant answered. 'I mean, that something is happening in Mus and that the girl has been taken there.'

Presteign nodded. 'I know your function in the Civil Service. I'm not supposed to, but I do. I accept your view of the validity of this affair. Do you think these criminals have taken charge at Mus?'

'That's my belief.'

'Do you suspect Professor Tangye of being involved?'

'No. That's not impossible, perhaps, but certainly improbable.'

'His reports give no indication of trouble.'

'They wouldn't, if Gabriel and Delicata are in charge,' Tarrant said a little drily. 'Aaronson seemed to detect something odd about Tangye's letters, though.'

Presteign nodded again. 'He knew Tangye better than I. It seems we have three alternatives. A request from our Government to the Algerian Government, asking them to investigate. A request from me to the Algerian Government on the same lines. And some form of private investigation.'

Tarrant started to speak, but Presteign held up a polite hand. 'I think the first course is useless. The two governments are not particularly friendly. The second course is possible. Before I financed Tangye and his team I had first to secure permission for the excavation from the Algerian Minister of Culture. It cost me a sizeable contribution to the new museum they plan to build. So I have perhaps some small personal influence there. But I doubt if investigation by the Algerian authorities would be swift. It might well be unwise. If this girl Dinah Pilgrim is in danger, together perhaps with Tangye and the rest, we can't afford to be clumsy.'

Presteign looked at Modesty Blaise. A slight smile touched his lips. 'I mentioned that I knew about Tarrant,' he went on. 'I also know something of you, Miss Blaise. You cost Selby his job as Minister, I believe, over that Kuwait affair.'

It was Tarrant who answered. 'Selby's head rolled because he refused to accept the information Miss Blaise almost lost her life to provide, and thereby left her to pull some very hot chestnuts out of the fire.'

'Yes.' Presteign's eyes still rested on Modesty. 'I should have said that Selby cost himself the job. He lacked instinct.'

'For what?' Modesty asked quietly. It was the first time she had spoken since the brief introductions.

'For knowing when to gamble. And on whom. I don't think I have that deficiency. What do you want me to do, Miss Blaise?'

'Arrange for the pilot of your supply aircraft to take out two passengers with him on the next regular trip. I'm sorry, I mean three.'

'Yourself, Garvin and—what was his name? Collier. Yes.' Presteign opened the big desk diary. 'The next regular trip from Algiers to Mus will be on Thursday, the day after tomorrow.'

'We'll fly out tomorrow, then. Who do we contact in Algiers?'

'My agent. I'll provide you with a signed carte blanche instruction for him, and I'll also telephone him myself tonight. He'll place the pilot under your orders.'

'Will they both keep their mouths shut?'

'Yes. I choose my people carefully, handpick them myself. In any event, nobody could get word out to Mus before you arrive there, since you'll be on the next trip.'

She nodded, satisfied. 'Is the pilot good?'

'I'd put him among the six best in Europe and the States.'

'That helps. I shall want him to put us down somewhere about ten miles from Mus, then continue the trip and forget us.'

Presteign raised his eyebrows. 'Is the terrain suitable?'

'Yes. The Sahara's only about one seventh sand dunes. There are quite a few hard flat areas of ground. But I'll leave it to him when the time comes. If he's doubtful, we'll use parachutes. We have to reach Mus unobserved, so that we can see what's happening before we get in the middle of it.'

Presteign studied Modesty curiously, then looked at Tarrant and said, 'I suppose you're used to this?'

Tarrant smiled wryly. 'Only to a degree. I still find Miss Blaise a little disconcerting.'

Presteign looked at Modesty again. 'So I should imagine. Excuse me for a moment.' He opened a drawer, took out a sheet of die-stamped paper. With a plain gold pen he wrote quickly and without hesitation for perhaps sixty seconds.

'Here's my agent's address in Algiers, and the necessary authorisation.' He got up and moved round the desk to give the paper to Modesty. 'Will that do?'

She read it through quickly. The writing was bold and clear. 'That covers everything. Thank you, Sir Howard.'

'When do you think we shall hear from you?'

'As soon as there's anything to report. We'll arrange a radio link with Sir Gerald's communications room.'

'I'm afraid that won't work.' There was a shade of apology in Presteign's voice. 'They tell me Mus is a dead area, whatever that means. Something to do with the mountains, the

Tademait Plateau. That's why I have no radio link with Tangye. We have to rely on mail.'

He paced slowly towards the window. 'Perhaps you could arrange a three or four station link to get round the problem—I don't know about these things.'

'No.' Modesty looked at Tarrant. 'It's too complex.' Tarrant gave a reluctant nod of agreement.

Presteign said, 'Perhaps it makes no difference, except to allay anxiety at our end by keeping us informed. If you did send out a call for help there would be very little we could do. You're on Algerian soil, and I wouldn't like to speculate on how long it would take me to get any action from the government there.'

Tarrant sighed inwardly. Presteign was right, of course. But he, Tarrant, very much wanted his anxiety allayed. As it was, he would know nothing until the whole thing was over. One way or the other.

'Give me three weeks,' Modesty said. 'I know it's a long time, but Mus is a long way from anywhere. I don't know yet what we'll find, or how we'll tackle whatever needs to be done. Have the plane continue its regular trips and give us three weeks.'

After a little silence Presteign said, 'And if we hear nothing by then?'

She stood up. 'You must assume we've failed. It will be up to you and Sir Gerald to decide the next move. To be honest, I've no idea what you can do that might be of use.'

'I have,' Presteign said quietly. 'If we don't hear from you in three weeks I shall take it that overt action can no longer do any damage. I'll fly out myself, with one or two Algerian Ministers and an escort. But I hope it won't come to that.' He looked at Modesty. 'I sincerely hope it won't come to that.'

It was midnight, and raining hard, Modesty was in bed when she heard the sound of the lift that served the penthouse. She took a firm hold on the anger that touched her, and lay waiting. A minute later there came a soft tap on the bedroom door. She called, 'Come in.'

Collier opened the door. She put on the bedside light. He stood just inside the room, a hand still on the door handle. He had taken off his mack. His hair and the bottoms of his trousers were soaked.

'Hope I didn't wake you,' he said quietly. 'I thought I'd better let you know I was back.'

She propped herself on an elbow. 'It's been five hours. Back from where, Steve?'

He gestured vaguely. 'Just walking. I couldn't sit still.'

'You might have left word with Weng or Willie.'

'Yes. I'm sorry.'

'It's all right. Come to bed. You look tired.'

He stirred uneasily. 'I put my bag in the spare room. I thought . . .' His voice trailed to silence.

'I noticed. Why did you do that?' Her eyes were gentle. 'Are you feeling unfriendly?'

'No. No, it's not that,' he said in distress. 'I'm sorry, Modesty. I don't quite know what I feel. But I can't stop thinking about Dinah.' His face twitched, and she could see the unrelieved tension in his thin, rather gangling body. 'I can't bear the idea of lying comfortably and safely in bed while Dinah——' His voice became uneven, then stopped.

She said, 'Nothing you do or don't do at this moment will help her, Steve. Accept it. Take a sleeping pill and come to bed. Or go to bed, if you'd rather.'

'Accept it?' he echoed, and an ugly spasm crossed his face. 'My God, I don't know how you do it.'

Her face became impassive. 'I learned how to do it.' She threw back the covers, got out of bed and moved towards him. She had never in her life worn nightwear in bed, and she was naked now, yet this in no way diminished her assurance. She knocked his hand rather sharply away from the door so that she could close it, then turned and sat on the edge of the bed, her hands beside her, looking at him.

157

'I learned how to do it,' she repeated. 'It's not easy, but I learned. That's just as well, for Dinah's sake.'

'For Dinah's sake? How much are you thinking about her?'

'Not much. For her sake, again. I'm thinking about how to make sure she doesn't end up dead.'

The anger ran out of him suddenly, and with a weary gesture he said, 'I'm sorry.'

'No, you're not sorry. You just don't want to argue.' She kept her voice hard. It was necessary to kindle his anger again, and then to feed it until she wrought an explosion that would bring him at least a few hours of relief from his screaming nerves.

'What do you mean?' he said stiffly. 'What is there to argue about?'

'Not a lot. But before you go, I'll tell you why you put your bag in the spare room. It's because you hate me a little, Steve.'

His anger flared anew. 'Don't be bloody silly!'

'Am I? You're frightened for Dinah. She's tangled up in something that doesn't usually exist in your world. But it exists in mine; it always has. And there's just a little bit of you that blames me for what's happened to Dinah.'

He looked at her coldly. 'That's quite ridiculous.' He paused, then went on, unable to prevent the words that would hurt. 'But perhaps you'll agree that friends of yours should walk a little warily. You seem to have an ambience that involves them in the most brutal kind of violence and danger.'

His face was very pale now. She had touched a deep and sensitive chord in him, for there was truth in her saying that he felt an element of accusation towards her, and it was a truth that he wanted to reject with his whole being.

She said, 'You could be right about my ambience. Maybe I'm not the sort that wise people choose as a friend.' Her voice grew chill. 'But listen, my sensitive and talented mathematician, and let's see if you can add up a simple sum. I didn't draw Dinah into this, remember? She met violence and murder, all on her own, no help from me. By the grace of God, or whatever you choose to believe in, Willie Garvin was there. Oh yes, complete with his ambience. And he pulled her out.'

She stood up and moved slowly towards him, throwing her words like sharp stones. 'They caught Willie and rigged him up to be blown to shreds, remember? They laid on a chopper-man to cut me in two. Never mind. We got out of that. We got Dinah away. Now the opposition turns out to be twice as tough as we thought, and they've taken Dinah again.'

She stopped in front of him, and even through his anger and confusion he was aware of the warm magnificence of her body.

'Dinah may die,' she said distinctly. 'Accept it. And give a thought to Willie. He's been hit harder than you. If you're not satisfied with the best we can do, then bloody well find somebody who can do better. But don't ever dare to blame *me*! Now go to bed.'

Her hand flicked across his face. In the nerve-snapping tension that possessed him, the response was automatic, as she knew it would be. He swung an open hand hard at her face.

Deep in his subconscious knowledge of her was the certainty that she would block or avoid the blow easily. But she did not move a muscle. The slap seemed to echo round the room. She turned away from him and walked towards the bed.

He made a sound, a choked cry. Then she felt his long fingers on her shoulder as he caught at her.

'Modesty . . . please! Oh, Jesus, I'm sorry. I've been half out of my mind. I didn't mean—— Please . . .'

She turned into his embrace and leaned back so that they half sank, half fell together on the bed. He was still talking incoherently, his whole body shaking. She put a hand to his cheek and stopped his lips with a kiss.

'Don't, Steve,' she whispered. 'It's nothing, darling. Nothing. I was a bitch, but it was the only way. You've got to get unwound or you'll be no good for anything. Easy now, darling, just a minute, just a little minute. Let's get your shoes off. There. Now these things . . .'

He was taut and shaking at first as she made love to him, then passively grateful under her gentleness. Later came the tumult of release, and he was limp, with every nerve and muscle unstrung, his mind empty, his breathing deep and regular like that of a man on the threshold of sleep.

She lay down beside him, pulled up the covers and settled his head against her breast, an arm about his neck.

'It's high time I made you put that bit about making an honest woman of me in writing,' she whispered.

His voice was slurred, barely audible as he muttered, 'Get a pen . . .' Then he sighed, and was asleep.

In the morning, when Modesty woke, Collier was sitting up in bed, placidly smoking a cigarette. His face was quiet, cleansed of all tension. She wondered if it was the dangerous quietness of despair, but then he turned his head and smiled down at her, and she knew with swift happiness that this was the quietness she had hoped for, the unstrained quietness of a man who had at last found his emotional balance; who would go forward now with neither foolish optimism nor fibre-sapping pessimism, but simply with that hard, neutral, unyielding persistence which was the core of survival.

He said, without undertones of irony, 'I'm truly grateful for the child-welfare bit last night. I was nearly over the edge.'

She smiled back at him, got up and started to put on a blue velvet dressing gown. 'How do you feel now, Steve?'

He considered. 'I think I feel the way you want me to. It's a little hard to describe.'

'I know.' She sat on the edge of the bed, facing him.

He said, a little awkwardly, 'That was a humiliating exhibition I made of myself last night. Do you think you could forget it?'

She shook her head. 'Not quite. It's important to me. You

needed a little help and I was able to give it. Being needed is important.'

He made a rueful face. 'All the same. It's a rather abject image of me for you to enshrine in your memory. True, perhaps, but unattractive.'

She looked at him, still smiling, but with a touch of wonderment now. 'You really haven't got a clue about yourself, have you, darling? Maybe that's part of what I love about you. Surely you can't think I have that kind of image of you? The way I see you is quite different.'

'How do you see me?'

She said very soberly, 'I see you down at the cottage, in the kitchen there. You've just watched Delicata rip out a steel screen that would hold six normal men. You know he's a killer. You know you haven't a ghost of a chance against him. But there's a blind girl in your care. So you push her out, shut yourself in with Delicata, and square up to him with a one-pint milk saucepan.'

She leaned forward, kissed him on the cheek, and got to her feet. 'That's how I see you.' Collier stared at her incredulously as she went across to the door of the bathroom. Then he said, 'But I was petrified. I was scared right through to the marrow.'

Looking back at him she gave a little sigh of exasperation. 'Don't you realise, you great stupid idiot? That's the whole point!' She turned and opened the bathroom door. 'Now you'd better start jumping about. We're off to Algiers in three hours.'

13

THE aircraft was a Cessna Skywagon, high wing and with a 300 h.p. Continental IO-520 engine. On each side a big door made for easy loading and unloading. The cabin had been stripped to leave only two seats, making room for the thirty-gallon drums of water which made up the main payload for the twice weekly flight to Mus.

The Cessna was a good little work-horse, and Willie Garvin approved as he stowed two roped bundles of gear on the deck. There were four drums of water and a crate of food. With three passengers that put the payload a little above what the book said, but not enough to worry about.

Modesty stepped up into the plane from the hot tarmac of the airfield, and Collier followed. Collier felt slightly fool-ish in the mottled fawn shirt and slacks he wore, with lace-up brown boots of soft leather extending to just below his calves. Modesty and Willie were dressed in the same way, but some-how they looked right in combat rig. And that, Collier thought resignedly, was hardly surprising. He sat down beside Mod-esty. Willie Garvin settled himself on the crate just behind them.

A man climbed in through the open doorway, a flying helmet in one hand. He was dressed in stained blue jeans and a faded shirt. His hair was streaked with grey, in odd con-trast to the face beneath, which was the face of a far younger man, fresh and unlined; the eyes presented yet another con-trast, for they were quiet and old.

Modesty raised her eyebrows and said, 'Well, hallo Skeet. We didn't know it was you.'

'Hi, ma'am.' The soft American voice was as placid and unreadable as the ash-grey eyes. 'Hi, Willie. Long time.'

'Quite a while,' Modesty said. 'How's business?'

'Regular, ma'am.' He pulled on his flying helmet and closed the door. 'You all set?'

'Yes. The agent said you knew a place where you can get us down safely about eight miles from Mus.'

'Sure. It's a little short, but we'll manage.'

Modesty nodded. If Skeet Lowry said it, that was good enough. When Presteign had classed him among the six best pilots in Europe and the States he had underestimated. Skeet Lowry flew. He flew any aircraft, and he flew in conditions that would keep most pilots on the ground. Yet he was no screwball flyer. He was simply a natural, who could do things with a plane that few men would attempt, and do them with quiet ease.

He had flown in air circuses, he had flown crop-dusting runs. At different times he had ferried Russian and American jet fighters for opposing sides in the Far East. He had flown big jets as an airline pilot. He had flown guns and gold and drugs and men on the run. Skeet Lowry flew for hire, legally or illegally, and he made no judgments about who hired him, or for what. He had no loyalties except to whoever was paying him for the job. He simply flew.

Modesty had used him on three occasions during the years when she ran the Network because he was utterly reliable, but he had never been a part of her organisation. He was a free-lance and a wanderer.

Willie said, 'How d'you make out for fuel on the home run, Skeet?'

'Spent every day for three weeks ferrying out gas and water before I took the people out.' Skeet Lowry edged through the crowded little cabin to the cockpit. 'Got a good store there.'

Modesty said, 'Skeet . . . have you noticed anything off-beat at Mus? People you didn't take out? Any signs of another aircraft? Has Tangye acted strangely?'

He paused and looked at her. For a brief moment some remote flicker of humour touched the incurious face, and then was gone. 'Me, ma'am?' he said politely. 'When did I ever notice anything? I just fly out and fly back.'

He went through into the cockpit and settled himself in the pilot's seat. Willie glanced at Modesty and said, 'Same as ever.'

The engine coughed and roared. Collier fastened his safety belt and said, 'An old friend, I gather? That's one more on our side anyway.'

Modesty shook her head. 'Skeet just flies. He's on nobody's side. But Presteign picked him and Presteign pays him, so he'll follow orders to the letter. Flying orders, that is. Outside that, he doesn't want to know.'

The Atlas Mountains lay far behind to the north. The Cessna had crossed the endless dunes of the Great Western Erg and now the brown, horizon-to-horizon carpet that lay below was peaked here and there by islands of grey rock thrusting up through the sand and gravel plains.

It was not excessively hot in the aircraft, but the glare of the sun from the port side had a ferocious quality. This, combined with the arid immensity below, produced in Collier an almost frightening sense of insignificance.

In the last three hours of the flight he had only once seen any sign of life—a string of ten camels, presumably with riders, strung like dots against the sallow background. Twice Modesty and Willie had seen gazelle, but though he strained his eyes Collier could not detect them.

'You have to tune your eyes for different terrain,' Modesty said. 'Jungle, desert, town, there's a different way of looking. It'll come with a little practice.'

The sun was low when Skeet Lowry set the controls on automatic and left the cockpit. The Cessna was a quiet plane, but he had to lift his soft voice a little to be heard.

'Putting you down in thirty minutes, ma'am,' he said to Modesty. His use of 'ma'am' was neither meek nor ironic, but a habit of indifferent civility.

'What's the spot like, Skeet?' she asked.

'Flat sand and gravel. Runs alongside a kinda low, twisty, ridge. No water.' He shrugged. 'No water for God knows how far. But I put on an extra drum for you like the agent said. Okay?'

'Thanks.'

He went back to the controls. Modesty said to Collier beside her, 'It's better than it might have been. That twisty ridge will give you shelter from the heat. With any luck we'll find a cave.'

Collier nodded. His role had been allotted. He would be in charge of the base set up some miles from Mus. They had enough food and water for ten days, more with careful rationing. Modesty and Willie would be going out the first night on foot to Mus; tonight, he realised with a little shock. There were no hard plans beyond that. They would do whatever their reconnaissance indicated.

'We'll leave most of the small arms weaponry with you, Steve,' Modesty had said. 'Once we know the score we'll come back and get what we need.' She smiled. 'You know how to use a CAR-15, and one thing we may need is an extra gunman, if you feel like it.'

Collier thought of another time and another place, when he had been initiated one terrifying night in the use of the Colt automatic rifle. And he thought of Dinah Pilgrim.

'Yes,' he said. 'I'll feel like it.'

The sun was very low now, and lying directly astern. Skeet Lowry had brought the plane round on an easterly course for the landing. They were losing height, descending into the twilight that already lay over the desert.

A ridge of rock loomed on their starboard side, and the note of the engine changed, softening a little.

There was no jolt, only the sudden vibration of the wheels on a gravelly surface as Skeet Lowry, an integral part of the machine he flew, kissed the ground with the Cessna as delicately as a butterfly settling upon a leaf.

Collier swallowed hard. They were still moving fast, and the ridge curved round sharply ahead. They were racing towards a wall of rock.

Modesty said, 'Don't worry. Not with Skeet.'

The plane halted exactly twenty yards from where a broad fissure split the sloping rock face. The engine died, the vibration stopped, and Skeet Lowry climbed lazily out of his seat.

Modesty said, 'Five minutes, Skeet. Get that drum of water unlashed please, Willie.'

She opened the door and stepped down. Collier followed. The sun was below the horizon now, and suddenly it was almost dark. Heat came up from the ground in stifling waves. He ignored it.

'You'll be hot, and at night you'll be cold,' Modesty had said. 'Don't let it register. That's what knocks you out. Exhaustion is fifty per cent mental.'

She was looking towards the fissure now. 'We'll take a look through there when we've got the gear out,' she said. 'It's promising.'

The beam of light hit Collier like a physical blow. It was a spotlight of some kind, and it shone down from the sloping side of the fissure to throw a great circle on the ground. In the middle of the circle stood Dinah Pilgrim. She wore a shirt and trousers and she was alone, facing them, twenty paces away. Something was tied across her mouth, and her hands were behind her back.

A brief rattle of fire from a submachine gun made sand and gravel spurt from the ground a few paces to her left. In the silence that followed, a voice spoke from the darkness beyond Dinah; a smooth, cultured, amused voice that made the sickness of despair rise suddenly in Collier's throat.

'Welcome to our little band of brothers,' said Delicata's voice. 'And sisters, too. I hate to labour a point that should be obvious, Miss Blaise, but the Pilgrim girl will have her pretty little guts blown out at the first hint of any belligerence from you or your two Sancho Panzas.'

Collier half turned his head, slowly, like a man with a stiff neck. He saw Willie Garvin framed in the doorway of the plane, a knife held by the blade between finger and thumb. He saw the Colt .32 in Modesty's hand, and realised she must have drawn it in the instant that the spotlight flashed on. He saw her slowly thumb the safety-catch on, and relax her grip so that the revolver hung from her finger by the trigger-guard. Then she bent unhurriedly, placed the gun on the ground, and straightened up.

Willie Garvin slid the knife back into the sheath under his shirt and stepped down to the ground from the low deck of the Cessna.

'Very good so far,' said the voice from the darkness approvingly. 'Concentrate on poor Miss Pilgrim's guts, and we'll get along splendidly.'

Skeet Lowry appeared in the doorway of the Cessna and lit a cigarette. Collier felt murderous rage sweep through him as he realised that Lowry had known precisely what was waiting for them.

Without turning her head Modesty said quietly, 'Why, Skeet?'

Collier saw a slight shrug of the pilot's shoulders under the faded shirt. There was even a hint of protest in Lowry's voice as he said politely, 'I fly for the guy who picks up the tab, ma'am. You know that.'

The huge form of Delicata moved through the pool of light and came towards them. His arms were so long that for a moment it seemed he was carrying two short clubs hanging down almost to his knees. And now, beyond him, there were other figures near Dinah, two at least, with submachine guns.

Delicata halted, smiling. He looked with interest at Modesty for several seconds, then turned to study Willie. After a little silence he said, 'I think you've improved with the years, young Garvin. How are the ribs?'

'They'll do.' Willie's voice was neutral. His eyes were on

Modesty, on the hand that hung by her side. Her loosely curled fingers straightened, then curled again. There was to be no action yet. Willie looked away. He felt bleak relief. The submachine guns were on Dinah, and she would be the first to go. Delicata knew how to handle things.

The big man moved towards Collier and stood in front of him, one barely existent eyebrow quirking upwards. 'The saucepan man,' he said. 'Oh dear. I really thought you were dead. I'm afraid you've been living on borrowed time.'

A vast hand flickered out and took Collier by the neck in a grip that seemed to paralyse every nerve.

Modesty said, 'I don't think that's wise.'

'No?' Delicata chuckled, and without seeming effort lifted Collier so that his toes barely touched the ground.

'No.' Her voice held a shade of contempt. 'He's an expert in what you want Dinah Pilgrim to do. The top expert.'

'Really?' Delicata twisted Collier's head towards him as if turning the head of a ventriloquist's dummy. With waves of pain and humiliation surging about him, and with the knowledge that he was only a moment from death, Collier forced a foolish grin to his lips and said, 'I didn't actually bring any references with me.'

Delicata stared. Then a roar of laughter erupted from his enormous chest. He released his hold, and Collier dropped in a heap to the ground. 'Oh, I liked that,' Delicata said, still shaking with amusement. 'I'm not sure that we need any experts, but we must certainly keep you around for a little while.'

He moved towards Modesty. 'I'm saving Garvin for later, too. Now do *you* have any convincing reason for being kept around, Miss Blaise?'

'No.' She was relaxed, but watching him carefully. 'There's this, though. If you're thinking of a demonstration killing, that puts an end to the options you hold.' Her eyes flickered to Dinah and the gunmen, then back to the immense face. 'I won't stand still to be killed, Delicata. I don't say you can't do it. But I'll guarantee to take your eye out.' She paused, then added, 'At least.'

'This becomes more fascinating all the time.' There was genuine pleasure in Delicata's voice. 'I think we shall all have a great deal of instructive amusement over the next few days.'

Collier had got to his feet. His body was trembling. He fought to control it, and to nurse the spark of an idea which, amazingly, had gleamed in his confused mind a few seconds ago, in the moment when Delicata prepared to kill him. He massaged the back of his neck, looked across at Modesty and said in an aggrieved tone, 'He's rubbed off that anti-sunburn cream I put on.'

Delicata gazed incredulously, then again exploded with laughter. 'Oh yes, we shall have a *lot* of fun,' he said, delighted.

Turning towards the fissure he lifted one arm in a signal. The two men there closed on Dinah and moved her aside. From the hollow beyond came the sound of an engine starting, and next moment a Land Rover drove out. Delicata looked at Skeet Lowry, still leaning in the open door of the Cessna, and said, 'You take the girl and her two guards, Lowry. Our new guests will return with me under escort in the Land Rover.'

Skeet Lowry extinguished his cigarette carefully and nodded. 'Sure,' he said.

Collier shivered. The rock wall against his back was growing cool with the coming of night, and he was naked. So were Modesty and Willie, in line next to him, their hands resting on their heads.

The chamber was well lit by two electric lamps. On a long trestle table lay their clothes. Two men stood on the far side of the table. Collier knew now that they were Gabriel and McWhirter. McWhirter wore rather long baggy shorts and looked ridiculous, but there was nothing ridiculous about the cruel laughter that sparkled in his bright blue eyes. Gabriel wore a tropical suit. His hands were busy searching

Willie's shirt. There was no triumph or laughter in him, only a chill malevolence.

With a screwdriver, McWhirter prised away the thick sole of one of Willie's combat boots. There were two recesses in the rubber. Into one of them was fitted a slim knife-blade with a threaded tang, and in the other lay a little flat hilt.

McWhirter wagged his head with a knowing grin. He lifted out the blade and hilt, screwed them together, and put the knife with a growing collection of other objects stripped from the clothing and footwear. Carefully he began to examine the heel of the boot.

Delicata lounged in a folding chair, smoking a cigar and watching with a remote, almost absent-minded manner. One hand rested on his knee, holding a heavy Mauser automatic pistol, an ugly weapon with a twenty-round magazine.

There was a fourth man. He wore neatly creased dark slacks, and a cardigan over some kind of gym vest. He stood very upright, hands behind his back, slowly rising on his toes and sinking back on to his heels as he watched.

The ride in the Land Rover under close guard had taken only twenty minutes. They had been driven through the broad cleft which, blocked by blown sand for so many centuries, was the gateway to the rock city of Mus. Darkness had prevented them seeing much of the valley, and they had been quickly hustled from the Land Rover into a hewn passage which led to this chamber.

Collier found himself in a strange state of mind. He was afraid, but his fear was well within bounds. He knew that Modesty and Willie were giving no thought to their present helplessness; knew that their minds were entirely occupied by an intense assessment of the future situation. Facts, deductions, possibilities, mental reconnaissance—this was the path that left no place for despair, a path Modesty had taught him to tread in other days, and he was trying to follow it now.

There must be a power source for the light. Useful to locate it. The guards he had seen were city Algerian, if his guess was right. They spoke no English, a little French. Their language was Arabic, which Modesty and Willie spoke fluently. Useful. The guards might well be open to bribes. His thoughts focused on Delicata, for it was here that he might be able to achieve something that was beyond both Modesty and Willie. He had already made a beginning, and perhaps saved his life thereby; he had made Delicata laugh, really laugh, and caught his interest. The big man would enjoy having a fool to amuse him, a court fool; and a man in that role might be somewhat privileged, perhaps.

Collier was preparing himself to continue in the role, but knew it must be carefully done. Now was not the moment to be stupidly amusing, for there was a change in Delicata's manner. He was watching the growing pile of objects as McWhirter and Gabriel worked their way methodically through every inch of the clothing, and there was an ominous coldness in the great smooth face.

Collier looked at the pile. There were some items he did not recognise, but most he knew; the Colt and the little MAB automatic; Willie's twin throwing knives sheathed in the leather harness, and two similar knives taken from the thick soles of his combat boots. An eight-inch metal tube from a thigh pocket in Modesty's slacks, which extended to make a bow; thin steel rods which screwed together to make arrows; a phial of anaesthetic nose-plugs; a sling, and half a dozen round lead balls. A kongo, the little dumb-bell shaped piece of polished wood that Collier had seen Modesty use with such deadly effect. McWhirter was listing everything carefully in a black notebook. It seemed pointless, and Collier registered that fact; McWhirter was a compulsive note-maker.

Gabriel felt round the cuff of Modesty's shirt, picked up a knife and ripped the seam of the cuff open. He drew out a rectangular piece of very thin lead that lay like a lining within the cuff.

McWhirter said, 'What the hell's that?'

Gabriel squeezed the lead into a lump and weighed it in

his palm. He said, 'Rip the sleeve off, and you've got something you can swing like a mace and chain.' His eyes rested with venomous hatred on Modesty.

McWhirter cackled. 'It's no wonder they wriggled out when we had 'em before,' he said, and threw Collier's shirt aside. 'Well, it's different now.' He glanced at the little heap of weaponry. 'That's all, I'm thinking. Oh, except one thing, just.' He walked round the table and across to Modesty, standing in front of her. Putting his hands on her breasts he gave a little push and said, 'Turn round, lassie.'

She obeyed. He reached up to the club of hair held by two strong elastic bands at the nape of her neck, and plucked the bands away. As the bound hair loosened he probed in it for a moment, then held up another kongo.

'Ye canna be too careful wi' some people,' he said with sprightly good humour, and turned back to the table.

Delicata said in a cool voice, 'Are they clean now?'

Gabriel nodded. 'They're clean.'

'No mistakes this time?' Delicata's smile was wintry and polite.

Gabriel's lifeless eyes glittered for a moment. 'Keep that for those who have to take it, Delicata. I told you they're clean.'

Delicata chuckled. 'Now I've offended you,' he said happily. 'I'm so sorry.' He stood up, smiling. 'You can turn round again, Miss Blaise.' She obeyed. Her face was calm and a little remote. Delicata hefted the automatic pistol in his hand. 'And now,' he went on with the air of one providing a great treat, 'you can get dressed and we shall proceed to the ceremony of initiation.'

14

This was a smaller chamber, no more than twelve feet square. The worn rock floor was bare. A timber frame and a heavy door had been recently set in the single narrow doorway. A rubber surround, cushioning the edges of the frame, ensured that no air could leak through. There was neither key-hole nor handle. Two thick metal bars secured the door from outside.

Collier heard the sound of the bars sliding into their sockets, and wondered how long the air in the small chamber would last three people.

Willie Garvin was at the door, his ear pressed to the solid timber, listening. Modesty was looking at one corner of the wall, high up near the slightly domed ceiling. Her face was without expression, and it was only because Collier knew her so well that he could tell she was puzzled. He followed her gaze, and saw a small vent about four inches square. It was simply a rough hole, and looked as if it had been made when the city of Mus was first cut out of the valley sides.

Willie had stopped listening and was running a hand over the door, assessing its strength. Still looking at the little vent, Modesty said in a whisper, 'Steve, you're the only one who's earned any marks so far. You're playing Delicata exactly right. Can you keep it up?'

'I think so.' Collier kept his own voice low. 'I don't know for how long. He's clever. And if he spots that it's an act . . .'

'You won't have to keep it up long. We haven't *got* long if we want to come out of this. How do you read Delicata now, Willie?'

'Hasn't lost a thing.' Willie's face was grim as he answered. 'And Gabriel?'

'Lost a bit of edge.'

'Who's boss?'

'Not sure.' Willie moved away from the door and looked at the vent. 'Can't see either of 'em working for the other.'

'No.' Though she still whispered, her voice was suddenly sharp with anger. 'My God, I let us walk into this one.'

'You?' Collier was startled. 'I don't see how you let us walk into it.'

'Haven't you caught on yet—?' She broke off as there came a soft hissing sound from the vent. It lasted for ten seconds, then stopped. They looked at each other. The room was filled with a fine atomised spray. Collier felt quick apprehension. He saw Modesty give a little start, then raise her hands to touch her face. At the same moment he felt his cheeks and brow begin to tingle. In seconds the tingling became a pain. Willie Garvin had his hands to his face and was looking at Modesty. '*Mace!*' he said huskily. 'Or something worse . . .'

A moment of panic swept Collier. 'For Christ's sake what is it?' he said, then winced and gasped as countless hot needles stabbed into his face.

'Anti-riot nerve gas.' Modesty moved towards him, her eyes slitted with pain. 'It's going to get bad, Steve——'

She saw that he was no longer listening but was holding his bowed head and grunting like a man under the lash.

Mace. A spray rather than a gas. It caused no permanent damage, but its power was ferocious. A few drops of the spray were effective for half an hour or more. It interacted with the oils of the facial skin and caused temporary displacement of oxygen in the lungs, bringing muscular weakness and breathlessness; but above all it brought pain, causing every pinpoint of skin covering face and skull to leap with the searing agony of acute toothache, of nerves laid bare.

Eyes streaming, pain dimming her sight, she pulled Collier to the floor and propped him with his back against the wall. Willie was beside her, helping, breath hissing through teeth clenched tight under the torment.

'Can you—can you drop out, Willie?' she panted.

'M'mm.' It was an affirmative, uttered with a long shuddering breath. 'What about Steve?'

'I'll put him out. Carotid.' Her voice wavered jerkily. 'Sit him between us. Upright. Keep blood from his head longer . . .'

Collier could hear himself groaning, whimpering now, but he did not care. Only the pain mattered, the unbearable pain. As if from somewhere in another world he felt Modesty's hands settle round his neck, felt the firm pressure of her thumbs. She was choking him . . . ? No . . . he could still breathe. What was she . . . ? Why——?

With unutterable relief he felt himself sliding into a pool of blackness, leaving the pain behind. Then there was nothing.

Modesty took her hands from his neck. Willie was squatting on Collier's right, his legs crossed like a tailor, his hands resting limply on his knees, palms up. His eyes stared sightlessly, and his face was becoming strangely blank.

Modesty took up the same cross-legged position, close on Collier's left. Now . . . the first effort would be the hardest, because it must be non-resistant, void of effort. She slowed her troubled breathing, not fighting the agony but letting it wash through her as river water washes through the meshes of a stretched net.

After sixty seconds the pain was something separate from herself; existent, observable, but not a part of her. Gently, not compelling, but allowing, she let it drift further away . . .

Now the pain was a small distant thing. She held it so, not letting go completely, for in one small part of her mind was fixed the necessity of movement in five minutes' time. By then the blood would return to Collier's sleeping brain, and he would begin to rouse. That part of her mind which remained in the here-and-now would guide her hands to the carotid arteries in his neck once again, to cut off the flow of blood and give him new oblivion.

Her breathing matched Willie's now, four inhalations to the minute. Their eyes were open, rolled a little upwards, the pupils so widely dilated as almost to obscure the irises. All tension had drained from their faces.

Like statues, nerveless and serene, they sat on each side of the unconscious Collier, and were at peace.

A finger and thumb were pinching the lobe of his ear. Collier grunted resentfully. He did not want to wake up. There was some misty recollection in his mind of coming close to the surface before . . . how many times? Six . . . seven? And each time, as he neared the surface, he had felt the beginnings of the pain that lay in wait for him above. But then had come —what was it? Pressure. Hands holding his neck. And he had sunk down again, deep down to where the searing agony could not reach him.

A nail dug into his ear. He jerked angrily, then opened reluctant eyes. He was lying on his back. Modesty and Willie crouched gazing down at him. Their eyes were strange. The pupils were big and dark, as if from the atropine drops used by oculists.

Memory came back to Collier and he sat up with an oath, putting a hand gingerly to his face. It did not hurt now. Nerve gas. *Mace*, Willie had said. An anti-riot gas. Collier shuddered at the memory of the pain. Modesty had put him out and kept him out. He had escaped all but the first onslaught.

'How long?' he asked thickly, staring at her.

'About half an hour.'

'Oh Christ.' He shivered. 'I'd have gone out of my mind.'

'That's more or less what we did,' she said, and smiled. 'Don't worry. We just dropped out till the effect passed off.'

He nodded slowly, remembering something Tarrant had once said . . . 'They don't survive by physical skills alone, you know. It's their mental posture that really counts. Their control goes so deep it's almost mystical.'

Collier said, 'Delicata's initiation ceremony. Oh my God, I wonder if Dinah went through that.' He started to get to his feet, but Modesty stopped him.

176

'Stay there,' she said in a low voice. 'They'll be coming for us any minute, and they'd better find us the way they expect to. Wrung out. Clubbed stupid by pain.'

There came the sound of the bars being withdrawn. Willie rolled away and lay with his face resting in the crook of his elbow. Modesty squatted against the wall, leaning her head back wearily against it, eyes half closed, breathing heavily, unevenly.

McWhirter entered. Behind him stood a a thin-faced Algerian with a submachine gun, an aerosol cylinder hanging from his belt.

'Useful stuff, heh?' said McWhirter briskly, rubbing his hands together. 'Fiercer than what the Yanks use. We got a boffin to tart it up for us a wee bit.'

Nobody answered. He surveyed the captives and grinned.

'We started off giving the others a treatment three times daily. Hardly need to use it at all now. Och, it's awful good stuff for makin' yesmen.' He gave a cackle of laughter, then looked suddenly lugubrious. 'It's just the one taste you'll be having,' he said regretfully. 'Yon Delicata's a crazy man. He won't have you three made zombies like the rest.' The rather high and singsong Scottish voice changed in a ludicrous attempt to imitate Delicata's deep, mellifluous tones: 'They'll be much more amusing this way, my dear Gabriel. Zombies are so depressingly dull.'

Willie Garvin lifted his head and stared heavy-eyed. McWhirter took a quick pace back and nodded to the man with the submachine gun, who lifted it menacingly.

'If it was me, I'd ha' shot ye to ribbons before this,' McWhirter said malevolently. 'Just offer a wee excuse for me, that's all. On your feet now.'

They got up slowly, listlessly.

'You'll be in what we call the commonroom, wi' the others,' said McWhirter. 'Recruits for the labour force. The water ration's fifteen pints per head per day. I'll advise you to drink most of it an' go dirty like the rest. A day's hard digging in this heat seems to take the juice out o' them.'

He turned and gave an order in appalling French. There was another armed man just outside the door. At gunpoint the three captives were herded out and along a short passage which brought them into the open. Collier, taking his cue from Modesty and Willie, walked with slumped shoulders and dragging feet.

The night air was cool. After the heat of the day it made the contracting rock groan eerily. They trudged along beside the eastern wall of the valley for a hundred yards, passing openings of various sizes cut in the rock. In some places the stone had cracked and fallen.

Ahead, in a square archway, stood a heavy wooden door. It was new, like the door of the gas-chamber, but much larger, hanging from massive hinges. Two more Algerians squatted by a huddle of rock outside, submachine guns resting in their laps. As the little party approached, the two guards got up and drew thick steel bars from brackets grouted into the rock face beside the door frame.

McWhirter said, 'Lights out in one hour. Oh, and best ask the Pilgrim girl about the rules. You'll not get much out o' the others.'

It was like an army barrack room, Willie Garvin thought as the door closed behind them. About eighty feet long and thirty wide, with a line of camp beds ranged along each side. Four rough pillars of rock had been left by the ancient builders to support the wide span of the roof, from which hung three electric lamps.

An elderly man with a shrunken face sat on one of the beds, gazing absently at his hands. Before leaving London, Modesty and Willie had studied a photograph of Professor Tangye, a man of fifty-seven. This man could have been twenty years older, and was barely recognisable as Tangye. He had not looked up when the door opened. None of the six other men who lay on the camp beds had moved.

178

Willie looked at the nearest man. He was probably young, but it was hard to tell his age. A beard hid his mouth and chin, a tangle of hair fell over his brow. The eyes were empty of everything but dull fear. After a moment the man said in a slightly shrill voice, 'I wrote my letter all right—I didn't put anything in it!'

Yes. They would have to write letters from time to time. And any hint of the truth, however obliquely given, would mean treatment in the gas-chamber.

Willie said, 'It's all right, matey. We're on your side.'

Collier felt sick. He had suffered only two minutes of pain. This man, all these men, had suffered a full half hour three times daily for a spell. They might have been strong men, brave men, but no human will could stand against torment of such dimensions. And though the torture was vicious, it was also subtle. The crude pain of whips and flame and instruments could quickly go beyond all physical bearing, and so bring its own relief, for the victim would pass out. The atomised spray did not burn or cut or gouge living flesh. It attacked the nerves, and imposed an agony void of the sudden physical shock which brought unconsciousness.

The cold and deliberate cruelty of it was barbaric. Collier found that his fingers were working as if they were about McWhirter's throat at this moment, or Gabriel's throat, or Delicata's. He burned to kill them. And he knew that even when this wave of passion ebbed, the wish for them to be dead would still remain, because such men should not continue to exist.

Beside him, Modesty touched his arm and said quietly. 'There she is.' The thoughts that seethed confusedly in his head were suddenly swept away. Dinah Pilgrim had emerged from what appeared to be an annex at the far end of the long cave, on the right.

Willie lifted his voice and said cheerfully, ''Allo, Dinah. Looks like we're in it again, love.'

She ran down the centre of the commonroom, lips pursed

in a barely audible whistle, and swerved round Tangye where he sat with legs extended at the foot of his bed. Willie gathered her into his arms.

There were no tears, but she was shaking uncontrollably and words broke from her in choking, disjointed phrases. 'Oh God, Willie, did they hurt you? They do something to people—it's terrible. I can't talk to anyone here, they're all just like dead. I didn't know what was happening when they took me out tonight. We just waited, and then I heard the plane land and Delicata spoke——'

She lifted her head and her nostrils flared a little as she snuffed the air. She was still shaking. 'Modesty's with you. And Steve. Oh, thank God. I thought Steve was dead until I heard him speak after the plane landed. I thought that man had killed him in the cottage. Are you all right, Willie? Talk to me, *please*!'

Willie said, 'I've been waiting to, love. Name a subject.'

She gave a sobbing laugh of relief and hugged him fiercely for a moment, then moved reluctantly from his arms and put out a groping hand. 'Steve?'

'The renowned bodyguard himself,' said Collier, taking her hand. 'I'm sorry, darling. He was a bit big for me.'

She shook her head in wordless denial of the need for his apology, then suddenly the tears came and she was crying silently.

Collier said, 'That's the girl, don't bottle it up.' He put an arm round her shoulders. 'We're in quite good shape, really. They put us through a nasty business with some nerve gas that should have been painful, but we frustrated that knavish trick pretty well.' He shrugged. 'I use the plural loosely of course. You'll have to apply to Modesty and Willie for details.' He lifted his forearm close to her face. 'Here. They seem to have taken my handkerchief, but you can wipe your nose on my shirt sleeve.'

She half laughed again, and sniffed. 'I've got one.' She took out a handkerchief, wiped her eyes and blew her nose, then

turned her face towards Modesty and said, 'How do we stand?'
Collier started to speak, but the blind girl sensed it and silenced
him with a quick gesture. 'No. You'll dress it up. So will
Willie. I'm asking Modesty.'

There was a little silence. At last Modesty said, 'It's bad,
Dinah, but it could be a lot worse. We're in one piece, all of
us, and it doesn't look as if Delicata means to sign any of us
off right away. So we have time and we have a pretty simple
objective—to get out, that's all.'

'Across that desert?' Collier said.

She shrugged. 'We'll get you across the desert alive.' Her
eyes went past Collier and her face grew thoughtful.

Willie Garvin, watching her, knew that her thoughts were
less hopeful than her words. The objective was not as simple
as she had made it sound. He did not doubt that they would
find a way out. There was always a way. As for the trek beyond, Modesty had lived in the desert and he had served with
the Legion there. They had both learned that the desert
would keep you alive, if you knew its secrets. To get Collier
and Dinah across the Sahara would be a fiercely exacting
ordeal, that was all. But there were the zombies, as McWhirter
had called them. Professor Tangye and his team. Yes, and
there was a Mrs. Tangye somewhere; he had forgotten her
for the moment. Escaping from Mus and crossing the desert
with a bunch of fearful, mindless creatures, two of them elderly . . . that was something else.

He looked at the men lying on the beds. None of them had
moved. Professor Tangye still sat at the foot of his bed as
before, frowning, rubbing the stubble on his chin with a
distant and troubled air, as if he were pondering some obscure
archaeological mystery.

Modesty said, 'Where's Mrs. Tangye?'

'We have a kind of separate place at the end.' Dinah nodded
down the length of the commonroom. 'She's not quite so bad
as the rest. McWhirter calls her the mem-sahib, and I guess
that's right. She's dried out and tough. They cracked her,

like they cracked everyone else. But I think she took a lot of their special treatment first. And she still talks sense a little, sometimes.'

Modesty took the girl's arm. 'Let's try her now. There's a whole lot we have to know before we can do ourselves much good.' She looked at Willie. 'Better not crowd her to start with. You and Steve pick yourself a bed apiece here in the men's ward and get settled in. See if you can get any of them talking.'

Willie nodded. She moved away down the commonroom with Dinah. Collier let out a long breath and said softly, 'Well, at least they didn't put Dinah through that bloody Mace thing, or whatever it is.'

'It might knock 'er off balance for locating what they're looking for. That's why.'

'We can still be glad about it,' Collier said with a touch of anger.

'Sure.' Willie looked at him. 'I'm glad. But she's still dead like the rest of us unless we can pull off a stroke.'

Collier rubbed a hand across his eyes. 'We forgot to ask her if they'd got her trying to locate anything.'

'We didn't forget. We can get what Dinah knows any time. What we need is a ton of information she doesn't know.' He glanced at the men on the beds. 'Let's try and open 'em up.'

As they started to move there came the sound of the bars being withdrawn outside the door. They turned to see the door open. A man came in carrying a bedroll and a small pack. In the seconds that the door was open Collier glimpsed in the moonlight one of the guards standing back. A submachine gun at his hip pointed at the doorway. In his free hand he held a small aerosol spray ready for use.

The door slammed and the bars slid into place. Collier looked at the newcomer. Shock and anger swept him. It was Skeet Lowry.

The American nodded amiably at Willie and said, 'You fellers got any special choice for beds?'

Willie shook his head, and Collier saw that his face was impassive. Lowry nodded and moved on past. He dumped his blanket roll on an empty bed and unfolded it, put his small pack at the head for a pillow, then lay down and took out a packet of cigarettes.

Willie strolled to the foot of the bed and Collier followed. Lowry held up the packet of cigarettes and lifted an eyebrow. Willie shook his head and said, 'You sleep here overnight, Skeet?'

'Sure. It was here or with that guy McWhirter. The big feller don't like anyone wandering around. I chose here. That McWhirter's too gabby.' He lit a cigarette.

Willie said, 'How's the Skywagon guarded?' When Lowry did not answer he went on, 'Is she tanked up?'

Lowry said plaintively, 'Now, Willie.' He meant that anyone who knew him should know better than to ask questions that called for answers which might be against the interests of his employer.

Willie nodded and moved on down the commonroom. Collier followed. At a point where there were three empty beds Willie sat down on one of them and gestured for Collier to take the next.

'Why the bloody hell didn't you break his neck?' Collier asked in a soft, seething voice.

Willie Garvin looked mildly surprised. 'I would if it 'elped get us anywhere, but it won't.'

'He's the one who put us in the bag, dammit!'

Willie shook his head. 'We put ourselves in the bag. Skeet just didn't warn us. He couldn't, because he's honest. He stays bought.'

Collier stared, baffled. Then he shrugged, stood up and moved down the commonroom to where Professor Tangye sat. 'My name's Collier,' he said pleasantly. 'We all seem to be in rather a mess here. I wonder if you could tell me what's happening?'

Professor Tangye eyed him furtively, then looked away and

said in a high-pitched, irritable voice, 'I'm tired. Can't you see I'm tired? And there's a lot of work to be done tomorrow.' He lay down on his side on the bed and pulled a blanket over him, drawing it up so that his face was hidden.

In the small room, Modesty sat beside Dinah facing a tall, rather thin woman with dry sunburned skin drawn tightly over the bone-structure of an aristocratic face. The lank hair, once blonde but now fading to grey, was rolled in a bun at the back of her neck.

Mrs. Tangye was speaking with an admirable attempt to maintain some degree of dignity, but her control was shaky.

'I'm very worried about my husband,' she was saying. 'He hardly speaks at all now. This has been a . . .' her voice quavered, 'a very destructive experience for him. And those poor boys. They were so keen and—and energetic, you know. I told Malcolm at the start that it wasn't wise to agree with Dr. Aaronson's idea. Withholding those pages from the translation of the Mus scrolls was very foolish.'

Modesty looked at Dinah, who sensed the movement and gave an uncomprehending shake of her head.

'There was something in the scrolls that wasn't published?' Modesty said with encouraging interest.

'Oh, yes. Malcolm, my husband, is a very strong Zionist, you know. That's why he agreed to keep the part about the Garamantes treasure a secret.'

'The Garamantes treasure?'

'Well, only the jewels came from the Garamantes, of course. The gold and silver and all the rest were accumulated over the years by Domitian Mus. I'm really very worried about my husband, you know. He hardly speaks at all now . . .' Her voice trailed on repetitively for a few moments, then faded to silence. She sat staring into space with empty blue eyes.

'She's gone,' Dinah said quietly. 'Sometimes she'll talk a while, then she just fades out like this.'

Modesty touched the girl's arm and stood up. Together they went back into the long room. Willie and Collier lay on

184

adjoining beds, silent. As they started to get up Modesty said, 'No, stay there.' She sat on the edge of Collier's bed, looking at Willie, who edged over to make a space for Dinah to sit and drew her down.

'No luck then,' Modesty said.

Willie shook his head. 'They've been conditioned all right, Princess.' He glanced along the row of beds. 'Skeet's here.'

She nodded. 'You talked to him?'

'He's getting thirty thousand bucks for the job. I offered sixty thousand.' A shrug.

'Yes. What about transport?'

'Those two Land Rovers, and some other truck. They're all kept in a sealed off bit of the valley beyond where the big boys have their quarters. Delicata holds the rotor arms. The Skywagon's immobilised too. Skeet has to take out the plugs, and Delicata holds 'em overnight.' There was a dry note in the last words, a subtle implication that Collier could not define.

Modesty sat silent for a while, considering. Watching her, Collier had a feeling he had known before, a feeling that for the moment he had ceased to exist for her. He had resented this once, but not now. She and Willie were communing on a level far beyond the words they spoke, and in a manner which he could only vaguely follow. They were stripping the situation to its bones, considering lines of action, rejecting some, putting others aside for further examination, assessing information needed, and ways of getting it. Their minds were linked almost telepathically, and there was no way of tapping that link.

Collier decided that Dinah Pilgrim, with her hypersensitive intuition, must have understood the situation. She was sitting with her hands linked in her lap, not speaking, listening carefully even during the silences. And on her face there was a strangely wistful look.

Modesty said, 'It's treasure, Willie. A lot of stuff, but she only spoke of the Garamantes jewels.'

Willie said softly, 'Christ.'

Collier searched his memory. He had read history at Cambridge. Garamantes . . . ? Yes. Garama had lost its name somewhere around the fourteenth century. Now it was Djerma, about four hundred miles east of here, in Fezzan. In the days when Rome ruled North Africa, Cornelius Balbus had struck south and conquered the Garamantes, to control the only corridor leading across the Sahara to the riches of Black Africa beyond.

Gold, silver, ivory, slaves . . . jewels? Yes. Now he remembered a line from Strabo, something about 'the carbuncles of the Garamantes'. He felt brief surprise that Modesty and Willie should know anything of ancient jewels which were possibly mythical and scarcely mentioned in historical records. Then he remembered the library of books in Modesty's lapidary workshop at her penthouse, and his surprise passed.

She was saying, 'There's something more important.'

Willie Garvin nodded, and his face hardened in an ugly look. 'More important for later.'

'Yes.'

There was a long silence. At last Collier said apologetically, 'I expect Dinah would like to be told what it is. I know I would.'

Modesty turned to look down at him as he lay on the bed. She smiled and said, 'Sorry, Steve. We're talking about Presteign.'

He propped himself on his elbows, staring. 'Presteign? I didn't hear you.'

'Well, thinking about him. Presteign handpicks his own people. He handpicked Skeet Lowry.'

After a moment Collier said, 'Well?'

She seemed surprised, and went on, 'Skeet works for the man who picks up the tab. Nobody else.'

'Aren't Delicata and Gabriel picking up the tab?'

'No. Presteign is. He chose Skeet. He said so himself. I

told you the whole conversation, Steve.' Again she stopped, as if she had said all that needed to be said.

Willie turned on his side to face Collier and spoke patiently. 'They were waiting for us. So someone told 'em we were coming. And the same someone told Skeet to drop us right in their laps. There's only one bastard could do that. Presteign.'

'*Presteign?*' Collier could not encompass the thought. 'But he's—dammit, he's got an industrial empire. He's the top philanthropist and hander-out of charity in the country!'

'He can afford to be,' Modesty said drily. 'Don't you know there are people who steal books and sell them, and give money to beggars? It's only a matter of degree.'

Collier had a wild desire to laugh. He quelled it and said, 'A matter of degree. I see. You know, there are times when I'm not sure whether you have a huge sense of humour, or whether I'm out of my mind.'

'Presteign told us this was a dead-spot for radio communication,' Modesty said. 'That was to stop us having a link with Tarrant. It's not a dead-spot. There was a radio in that room of Delicata's, where they searched us. Didn't you see it?'

Collier closed his eyes and said wearily, 'Yes, I saw it, but it didn't register. I suppose it just looked right, standing there.'

'Probably a direct link to Presteign,' Willie said grimly. 'And that's 'ow Presteign told 'em we were coming.'

Gradually Collier accepted the inevitability of the conclusion. Aaronson had become worried, had spoken of his suspicions to Presteign, and had been killed by Delicata. Then Modesty Blaise had appeared on the scene, with well-founded suspicions, wanting to investigate Mus. How very convenient. No need to send for Delicata again, just send the victims out to him.

'But for God's sake, he can't get away with this!' Collier said with sudden rage. 'Tarrant knows we're here. *Everybody* knows Tangye and his team are here. Presteign can't get away with it, even if he kills off the lot of us.'

'That's his intention,' Modesty said absently. 'He'll have given Delicata orders to kill everybody as soon as Dinah turns up the treasure. And why can't he get away with it? We all just disappear. A Marie Celeste mystery. Or maybe a cave collapses and buries us all. Presteign will get away with it all right. Who'd suspect him?'

There was a silence, then Dinah said, 'Looks like I'd better hold off finding that treasure.'

Willie Garvin put his hand over hers. 'Can you fool 'em, love?'

'I guess so.' Her face was pale in the dim light of the commonroom. 'They mark out an area for me to cover each day. First it was too big. Looking for precious metals I get so I'm nearly jumping through my skin, and then I can't locate anything. They must have seen I wasn't fooling, because they cut down the daily area by half. I just do three spells of half an hour.'

Modesty said, 'How long will it take to cover the whole of Mus at that rate, Dinah?'

'I can't see how big it is. But McWhirter says another ten days.'

Modesty and Willie looked at each other. Again they seemed to withdraw into their own strange communion. After a little while Willie said, 'Delicata,' and Modesty nodded.

Collier sat up. 'Delicata *what*?' he said in a low, furious voice. 'Dinah and I don't mind missing the silent councils of war, but we do want to know what the hell to expect. So Delicata *what*?'

'Delicata's employed by Presteign,' said Modesty, her eyes still on Willie. 'He's probably in charge up to the time the treasure is unearthed. Gabriel's been brought in to take charge of disposing of it.'

'That's not what Willie meant.'

'It was part of it. We couldn't figure either Delicata or Gabriel working for the other. Now we can see it. The only important aspect is that Delicata's in charge of this part.'

'So?'

'So he's a very clever man who can do any job he's given and still find time to do it in a way that amuses him, a way that provides him with his own kind of kick. Dinah said ten days just now. That doesn't mean we have ten days to find a way out.'

She took her eyes from Willie and looked at Collier. 'Delicata will start having his fun long before then. Why else do you think he kept us alive?'

15

WENCZEL had placed an upright plank against a crumbling pillar which had once formed part of a small colonnade. On the plank were chalk circles at varying heights. Épée in hand, Wenczel was practising lunges against the little targets on the plank. He had been at it tirelessly now for over an hour.

Twenty paces away a guard sat with a Halcon submachine gun, an Argentinian weapon with a folding stock and a 30-round magazine of .45 calibre cartridges. He was watching a working party consisting of Modesty Blaise, Professor Tangye, and three young men of the archaeological team. They were working in the necropolis area of the miniature city.

A quarter of a mile away, Willie Garvin, Mrs. Tangye and the rest of the team were digging among the ruins of a small temple, close to the dusty oval which had once been a circus or arena. They were using light block and tackle mounted on sheerlegs of tubular alloy to lift some of the heavy stone flags.

Between the two parties Dinah moved slowly along a marked strip of ground. In each hand she held a locator of copper tubing and steel wire. Gabriel was at her elbow, wearing a straw hat and with his shirt sleeves rolled down. There was no sign of Delicata, or of Steve Collier.

McWhirter paused by the necropolis working party. He wore his baggy shorts, a sun helmet, no shirt, and a crumpled khaki jacket hanging open. After watching for a few moments he took out his black notebook, ticked something neatly on one page and wrote carefully in cramped writing on another. Mc-Whirter was a methodical man, and his notebook was the bible he lived by.

Wenczel came across from the upright plank, the épée in his hand. McWhirter grinned and said, 'Stage three, section four, very near completion.'

'I cannot understand Delicata,' Wenczel said brusquely. 'It is little use to continue digging by guesswork. Better to wait until the blind girl has found the location.'

'An' you an army man,' McWhirter sighed. 'D'ye not know the value o' keeping prisoners occupied?'

'These prisoners?' Wenczel said with contempt. 'Do you think Blaise and Garvin can stir them to revolt?'

McWhirter cackled. 'Maybe not.' He glanced towards Modesty Blaise, a few paces away. She was prising a stone from the baked ground with an entrenching tool. 'If it was just you an' Garvin, lassie, I'd sleep awful light. But you're carrying too much weight this time, heh?'

She did not answer. Wenczel eyed her thoughtfully then moved across the rubble towards her. He was not worried about the tool in her hands. She could use it against him only if she were set on suicide for herself and death for one or more of the others. The working parties were always split; one group was security for the good behaviour of the other. And quite apart from this, Wenczel was very sure that the épée, in his skilled hand, would be faster than any crude weapon.

He said, 'I have heard that you fence.'

She did not look up or stop working. 'A little.'

'Then we shall fence together. I have another épée.'

She straightened up. 'Do I take orders from you or from Delicata?'

Wenczel looked angry. McWhirter said. 'You take 'em from Delicata or Gabriel, lassie. I don't fancy they'll say yes. Wenczel uses swords without buttons, or whatever you call 'em.'

'We would fence under the rules for foil,' Wenczel said stiffly. 'I have a jacket of lightweight mail you would wear to protect the target area.'

She looked at him with raised eyebrows. 'And you?'

He smiled without parting his lips. 'My sword will be sufficient.'

Modesty looked at McWhirter and said, 'Do I have to?'

'Only if the big feller or Gabriel says so.' McWhirter was enjoying Wenczel's annoyance.

She turned to resume her work, then saw that Professor Tangye was gently brushing sand away from a buried stone which bore a Neolithic rock carving of a giraffe hunt. His fingers trembled as they touched the worn grooves, almost smooth now, which had been carved five thousand years ago, when the Sahara had been fertile jungle.

She moved to where he knelt, and said gently, 'You'd better study it another day, Professor. All we must do now is dig.'

He looked up, bewildered for a moment, then saw Wenczel and McWhirter watching. Sudden fear touched the dazed, sunken eyes. He got to his feet laboriously, nodding his head and reaching for the shovel he had laid down. 'Yes. We must dig. Dig.' His voice was high and shaky. He turned to the three younger men. 'Dig, gentlemen.'

One of them looked at him dully, without curiosity. The other two seemed unaware that he had spoken.

McWhirter giggled and walked away in the direction of the other working party. Wenczel, tight-lipped, returned to his practice lunges.

Modesty Blaise put down her entrenching tool and began to shovel loose rubble into a wheelbarrow. This was the third day, and she was finding the need to use careful control against the subtle beginnings of despair. She had learned many things in the past sixty hours, but so far nothing had offered any line on which to base a plan of escape, nothing at all.

She and Willie had tested the guards warily, and found that there was no hope of bribery. All eight Algerians had been tried. Not one was interested. The promise of payment at some unspecified time in the future held no attraction for them, but above all they were afraid of Delicata. They had reported the attempts at bribery to him this morning, and Delicata had been greatly amused. He had also given instructions that Blaise and Garvin and Collier should suffer another treatment in what he called the initiation chamber when the day's work was done.

Modesty thought about that briefly. She would have to be careful about keeping Steve unconscious. Too long a pressure on the carotids could cause damage to the brain.

The barrow was full now. She trundled it over the rough ground to the growing pile of rubble beside the ruins of the temple. In that rubble were many fragments of archaeological treasure; a bone fish-hook, a finely chipped arrowhead, pieces of pottery, a broken axe-head; and, from later centuries, the iron boss of a Roman shield, a corroded knife-blade, the obtuse point of a Roman sword.

Halfway across the valley, the small figure of Dinah moved slowly along the marked strip, the locators held in front of her. Modesty felt a little wave of affection for the girl. Dinah could have been the biggest problem of all. The daily strain of location was an ordeal that shredded her nerves. Yet at night, when they were all together in the commonroom, she showed no sign of breaking down, made no troublesome scenes. She would sit quietly on Willie's bed, her hand in his, not talking much, but listening thoughtfully as the others pooled whatever grains of information they had gathered during the day.

That was something to be grateful for. Dinah was no fool; she knew that they would all die when their purpose had been served. But she seemed to have created an inner shield which prevented that knowledge eroding her nerves and her mental balance. Her trust in Willie was immense, yet Modesty had a strange feeling that it was Steve Collier who helped her most. His dry, sometimes sour humour, his pretence of bewilderment, of being a lamb fallen among jackals, his protestations of fervent cowardice—all these things brought moments of laughter for Dinah, even under the sharp menace of their situation, and at the same time seemed to rouse a curiously protective instinct in her.

Modesty wheeled the empty barrow back and picked up her entrenching tool. Her thoughts switched to Willie Garvin, and at once she had to beat down a twisting stab of fear. Immediate danger hovered closer to Willie than to anyone else, danger from Delicata. Slowly, enjoying every prolonged moment, Delicata was working up to a showdown with Willie.

There was the constant prodding and needling from that suave tongue, the oblique reminders of the past, the smiling insults and the hints of challenge.

Yesterday Willie had been struggling to lift a block of stone bedded in the ground. It was a task that would have tested three men, and the lifting gear was in use elsewhere. Delicata had watched for a while, then stepped down into the trench and heaved the stone out with seemingly small effort. He had straightened up, smiling, and said, 'Don't do yourself a mischief, Garvin. I'd hate to be forestalled.'

Modesty had not seen the incident. Collier had told her about it, his face gravely troubled. He knew nothing of Willie's past battle with Delicata, but he was sensitive to atmosphere and knew that something peculiarly bad was brewing.

Modesty reminded herself thankfully that in spite of it all Willie was handling himself with immaculate care. He absorbed the needling and insults and challenge with apparent unconcern, going placidly about his work and doing as he was told. He was cheerful with Dinah and Steve; gentle with the zombies. And with Modesty herself he was as coolly realistic as he had always been when on a caper.

He knew, as she did, that it was Delicata's intention sooner or later to take up where he had left off many years ago, and to kick him slowly to death. He had accepted that this would happen unless they escaped soon, and he had set that certain knowledge aside, at a distance, to concentrate with her on finding a way out.

But so far they had found nothing, and this was the third day . . .

Modesty picked up her shovel. With a conscious effort she eased the tautening in her stomach that was making her feel sick. It could be worse. Steve Collier was helping to postpone the showdown. He was providing Delicata with amusement, and doing it with considerable skill. He had become the court fool, an obtuse and frightened man, but of some culture and breeding, an ideal butt for Delicata. She wondered how long he could keep it up.

In the distance she saw McWhirter pause to speak to Gabriel and make another entry in his notebook. By the crumbling pillar and the plank, Wenczel was thrusting and recovering, thrusting and recovering.

A slender thread of thought formed in her mind, a sudden linking of unrelated trivia. McWhirter and his notebook; Tangye and the zombies; Wenczel and his sword; Skeet Lowry and the Skywagon; McWhirter pawing her when she was stripped and searched; Delicata and Willie Garvin.

The thread thickened and began to form an intricate pattern.

A safety-valve for Delicata; take the heat off Willie. An angle to play for Skeet, who couldn't be bought. Yes . . .

She realised that she was standing immobile, staring at nothing, and quickly bent to resume her shovelling. The last vestiges of tension faded from her nerves and muscles, leaving the cool tranquillity that came from decision. A move could be made, and the blind groping was over.

The pattern in her mind built up smoothly. She studied it. There was one piece missing, one vital piece. But that could well emerge in the working out of the rest. She paused and drank from the waterbottle that hung at her hip. Each prisoner was served with ten pints during short breaks in the working day. The remaining five pints came in bulk to the prisoners each evening, in jerricans.

195

She stoppered the bottle and reviewed the pattern again. Willie Garvin wouldn't like it. Steve would be at once furious and frightened. She decided it would be better to say nothing until after she had taken the first step. Then argument would be pointless.

The plastic plate held an enormous pile of food, cold food from cans kept in the cool interior of the ancient stone tanks built two thousand years ago.

Collier set the plate on the table in front of Delicata._In setting it down his hand came within inches of the knife. He could have snatched it up and tried to drive it into Delicata's throat, and failed. Delicata was half hoping for it, and Collier knew that the attempt would end in those huge hands breaking his arm.

Collier stepped back and said with an anxious grin, 'Is that all right?'

'If ever there's anything wrong,' said Delicata, picking up the knife and fork, 'you can be sure I shall let you know in one way or another.' He nodded to one of the folding canvas chairs. 'Sit.'

Delicata ate enormously but not gluttonously. It amused him to have Collier present. Collier was entertaining.

'You have probably observed,' said Delicata genially, 'that when I stand up my hands reach almost to my knees. Now what does that remind you of, Collier?'

Collier looked anxious and a little frightened. It was important that he should do so, and he did not find it hard. Keeping the right balance on the tightrope he walked with Delicata was a frightening business.

'Well,' he said tentatively, 'it reminds me of . . . of an acrobat.'

'Really?' Delicata was enchanted. 'Why?'

'I'm not quite sure.' Collier put a touch of desperation into his voice. 'I suppose hanging on trapezes and things would make their arms long.'

'It doesn't remind you of an anthropoid ape?' Delicata asked with a jovial smile.

'Jesus, no!' Collier said hastily. He plunged on, changing the subject with carefully judged clumsiness. 'I say, did you know about the Tuaregs? They pair off with women any old how, and no questions asked. There was a chap called de Foucauld who made a dictionary of their language, Tamahaq, and there just wasn't any word for virginity. Sort of complete absence of moral concepts.'

'An attitude I approve,' said Delicata, chewing steadily. 'You're sure I don't remind you of an anthropoid?'

Collier rasped at the three-day stubble on his cheeks. 'No.' He hesitated. 'But McWhirter does. A small, busy one.'

Delicata shook with laughter and mopped a moist left eye. 'You're what used to be called a proper caution, Collier. You really are.'

Collier wiped his brow, grinned with relief, and said nothing. The flies buzzed about his face. They were worse than heat and thirst, sometimes even worse than fear in their maddening persistence. He kept flicking them away. Delicata did not flick them away. They crawled unhindered over the great landscape of his face. He seemed immune to their irritation.

'When I was a young man at college,' Delicata said reminiscently, 'I was dubbed King Kong. I didn't like that at all.'

Collier contrived to look shocked in a manner which revealed the contrivance.

'It upset me very much,' Delicata went on amiably. 'You'll hardly believe this, Collier, but I became almost suicidal over my freakishness.' He beamed with amusement. 'You know the works of Housman?'

'Er . . . well, I remember bits. "The troubles of our proud and—and something dust are from eternity and shall not fail . . ." That sort of thing. I always found Housman a bit morbid.'

'Angry dust,' said Delicata, and grinned. 'He suited my

youthful torments. I remember very clearly how I'd look at my graceless shape and agree with poor sad Mr. Housman's lament . . . "There's this to say for blood and breath, they give a man a taste for death."'

Collier stirred unhappily in his chair. 'Well, as I say, he was a bit morbid.'

'And then do you know what I discovered?' asked Delicata with a benign, teasing air. 'I discovered that I was rather clever, quite remarkably strong, and to a large degree invulnerable. My threshold of pain is perhaps uniquely high. Nothing hurts. I believe there's a medical term for it.'

Collier looked vaguely baffled. 'You couldn't suddenly discover that. You must have known all along. About the pain thing, I mean.'

'Oh, I did. But my freak appearance inhibited me from seeing the significance of it. So it came as a discovery.' The chair creaked under Delicata's soundless laughter. 'Six of my contemporaries decided to debag King Kong. It developed into a somewhat vicious affair, and they were badly hurt. But I wasn't hurt at all, even when they became quite desperate.'

'And then it dawned on you?' said Collier.

'Then it dawned on me. My freakishness lay not only in my shape. It went deeper. Apart from scarcely feeling pain, I could sustain blows which would have maimed or killed another man.' He grinned. 'Garvin found that out, some years ago.'

Collier nodded. It confirmed a suspicion he had, that Willie and Delicata had clashed before.

'I also realised,' Delicata went on, 'that I had a certain mental invulnerability as well. Neither drink nor drugs nor women had an addictive effect on me. I could use them without the slightest fear of bondage.' He looked at Collier with amusement. 'So I changed. Quite radically.'

After a moment Collier said with feeble approval, 'Well, it must have been nice to get yourself sorted out. Farewell to Mr. Housman and all that, eh?'

'Farewell to Mr. Housman,' Delicata agreed, and put the last forkful of food into his great mouth. When he had chewed and swallowed it he said happily, 'Except that to some extent I retained the taste for death he mentioned. Only it wasn't my own death any longer. It was other people's. Now isn't that an interesting story?'

'It's—er—well . . .' Collier giggled. 'It's a bit alarming in a way.'

'You're very shrewd. It is indeed most alarming for you.' Delicata put his knife and fork together and sat back, surveying Collier with a peculiarly absent-minded stare.

Collier felt hot and thirsty and frightened, and he let it show. There had been a similar session with Delicata at lunchtime yesterday. That one had been easier, because part of it had been spent in reading several photostat sheets—the missing pages from the translation of the Mus scrolls. It had amused Delicata to reveal the immensity of what lay hidden in Mus, because the very size of it implied that no witnesses would be left to talk of what they knew.

The extract began:

. . . Therefore I, Domitian Mus, a Tribune of Rome, Son of Fabius, Praetor of the Province of Numidia, did with my bodyguard of hastati travel in the Unknown Lands beyond Africa Nova and came well to learn of the Princes of the South who rule the Aourigha peoples that do dwell in those parts. With some did I make good bonds of Friendship and Alliance, for with this was I charged by my father, Fabius. The Lands were barren, yet in strange Places did Water gush forth making the Trees to grow . . .

In the third year of his travels Domitian Mus had come upon a tribe of the Berber people occupying the valley which would later bear his name. He had married the daughter of the amekkeran, the head of the tribe, or 'Prince' as the young tribune called him. And soon, with typical Roman expertise and thoroughness, Domitian Mus was running a tiny empire of his own. Slaves were brought from the south, new gods were proclaimed, and Roman administration was applied.

But that was not all. The young Mus served his father faithfully; which was better than his father served Rome. Fabius, as Praetor of the Province of Numidia, was making plans to feather his own nest. This was warmly justified by his son, on the grounds that Fabius had been passed over for promotion to a position in Rome itself, a position he well deserved.

And so, for the next ten years, Fabius scoured Africa for treasure and sent it by caravan to his son, to be stacked away against a rainy day. There was plenty of loot for a clever man to pick up. Rome was taking the accumulated wealth of Carthage and of every other city worth the picking from Fezzan to Mauretania. Much of it passed through the hands of Fabius. Much of it stuck.

Fabius died by assassination. His son decided to remain where he was, a good safe distance even from Rome's long arm. For two thousand years the treasure had lain buried somewhere in the city of rock which housed the strangely blended community of Roman and Berber.

In his later years Domitian Mus had listed the treasure. There was gold and silver, coin and plate, barbaric vessels and ornaments; there was ivory and there were ceremonial weapons and armour, of gold and silver set with jewels; and there were gems. The jewels of the Garamantes were specifically listed, '. . . *Carbuncles of great purity and of such size that a man can scarce contain ten in his two cupped hands, and of these are there close to six hundred.*'

There were other gems. Over the centuries, Phoenicians and Persians, Greeks and Carthaginians had reigned on the African coast in days when men carried their wealth with them. Some of the gems, to judge by their description, had been cut and polished in the East. And these, seized by the Greeks, lost to the Roman conquerors, carried in the private treasury of a general, and lost or stolen in some battle fought against Carthage before the young Mus was born, had come to rest at last under the stones of the city he had built.

Today even their intrinsic value would surely run into millions sterling. But Domitian Mus had died without entering in his journal the secret he had guarded so well—the exact location of his hoarded wealth.

'Interesting, I think you'll agree,' Delicata had said when Collier finished reading. 'That silly little man Aaronson suppressed the pages about the treasure. He was a Jew, and Tangye is a Zionist. They had the quaint idea that in due time, when Tangye found the loot, they'd hand it over secretly to the Israeli Government for development of the Promised Land.' A wide grin. 'They could hardly tell the Algerian authorities that. But they had to tell Presteign in order to get his backing for the dig. Presteign, of all people. Oh dear me!'

Delicata had been immensely entertained by the idea.

Collier brought his thoughts back to the present, to find Delicata staring at him.

'That's very odd,' Delicata said softly. 'In repose just now you looked rather intelligent.'

Collier cursed himself. Avoiding a sudden change of expression he slowly sat up straight and looked at Delicata with an air of bafflement tinged by indignation.

'I don't think I've ever been considered a fool,' he said stiffly. 'In repose or otherwise.'

Delicata smiled. 'Perhaps not,' he said. His manner was thoughtful. 'Perhaps not.'

Huge fingers drummed on the table for a moment, then he gestured at the empty plate. 'Clear this away and we'll see how the working parties are getting on.'

16

COLLIER said politely, 'Did your husband form any ideas about the water supply of Mus in the old days, Mrs. Tangye?'

She was sitting beside Professor Tangye, on his bed. This was where she spent most of her time, except when she slept at night. Tangye rarely answered when she spoke to him. If she persisted he became irritable. Collier had the feeling that Tangye's mind had been damaged beyond repair.

The younger men of the team sometimes talked a little among themselves, but in a remote and desultory manner, usually about past excavations they had worked on, never about the present. The present was a nightmare from which they had mentally withdrawn. They spoke barely a word to the four strangers among them, but for the most part eyed them furtively, with suspicion and fear.

It made Collier shiver to realise that he could easily have been bludgeoned into this same lifeless inertia. Even knowing that Modesty would put him out when they were herded into the gas chamber that evening, he was still nervous and a little afraid.

This was the long midday break. The prisoners worked from dawn until noon, then were given their food and locked in the big stone commonroom until four, when the sun had ceased to beat directly down into the valley. At four they began to work again until seven.

Mrs. Tangye's face was more gaunt than ever. She looked at her husband, then at Collier, her faded eyes anxious and bewildered.

'Water?' she said vaguely. 'Yes, we discussed that, I think. But you mustn't trouble him now. He's not himself, Mr. . . . I'm sorry, I can't quite remember your name. I'm really very worried about him.' She patted Tangye's arm soothingly with a hand roughened by labour.

'Perhaps you remember what was said about the water supply?' Collier suggested.

She brushed a fly away from her face. 'It was just . . . you know, the *foggara* system.' Collier did not know, but Modesty would tell him later. 'That was unusual because we thought the *foggara* began much later,' Mrs. Tangye went on. Her voice was thin and disinterested. 'We were going to trace the source. A river nearby, or wells. They must have dried up over a thousand years ago, but there would still be signs. And then those . . . those men came.'

She closed her eyes and her face twisted in a sudden grimace. Collier realised that she was trying not to cry. He said gently, 'Don't give up hope, Mrs. Tangye. I'm sure everything will work out all right.'

As he walked towards the smaller room to find Dinah, he echoed the last words to himself with sour contempt. Everything would work out all right. All it needed was a few miracles. Sweat broke out on him at the prospect of another session with Delicata that afternoon. He hoped he would be put on a working party instead. Anything was better than the strain of amusing Delicata.

Carefully he subdued the wave of apprehension and concentrated on the idea that had come to him. It was no doubt a useless idea, but at least it served as a diversion. He went through the arch into the little room.

Dinah was stripped, gently scouring herself with handfuls of sand. This was their substitute for a bath, the Tuareg way that Modesty had taught them, and it worked well enough. All their small-kit and toiletry had been withheld. Conditions were primitive. The latrine was at the end of a ten-foot blind passage leading off one side of the commonroom. It was simply a deep natural crevice in the ground with a pile of sand beside it and a length of sacking strung across.

Tangye's team no longer cared that they were dirty. But

Collier and Dinah, Modesty and Willie, kept themselves clean with sand-baths, which was at least good for morale.

In the archway, Collier stopped short as he saw Dinah and said, 'Oh, sorry.'

'It's all right, Steve. I'm way past worrying.' She brushed the sand from her skin. 'Come and talk. I'm just finished.' Before Collier looked away he saw that her small body was firm and very shapely. He strolled towards the bed, looking at the locators which lay there, and said, 'Was it a rotten morning?'

'Not too bad.' She clipped her bra in place, pulled on briefs and slacks, then turned to him, picking up her shirt. Her face was troubled. 'I keep thinking about the gas treatment waiting for you this evening——'

'Don't let that worry you,' he broke in easily. 'Modesty will take care of it, or rather she'll take care of me. And she and Willie can take care of themselves.'

'Yes.' There was a wry twist to her smile. She sat down and patted the bed beside her. 'It's tough on them that the rest of us are just deadweight they have to carry. I don't see how they can get us out of this.'

'You're too impatient,' Collier said, trying to put confidence in his voice. He sat down on the edge of the bed. 'They'll come up with something. But meanwhile I've had a thought, Dinah. It's probably a waste of time, but will you try an experiment for me?'

In the big room Willie Garvin sat with a flat stone on his knees. He was using it as a miniature anvil on which to renew the edge of a flint arrowhead by delicate chipping.

One arrow was complete, with a shaft of smooth bamboo stolen from one of the big wicker baskets used for hauling rubble out of holes and trenches. The arrowhead was carefully balanced, leaf shaped, and with a central tang. The tang had been inserted into the head of the shaft and secured there by a whipping of thin wire, also stolen.

The bow was not quite finished. He had made it from a length of thala wood left by the Arabs who had first come to Mus after the discovery of the scrolls, and who had dug away the mass of sand blocking the valley entrance. It had probably formed part of a tent, and was good wood for a bow, but it needed more work in shaping and tapering. The string was an inch-wide strip of nylon, cut in a spiral from one of Dinah's stockings, and tightly twisted.

Modesty sat on Collier's bed, facing Willie. She held a knife Willie had made. The hilt was of wood, bound with thin wire. The blade was of iron. Its edge had been eaten away over the centuries, but she was patiently honing it with a stone.

Willie glanced at her uneasily for a moment, then looked down at the arrowhead again. There was nothing to be read in her face, at least by the casual eye. But he knew every nuance of her every mood, and there was a quiet serenity within her that made him apprehensive. He was quite certain that she had found a line of action. What troubled him was that she had not laid it out for him, and this could mean only one thing; whatever she was planning, it involved her in something that would scare him if he knew.

Sombrely Willie Garvin reflected that this was a bastard of a caper. He thought it likely that Delicata would kill him very soon. That would leave the Princess to cope on her own. He decided that somehow he would have to damage Delicata as much as possible when the crunch came. It might help her a little. Even so . . .

He sighed inwardly. There had to be a last caper sometime. They had always known that. But this was a lousy one to go out on. There was Steve Collier, too. And Dinah . . .

She was pacing slowly along the length of the commonroom now, with Collier following her. In her hands she held the locators. Vaguely Willie realised that she had been pacing like this for some time. He guessed that Collier had cooked up something to keep her occupied, to make her feel useful.

Willie felt a dull ache in his chest. Dinah hadn't asked

205

for any of this. She was small and lovely and brave and blind, and they would kill her when her work was done . . .

Modesty said, 'Did you ever know a girl in Barcelona, Willie love?'

Willie Garvin caught at himself quickly. He had let his thinking slip dangerously, and she had sensed it. He examined the flint edge of the arrowhead and let his mind roam back over the years, then said, 'Not Barcelona. But I was in a circus once, with a girl from Cadiz.'

'A circus?' Her surprise was genuine.

'Didn't I ever tell you?'

'No. Tell me now.'

'It was only a couple of weeks. I was trouble-shooter in this little tenting circus. She was a trapezist, and 'er catcher went on the bottle, so I took over.' He grinned, remembering. 'Flying Francesca, they billed 'er. I could've told 'em a better word.'

'You hung upside down on a trapeze and caught her?'

'M'mm. It's not too bad once you've got the timing right. We used to practise 'alf the night at first.' He looked up from his work. 'I bet I'm one of the only two men in the world that ever got seduced at three in the morning on a trapeze.'

Modesty stared. Then her shoulders began to shake and her face lit with laughter. 'It can't be done. It *can't*, Willie!'

'Honest, Princess. Upside down, like a bat. I don't say it's easy. You got to concentrate. But Francesca was crazy about it.'

'Well . . . it's new. But I can't see it becoming a trend. Who was the other bat-man?'

'Pedro. The catcher I stood in for. I think she was a bit too keen for 'im. That's why he went on the bottle.'

'And what about yourself, Willie?'

He rasped a hand across his stubbly chin. 'I think it might 'ave grown on me,' he said reminiscently. 'But the third time, we fell off. Always 'ad a safety net for practice, but a double

206

fall's dodgy, even with a net. So I quit before I did meself
a mischief.'

His voice was cheerful now. Behind him Steve Collier said,
'I only heard the last bit and I'd love to hear the rest sometime. But what's a *foggara?*'

'Channel cut underground for bringing water across the
desert,' Willie said, looking up. 'They used to leave chimneys
every so often so the diggers could breathe, and to aerate the
water. Underground, it didn't evaporate like it would in an
open channel. There's still a good couple of thousand miles of
foggara in the Sahara. You can see the lines of chimneys
sticking up like 'ollow sandcastles.'

Modesty said, 'What made you ask, Steve?'

'Mrs. Tangye used the word. I was asking her about water.
And I think we've found something. Or rather Dinah has.'

Dinah moved between the two beds and sat down beside
Willie. She said, 'There's an aqueduct of some kind running
under this commonroom. It hasn't carried water for . . . I
don't know. Centuries, I guess. But it used to carry water.'

Modesty and Willie looked at each other. Collier said, 'It
dawned on me that this place must have been well supplied
when our friend Mus and his people were here. And whenever
you got a couple of Romans together they always started building an aqueduct.'

Modesty slipped the crude knife and the stone into the
folds of her blanket.

'Under here?' she said, tapping the sandy floor with her
foot and looking at Collier. 'Isn't it solid?'

'Mostly.' Collier pointed to one long side of the chamber.
'But when Dinah found the run of the aqueduct we brushed
away some sand and took a closer look. We found a double
line of stone flags bedded in the ground over there, parallel
to the wall.'

Willie Garvin put his working tools aside and stood up. He
scooped Dinah up in his arms and kissed her heartily. When
her lips were free to speak she said, 'It was Steve's idea.'

'I'm not going to kiss Steve.' Willie put her down and unfolded his blanket. In it lay a variety of small objects—flint and bone arrowheads, corroded pieces of iron, a coil of wire, two strips of flat metal broken from the beds, a jagged piece of glass, a sling he was fashioning from a strip of leather, and several smooth round stones. He picked up one of the metal strips. It was slightly curved at one end, and this end had been ground to an edge, like a jemmy. He said, 'Let's 'ave a look.'

Even with the sand brushed away it was hard to see the flags. They had been set dry, but dust and sand had filled the joints. The run of the flags was L-shaped. At one end they stopped against the rear wall. The short horizontal stroke of the L stopped against one of the long walls, near the door.

Without discussing the matter, Modesty and Willie concentrated on the flags near the rear wall. It took them half an hour to rake out the joints with their crude tools, and another hour to lever up the first flag. The second came up easily.

Below lay a channel with square sides, cut from the rock, its edges recessed so that the flags lay snugly. The channel was perhaps sixteen inches across and the same depth. It was bone dry. Modesty knelt and put her head down the hole. After a moment she got up and started to unbutton her shirt. She said, 'You're too big for it, Willie. Lift another couple of flags and I'll give it a try.'

Collier looked at the dark hole with repugnance. It ran under the wall, and then God knew where. It was too small to crawl through. Modesty would have to wriggle on her stomach, arms outstretched in front of her. And it would be impossible for her to turn. She would have to come back feet first.

She had taken off her slacks, leaving only her boots, bra, and opaque black nylon briefs. Now she knotted Willie's handkerchief over her hair.

Collier said, 'Why not keep your clothes on for God's sake? They might save a few scratches.'

'There's no cleaning service and I don't want to look as if

I've been along a tunnel.' She lowered herself into the enlarged hole, her back to the wall, slid her feet forward until she could lie down, then twisted on to her front. Collier expected her to inch forward, but to his astonishment she vanished quickly. He realised that she was moving by supporting herself on her forearms and toes, her body only an inch or two above the bottom of the channel. The strain would be enormous. He wondered how far she might get, wondered if the aqueduct was blocked at some point . . .

They stood waiting. Willie was whistling very softly between his teeth, not tense, not impatient, just gazing placidly down at the dark oblong hole. Collier, craving a cigarette, sensed a more natural relaxation in Willie than there had been for the past three days.

A man wandered slowly towards them across the common-room. Collier did not know his name, but he was the only man of Tangye's team who had spoken a few words to them. He looked at the hole with dull eyes and muttered, 'What's that?'

Before Collier could answer, Willie Garvin said softly, viciously, 'It's nothing. You're bloody well imagining things again. Now go back to your bed an' lie down, or I'll put in a squeak to the big man and get you stuck in that gas-chamber till your whole bloody 'ead burns off!'

The man went very pale, gestured placatingly with a shaky hand, then turned and shambled away.

Dinah said in a small, trembling voice, 'My God, that was awful, Willie. Did you have to frighten him so?'

'No, I didn't 'ave to.' Willie took her hand. 'I could just write 'im off instead.'

'I don't get what you mean.'

'Tangye's lot are too far gone to be any 'elp,' Willie said patiently, 'so it's better for 'em to stay zombies for now. Then if we get a break they'll do as they're told, an' no arguments. That's the only way we stand a chance of getting 'em out alive.'

Collier said slowly, 'All of them? It's hopeless, Willie.' He looked down at the hole. 'If this leads out somewhere clear of the guards at the valley entrance, it means Modesty and Dinah could go. That's about all.'

'No,' Dinah said flatly. 'No.'

'There's little point in us all going down with the ship and singing *Rule Britannia*, darling. Be sensible.'

Willie said, 'Leave it. Modesty's got something in mind. I don't know what it is yet. I just know that if anyone's left be'ind, they're dead. And she won't want that.'

'Nobody does,' said Collier. 'But why the hell should *she* feel responsible for every last one of us, zombies and all?'

Willie glared suddenly. 'Christ knows,' he snapped. 'She gets no bloody thanks for it. Now belt up, will you?'

Half an hour later there came a faint scuffling sound. Modesty's feet and legs appeared in the narrow hole. She backed into view, turned, and sat up. Willie reached down and lifted her out. Her sweating body was plastered with dust, but there were only two slight grazes. In her eyes was a deep, steady glow of excitement.

She wiped thick dust from her lips before she spoke: 'It's good. Lay those flags back, Willie love. I'll get cleaned up.'

In the smaller room she stripped and rubbed herself down with sand. Dinah helped, gently scrubbing away the dust and sweat from her back. She rinsed her mouth and nose with water, then drank a full pint.

Collier watched, not speaking. There was something in her face and in her manner that he did not like, a kind of animal ferocity, a controlled fury against her enemies which made her incapable of compromise.

Willie came in and nodded. The flags were laid. There was still half an hour to go before the midday break ended. Modesty put on her clothes, pulled the knotted handkerchief from her head, and sat down on Mrs. Tangye's bed. Dust had crept under the handkerchief, and Willie began to comb out her hair with a crude comb fashioned from a fanshaped piece of bone.

'It's a good ten minutes' crawl,' Modesty said. Her voice and her face were both very quiet now. 'And it pinches in places. But I can get through, and there's daylight at the end. I stopped a little short to be on the safe side, but the aqueduct runs pretty straight and I think it comes out in a dry gully . . . outside the valley.'

There was a little silence. Collier said, 'So you and Dinah could make it?'

She looked at him blankly. 'Don't be damn silly, Steve.'

'I'm not. I'm just being objective and quite disgustingly heroic, darling. If you think I enjoy the thought of Delicata's reaction when he finds you gone——'

'Forget it,' Modesty said abruptly, and again he saw something flare deep in her eyes, like the momentary red glow of a dog's eyes picked out by headlights in the dark; or a wolf's eyes, Collier thought. He knew that it was the feral glow of her will, that this quality alone had kept her alive against all odds in early childhood, and that this alone might save his own life now, as it had done before.

But still, in some strange way, it repelled and saddened him. She had been all things to him and he loved her, but this was a part of her with which he could make no contact. He knew that she had surprising depths of charity and compassion, of humour and warmth; that she was intelligent, with a serene but joyous zest for life; that she could give a man supreme happiness, or give him rest; and that, despite her dangerous skills, she was wholly feminine. But this, now, was something else. She was on ground where he could never hope to walk with her, where perhaps Willie Garvin alone could walk with her.

Collier felt no resentment, attached no blame, made no judgments. In childhood she had lived like a wild creature, fought for survival like a wild creature. These years had shaped her. The wonder was that they had not shaped the whole of her, nor even the dominant part of her character, but only the unyielding steel core that lay hidden deep within her . . .

He had missed what she was saying, and came to himself with a little start, then realised that she was speaking to Willie. '. . . and concentrate on finishing the bow, Willie love. By tomorrow night at the latest.'

'Right.' Willie put away the comb and stood up. 'I can get in 'alf an hour on it now. Might be a good idea if we cached what weapons we've got under those flags, Princess. There's been no search so far, but there might be.'

She nodded. 'Do it, Willie.'

He went out through the archway of the small chamber. She waited for a few moments, then spoke softly to Collier. 'Are you listening now, Steve?'

'Sorry. Did it show? I sort of drifted away a bit.'

'It doesn't matter, but this is for you.' Her eyes looked through him, distant with speculation. 'Delicata's working up to a major piece of amusement. He's relished the anticipation for just about long enough now.'

'That's right,' Collier's mouth was dry. 'What do you think it will be?'

'It'll be Willie.' She reached out and gripped Dinah's hand hard. The girl's face had gone very pale. 'Now don't worry about it, Dinah, because I'm not going to let it happen. I promise.' She looked at Collier again. 'You're closest to Delicata. You know his moods best, Steve. Let me know when you think he's going to start trouble.'

'All right.' Collier swallowed. 'How do I let you know—I mean, if I don't have time to talk to you?'

'Make some kind of scene. Pretend you've hit your foot with a pick, and make a big song and dance. Anything. You'll have to play it whatever way offers.'

Collier nodded. 'It could be any time,' he said in a low voice. 'Today he talked about having a taste for death. I think he's just about ready to indulge it.'

Modesty thought. When she spoke it was with seeming irrelevance. 'Skeet Lowry flies in tomorrow night, doesn't he?'

'He should do. He's making trips alternate nights now, bringing in extra water and food. And he was here last night.'

Again there was silence. Collier could almost feel the intensity of her thoughts. He wondered about their shape, and fear squirmed sickeningly in his stomach. At last she said slowly, 'Yes . . . that ought to do.'

The absorption vanished from her face and her teeth showed white in a sudden smile. She was still holding Dinah's hand, and now she gave it a little shake. Her eyes still on Collier, she said, 'Stop looking miserable, you two.'

'I feel miserable,' Collier said uneasily. 'What the hell are you cooking up?'

The smile changed slowly until she was looking at him with a kind of wry compassion. 'You'll have to brace yourself for one or two shocks I'm afraid, darling. But just try to remember there's no other way.'

His unease became sharp alarm, and he sat up straight. 'That's no bloody answer!'

She leaned forward and kissed him. 'I know, and I'm sorry. But it's all you're going to get just now.'

━━━━━━━━━━━━━━━━━━━━━━━━━━━━━━━━━

17

Iᴛ was almost seven and the sky was tinged with pink when Modesty Blaise saw Delicata and Steve Collier emerge from the guarded branch-valley which held the comfortable quarters where the big man and his colleagues lived. Delicata was speaking, waving one long arm in an expansive gesture.

Modesty lifted a rock from the trench she was digging. There was something new and energetic in Delicata's manner. She could see it even at this distance, and the back of her neck crawled in a danger signal.

Willie Garvin was working with his party three hundred yards away, on the forum area. Wenczel was shadow-fencing a little behind her and to her left. Some of Tangye's people were digging nearby. She saw Collier and Delicata begin to walk along the top of a long ramp of sand and rubble which sloped down a few feet to a lower level. Collier appeared to miss his footing. He slithered and rolled down the ramp. Faintly she heard his voice, shrill with pain and indignation. 'My ankle! Jesus, it's broken! Oh, look here, it's all very well to laugh—!'

Wenczel turned round, stared at the distant scene, gave a contemptuous shrug, then squared up to the vertical plank again, his épée poised.

Rather indistinctly he heard a voice say, 'Stupid bastard, prancing about with his toasting-fork.' His head snapped round. Modesty Blaise was looking at him. She dumped a small rock on the ground beside the trench and turned away. Again he heard the same voice, 'Amateur . . . nine hours a day with that sword . . . the d'Artagnan of Mus. Oh, Christ . . .'

Wenczel froze. It was the Blaise woman's voice, he was certain of it. Anger made his lips pallid as he strode towards her and halted, looking down. 'You *said* something?' There was incredulity in his voice. She glanced up at him, shrugged with finely judged disdain, and bent to lift another rock.

The sword lashed down sharply across her shoulders. '*You said something?*'

She was out of the shallow trench, facing him across it, her eyes flaring with angry contempt. Twenty paces away the guard stood up and cocked his Halcon submachine gun. Wenczel thrust his head forward. There was something in this woman's manner that made his blood pound with rage, a blend of scorn and insolence beyond all bearing.

'*What did you say?*' His voice rose in the shrill bark that he had once used on a barrack square.

The angry glare had gone from her eyes, and she looked at him now as if he made her weary. 'Perhaps I was thinking aloud.'

'And *what* were you thinking aloud?'

She looked away, blinked, then stifled an absent-minded yawn. The sword lashed at her like a whip, but astonishingly she was out of distance, poised on the balls of her feet. Wenczel followed up and swung the sword again. For the second time the blow missed its mark.

She backed rapidly, sure as a cat over the rough ground, and Wenczel came after her. The guard moved uncertainly behind Wenczel, his Halcon held at the low port in front of him. Now the scene had become a fast-moving scramble.

Deliberately she kept her hands behind her, backing, weaving, dodging, but making no attempt to strike back. Twice Wenczel caught her with stinging blows of the thin blade, once on the leg and once on her ribs.

She knew that Delicata must have seen. He must surely have heard that last shout of Wenczel's. The Hungarian was cursing in his own language now as he pursued her.

Delicata's voice boomed from fifty yards away. 'Major Wenczel! Desist, if you please.' The sword hissed again. Delicata's voice was nearer when he spoke again, yet it was quieter and almost sleepy with pleasure. 'Do please subdue your passions, Major Wenczel, or I shall feel bound to take a rock and smash your hands to a paste.'

Wenczel stood still, panting, and lowered his sword. Delicata came up, not hurrying, yet covering the ground quickly on his short massive legs. Collier came way behind him, remembering to limp.

'Oh dear me.' Delicata's voice held a happy note. 'What have we here? Insubordination to the gallant Major, Miss Blaise?'

Wenczel's eyes were still on her, and they were burning. 'She—she insulted me!' He had difficulty in getting the words out.

'Never!' Delicata said with mock horror.

'I tell you she insulted me!'

Delicata looked at Modesty. 'We can't have you being rude to our Major Wenczel.'

Modesty rubbed a hand across her eyes. 'That sword,' she said tautly. 'All day, every day, waggling that bloody sword.'

The veins stood out on Wenczel's neck.

'Waggling?' Delicata sounded shocked, but he was grinning hugely. 'Waggling? My dear Miss Blaise, that's no way to speak of a fencing master.'

'A what?' The nuance of contempt in the two quiet words was razor-edged. Wenczel drew in a hissing breath and his sword-hand lifted.

Delicata said, 'No.' The inflexion was flat but the word was like a hammerblow. Wenczel lowered the épée, seething.

Gabriel came on the scene, walking quickly, hustling Dinah along beside him. His putty coloured face was still untouched by the sun and his white shirt was clean and freshly pressed. He snapped, 'What's happening?'

'A touch of feminine temperament,' Delicata said happily. 'Poor Miss Blaise finds Major Wenczel's performance with the sword nerve-racking, and Major Wenczel feels she has insulted him.'

Gabriel's pale dead eyes were on Modesty. 'Kill her,' he said abruptly. 'She's up to something.'

Delicata sighed. 'I wish she were,' he said with regret. 'But I'm afraid you're overly mistrustful, Gabriel. Women, bless them, even women like Miss Blaise, are highly strung creatures. The sword-waggling—oh, I do beg your pardon Major Wenczel—I mean the sword-*wielding* frayed her nerves. Now isn't that delightfully feminine? There may even be something Freudian about it don't you think?'

'Kill her,' Gabriel said again, this time with a hint of anger. 'Do it now.'

Delicata shook his head reproachfully. 'One mustn't gulp one's pleasures. First the bouquet, then the palate and finally the departure. Ah, the departure—observe the double-entendre.' He smiled with jovial malice at Gabriel. 'And do remember the administrative system. Once the loot is above ground you can do everything in your own pretty way, Gabriel. But until then I shall try to bring some style and panache to our endeavours.'

He turned to look at Modesty, and his voice became solemn. 'Our Major Wenczel is one of the world's finest swordsmen by all accounts. And you have spoken lightly of him, madam. Can it be, can it possibly be, that you fail to recognise his skill?'

Modesty pushed a wisp of hair from her brow. 'I don't know about his skill.' She glanced at Wenczel and shrugged. 'But I doubt if the plank's been cut yet that he couldn't beat the hell out of.'

There was a moment of complete silence. Dinah's face was white; so was Wenczel's, from a very different emotion. Collier was screaming in his mind, *'God Almighty! Stop it you crazy bitch, stop it!'*

Then, as Wenczel moved, Delicata gave a shout of laughter. His huge hand shot out at the end of an incredibly long arm and caught Wenczel by the shoulder.

'No, no, Major Wenczel.' Delicata spoke between rigours

of mirth. 'I must admit . . . I really must admit that she's very provoking. But surely you prefer to wipe out the insult in due form?'

Wenczel turned his head slowly to look at Delicata. The murderous fury subsided, and in its place dawned a consuming eagerness.

'In due form?' he said hoarsely.

'You have two épées, I believe?' Delicata dropped his hand from the shoulder. 'A duel, Major Wenczel. A splendid duel. Ah, the glory of the sword as a weapon. I can almost feel your little pink heart leap with the joy of it.'

The ironic phrases were lost on Wenczel. He was staring at Modesty, his face agleam with the sudden sweat of longing.

'When?' he whispered.

Delicata glanced up at the sky. 'The light is going, and we must all have time to relish this happy prospect. In fact we'll cancel the nerve-spray treatment this evening, so Miss Blaise and her friends can look forward to the event undistracted. Shall we say tomorrow, but an hour earlier, on the ground of the old arena?'

Gabriel took a pace forward. The pupils of his eyes were pinpoints of anger. 'You're out of your mind, Delicata,' he said harshly. 'I don't care if Wenczel's the greatest ever, *she might still kill him.*'

Delicata looked hurt. 'Oh dear me, no. Major Wenczel is going to wear that steel mesh jacket.'

Gabriel's anger faded, and he began to grin. Wenczel, stiff with outrage, said, 'I refuse! It is utterly unnecessary for me to wear the jacket!'

'I'm sure it is,' Delicata agreed, smiling upon him. 'But you'll wear it all the same, Wenczel . . . just to please me.'

Tangye's team kept well away from the woman who was going to die, and from her friends. When the heavy door closed they ate their evening ration of food, drank water, and lay in silence on their beds. Mrs. Tangye sat with her husband.

In the smaller room Collier said bitterly, 'So there was no other way?'

'I told you, Steve.'

'I know. You didn't tell me that this way meant getting yourself run through by a sword-mad fanatic. You and Dinah could get out tonight through that hole. But no. Oh, bloody no. You go and do *this*!'

'It's the only way to get us *all* out.'

'The zombies too?'

'All.'

'And you won't settle for less?'

'I would—if there wasn't a chance to do more.'

'You call this a chance? How the hell does it help, anyway?' Collier locked his fingers together to stop them twitching. His body felt cold with sweat.

She said apologetically, 'I'd rather not lay it out for you, darling. You're so much more effective when you don't have to pretend. Truly. Your face was worth rubies when I baited Wenczel just now. One look and Delicata knew we weren't acting out a put-up job.'

She was lying on her bed, hands behind her head. Willie sat on the edge. Collier and Dinah sat side by side on Dinah's bed, facing them.

Collier wiped a hand over his damp face. His anger, an anger that stemmed from shock, seemed to drain suddenly away, leaving him limp and a little woolly-headed.

Willie had not spoken since the guards had herded them into the commonroom for the night. He said to Collier in a neutral voice, 'You're alive now because the Princess wouldn't settle for less once before. Remember?'

Collier nodded wearily. 'All right. I know. But is *she* going to be alive by this time tomorrow night?'

'Stop that.' Modesty lifted her head a little. 'Keep your imagination starved, Steve.'

Dinah said in a quiet voice, 'I'm too scared and too con-fused to know what I think about anything. I just figure you ought to quit beating Modesty over the head, Steve.'

'So do I,' Modesty said amiably. 'Now listen, I'm going along that aqueduct as soon as it's really dark outside, and I'll be gone quite a while. You carry on with the bow, Willie love. Steve, maybe you could start fixing a hilt on that other knife-blade Willie picked up. He'll show you how. Oh, and don't forget to show a bit of a limp tomorrow or Delicata might start wondering if you faked that fall this evening.'

Willie leaned forward and touched Dinah's knee. 'Reckon you could bind the edges of the sling with a bit of leather thong, love? I got a fish-bone for making holes.'

'Sure, Willie. Get me started and I'll manage.' Dinah spoke as if her thoughts were elsewhere. Her face was drawn and tired. After a little pause she went on, 'I don't know if this is good or bad, but you'd better hear it. I'm going to make the strike tomorrow.'

'Find the loot?' Collier stared at her. 'How do you know?'

'I felt it tugging a little. It's just outside that last strip I covered today. In a corner of the forum area, as near as I could figure.'

There was a silence. Modesty said, 'Is it deep?'

'No . . . I don't think I'd have felt the tug if it was deep. What do you want me to do?'

Modesty sat up and swung her feet to the ground, her face thoughtful. After a few moments she said, 'Don't hide any-thing, Dinah. Make the strike. But fix things so you make it . . . let's see. Just before six tomorrow. If you've had to cover the area before then, say you want to double-check or some-thing.'

Collier's heart jumped a little. Just before six . . . that would be shortly before the duel. It would distract Delicata, over-ride everything else——

'It won't put Delicata out of stride,' Modesty went on. She was staring into space, and seemed to be thinking aloud. 'He's not likely to start digging right away, just before dusk . . . especially if you tell him it's pretty deep, Dinah. Yes, do that.

He'll be well enough pleased to know you've found it. Extra spice for the evening's amusement.'

Collier felt his stomach heave, and clenched his teeth against the wave of nausea. He said, 'Why tell Delicata anyway?'

'Because it will focus everyone's attention away from us overnight. They'll think of little else. And because Delicata will probably set a man to guard the forum area, mainly to needle Gabriel by implying mistrust. That means one guard less elsewhere, which might help us.'

Dinah said, 'Gabriel will want to set up lamps and have everyone start digging all night.'

Modesty looked at Collier. 'Yes. But Delicata won't, will he? He knows from Presteign that he's got a couple of weeks to play with before anyone comes looking for us. And once the treasure's lifted he has to hand over control to Gabriel. The way I read Delicata, he'll want to have his fun first.'

Collier said tiredly. 'His fun. Yes. I'm sure you're right.'

Nobody spoke for a while. Collier found Willie Garvin's eyes on him. The gaze moved to Dinah then back to Collier in a silent message. Collier nodded and stood up, taking Dinah's hand. With an effort he spoke in some semblance of the manner that had belonged to him what seemed a lifetime ago: 'Well . . . I'm going to have a bath. And Miss Pilgrim is awarded the ineffable privilege of scouring my back. Small sachets of the used sand will later be on sale to admirers at fourpence each.'

Dinah made a little sound that began as a laugh and ended as a sob. She said quickly, 'I'm sorry,' then stood up and moved slowly away with Collier, holding his hand.

Modesty lay back on the bed again and closed her eyes. She said, wonderingly, 'You've got to hand it to them, Willie. I'd like to think I could do as well if I was starting from scratch.'

He did not answer, and when she opened her eyes she saw that he had not heard her, but was staring blankly at the ground. After a while he said, 'It doesn't get us anywhere, taking the heat off me and switching it straight on you, Princess.'

'Don't be thick, Willie. It's much better this way. Wenczel doesn't have any p.d. over me.'

He looked at her. 'The sword's his weapon. Wenczel lives for it. You only play at it, Princess. He's going to be better than anyone you've ever met.'

'A better fencer, yes. Just figure how that limits him.'

Very slowly the lines of Willie Garvin's face relaxed, and a speculative glint replaced the deep anxiety in his eyes. 'Ye-e-es . . .' he said thoughtfully. His mind raced suddenly, evaluating a dozen possibilities her words had shown him. 'Yes, by God.' He started to smile, then caught his lower lip in his teeth and frowned. 'But that bloody steel jacket, Princess. It gives him a hell of an edge. You reckon you can take him?'

She said simply, 'I haven't thought about whether I must.'

He nodded. Perhaps this was the quality above all others in her that made him proud to sit at her feet. It was a quality rarely needed, except in a killing crunch like this. Others might not admire it. They had never been in a killing crunch. He said, 'It's a double shot isn't it? There's something else?'

Her face changed again. A brilliant smile, sparkling, almost mischievous. For the moment it swept away all the burden of doubt that lay upon him. 'There's something else all right, Willie love.' She closed one eyelid, and punched his arm gently. 'If I've added things up right, we're all going to be out of here tomorrow night.'

'All?'

'Yes.' Her eyes narrowed and she stopped smiling. 'We're leaving nobody for Delicata. Nobody, by God. Now, this is how it works . . .'

She laid it out for him. He schooled himself to listen objectively, without emotional reaction. Collier would have thought the plan mad. Willie Garvin could see four points on which it might fail. He knew that Modesty was aware of those points. He also knew that failure was far less likely than it might seem. Three points turned upon how particular people would behave under given circumstances—Delicata, McWhirter, Skeet Lowry. That was a matter of judgment, based on observation, intuition, and simple psychology.

Willie thought it through, and decided that her assessment was right on all three points. The fourth point of possible failure was simple and brutal. It turned on whether Modesty Blaise would kill Wenczel, or Wenczel would kill Modesty Blaise.

Thirty minutes later she lowered herself into the narrow aqueduct. This time she wore clothes and had dirtied her face for night work. There would be plenty of time to clean up before morning.

Only two branches joined the aqueduct. She kept to the main channel, as she had done before, slithering forward in the blackness, pausing to rest for thirty seconds in every two minutes.

At last the total darkness took on a different quality, and she saw ahead a few bright stars in a small patch of black sky. The channel debouched into a thin natural gully, with the remains of some brickwork which had once guided the trickle of river-water into the system made by the builders of Mus.

As she stood up in the chill night air, the sudden sense of freedom was overwhelming. She waited for the emotion to pass, then began to move carefully along the flank of the mountain, the outer side of the escarpment which enclosed Mus.

The reconnaissance lasted two hours, for she moved slowly and with infinite care. The airstrip was unguarded. That fact might not obtain when the Cessna was grounded there overnight. One guard was mounted on the valley entrance. She waited for an hour to discover when he would be relieved. The change was made at midnight. She had no watch, and no need of one. Her sense of time, like her sense of direction, was uncannily sure.

A hundred yards from the valley entrance she found a very large cave. It had presumably been used as a dump for stores when Tangye's expedition first arrived, before the access to the valley had been fully cleared. It was still used as a petrol store. In the moonlight reflected through the wide entrance she could see the stack of thirty-gallon drums. There were forty-two of them.

Beside the drums was a hand-operated pump on wheels, a stack of timbers, some coils of nylon rope, and a pile of folded sheets in very light rubberised nylon with eyelet holes round the edges. Tangye had evidently planned to set up temporary awnings so that his people could have shade while working. Delicata was less considerate. There was also a trolley, or perhaps a trailer, and in the darkness she examined this as closely as possible, a new thought taking shape in her mind.

It was a trolley, a flat triangular platform mounted on three wheels with desert tyres. The two rear wheels were large, the front wheel was smaller and mounted beneath a tiller steering bar. Between the strong angle-irons of light alloy which joined to form the apex of the triangle she found the base of a long hollow pipe, like a metal scaffold pole. It was made of the same light alloy as the chassis of the trolley. The base of the pipe pivoted on a steel pin between the angle irons, and its twelve-foot length could be raised to an upright position, or to any angle above the horizontal, and fixed there by bracing bars.

It was only when she felt the other end of the metal pipe, and found the block and pulley there, that she realised the trolley served an ingenious double purpose. It was a simple mobile derrick. With the arm raised, cargo could be swung easily from the Cessna to the trolley, moved to its place of storage, and lifted safely down.

She stood thinking in the darkness, rearranging a dozen

factors in her mind. Yes . . . Willie would be in his element with this.

The return journey this time was easier than on her first exploration of the aqueduct, for now she could move head-first.

When she emerged, Willie was squatting near the hole with his back to the wall, the limb of the bow in his hands, using a rough piece of mud brick as a rasp to complete the shaping. As he stood up and helped her rise from the hole, Collier and Dinah came across from the bed where they had been sitting and working.

Modesty said, 'There's even a bonus with it, Willie. Maybe we're coming into a run of luck at last.'

Collier stopped himself asking a question. She would tell him anything she wanted him to know. When she stripped off her clothes he took them from her and moved away to start beating and brushing the dust out with a few thin dry twigs he had gathered. Dinah helped Modesty take a sand-bath. Willie continued work on the bow.

Modesty said softly to Dinah, 'Don't feel shut out. It's better if you and Steve don't know everything we're trying to do. That may not make sense to you now, but it's true. Just try to believe that Willie and I will do what's best. For all of us, pet.'

The unexpected endearment touched Dinah more deeply than she would have believed possible. She felt suddenly close to Modesty Blaise for the first time, close in an intuitive female way that not even Willie Garvin could ever know.

'I don't feel shut out,' she said. 'I just wish I wasn't so much of a passenger.'

'Passenger? My God, you found the aqueduct. Passengers we'll have plenty of. But not you.' Modesty paused, then went on slowly. 'I'm going to need you, Dinah. Try to help Steve as much as you can, all the way through. He's frightened for me, and he's wearing a little thin. The best way you can help is by leaning on him.'

'I do that now. He's awfully good.'

'I know. Lean a little harder. I don't want him to think about tomorrow.'

Dinah remembered the sour metallic smell of Wenczel; the cold singing sound of his sword. 'I don't want to think about it myself,' she said dry-mouthed.

Through the hot hours of the morning there was a strong undercurrent of tension in the valley. McWhirter was grinning and verbose as he walked bouncily from one working party to another, his crumpled jacket flapping. Gabriel was as taciturn as ever, but looked coldly satisfied. Delicata had an air of lazy contentment, like a cat toying with a crippled mouse.

Modesty and Willie were switched to each other's working party, to separate her from Wenczel. The brain-washed prisoners were nervous. The Algerian guards were intrigued and a little excited at the way in which the monotony was to be broken.

Collier suffered only an hour of Delicata's company and was then sent to join Wenczel's party. Dinah started work on the day's location area by pacing cross-sections instead of the usual lengthwise strips, and Gabriel raised no objection. That was another small bonus. It meant she would reach the corner of the forum towards the day's end.

There came the midday break.

Except for sleeping, Mrs. Tangye had moved out of the smaller room now, leaving it for the four strangers. Collier sat grinding the edge of the knife he had made. Willie Garvin was shaping vanes for the two arrows, cutting them from a moon of thin plastic ripped from the peak of a desert cap which had belonged to one of Tangye's men. He would have preferred turkey feathers for the fletching; he would have preferred many impossible things.

Dinah sat beside Collier, patiently twisting long linen threads from a jacket which had also been commandeered from Tangye's group. Willie had decided against nylon for the bowstring. There was too much stretch in it, which made for loss of power. Hemp would have been best of all, but linen was a good second best.

Modesty sat on her bed cross-legged. She seemed to be asleep except that her eyes were open. They did not blink. The pupils were huge. Her breathing was so slow that it was hard to detect the rise and fall of her breasts.

Collier had found the combination of her physical presence and mental absence a little eerie at first. But after the first ten minutes he had grown used to it. Looking at her face he saw the slowly increasing serenity, the tranquillity of a mind cleansed of all stress and burdens. Apparently there was no fear of disturbing her, for Willie talked casually as he worked, paying no heed to her. His conversation seemed unforced. He talked of ordinary things.

After an hour Modesty drew in a long slow breath and stirred. Her eyes focused. She stretched, sighed, and lay down on her face on the bed.

'Let's have a session of the magic fingers, Willie love.'

'Sure, Princess.' For half an hour he probed and kneaded with assured skill, his fingers coaxing every muscle to supple efficiency.

At last she said, 'That's fine. How about the fletching?'

'I'm just going to glue the vanes on. They'll be set by this evening.'

Last night, in the early hours, Collier had woken from a nightmarish sleep to find Willie crouched over a tiny fire he had made by coaxing a spark from flint and iron. He was boiling ancient fragments of animal bone in half a mug of water.

Now, twelve hours later, there was a thin film of glue set hard in the bottom of the mug. Collier watched as Willie knelt with a little ball of dry wool from one of the blankets and began to strike a flint with one of his hoarded pieces of iron.

'I didn't think you'd get any glue out of those bones,' Collier said. 'They were too old. Dried out.'

'Only the fat gone. Saved me getting rid of it first.' Willie put a few drops of water in the mug and fed the tiny flame with shreds of dry twig.

Ten minutes later three vanes were glued in position an inch forward of the butt of each arrow. When he was satisfied Willie went out and laid the arrows carefully across two stones in the aqueduct where he had hidden the rest of his primitive armaments.

He returned, stretched out on Mrs. Tangye's bed, and picked up a tattered magazine Skeet Lowry had left behind two days earlier. For a while he frowned over a crossword puzzle, then said, 'How many S's in possession, Princess?'

Her brow wrinkled. 'I don't know much about spelling, but I know what I like. Three's enough, surely?'

'Well, it fits okay with three. But that makes five-across E something L. What's a night bird spelt E something L?'

Modesty looked at Collier. 'There isn't one, is there?'

He felt a spurt of irrational anger and said, 'I'm not passionately interested in orthography at this moment, or even ornithology. I can't think why. Perhaps it's the weather.'

Her smile was mischievous. 'Go on, get angry some more, Steve. I love it when you're scathing.'

'For God's sake don't baby me!'

'All right. But you might help a little. *Are* there three S's in possession?'

He stared at her dazedly. Dinah said. 'I guess we don't understand something, Modesty.'

Willie rolled on his side. 'Adrenalin fatigue,' he said. 'You sit fretting, and you use up more juice than running upstairs every five minutes. We'd rather do crossword puzzles and save the juice, that's all. Now, 'ave you got any night birds in Canada, love? Any you spell E something L?'

The tension grew sharper as the long afternoon wore on. At

a little before six there was a sudden hubbub of excitement from the forum area. Modesty was in the working party nearby. She saw Gabriel, McWhirter and Delicata gathered about Dinah. Wenczel came running across.

She could hear scraps of an altercation between Gabriel and Delicata. The big man was laughing. Gabriel was bristling.

'. . . rig lamps and we can start digging tonight!'

'. . . gulping again, Gabriel. No, no . . . we'll begin tomorrow.' Something said with a splutter of laughter.

At last an angry shrug from Gabriel. She saw Delicata glance towards her and heard his voice clearly now. 'Besides, we can't deprive Major Wenczel of his righteous satisfaction, can we? Nor me of mine.'

He moved towards Modesty, his long arms swinging, and halted in front of her. 'Rainbow's end, if Miss Pilgrim's talent may be trusted. Isn't that a splendid apéritif for the main course of the evening?' His smile was benign. 'You have an appointment, remember? Our Major Wenczel is going to waggle his sword about in you.'

18

THE sandy ground of the small oval arena was still warm from the day's sun. To her left, the huge bulk of Delicata sat on a low dais of stone, the smaller figure of Gabriel beside him. Gabriel's anger had passed now. He was enjoying himself.

To her right, on the opposite side of the oval, all the captives were grouped on the first two tiers. Dinah sat between Collier and Willie Garvin. Tangye and the others sat behind, not moving, not talking. It was hard to tell whether they had any clear idea of what was happening.

A little higher on the worn tiers were the Algerian guards. Some were sitting smoking. Two were standing, their submachine guns cocked.

It was unlikely that there had ever been gladiatorial combats in ancient Mus. The mixed and miniature population could never have sustained a true Roman circus. The arena had been used for sport, no doubt; races, cockfights, training and mock combat. Strange now to think that she and Wenczel might well be the first ever to meet here in a death-duel.

McWhirter appeared at the far end with an épée. She took off her boots, then her slacks and shirt. For this fight she preferred to be barefoot; a boot could slip on the thin layer of sand that covered the baked ground. As for the rest . . . that was something else.

She unclipped her bra, and stood wearing only the plain black briefs. McWhirter halted at a careful distance from her, staring. 'Is it targets you're offering him then?'

She did not answer. He looked at her curiously and said, 'Ye'll not distract Wenczel.'

Her voice held distant contempt. 'I don't want cloth fibres

driven into a wound.' It was a sound enough excuse. In the old days of duelling men had died from the poison set up by dirty cloth fibres, and surgeons had advised contestants to strip to the waist for that reason.

McWhirter gave an incredulous cackle. 'Holy God! D'ye have some notion this is going to stop at first blood? He'll make a colander of you, lassie!'

She looked through him, yet saw that his eyes were lingering on her naked torso and his face held a hint of desire. She had judged McWhirter as being at the sexual level of a schoolboy. His manner now confirmed it. A crude eagerness to touch her warred with some long-forgotten prohibition within him—a Presbyterian boyhood, perhaps.

He held out the épée to her, gripping the hilt so that she had to take it by the blade, then stepped quickly back out of distance. McWhirter was a cautious man. Four paces was the closest he ever allowed himself to come to Modesty Blaise or Willie Garvin unless they were at gunpoint.

'Och, it's a waste o' good flesh in some ways,' he said, grinning. 'But I'll be glad to watch you go, Blaise. There's an awful lot to be paid for.' His grin twisted with sudden malice and he turned away to join Gabriel and Delicata on the seat of the dais.

The handle of the épée was orthopaedic in design, moulded so that the fingers closed about it like a pistol grip. She tried the balance, and at once the sword came alive as if it were an extension of her arm.

She let the point rest lightly on the ground and waited, detached. There was nothing to think about. For what it was worth, her strategy was already decided. The tactics would have to wait until she had taken Wenczel's measure.

He would be a better swordsman, that was certain, and he would have the advantage of reach. She hoped that his pride might be strong enough to withstand Delicata's order to wear the sleeveless jacket of featherlight chain mail, but this hope was minimal.

She held two advantages. One was that Wenczel would never try to kill her in the first few engagements. This whole prospect, the use of the sword for killing in a duel, was a fanatical desire in him. He would want to savour it, to use all his skill in slowly, delicately reducing her by small wounds to a bloodied and weakened condition before making the final thrust. For Wenczel, this would be like the prolonged love-play that leads to the ultimate climax.

So at least she would gain time; time to exploit her second advantage, which lay in Wenczel's conception of fencing as an art form. By instinct he would tend to fence according to the rules by which he had fenced all his life. To brawl with swords would disgust and infuriate him.

It would not disgust Modesty. Wenczel might well have realised that, and be alert for any unorthodox trickery. Yet this in itself would lay some degree of inhibition on him.

She heard McWhirter say 'Ah!'

Wenczel was passing between the broken stone pillars which had once framed the entrance to the arena. He wore white breeches, fencing shoes, and a superb tunic of fine mesh steel reaching to his thighs. The twin of Modesty's épée was in his right hand.

On the flaking stone seats of the first tier, Dinah whispered, 'What's happening?' Her hand groped for Willie's and found it.

'Wenczel,' he said, barely moving his lips. 'Any minute now. Don't talk, love.'

On her other side, Collier dragged his gaze away from the figures in the arena for a stricken glance at her tense, puckered face. Every nerve in his body was jumping. He felt sick and bloodless. For a moment he almost envied Dinah her blindness. To watch this was going to be torment, yet it was impossible not to watch. Perhaps for that reason it was even more horrible for Dinah—hearing the sounds, feeling the tension, aware of every gasp or intake of breath from those watching around her, yet unable to see, not knowing, only able to imagine. Collier was aware that his own imagination had reduced him to shuddering nausea already.

He looked at Modesty again. The lines of her athlete's body were firm and beautiful. There was little rise and fall to the taut breasts even as she moved, walking now towards the centre of the arena.

Willie Garvin was sitting quite still, one hand resting on his knee. Dinah's hand was enveloped in the other. His eyes were on Modesty Blaise, and his face was empty of all emotion.

In the arena Wenczel halted ten paces from Modesty, faced the dais and raised the épée vertically in front of him in a flamboyant salute, then turned to salute Modesty in the same way. If her nakedness surprised him, his face showed no reaction whatever.

She said quietly but distinctly, in a voice that carried to every ear, 'Lovely style. Now try sticking it up your arse.'

McWhirter giggled. Delicata shook with merriment.

Collier felt brief bewilderment; then he realised that her crudeness was calculated. An insult to the sword was more likely to unbalance Wenczel than an insult to himself.

Modesty saw the arrogant face clench with anger. Then it relaxed, and Wenczel was studying her body impersonally, analytically, like a surgeon studying the working area of an operation.

Delicata's deep rich voice said, 'Please don't keep us waiting.'

Wenczel raised his blade and dropped into the on-guard position. Modesty followed him. The blades crossed.

There is, in fencing, a flow of awareness between the adversaries that comes with the first contact of the blades, as if electric current had passed. In the brief instant of that first feathery engagement Modesty knew that she faced a master whose skill was complete.

Then there was no more time for thought. Wenczel had

attacked with a speed and ferocity that gave her no chance to riposte. Her parries were daringly economical, the barest deflection of his blade. She could afford no more, for his attacks on the blade, changes of engagement and redoubles were so blindingly swift that she could only give ground steadily, defending, keeping the fencing measure as wide as possible between them.

On the piste, she would already have been driven over the rear limit. Here there was no regulation limit, but there was the low wall at the end of the oval, and she knew it must be close now. She stood her ground against Wenczel's darting blade.

Lunge, reprise, redoublement, recovery—his recovery was a miracle, a fluent snapping back to the on-guard position, effortless, as if drawn by a spring. She gave ground again before a sudden balestra, a two-footed jump forward, and in the smooth following lunge it seemed that his body, arm and blade extended beyond all possibility.

Because she had thought herself out of distance her parry was fractionally late, and the sharp point of the triangular blade ripped across the outside of her thigh. Wenczel recovered and stepped back out of distance. He looked at the widening red line on her flesh, laughed abruptly, then turned and walked away, watching her over his shoulder.

Modesty flexed her leg. The muscle was unharmed. Her body glistening with sweat, she walked back to the centre of the arena, where Wenczel waited. She was not dissatisfied. In fighting with the épée it is the arm that takes most of the hits, the sword-arm. Wenczel had been trying for that, but she had at least forced him to draw first blood elsewhere. And she had emerged with only a deep scratch from a lunge intended to penetrate the muscle.

There was something more. Wenczel had been showing off, partly for his audience and partly to establish total domination by his speed. A good tactic in itself, but not for a long fight. No man could maintain that degree of speed. Even so, if the fight continued in the orthodox pattern Wenczel would certainly kill her. But it was necessary, for her own designs, to let that pattern continue for a while and establish itself. Her task was to stay alive during that time.

She took up her position, and again the blades engaged. Wenczel began to play counter-time, the basic tactic of the épée, using the intentionally uncovered feint or the half-lunge to draw her counter-attack stop-hit, so that he could take the blade and attack. But now that the pace had slackened a little her combat brain was able to work above the level of instinct.

She played carefully with his blade, appraising, assessing, spotting the half-lunge, never allowing herself to be drawn. When he began to use the beat, to exploit his advantage of strength by tiring her, she took up a line with hand and blade well out to sixte, so that he found difficulty in making contact.

She learned a great deal about Wenczel during this phase, and above all she discovered his cadence, his natural speed in a sequence of movements as opposed to his speed-tactic in the first phase.

On the broad stone steps, Stephen Collier had retched and almost been sick during the first terrifying attack. Now he sat drawn and sweating, fingernails driving into his clenched hands.

Dinah Pilgrim was trying to blot out the pictures that kept forming in her mind from the clash of the blades, the little wordless sounds from Steve, the changes in Willie's breathing. The hand Willie Garvin held was hurting badly, for he was almost crushing it. She did not tell him. The pain helped to blur her imaginings.

Not a muscle of Willie's face had moved, but now there was the slightest glint of excitement in his eyes. The first onslaught had frightened him, but that was past. The longer the fight continued, the better the chances for Modesty. Wenczel might be the greatest fencer ever, but fencing was only a form

235

of combat. The great thing in combat was to know your enemy. And to Willie Garvin it was axiomatic that Modesty would know more of Wenczel in two minutes than he would know of her in two weeks.

Wenczel attacked again, this time with cold and beautiful precision. Modesty gave ground, but now the retreat was intermittent and controlled. Her ripostes were rare, and more for experiment than for business. With her trunk naked, she would be mad to commit herself rashly, especially when her only targets were Wenczel's head and limbs.

This was a long elegant phrase in which Wenczel used every classic stroke. By her own response she encouraged him, knowing that he was exulting in the artistry of it. Twice his point got home. They would have been mere touches on the piste, with buttoned point against a protective plastron; but not so here. When she at last sprang back out of distance there was a small round flower of blood above her right breast and an ugly gouge along her ribs.

He surveyed her for a moment through narrowed eyes, a hint of grudging respect on the haughty face. Then he moved in on guard, and with something new in his demeanour. Wenczel was getting down to business.

She engaged, and for the first time went into the attack, taking him marginally by surprise. Her move was a prise de fer, an envelopment of his blade. Against his strength of wrist and fingers it should have been a bad tactic, but in all combat movements there is a moment of truth, a moment of unity when mind and muscle and intention combine irresistibly.

Her narrowly circling forte corkscrewed down the foible of his blade, gathering it, swinging his point wide. His reaction was against instinct, for it was against the rules; but it was just quick enough. To go back would have left him wide open to a lunge. He went forward, in the forbidden corp-à-corps, their bodies almost touching.

For a moment they were perfectly still, faces inches apart,

blades locked at the pommels and pointing vertically up. It was then that Modesty Blaise lifted her knee and hit him very hard in the crotch.

She knew, as the blow landed, that it was at best a partial success. Wenczel was wearing a light box of some kind, probably plastic. She felt it give as her knee drove home.

He gasped and thrust her away with all his strength, falling into a low crouch but with his blade still in line. She attacked fiercely, but he retreated, parrying, parrying with minimum movement, his face shining with the sweat of pain, concentrating solely on guarding his head and limbs. Twice she could have run him through the body but for the mesh jacket protecting his trunk.

After ten seconds of driving attack she knew that her throw had failed. The shock and the pain were ebbing. Wenczel was recovering. If she continued, he would take her with a stop-hit or a riposte.

Stephen Collier whispered, 'Oh, my God . . .'

Willie Garvin said tautly, 'Shut your mouth.' Then, gently, to Dinah, 'It's all right, she's still there.'

In the arena, Modesty kept up a steady but more wary pressure. Wenczel was defending with greater ease now. The mask of pain was changing to one of murderous hatred. Soon, she knew, he would go over to the attack, this time to kill her. There would be no more exhibition fencing, no more pretty play.

She could feel Wenczel's renewed confidence, feel it in his blade. There was good reason for it. He knew she had fought long, hard and exhaustingly to establish a pattern of salle swordplay so that in the end she could take him unawares with a rough-house trick. It had failed. So now she would quickly crack. The reaction was psychologically inevitable. Wenczel had no vestige of doubt about it.

If he could have taken his gaze from her blade and body for a moment he might have been less certain. The blue-black eyes held neither despair nor defiance, only a limitless will to endure, to outlast, to begin all over again. And then, if need be, again.

He attacked savagely. She was driven back . . . and suddenly realised that Wenczel was developing a habit. Three times within twenty seconds he had lunged in sixte. All her knowledge of his personality ran through the fighting computer of her mind, and told her why. He was out for the kill, and because he was Wenczel the kill was to be made with classic perfection—a lunge penetrating the heart, a story-book finish.

She knew now that no riposte or stop-hit she could make would succeed. He was too good. Her only hope of reaching him was to secure his point—in her own body.

So be it. In the salle, only Wenczel's hit, the first hit, would count. Here, the hit that counted would be the hit that killed.

He feinted in the low line and she made a semi-circular parry to the line of octave, but delaying it by a fraction and then using sudden needless pressure as if from panic. Wenczel disengaged smoothly into sixte.

'Hélà!' The panting shout of triumph broke from him as his whole body extended in a perfect lunge for the heart. And it was then, in the last instant, that she turned slightly in co-ordination with the lunge and took his point in the upper part of her sword arm, four inches below the shoulder.

The steel bit into bone and the blade curved in an upward arc. She leaned into the thrust, crouched, bringing her left shoulder round a little, the épée dropping from her right hand. For once Wenczel did not make his usual swift and immaculate recovery. He held the lunge, staring, new resentment burning in his eyes as he realised that his classic kill had failed; that she was only wounded and disarmed; that the end now would have to be simple butchery.

He was still staring when she caught the hilt of her falling épée in her left hand and drove the blade forward, angling upwards, so that the point went in above the high collar of his mesh jacket, in under the chin and up into the brain.

Still extended in the lunge, Wenczel fell sideways. His

hand, locked on the épée, wrenched the point from her shoulder, and his fall dragged her own deep-driven épée from her grasp. His legs twitched in one fierce convulsion, and then he lay still.

The only sound was the whisper of wind-blown sand across the floor of the arena. The whole scene, grotesque and unreal, became a silent tableau.

Dinah felt Steve Collier shivering beside her, heard the moan of a long indrawn breath in his throat. Willie's voice whispered exultantly, 'It's over, love. She 'ad to take one in the arm. *But she's killed the bastard!*'

On the dais, Delicata began to shake, then to chuckle, and finally his head went back in a booming laugh. His mirth was wholly genuine. Gabriel turned lizard eyes upon him and said viciously, 'Is it *funny* to lose Wenczel, you crazy fool?'

Delicata's face was creased with merriment, and he was still gasping a little as he spoke. 'Why not? Oh, what an epic surprise! Such moments are surely the spice of life, Gabriel.'

'Wenczel's *dead*!'

'You're a shrewd observer. He wasn't good enough, was he? Oh dear, oh dear, how humiliating for him.' Delicata stopped wheezing and looked at Gabriel with a whimsical air. 'All things considered, I feel very little sense of loss. Major Wenczel's value to us decreased as our project prospered. I had no further use for him myself. Had you?'

Gabriel turned his head towards the arena. 'All right,' he said slowly. 'What about Blaise?'

She stood with her hand clamped over the wound in her upper arm, looking down at Wenczel. The wound was deep but small, not bleeding fast. She swayed a little, as if from reaction, and her ears strained for Delicata's reply. His voice came clearly in the silence.

'Ah, yes. Miss Blaise. We must think anew about her, mustn't we? But do let us avoid any anti-climax to this splendid drama. Tomorrow is another day. Suppose she were towed at speed behind a Land Rover, h'mm? It's only a suggestion of course . . .'

His voice flowed on. Modesty turned and began to walk back to where she had left her clothes. Her feet dragged, and she staggered a little. McWhirter jumped down hastily from the dais and started towards her with springy strides. His face held a look of prurient anticipation.

Steve Collier started to rise. Willie reached across, caught his arm in an iron grip and dragged him down. Collier said savagely. 'Let me go to her, damn you—she's hurt!' Willie's grip did not relax. He spoke in a whisper without moving his lips. *'Keep still. This is why she did it!'*

Collier sat back limply, his mind in chaos, wondering if he had gone mad. Something was happening that he could not see. Or something was going to happen. And this was why she had fought Wenczel. *This?* But what? It made no sense. Even if it made some kind of sense that was beyond him, it was still unbelievable.

He saw Modesty reach her clothes, bend slowly and pick up her shirt. A thin stream of blood ran down her arm. Her breast, thigh and ribs were already smeared with blood from the minor wounds. She swayed, recovered, swayed again. As McWhirter reached her she crumpled to her knees, falling against him. He caught at her, his hands steadying her but moving eagerly on her flesh, pressing against her breasts. She pawed weakly at him, trying to get to her feet.

McWhirter did not help her up. His hands were clamped on her body now and he was looking down at her. Gabriel called in a menacing voice, 'McWhirter!'

Holding her for a moment longer McWhirter said, 'It'll be different tomorrow, clever lassie.' He put a hand against her face and gave a shove that sent her sprawling, then turned and strode briskly away, grinning a little to himself.

Modesty got slowly to her knees, still holding her bundled shirt. Her body was bowed and her head hung down as if with exhaustion.

Delicata called across the arena to the guards, 'Ne tirez pas.' Then, jovially, 'You can give her a hand, Garvin. And make sure she gets a comfortable night. We have a full and varied programme tomorrow.'

19

It was an hour since the commonroom door had closed upon them. Modesty sat on her bed, moving her arm gently to keep it from stiffening. Willie Garvin had cleaned her wounds and bandaged the deep one on her arm with a strip of shirt he had boiled. There was ample water. One third of the ration was put into the commonroom each evening with the ration of food. Five pints each for twelve people, in two plastic jerricans.

Nobody had drunk any of the water ration that evening, except Modesty, and nobody had eaten. Willie had forbidden Tangye and his team with a ferocity that quelled all thought of protest. He had offered no explanation. Now he was kneeling beside Dinah's bed. McWhirter's black notebook was open in front of him, and he held the pencil that slotted into the spine of the book. For thirty minutes he had been practising to imitate the neat, cramped writing. The margins of the magazine Skeet Lowry had left were covered with it.

McWhirter's notebook was written up in abbreviated longhand. The earlier pages contained a detailed plan of the whole operation, with spaces left for adjustments and comments as each stage was completed. The later pages were in the form of a daily situation report.

Collier sat a little hunched, his elbows on his knees, hands hanging limply. He felt as if all his nerves had been destroyed, leaving him numb and empty. He said slowly, 'You engineered the fight with Wenczel . . . for that?' His eyes moved to the notebook.

Modesty rotated her arm and shoulder. Her body felt sore, and the wound in her arm was beginning to throb, but there was no weariness in her. She said, 'It was the only way I could ever hope to get close enough to McWhirter.'

He shook his head as if to clear it. 'But you couldn't *know* he'd maul you . . .'

'Yes I could. He has an adolescent urge to paw me about. He did it that first night, when we were searched. I knew if I was stripped, and if I played shaky at the end of the fight, he'd come and get his hands on me.' She made a grimace. 'I wasn't too happy about having to take a hit in the arm at the end, but that couldn't be helped once the knee-jab failed. Anyway, it made a good excuse for staggering about a bit.'

Collier kept looking at her blankly. He felt as if something had broken inside him. 'But . . .' he said, and shook his head again, 'but you couldn't know that you'd *win*.' She looked with compassion at his haggard face, then leaned forward and took it between her hands. 'I know now, and that's all that matters. Come on, darling. Snap out of it. One more big heave and we're free-wheeling home.'

Willie knelt up and looked at what he had written in the notebook. There was an early page which referred to the plan of action after the treasure had been raised. It read: *G. takes over. Prep. and execute rock-fall burial Tangye and pty. (Recce suitable sit. prior)*.

Here a space had been left, and at the top of the space came the insertion: *M.B. and pty? Ck. with G. on alternative dispsl.*

The next entry might have been in the original or an insertion. It read: *Dispsl. S.L. and Cessna. T-bomb for expl. in transit.*

Willie Garvin had made that entry with considerable skill. He passed the notebook to Modesty and began to burn the magazine on the little fire he had made for boiling water. She studied the forgery carefully, then smiled. 'That's fine, Willie love.'

Collier said, 'What happens when McWhirter misses his notebook. Suppose he guesses you picked his pocket?'

It was Dinah who answered, sitting beside him. She said

243

quietly, 'Would you guess, Steve—in a million years? After that fight, and Modesty with a hole in her arm? No. McWhirter will look all over for it. But not here.'

'I got a clever girl there,' Willie said with pride. 'Beautiful, sexy, and clever with it. I'm a great picker.'

Dinah ran her hands down her cheeks. 'You're kidding,' she said. 'I've shrunk too much to be beautiful. My bust's shrunk too, so I can't even look sexy.'

Willie grinned. 'You're fine,' he said gently. ' "... *The little hills rejoice on every side.*" Psalm 65, verse 11.'

It was half an hour later when they heard the distant sound of the Cessna landing on the strip beyond the valley entrance. Another hour passed. The guards would be unloading, securing the aircraft with ropes against the steady wind that blew across the barren plain, a wind that could rise suddenly to a fierce gust. They would be filling the tanks. Modesty knew now that the tanks were topped up on landing; when Skeet Lowry had gone out of the commonroom two mornings ago she had heard the take-off only ten minutes later. That would be the time needed to put the plugs in—the plugs that were held by Delicata to keep the plane immobilised.

Skeet Lowry entered. The door closed behind him and there came the sound of the steel bars sliding into place. He strolled to an empty bed, put his bed-roll down on it, and lit a cigarette. His gaze roamed idly along the commonroom.

Modesty said, 'Hallo, Skeet.'

'Hi, ma'am.' He took out his pack of cigarettes and ambled along to where the four of them sat on the beds that Willie and Collier used. 'Smoke?'

They all took one. Skeet said with only vague interest. 'I hear you tangled with Wenczel, ma'am. Took him out, huh?'

She nodded. 'Took something else out too, Skeet. Ever seen McWhirter's notebook?'

He smiled faintly. 'Tired of seeing it. The guy writes down when someone blows their nose.'

Willie handed him the notebook, open. 'We mean the

inside. 'Ave a look. There's a bit might interest you.' Skeet's eyebrows lifted a fraction. He took the notebook and studied the page, lingering unhurriedly over the abbreviations. Then his face became suddenly expressionless, and he read the whole page through again. At last he looked up and said softly, 'Just shows. Third time I've worked for Presteign. Didn't reckon on a gold watch. Didn't reckon he'd finger me for the high-jump neither.'

Modesty said, 'We think this must be too big for him to leave any witnesses. Even you, Skeet.'

'I just quit.' He handed the notebook to her.

'You just found another job. You fly us out, Skeet. For twenty thousand dollars.'

He pondered, pinching his lower lip. 'Too risky, ma'am. I sure appreciate you giving me the word, but I never did like showing appreciation the hard way. Guess I'll just shuffle off tomorrow and not come back.'

She shook her head. 'We're breaking out in a couple of hours. It's all set and there'll be no noise. Twenty thousand dollars, Skeet, if you play it my way. If you don't, we rub you out here and now. Willie can handle the Cessna.'

Skeet Lowry sighed. He said, 'She won't fly ma'am. Delicata holds the plugs.'

'That's right.' Modesty inhaled on her cigarette. 'And you're carrying a spare set in your kit, Skeet. And a plug-spanner. You'd sooner lose an eye than let someone else control your plane, flying or grounded.'

To Collier's surprise a smile tugged at Skeet Lowry's lips. He gazed at Modesty for what seemed a long while, and said at last, 'Looks like you know me too well.'

'It looks just like that. A deal?'

'A deal, ma'am.'

Collier felt a sudden glow of relief expanding within him. He realised that the last words of this strange man had put betrayal beyond all possibility. Skeet Lowry's peculiar loyalty would be to Modesty Blaise now. She was picking up the tab.

The American exhaled a long feather of smoke and looked round the commonroom. Collier had the impression that he was about to ask a question, but Modesty stood up quickly, easing her shoulder, and said, 'There are one or two wrinkles that need ironing out. Walk a little with me, Skeet. I don't want to stiffen up.'

'Sure.' He strolled slowly away towards the door with her.

Willie said, 'Right. Now we start rigging a target. We can prop a bed up an' tie a wad of folded blankets to the springs. Get off your backside, Steve matey.'

Collier stood up. 'A target?' He could not think what Willie meant.

'A soft target. She's got to try the arrows in case the vanes need trimming, and she won't want to break 'em.'

It was ten minutes after midnight when Modesty Blaise emerged from the aqueduct into the cold chill of the desert night. She had made the journey at an easy pace, partly because of her wounded arm and partly because she was pushing the bow-stave and arrows ahead of her. In her pocket was a kongo Willie had shaped for her from a piece of hard wood.

Carefully she strung the bow. The limb was flat in section, with the outer side a little narrower than the compression side. The centre of the grip was an inch below the centre of the bow, which gave the balance she preferred. It was a beautiful piece of work. So were the two arrows. She marvelled that only one of them had needed a final touch of adjustment when she had tested them in the commonroom. Even for Willie Garvin this was a notable achievement with such crude tools and materials.

The test of the bow and arrows had also been a test of her wounded arm. It hurt when the muscle contracted, but there was still ample power.

The moon shed a pale light over the flat, stony ground as she moved round the curve of the escarpment. For a while she lay in the shadow of the mountain, watching the strip where the Cessna stood. She had allowed half an hour for this. If a guard did not move in half an hour, he was asleep.

He moved after ten minutes. She saw the flare of a match as he lit a cigarette, then he emerged from the shadow of the aircraft and began to stroll slowly towards the valley entrance which lay a hundred yards away to her right.

She moved along the face of the rock, on a converging path. When he had covered half the distance he was thirty paces from her. She nocked an arrow on the string. Her feet were a little astride, her left shoulder pointing directly at the target, her weight slightly forward. The man was no longer a silhouette now. She could see his profile clearly. As she raised the bow and drew it in one smooth movement she made a clicking noise with her tongue; a meaningless, puzzling noise.

The man turned and peered. She loosed instantly, and heard the soft thud of the arrow striking home. He sank to his knees, then fell forward. The submachine gun slung on his shoulder made a little noise as he hit the ground. She waited, the second arrow nocked on the string. He did not stir. Nobody moved in the valley entrance. After sixty seconds she moved forward warily.

The man was dead. The twenty-six inch arrow had driven through his chest, a little off-centre of the heart. She left his gun, for to use it meant noise, and noise meant failure. Moving back to the mountain wall, she edged slowly along towards the valley entrance.

It was unguarded. The dead man must have been covering both the entrance and the Cessna. She passed through the broad cleft. Five minutes later, keeping close to the irregular rock face, she saw the door that sealed the common-room. It lay directly ahead, facing her obliquely, for here the wall curved inwards.

A guard in a sheepskin jacket paced slowly back and forth, a Schmeisser MP 40 slung on one shoulder. After a little while she realised that he was alone. Before, whenever the door opened, there had been two guards present. It seemed that Delicata had taken one away to guard the location of the treasure.

The ground here was rock, and she was concerned about noise from the man's gun when he fell. For five minutes she waited, hoping that he might sit down for a spell, or unsling his gun and prop it against the wall.

His steady pacing continued. She had just decided that she would have to crawl in close, then make a final rush and use the kongo, when the man paused in his pacing and moved towards the door. He turned his head, pressed his ear to the door, and stood listening. Her arrow, loosed with the full power of the bow, slammed his body against the door as he died, its head penetrating an inch into the wood.

He sagged, dragging the arrow down. She reached him just as the arrowhead snapped off, and took his weight to ease him silently to the ground. The wound in her arm jumped with fierce twinges of pain. She ignored it, and drew the steel bars from their sockets.

Skeet Lowry was facing her when she opened the door. Beyond him the commonroom was in darkness. She whispered, 'Has Willie got them all set?'

His voice was a murmur. 'Got them scared rigid, ma'am. They'll do just like he's told them.'

She nodded and jerked her head. Skeet Lowry moved out and began to walk at an unhurried pace along the side of the rock face leading to the valley exit, his bed-roll under his arm.

Stephen Collier and Dinah followed. He was holding her hand. Modesty saw his eyes rest for a moment on the dead guard with the arrow sticking out of his back; then he looked at her and gave a little nod of grim approval. Without speaking, obedient to Willie's orders, he moved on.

Mrs. Tangye was holding her husband's arm as they walked. He had a gag tied round his mouth. Willie had decided that the old man's wandering mind was too much of a danger for

248

him to be allowed the power of speech. Behind the Tangyes came the other six members of their team, in pairs. They walked with almost ludicrous stealth, and their faces were taut with fear.

Willie Garvin brought up the rear. He carried a blanket-wrapped bundle lashed to his back and a four-gallon plastic jerrican of water in each hand. He winked at Modesty as he passed, then his face took on a glare of menace and he moved up to walk beside the little crocodile of zombies.

Modesty took the guard's Schmeisser, dragged him into the commonroom, left him there with her bow, then went out and barred the door.

Collier sat on the ground wondering how much longer fifteen minutes could last. That was the time needed by Skeet Lowry to unpeg his aircraft and screw the plugs in.

Tangye and his team were squatting on the ground in a small circle. Collier and Dinah were part of the circle. Every few moments Collier would glare round at the blank, scared faces with what he hoped was a look of unutterable menace. He knew that he should feel sorry for these people, but he had no capacity for it at this moment. He would feel sorry for them later. Nothing mattered now except that they should stay quiet and obedient. His nerves were screaming with impatience.

Beside him, Dinah had a blanket pulled about her, but he could still feel her shivering. He wanted to speak, but it was forbidden. Nobody had spoken a word since the exodus from the valley. Modesty and Willie were helping Skeet. There was nothing for anybody else to do except wait.

Five minutes or five weeks later, Modesty touched Collier's shoulder and gestured. The door of the Cessna stood open. For the first time she spoke, her voice a whisper. 'You and Dinah up front with Skeet.'

He nodded, and drew Dinah to her feet. The empty drums of water and petrol for the return trip had been lifted out of the plane. Even empty they were heavy. Collier, guiding Dinah up the step, wondered how Willie had managed it in near silence. Skeet Lowry sat at the controls. He gestured for Collier and Dinah to sit on the deck of the cockpit in the little space on his right.

Already the others were crowding aboard. Crowding was the word, Collier thought. The Cessna was supposed to carry a pilot and five passengers. Now it had to carry a pilot and twelve. *Twelve* . . . that was a hell of a load. He had not thought about it till now. With a stab of unease he wondered if they would ever get off the ground. There would be a fair safety margin above the normal loading, of course, but even so . . .

He shrugged mentally, and hunched up as the bodies crammed closer until they were packed like worms in a jar of bait. A lot of weight . . . but Modesty would have worked out all the problems with Skeet Lowry, and apparently Lowry was just about the best flyer in the business. It was bound to be all right.

The men beside him were half-crouched, unable to sit. Beyond them he heard the click of the closing door. Lowry sat gazing absently through the windshield. Collier fretted, wondering why the hell he didn't get started. Two minutes passed. Skeet Lowry stirred, and began to do mysterious things with the controls.

The sudden roar of the engine made Collier jump. He felt Dinah quiver beside him, and held her hand tightly, then craned his neck, trying to see Modesty. All he could see was the grubby shirt of the man crouched next to him, six inches from his eyes. Skeet sat watching his dials. Nothing happened. Collier wanted to scream. The sound of the engine would penetrate the valley. The guards would hear. Delicata would be roused. They would come charging out of the valley with guns.

Skeet Lowry glanced down at him and smiled faintly. 'Needs to be warmed up,' he said, lifting his voice above the noise of the engine. 'Oh, brother. She sure needs everything for this load.'

Collier nodded, with a smile like a snarl. Another thirty seconds passed. Skeet Lowry's hands moved. There came a bumping as the plane began to taxi forward. Collier exhaled a long breath. He visualised the ground ahead. It was flat and unbroken. There would be space for a fairly long take-off.

He looked at the pilot. Lowry's face was as passionless as ever, yet it held a blank intensity as if his nerves were reaching out through the sinews of the plane to make himself a part of it. The engine screamed and the bumping went on endlessly.

Collier found himself sweating. It was hot in the aircraft, and too much humanity was breathing too much air. He wondered sickly what would happen if the Cessna failed to take-off. Would they crash? Or just stop? Or——?

Dinah said in a voice that was a little shrill, 'We're off!'

He realised that the bumping had ceased. Looking up, he could see one or two stars through the windshield. By aligning a star on the upper edge he was able to tell that the plane was slowly climbing.

It was three minutes later when Skeet Lowry's hunched shoulders relaxed. He glanced down at Collier again, grinned suddenly, and called above the noise, 'Glad you guys lost a little weight.'

Something exploded within Collier, a wild, unimaginable joy. They were free. Delicata and Gabriel and the hard-faced men with guns were down there below, earthbound, helpless to hurt or torture or kill. Crammed tightly beside him, Dinah was pounding a small fist on his knee in the same sudden release of emotion.

He craned his neck again and yelled, 'Modesty!' Still he could not see her. Skeet Lowry touched his shoulder. When he turned, the pilot pointed down and said. 'No. She and Willie, they're walking.'

'*What?*' Collier tried to get to his feet. Lowry's hand pushed him down.

'The weight,' Lowry said, lifting his voice and speaking patiently, as if explaining to a child. 'Had to leave two. I said leave *four*, but she argues pretty tough. Man, if you'd felt that take-off you'd be real glad we didn't have an extra pack of cigarettes aboard.'

Collier screamed, '*But Christ Almighty, she's hurt!*'

Skeet Lowry shrugged. 'She's been hurt before. And Willie's there.' He patted his shirt pocket. 'Anyway, she's picking up the tab. Wrote a cheque on a page from that goddam notebook. And wrote some orders for you, when we land.'

Collier sank back, shaking. He felt a pain in his arm and realised that Dinah was gripping it, her nails digging in. When he looked at her face he saw that it was twisted with anguish and she was crying uncontrollably. Slowly he eased his arm about her and drew her head down on to his shoulder. Her palm beat on his chest with impotent bitterness and she cried, 'How much more? Oh for God's sake, Steve, how much more?'

He sighed and began gently stroking her brow. For him the moment of anger and protest had passed, leaving only emptiness. His lips were close to her ear. He said wearily, 'I don't know, sweetheart. As much more as they have to take, I suppose.'

The Cessna Skywagon had been gone for a full half hour before the distant voices from around the valley entrance faded and all movement ceased. Two men had picked up the dead guard from the airstrip. McWhirter, carrying a big flashlamp, had looked into the petrol store. There had been no search. Delicata's voice had been raised once, in a commanding shout that stilled the hubbub of voices.

Now all was quiet.

Modesty Blaise and Willie Garvin moved out from the narrow cleft beyond the store cave, where they had lain hidden. Willie carried the blanket bundle and the two jerricans of water. The blankets were wrapped about a square biscuit tin containing the whole of the evening ration of polythene-packaged food. There was also a large folded sheet of polythene that Willie had found on Professor Tangye's bed two days ago. He guessed that it had been used for handsorting precious fragments from sand and rubble during the first days of the dig.

Modesty carried the Schmeisser and two water bottles.

She had felt enormous relief as the Cessna droned away into the night. The dragging burden was lifted at last. She and Willie were on their own.

Delicata would be on the radio to Presteign by now. This did not worry her. Skeet Lowry was heading not for Algiers but for Tangier, and on arrival at the airport there Steve Collier would call Tarrant in London. He would also call the Moroccan Minister of Justice. Modesty had a villa on The Mountain in Tangier. She lived there for a part of every year. The Minister of Justice was a calm, intelligent man who had been a police inspector in Tangier when this was her headquarters. Even in the old Network days he had not been an enemy, for she was wise enough never to make trouble on her own doorstep but rather to abate it. Now he was a friend, and a powerful one.

Presteign would be too late to deal with Skeet Lowry, or Steve and Dinah, or the Tangye team.

The arm holding the Schmeisser throbbed sharply. In her free hand she held a small torch Skeet Lowry had given her. Willie picked up one of the featherlight awning-sheets of rubberised nylon and laid it on the trolley. He selected four of the long two-by-two timber spars and loaded them lengthwise. Two coils of rope were added, together with the jerricans of water.

He took the steering tiller, and the trolley moved smoothly, almost soundlessly over the stony ground. The light alloy of its construction gave it an unladen weight of only two hun-

dred pounds. Modesty switched off the torch and followed
him out. When he had towed the trolley for a mile, keeping
to the long curve of the mountain, he halted and said, 'Ought
to be okay 'ere, Princess. I won't make much noise.'

'All right, Willie love. I might be a bit slow with this arm,
but tell me if I can help.'

She turned her back to the steady wind that whipped across
the flat ground. It was a cold wind now, but by day it would
be at oven heat. She visualised the terrain to the north. There
were two regular routes across the Sahara, the Ligne du
Hoggar and the Ligne du Tanezrouft. The first ran north to
El Golea, a fairyland of fountains and flowers lying incredibly
in the vast dry wastes of the desert, then on through Ghardaia
and through the Saharan Atlas to Algiers.

The more westerly route ran for two hundred miles over
one of the completely flat alluvial plains that the Arabs called
reg, to Adrar, then on to Colomb-Béchar and through the
mountains to Morocco. There were three kinds of terrain in
the desert. The flat wilderness of gravel called *reg*; the immense seas of sand shaped by the wind into dunes, the *erg*;
and the landscape called *hammada*, a broken waste of rocky
plateaux and labyrinthine ravines, where time and weather
had bared the very crust of the earth.

She planned to take neither of the regular routes, for they
could prove to be linear traps. There was no way of knowing
how far Presteign's power extended, but if he controlled agents
along either route they would soon be scouring the two narrow ribbons that ran across the desert. Along those ribbons,
news travelled fast. In five hundred miles it would be easy to
pick up a man and a woman alone.

So they would break the iron rule of desert travel, and leave
the known routes, striking across to the northwest, crossing
the Ligne du Tanezrouft. For a hundred and fifty miles there
would be flat *reg*. Then they would have to face the areas of
sand dunes and *hammada*.

A stranger to the desert might with luck survive for twenty-four hours on such a journey. A stranger would not cover up his body to preserve the sweat; would not know how to make the sand yield water; would not eat lizard or locust or chew the tough grass called *drinn* that camels eat; would not lick the sweat from another's body for the salt; would not be able to bring down a gazelle with a sling-shot, as Willie could if the chance came.

A stranger making this journey might well not start with the advantage of a food reserve, enough for many days if eked out carefully, and a reserve of almost eight gallons of water in containers which prevented evaporation.

A stranger making this journey would scarcely hope to cover the first hundred and fifty miles or more at better than a walking pace—and sitting or lying down.

Willie Garvin said, 'Could you just 'old this steady, Princess?' She held the end of a long spar of timber while he lashed its centre to the horizontal derrick, just above the base. Together they moved to the rear of the trolley, and Willie Garvin made fast a short piece of rope to the middle of a second spar, with a loose bight round the upper end of the long metal pipe.

Ten minutes later he had spread the big square awning-sheet across the trolley and was threading ropes through the eyelets at top and bottom, spiralling the rope round the two spars. He worked efficiently and without pause, as if the whole operation had long been planned in his mind.

A length of rope was fixed to each end of the base spar, the free ends were coiled and placed on the platform of the trolley. With his home-made knife he began to cut shorter lengths from the main coil. Modesty lost track of his work. Her head felt hot, but every few minutes a shiver ran through her body.

There came a time when he said, 'Right. Let's see 'ow she looks.' He climbed on the trolley and laid hold of a rope. The slender metal arm of the derrick rose to the vertical, and he locked the bracing bars. The two cross-spars and the awning-sheet lay in a long bundle across the base of the derrick. Willie reached down a hand to help Modesty aboard.

Moving to the rear of the trolley he crouched down by a bar mounted an inch or two above the platform, where a number of rope-ends were made off.

Modesty heard the faint rattle of the pulley at the top of the derrick. The big square sail rose up the mast. It filled instantly, and the trolley began to move. Willie Garvin said, 'Jesus! Grab that tiller, Princess!'

She sprawled forward and caught the tiller, bringing the small front wheel round so that the trolley was on a straight course. Behind her Willie was mingling oaths with exclamations of delight as he fought with his variety of ropes, slackening one here, taking in another there, trimming the clumsy sail to gain the full benefit of the steady wind.

At last she heard him give a laugh of sheer exultation. 'Must be making twelve knots, Princess! How's she feeling?'

'Pretty good. But you have to hold her.' She looked over her shoulder at him. 'Maybe you could lash the tiller leaving just a few inches of play. Then if we hit a bump she won't swing hard round and maybe break a spar.'

'Sure.' He crawled up beside her with some rope. The trolley was trundling along over the sand-polished gravel of the *reg* with remarkable smoothness. They would have to be alert for sudden gusts and they would have to watch their course, but there was almost nothing else to worry about for a long time to come.

Unless their luck was very bad, the wind would hold; they knew that for only six days in a hundred does the wind in the desert drop. On the *reg* there would be no obstacles. They would have a flat world to themselves, from horizon to horizon. And later, where the plain began to merge with the sands of the *erg*, their crude sand-yacht would be even better than a truck. *Fesh-fesh* was the nightmare of men who drove along the desert tracks; *fesh-fesh* was the name for those patches of crusted, treacherous sand where the wheels spun vainly and a truck could sink to its axles. The trolley had no driving wheels, it was powered by the sail, and would skim over *fesh-fesh* as easily as over the hard gravel of the *reg*.

Willie finished the safety lashing on the tiller. 'Course all right, Princess?'

'Yes.' This was her gift. Without stars or compass, even blindfold, she could have laid their course unerringly. She held out a hand for Willie's knife, glanced at the sky, and scratched a line obliquely in the thin planking of the platform. 'Keep that on the Pole Star and we won't go wrong.' He nodded, went back to trim the swollen sail again, then unfolded a blanket and spread it along the trolley beside the spare spars. 'You might as well get your 'ead down, Princess.'

They could both of them sleep at will, on a bed of flints if need be. The steady trundling of the trolley would not disturb her. She stretched out on the blanket. 'Call me if you have to play cat's cradle with those sheets and halyards, Willie love.'

'Sure. How's the arm?'

'Not too bad.' She closed her eyes. 'It's turned out to be quite a caper. I wish we could have stayed around to take out Delicata and Gabriel.'

'So do I. But not with that arm. And with none of our gear. No sense taking daft risks.'

'No. No sense taking daft risks.'

She slept, and the trolley rolled steadily on beneath the stars.

20

Soon after midnight on the second day, nearly two hundred miles from Mus, the trolley's usefulness came at last to an end. They had pushed it up one or two mild gradients, but the last eight miles had taken two hours, and from now on the effort was no longer worthwhile.

They filled one jerrican to the brim, topped up their water-bottles, and drank what was left in the other jerrican. Willie tied the biscuit tin of food to his belt and lashed the full jerrican on his back with the awning-sheet rolled above it. From two blankets they had made rough cloaks and hoods, to retain the sweat on their bodies by preventing evaporation. Willie took his sling, his knife, and the sheet of thin polythene. Everything else they abandoned, even the Schmeisser; the chance that they might need it was not enough to warrant the extra weight.

Now they would cover twenty miles every twenty-four hours, moving by night, resting through the heat of the day. Through the sun-split rocks and dry ravines of the *hammada* they would find shade to rest in; amid the dunes of the *erg*, they would make a rough lean-to of the awning-sheet.

At dawn, after the night's march, they halted. Willie Garvin began to scoop a hole in the sand. He would have been quite content, but for Modesty's arm. It was swelling and the flesh was angry. Her eyes were too bright, and he suspected a fever. It was difficult to sleep soundly in the savage heat of the desert day, but even so her sleep was unnaturally troubled. He was deeply worried now as he watched her stir restlessly, muttering sometimes in her sleep as she lay under the shade of the awning he had rigged from a tall stump of cactus.

He had almost finished scraping a deep hole with his hands

in the fine sand a little way from the lean-to. The hole was ten feet across at the top and sloped down conically to a depth of three feet. He had been digging for an hour now.

Opening the biscuit tin, he put the packages of food on its lid in the shade and set the tin in the bottom of the hole. With his crude knife he cut fleshy hunks of cactus and placed them around the sloping sides. He spread the thin polythene sheet over the hole, allowing it to sag down in the middle, and heaped sand over the edges to secure it. A handful of pebbles tossed into the sagging sheet served to weight it down in the centre. He surveyed his work to make sure the polythene was not touching the tin beneath it or the sides of the hole, then edged into the shade beside Modesty. Methodically he began to strip his mind of worry, his body of discomfort, so that sleep would come quickly. Sleep helped to slow the metabolism, conserving energy and body-moisture. Sleep was vital.

Throughout the day the fierce sun would shine down through the polythene sheet, vaporising the moisture that remains even in the Sahara sand, vaporising the moisture in the cactus flesh. That vapour would condense on the underside of the polythene, would trickle down to the weighted base of the sheet, and drip into the biscuit tin below. By nightfall there would be two or three pints in the tin. Not much, for desert travel, but it helped to conserve their precious reserve.

Willie Garvin slept, and the sun burned its slow frightful way across the milky-blue sky.

The truck was fully laden. It was a massive Alvis Stalwart, a 5-ton high mobility load carrier, adapted to take a canopy. Half the load consisted of spare petrol and water. Delicata stood by the cab, smoking a cigar, his great round face pensive.

Gabriel came walking across from the valley entrance. There was malignant satisfaction in his eyes as he looked at Delicata.

He halted and gazed at the big man in silence for a few moments before he spoke. 'All right. We'll get moving.'

Delicata inclined his head politely. 'Certainly. What about our Algerian friends?'

'I've told them they can take the two Land Rovers and go to hell. You can get this truck to El Golea, can't you?'

'Without a doubt.'

A spark burned in Gabriel's eyes. 'How does it feel, not being Presteign's blue-eyed boy any longer?'

'You think that's the case?' Delicata flicked ash from his cigar, his face expressionless. 'I found the loot for him.'

'You found trouble for him. What happens when Blaise and the others talk? They'll be talking *now*.'

'I doubt if Tangye and his people will have anything coherent to say. Nothing that links Presteign to their discomfiture, certainly. Blaise and Garvin won't talk; they'll try to handle things their own way. If they intended to talk they'd have taken that Scots fool's notebook. Lowry can't talk without revealing his own involvement.' Delicata smiled a small tight smile. 'I don't think Presteign will be greatly troubled.'

'Maybe not. And he won't be greatly inclined to put you in charge of a job again. You like your amusements too much.'

'I certainly like them,' Delicata said, 'and he's had no cause for complaint before. Shall we go?'

Gabriel looked up at the cab of the Stalwart. 'Where's McWhirter?'

Delicata shrugged contemptuously. 'Underneath. Counting the nuts and bolts for his notebook, perhaps.'

Gabriel moved round to the other side of the big six-wheeler. McWhirter lay on his back beneath it, his feet sticking out. Gabriel bent to speak, but the words caught in his throat, which was suddenly dry with shock. There was something unnaturally still, unnaturally limp about the booted feet on the end of the skinny legs.

Gabriel was straightening, reaching for the gun under his

jacket, when Delicata's terrible hand closed upon the back of his neck.

For three nights they had trudged across the desert under chill moonlight. For three days they had rested and slept in whatever shade they could make or find. Their movements were deliberately lethargic and they spoke hardly at all, hoarding every scruple of their energy.

On the second day Modesty had seemed a little better. On the third day, worse. Willie Garvin found himself keeping a careful check on their direction by the stars. It was a relief to find that her instinct was still good, that they were not straying from their route.

On the fourth day, when they halted at dawn, Willie Garvin stood and turned slowly in a circle, making his customary survey of the great emptiness that encompassed them. To the north-west there was an area of *hammada*, where tilted plateaux and grotesque towers of rock mingled with outcrops of chalk and sandstone. There was something familiar to Willie about the configuration of this landscape, a pattern he recognised. He searched the memory-banks of his mind.

The fort. The ancient, rather small French fort. There were many of them scattered through the desert. The Arabs called them *bordj*. On the main trans-Saharan routes they were still used as points of call. The forts were no longer garrisoned but there was usually a watchman, and they were places where travellers could at least find shelter for the night.

Bordj Kerim. He remembered now. A lonely outpost far off the regular caravan routes. He had spent two months there during his time in the Legion. Willie Garvin shielded his eyes to gaze at the freak configuration that had jogged his memory. Gauging distance was no easy matter in the desert, but he knew the fort lay at the foot of a long slow gradient that curved round the edge of the *hammada*. It would be six or eight miles away.

He turned to Modesty, feeling the parchment skin of his

face move stiffly as he started to grin. She had been unrolling blankets, but now she was standing up, a hand to her head, staring anxiously about her. As he turned she said, 'Where's Steve got to? And Dinah?'

Willie felt the serpent of fear twist suddenly in his stomach. He went to her and put a hand on her good arm, speaking casually. 'They're okay, Princess. They went on ahead. Let's 'ave a look at that arm.'

'No, it's all right.' Her voice was almost petulant, and her eyes were not quite focused.

'Then it won't matter if I look. Come on now.' She resisted a little, and he had to use gentle force to make her sit down. Her weakness shocked him. She stared at the ground, making no move to prevent him as he pushed back the blanket cloak and started to unbutton her shirt. Twice he felt her wince as he eased the sleeve down her arm and drew it off.

Willie Garvin stared, his heart thumping with fright. From shoulder to elbow the arm was huge. The swelling bulged above and below the bandage, the skin was tight and shiny with streaks of inflammation creeping out under the paler skin beyond the swollen redness.

He left the bandage on and drew the shirt loosely over her shoulder, then settled the blanket cloak about her.

'I've got to open that arm, Princess.'

She looked at him with dull, feverish eyes, then nodded.

He said, 'There's a *bordj* pretty near. Two or three hours. Water there, and a decent bit of shelter for a change.'

There would be shelter if the fort still stood; water if the well had not dried up. He had no hope of finding a resident watchman, or food, or medical supplies, not in this forgotten outpost.

The journey under the naked heat of the sun was cruel torment. He carried the blankets and jerrican, water bottles and food tin hitched to his body, and held her good arm to support her as she plodded on blindly now, stumbling a little.

The fort still stood. He saw it from the top of the long slope down. Another thirty minutes passed before he half carried her through the gateway. The gates themselves were gone, broken up and taken away by nomads. He knew it would be so, knew the wandering Arabs would have stripped the fort of everything that might be of the remotest use to them.

Here was the courtyard, just as he remembered it, but silent now; the big two-storey block in the centre; the crumbling steps which led to the ramparts; the long low barrack rooms running along two sides; the ammunition store; the camel pen and the officers' quarters. No doors remained. Everything that was not built of stone or mud-brick had been taken.

He stripped off the gear strapped to his body, picked Modesty up in his arms and carried her into the Colonel's quarters. These had been sited in the permanent shade offered by the right-angle of the thick high walls, and lay half underground, like a sub-basement, for extra protection against the heat. In the same corner of the fort stood a small brick housing, open on one side, which had once sheltered the well. Now the timber roof of the housing had gone.

The well was a thin shaft driven fifty feet through layers of rock to collect the underground water that seeped down from the *hammada* to the south. A stone trough stood by the well. The pump that once served to fill the trough was gone. But the nomads had left the thick timbers which covered the well and prevented blown sand gradually filling the shaft. No desert dweller would endanger a water supply.

Beyond the well was a strip of vegetation. This had been the Colonel's tiny garden, hand irrigated by sweating legionnaires, the fine sand thickened by camel manure and kitchen compost. Colonel Jodelle had grown roses there. His roses had been dead for many years now, but some tiny measure of moisture still reached the surface, for a colocynth, a bitter apple plant, rose from deep roots between a straggling thala tree and some tall euphorbias, and in their shade was a scattering of other desert flora.

The room where Colonel Jodelle had slept lay at the end

of a passage and down a short flight of stone steps. It was insulated by two low storeys above it. Here the air was pleasantly cool after the shrivelling heat of the courtyard. There was a long horizontal aperture halfway up one wall of the partly sunken room, giving light reflected from the wall of the fort. This aperture had been a window, and pierced the thick wall at ground level outside. The shutters and the insect screen had gone.

Modesty sat propped against the wall while Willie made a mattress of sand on the floor and covered it with the blankets. She lay down obediently at his word. He went up to test the well, and heard a splash from the small pebble he dropped. Water was there when he needed it. For the moment he had enough in the jerrican for what was to be done.

With the knife and the flint that he still carried, he started a fire and began to boil water in the biscuit tin. Half his shirt he tore into strips, putting them in the water.

While the water boiled he cut stems from the euphorbia plants; Tuaregs used the sap for cuts and sore places on their camels. It was a strong vesicant, and he diluted it to prevent blistering.

There were still some dry biscuits left in his food store. He crumbled several of them, rolled the fragments in a piece of his shirt and put them into the water to soften.

Ten minutes later, carrying the container of boiling water in a little cradle of rope, he went down to the room where Modesty lay. Her eyes opened as he came in. She was gaunt with fever and the rigours of desert travel. Her face was flushed under the dark tan. She smiled at him vaguely as he knelt beside her, and said, 'Hallo, Willie love.'

''Allo, Princess.' He began to soak the bandage from her arm. It came away. The big blotch of yellow matter in the centre of the swelling made him draw his breath sharply. He managed to smile, and said, 'Not too bad. This is going to 'urt a bit though, Princess.'

'Is it?' Her voice was far away. 'All right, Willie.'

He took the freshly honed and sterilised knife from the steaming tin of water. This was the third lot of water; he had scoured his hands red in the second. Carefully he made six small cuts in the swollen flesh with the knife-point, then opened the centre with a longer incision. She neither moved nor spoke; a sudden blankness in her eyes was the only reaction. He swabbed and cleaned; squeezed, swabbed and cleaned again. And again. Impossible to be gentle now, impossible to stop until the wound was clean, at least to the eye.

An age later he wiped away the last of the ugly matter, then kept working and squeezing the flesh until blood ran freely. 'Can you 'old your arm up while I get a poultice on, Princess? Don't let it touch anything.'

'All right, Willie.' The same gentle, remote voice.

The soaked biscuits in the piece of rag were a soft pulp now. He squeezed out the surplus moisture, scalding his fingers, then opened the rag and spread diluted euphorbia sap over the pulp with a scrap of sterile cloth. When he laid the hot poultice on the wound she blinked once, but that was all.

He took two strips of sterilised rag and bandaged the dressing in place. Sweat was running down his face as he sat back at last on his haunches. He would poultice the wound afresh every two hours for as long as the biscuits lasted. After that he would leave the dressing in place and use a shirt-sleeve of hot sand to continue the fomentation treatment.

This should draw out the poison. He knew that her body's resistance to infection was very high, and with the healing aid of the euphorbia sap there was a good chance that the crisis would be past in another twenty-four hours. He did not know whether he had done the best that was possible, only that it was the best he could do.

He said, 'You'll 'ave to drink plenty, Princess. Don't worry about the water. There's enough 'ere for a garrison of thirty.'

'All right, Willie.'

He lifted her head and held the water bottle to her lips again and again while she drank slowly but deeply.

'That's a good girl. Now you go to sleep.'

'All right, Willie.' Her eyes closed. He watched her for a little while, then went out into the courtyard to make a rope from his blanket long enough to lower the biscuit tin down the well.

It was an hour before dawn the next day when Willie Garvin knew at last that she was safe. The swelling had gone down and the ominous red streaks that spread from the swelling had disappeared. The fever had broken and she slept quietly now. He knew that she would be as weak as a baby when she woke. But that would quickly pass. She had the recuperative powers of a cat, and with the infection gone there was nothing to hinder them now.

He would have to find food, but that did not trouble him. He would find it. In two days she would be on her feet. In four she would be fit to travel.

He felt tired after the long night vigil, but the lightness of his spirits made it a pleasant tiredness. Soon after dawn she woke, turning her head to look at him. Her voice was weak but there was no delirium in it as she said, 'Hallo, Willie . . . did I walk out on you?'

'Only for a bit. How's the arm feeling?'

She moved it slightly and gave a comfortable little sigh. 'Feels good now. I'm still a bit dozy. Where are we?'

He grinned. 'I found a fort. We're the only tenants. Plenty of water. You go to sleep again and don't worry about a thing.'

She managed to nod, and her eyes closed once more. He went out to draw more water from the well, annoyed with himself because he should have made her drink before she slept again. Later he filled the stone trough and washed his body thoroughly, then pulled on his slacks and boots and began to explore the fort. He was stripped to the waist now, for there was little left of his shirt.

When he was on the ramparts he looked across towards the

266

tangled rock of the *hammada*. That was the most likely place to find food. There was wild life in the desert, not only the lizard and the rat, but small birds, hares, and with luck a goat or a gazelle.

He went down the broken steps and continued his exploration, looking for anything that might help on the journey to come. An old sack would have been a godsend, or a jacket to replace his shirt. A bucket would have delighted him, for the biscuit tin was beginning to leak and he needed a container for his hole-in-the-ground water trap.

There was nothing. That was a pity, but not surprising. Nomads had little to learn from locusts. He came out of a long barrack room and began to walk towards the Colonel's quarters. It was mid-morning. He would get a little sleep, and perhaps make a trip to the *hammada* a couple of hours before dusk.

He was twenty paces from the well when Delicata's voice said, 'So we meet again. That seems a suitably dramatic comment, don't you think?'

Willie turned slowly. The big man sat on the low stone bench that the legionnaires had used in time past when scrubbing their equipment. He wore slacks and a shirt, but no hat. His boots were dusty but showed little sign of wear.

Useless to wonder how the man had got here. It did not matter. He was here. Willie Garvin, stripped to the waist and without a weapon, stood gazing with empty eyes, and despair rose like a grey tide within him.

'So they all flew away and left you behind,' Delicata said, and smiled. 'I should have realised at once, of course. You're the heaviest. Even our laconic friend Lowry can't work miracles, and that was quite a load for the Cessna.' He paused and looked at the watch on his wrist. 'I was greatly intrigued when we found next day that the trolley had vanished. What on earth did you do with it, Garvin?'

Willie said nothing. A spark of hope had come to life within him. Delicata had found him alone, had assumed he *was* alone. It was a natural assumption. Absurd for Modesty Blaise to face the desert journey with a wounded arm unless there was no other choice.

Delicata did not know that there had been no other choice.

'Don't be shy,' Delicata said. 'What did you do with the trolley?'

'I made a sand-yacht.' Willie spoke softly. 'It was Modesty got the idea. She reckoned it'd get me a good long way over the *reg* in the first twenty-four hours. Save about ten days' march.'

Delicata's eyes shone like jewels, and his bulk shook with laughter. 'She's very good. Very good indeed. I shall be more circumspect with her on the next occasion—which I have every hope will be soon.' He looked at his watch again. 'I'm afraid I have a rather tight schedule, so I can't spare you a lot of time, but let us relish what remains to us, Garvin. What strange impulse made me pause in passing, I wonder? This edifice has little architectural merit . . .' His voice rolled smoothly on.

The spark in Willie Garvin glowed steadily. Delicata was in a hurry, and presumably alone. He had not travelled on foot. There must be a truck outside the fort. Why no sound of its approach? The answer was simple enough. A driver in the desert nurses his engine, especially his radiator. He turns the bonnet to the wind when he parks. On a long downhill gradient he cuts the engine and coasts. There was a long gradient running down to the fort. The truck had approached in silence.

Soon, Willie knew, Delicata would take up where he had left off ten years ago. They would fight. The big man, with his enormous strength and invulnerability, would kill him. But then Delicata would drive off. He had a tight schedule, and he would not waste time exploring an abandoned fort; he would not find Modesty.

Down in the room where she lay sleeping, a jerrican of

water stood within arm's reach, and the remains of the food. For Modesty Blaise, that would be enough. She would recover her strength. Somehow she would survive.

Willie Garvin said, 'Where's Gabriel?'

Delicata broke off in the middle of a rounded phrase, and frowned. 'The noble Gabriel and his highland laddie have laid down life's weary burden,' he said gravely. 'One doubts that the trumpets sounded for them on the other side, but I spoke privately with my employer and persuaded him that this was the best course under the changed circumstances. However, you interrupted me, Garvin. Can it be, can it possibly be, that you were paying no attention to the oration I was delivering in your memory?'

He stood up, the great arms hanging, and began to move slowly forward. 'Words are wasted on you, I fear. But 'twas ever thus, and I can delay no longer. My feet itch for the crunch of your ribs once again——' He stopped short, staring past Willie, his eyes widening. Then, in a soft joyous voice, 'Why, Miss Blaise! It seems our friend Garvin has been deceiving me by *suggestio falsi*.'

Willie's head snapped round, and a wave of sick rage engulfed him. She was on her hands and knees in the doorway, twenty yards away. Her face was pale, her eyes dark and huge. She was shirtless, and the crude dressing stood out on her arm. God alone knew what instinct had roused her. But she had heard, through that ground-level slit of window, and she had crawled slowly up the steps and along the passage.

Neither man moved. She eased herself shakily into a sitting position against the side of the door, her eyes on Willie, and let her hands fall limply on her lap. With a final effort she lifted her voice and said feebly, 'Well . . . you'll have to win now, Willie love.'

Delicata laughed. Something deep down in Willie Garvin bared its teeth, and his face became strangely quiet. In his mind there was a sudden cool clarity.

So.

Close quarters with Delicata would be fatal. The gorilla arms were incredibly quick. If the hands once found a grip, Willie Garvin was dead. How to get past those long arms? There was no way that did not invite disaster. Once the hands laid hold . . .

The hands. Yes.

Willie Garvin began to move slowly forward, poised like a cat. Delicata smiled, and held out his hands in front of him, keeping them a little low to protect his crotch, the fingers spread and curved like the teeth of a steel grab.

There is a move performed by acrobats in which they spin horizontally on the axis of their hips, seeming for a moment to defy gravity. Willie Garvin judged his distance, then suddenly whirled with outspread arms and legs. One booted foot smashed against Delicata's right hand, and in the same instant Willie touched the ground with his palms and whirled again, taking himself well out of distance.

His foot had made contact with all the power of a rock swung on a length of cord, and he had heard a distinct crack of bone. Delicata was still smiling, but with a touch of puzzlement. He shook the hand as if trying to sense feeling in it, then began to move in again, more quickly this time.

The same whirling cartwheel. Delicata snatched his hands back to his chest. Willie jack-knifed, dropped, rose in the air like a bouncing ball and shot both feet out in a perfect dropkick; not to the head but to the hands, the massive hands, smashing them against the barrel of Delicata's chest.

The big man staggered back a pace, but kept his footing. Another man would have been hammered to the ground.

Even from where she sat, Modesty had heard the crunch of bone. There was no strength in her, no way she could help. Before beginning the long crawl out into the daylight, she had looked with blurring eyes for Willie's knife, but there had been no time to search. It was doubtful that she could have thrown it to him. The weakness following high fever is almost total, and she had drained her tiny reserve of strength in crawling along the passage to the doorway.

Now, after the first few seconds of the fight, she understood the pattern. Willie was going for Delicata's hands. It was a difficult tactic, only possible to a fighter of the utmost accuracy and speed. He had already done some damage, but she did not deceive herself that he had won the advantage yet. He would have to do far more damage before the odds became level. And Delicata would not be fooled twice in the same way. Willie would have to out-think him, find new ways of hammering at those monstrous hands while at the same time keeping beyond their clutch.

The two men were circling, poised. Willie moved in fast, and seemed to slip. His feet shot from under him and he was on his back. Delicata lunged forward and down. Willie's feet streaked out in a kick for the groin. The huge forearms flashed across in a protective block. But the groin-kick was undeveloped, a feint; instead came the business kick, below the crossed forearms, heels thudding against the fingers of Delicata's right hand. A flowing back-roll and Willie was on his feet and out of distance again.

It was an ugly fight. When men fight to kill with bare hands it cannot be other than ugly. Delicata began to use his arms like clubs, like flails. Willie Garvin stopped attacking and relied on counters, boot against hand, using Delicata's own strength to provide impact.

Once a glancing blow caught him on the shoulder and he went down. Incredibly fast for so big a man, Delicata jumped in to kick. Willie Garvin took the kick rather than risk a broken arm trying to block it, but he took it rolling fast, riding the impact, and came up with a patch of skin ripped from his side but with bones intact.

Once Delicata lured him to close quarters by turning suddenly and heading for Modesty. Willie Garvin landed on the enormous back like a pouncing wild-cat, feet drawn up, fingers sunk in the deltoid muscles. When an arm reached over

271

and back to clutch at him, he let go with one hand and chopped with the edge of that hand across the groping fingers, once, twice, until with a bellow of rage Delicata flung himself back to crush the tormentor beneath his weight. Willie threw himself clear, landed in a crouch, and kicked for a hand again as Delicata came to his feet.

The longer it went on, the more Modesty lost the impression of two men fighting. It was man against gorilla. Delicata had little combat technique; he had never needed it. His strength and invulnerability had always been enough. A man cannot break a gorilla's arm or neck with a leverage hold, cannot disable with a karate kick or chop, cannot dare to close in for a throw.

To follow the tactic he had chosen, Willie Garvin was having to take risks of hairline calculation. There were long crimson streaks on his body now, where the great clutching fingers had almost found a grip, and purple blotches where the swinging fists had grazed. Even Delicata's near misses were viciously punishing, and there were many of them as the minutes passed. But time and again Willie found his chosen target. The hands.

There came a moment when he misjudged fractionally, and Delicata's hand clamped on a forearm. But the hand was battered and bloodied. One finger stuck out at an unnatural angle now. Willie Garvin snatched at his own wrist, wrenched twistingly with desperate strength . . . *and broke free.* He stepped back, and for the first time he did not move immediately out of distance. His eyes rested on the big man with quiet assessment.

Delicata stood still and blinked. He lifted his mauled hands and gazed at them. Something happened to his face. After long seconds he smiled. It was a synthetic grimace, a caricature of the amused and utterly confident smile that had come so readily to him for so many years.

'I think,' he said, breathing a little heavily, 'I really think you've earned a draw, Garvin——'

Willie's feet hit him full in the face. Delicata staggered blindly, an animal sound breaking from his throat, a sound that ended with something close to a whimper.

Modesty Blaise sagged against the wall. In her heart she had not believed that Willie could win. It was hard to believe even now, when the issue was no longer in doubt. Delicata's p.d. was broken; Delicata's weapons, the hands at the end of those grotesquely long arms, were broken.

She closed her eyes for a moment, and when she focused them again it seemed that she was looking upon some kind of hallucination. The whole great bulk of Delicata hung vertically in the air, head down, a yard above the ground; and Willie was bent, poised on one straight leg, his forearms locked about Delicata's head.

Understanding came to her. This was the spring-hip throw, the enormously difficult development of the cross-buttock, in which the thrower must find perfect balance on one leg while using the other as a spring, doubled at the knee then thrusting out and up against the opponent's belly, to toss his lower trunk and legs high in the air. Willie had done it with Delicata's 280 lbs. plus, and he had done it in reverse, from behind Delicata. It took three-fifths of a second, and she had missed the crucial instant of the throw.

Now, still keeping his hold, Willie dropped to one knee as Delicata fell. Headfirst, vertical, the great bulk of the man drove down like a pile-driver, and it seemed that the rocky ground quivered under the impact. There came another and softer thud as his inverted body toppled like a felled tree.

Willie stayed on one knee, the breath sobbing in his lungs. Then, methodically, he checked that Delicata was dead. It was not a long task. The skull was caved in and the neck broken. Willie got to his feet and walked slowly to where Modesty sat slumped against the wall.

It was then that reaction hit him. He began to shiver as if from sudden cold, his mind recoiling in horror from what might have been. He stood swaying a little, his blood-smeared chest heaving, looking down at her with a kind of frenzied exasperation. And perhaps because he had never spoken to her in such a way before, he stammered a little as the words broke from him. ''Ave you lost your m-marbles, coming out like that? You were *safe* down there! And you—you bloody near got yourself k-killed! He'd 've done you *slow*!' He ran shaking fingers through hair matted with dust and sand. 'You knew it'd need a bloody miracle . . . for Christ's sake don't ever t-take a crazy risk like that again!'

A shaky laugh rose from within her, but weakness betrayed her. She caught her lower lip in her teeth for a moment and closed her eyes tightly. Tears welled out from under the lids and ran down her gaunt face. 'Don't go on at me, Willie love . . .' Her voice failed.

Willie knelt and put his arms around her. 'I'm a bastard,' he said, appalled. 'God, I'm sorry, Princess. Easy now. Everything's fine . . .' He held her until the spasm of weeping had passed, then stood up, lifting her easily in his arms with sudden buoyant strength. 'Let's get you back to bed while I 'ave a look round. I got a feeling this is our lucky day.'

Five minutes later, as she lay exhausted but at peace in the cool room, she heard the sound of a truck driving into the courtyard. Willie came in, his bruised face wreathed in a huge smile.

'I'll tell you what we got for dinner,' he said, squatting beside her and taking her hand. 'Soup, chicken, spuds, green veg. All canned, but never mind. Biscuits, chocolate, canned fruit, dates, cheese, nuts, raisins—just name it, we've got it. You'll be fit to fight a bear in a couple of days.'

She smiled at him. 'Just what I've always wanted.'

He grinned joyously. 'That's only a start. There's all our own gear—guns, clothes, small-kit, everything. Thirty gallons of water, and containers for another thirty we can fill from the well. And a king-sized medical kit—bandages, antiseptic, penicillin, the *lot*.'

'And a truck to drive home in.'

274

'A truck? Blimey, wait till you see it, Princess.' His voice became dreamy with pleasure. 'It's an Alvis Stalwart. Six-wheeler, all-wheel drive. Carries five ton, easy. Hundred gallon fuel tank, three-quarters full now, but there's another fifty in jerricans. Rolls Royce B.81 engine, 220 horse power. She's carrying all special accessories for desert travel. They've even installed a fridge, working off the battery. She can cross a five-foot trench . . .' He shook his head and grinned again. 'And just in case we strike a river, she's amphibious!'

Modesty was looking at his body. She said, 'Get the medical kit first and do something about those skinned ribs and claw-marks, Willie.'

'Sure.' He stood up. 'I'll just get rid of Delicata and finish checking the load. There's three big crates be'ind the rest of the stuff. I 'aven't looked in 'em yet.'

She began to laugh, feebly still, but this time the laughter did not break. When he looked at her, puzzled, she said, 'Have a guess.'

'Did I miss something?'

'Forgot something. But you've had a lot on your mind, what with me to take care of. And Delicata. You forgot Domitian Mus. It's the loot, Willie. The loot.'

He stared, then said slowly, 'Yes. It's got to be. Well . . . we can take a look later if you feel like it. I'm a lot better pleased about the truck and the grub.'

'So am I. And our kit. Soap. God, I want to feel clean, Willie. But go and patch yourself up first.'

An hour later he carried her out to the stone trough, stripped off her clothes and bathed her in the sun-heated water, lathering the sweat and grime from her body. The medical kit provided antibiotic ointment and a fresh dressing for her arm. He washed and dried her hair, brushed it out, then plaited it in two pigtails. There were clean clothes in the kit they had brought with them on the Skywagon. He dressed her and carried her down into the cool room again.

'You're going to eat like a horse and sleep like a log for the

275

next couple of days, Princess. Then we'll be on our way.'
He drew a long breath of satisfaction. 'Looks like this caper's
just about finished.'

'Just about.' She had been smiling, revelling in the comfort
of being clean and groomed, but now a shadow of bleakness
replaced the warmth in her eyes. 'Just about,' she repeated.
'There's only Presteign.'

21

'I RATHER expected you to call on me before this,' said Presteign. 'It must be almost a month now.'

Tarrant nodded but did not speak. It was twenty-six days since Collier had rung him from Boukhalf-Souahel, the airport for Tangier.

The empty bay spread below them, a small bay between Cannes and St. Raphael. Presteign's bay. The long red-tiled villa hung on the sloping cliff, fifty feet above the level of a quiet sea, dark blue under the full summer sun. Curving steps, broad and shallow, made an undemanding path down to the flat rock where the boat-house stood near the little white jetty.

The two men sat on the flagged terrace, a low table between them. Tarrant was in a lightweight navy suit and a plain white shirt with a club tie. Presteign wore a white towelling beach-robe over his trunks. He looked at his wristwatch and said, 'Is this an official visit?'

Tarrant shook his head. 'There'll be no official visit. Tangye and his people could only tell the police what you've no doubt read in the papers—that a gang of men took over in Mus and behaved in a most brutal fashion. Their story is rather incoherent.'

'Yes, it would be,' Presteign agreed. 'Collier and the blind girl?'

'They've said nothing. Except to me, of course. They were waiting hopefully for Modesty Blaise and Willie Garvin to appear.' Tarrant paused. 'Which happened just over two weeks ago.'

Presteign said, 'Ah.' His face did not change as he gazed

out over the sea. 'They've managed to lie very low. Did they have any news of Delicata?'

'Yes. He killed Gabriel and McWhirter, presumably on your orders as a result of the changed situation, then set off in a well-laden truck for parts unknown to me, but possibly known to you. Caught up with Modesty Blaise and Willie Garvin. And is now buried somewhere in the Sahara. The grave is unmarked, I understand.'

'And the contents of the truck?'

'Likewise buried. The interesting portion of the contents, that is.'

'I see.' Presteign was silent for a while. It was not a troubled silence. At last he said reflectively, 'I always had the feeling that Delicata was indestructible. They must be very good indeed.'

'Yes.'

Presteign looked at him. 'You have considerable influence, of course. Access to the Prime Minister, even. But if you intend to lock horns with me, I think you'll lose. I have what the newspapers call an industrial empire. It gives me a great deal of hidden influence, greater than your own. And I don't think you would be believed, Tarrant. Some things are simply unbelievable.'

'Perfectly true. That's been your strength for a long time, I imagine.'

Presteign nodded and looked at his watch again. 'I always swim at eleven, so in five minutes I must ask you to excuse me. Could you come to the point of your visit?'

Tarrant shaded his eyes and gazed at a ship just visible on the horizon. 'A long time ago,' he said, 'there existed quaint but rather civilised customs. If a gentleman was found to have embezzled the mess funds or something of that sort, he was given a service revolver and invited to withdraw to his bedroom, where he blew his brains out rather than endure disgrace.'

Presteign shrugged. 'As you say, quaint. But very archaic.

278

And after all, I'm in no danger of discovery or disgrace. I can certainly think of nothing to which shooting myself would be a preferred alternative.'

'I can,' Tarrant said pleasantly. 'Modesty Blaise will kill you if you don't.'

Presteign stared with a touch of curiosity. 'Revenge? Retribution? Or self protection?'

'Oh, not revenge.' Tarrant waved a protesting hand. 'She doesn't object to the human predators of this world trying to kill each other off. And since she places herself in that category, she considers that she's fair game. Personally I feel she's less than just to herself there, but no matter. Retribution? No again.' He smiled to himself. 'She certainly doesn't see herself as an instrument of justice. Self protection? I think not. It just isn't her style.'

He looked at Presteign. 'She simply says you have to go. If you don't, you'll murder more people. Little, harmless people. Like Aaronson, like Dinah Pilgrim's sister. Like the whole of Tangye's team, if you hadn't been prevented. That's why she'll kill you, Presteign. As a deterrent.'

Presteign shook his head. He seemed genuinely baffled. 'I know one adopts attitudes for public consumption concerning what you call little people. But really, Tarrant. Are you pretending they have any importance?'

Tarrant studied him. 'I'm not pretending,' he said. 'Not for one moment, Presteign. More to the point, neither is Modesty Blaise.'

Presteign moved his shoulders. 'I find this extraordinary. I've killed nobody.'

'That's rather worse.'

'I beg your pardon?'

'You do your killing by proxy. You employ a man like Delicata to achieve certain ends, and you grow fat on his killings. She won't have it.'

'I rather thought she had done the same sort of thing in her time.'

279

'No.'

Presteign sat silent, his face impassive. After a while he said, 'I've no intention of living under threat. It's quite intolerable.'

'You won't have to wait long,' Tarrant said grimly.

'Indeed I won't. I shall at once make comprehensive arrangements to get rid of her. And meanwhile, I shall ensure full security for myself.' Presteign reflected for a moment. 'I shall also see that close surveillance is kept on any of her old contacts she might hire to carry out her threat.'

Tarrant sighed. 'You have the wrong sow by the ear, Presteign. Forget her old contacts. Modesty Blaise won't kill you by proxy. She won't even send Willie Garvin. She'll do it herself. Not without distaste, but she'll do it.'

Presteign sat back in his chair and smiled faintly. 'She'll have to be very quick,' he said, and pressed a button set in the table. A buzzer sounded somewhere in the villa. Twenty seconds later a man in a white jacket walked soft-footed on to the terrace. He was dark, with smooth black hair, and he halted two paces from Presteign with a look of polite inquiry.

'I want calls to the special numbers in London, Paris, Zurich, Rome and Marseilles.' Presteign stood up as he spoke. 'In that order, and at five minute intervals from eleven-thirty onwards, Bernard. Oh, and get Sir Gerald a drink before he leaves.'

Bernard inclined his head, then looked at Tarrant. 'M'sieu?'

'A whisky and soda please.'

Bernard went silently away. Presteign said without emphasis, 'I choose to work by proxy. We'll see which way is best. Frankly I don't think she has any chance at all.' He began to unfasten the belt of his beach-robe.

'And you won't consider taking a revolver to your bedroom?' Tarrant asked. 'I'm sure she would prefer it.'

Presteign frowned slightly. 'Please don't be naïve.' He put the robe on the chair, his watch on the table. 'I'm glad you called Tarrant. Goodbye.' He turned away.

Tarrant watched him go down the long curving steps to the jetty. Presteign did not hesitate there, but walked to the end and dived in. With an old-fashioned but powerful overarm stroke he began to swim steadily out towards the point, two hundred yards away.

The man called Bernard came out with a whisky and soda on a small silver tray and put it down on the table. Tarrant did not touch it. As Bernard went back into the villa Tarrant got up and followed him slowly, pausing in the open french windows. Bernard was at the far end of the room, picking up the telephone.

'I've changed my mind about the drink,' Tarrant said, and leaned in the doorway gazing absently out over the bay. 'I'll be getting on my way.'

'As you wish, m'sieu.' Bernard put down the telephone and stood waiting for the Englishman to go.

A hundred yards out, Presteign's arms beat the water in slow rhythm as he swam on. Then the rhythm faltered for a moment, and quite suddenly he was gone. There was no flurry, no warning. He had simply vanished beneath the rippled blue surface.

Tarrant turned and walked slowly across the room. 'I must let you get on with your telephone calls, Bernard,' he said.

Half a mile away, round the western point of the bay, Willie Garvin sat in a small motor boat smoking a cigarette. He wore old clothes and a floppy straw hat. The boat was moving very slowly on a set course. Beneath it, on thirty feet of rope, hung a small waterproof red lamp flashing inter-mittently.

Ten minutes later a wooden toggle rattled against the gun-wale as the rope was tugged. Willie Garvin closed the throttle and looked about him. The sea was clear. He lifted binoculars to his eyes and studied the rugged cliff face that sloped back from the rocky strip of beach.

When he was satisfied he tugged twice on the rope. Ten seconds later Modesty surfaced, water glistening on the black neoprene hood of her scuba suit. Willie lifted the contour tank from her back. She climbed quickly aboard and began to strip off the scuba suit. He opened the throttle, passed her a bundle of clothes, and turned to haul in the rope with the lamp at the end.

The little scars where his knife had cut still showed faintly on her arm, but the flesh of her face was no longer stretched tightly over the bones as on that grim day when they had entered the fort. She looked a little tired in spirit as she pulled on the clothes, a little sombre. He wished very much that she had let him take care of the Presteign bit.

He said, 'All over?'

She nodded. She had taken Presteign by the feet and drawn him straight down. He could not reach her to fight, and in fact he had barely struggled. She thought his lungs must have filled with water almost at once. If his body was found, there would be no mark on him, just as there had been no mark on Aaronson, or on Judy Pilgrim.

'All over,' she said. 'Let's go home, Willie. We've had enough of trouble . . . and Steve and Dinah have had enough of waiting.'

The early morning sun gleamed from the rough white walls of the cottage in the valley, giving the promise of a fine day.

She came from the bathroom with her body still a little damp, pulled on a shirt and a coarse tweed skirt, and picked up an old jersey. Barefoot she went downstairs and made coffee in a saucepan. While it was cooling she spread an Ordnance Survey map on the kitchen table and stared at it for long minutes, her mind translating the contour lines into a relief of the countryside. With a pencil she traced out her route. Just over twenty miles, through common and woods and pasture, only twice crossing a secondary road.

She fixed the route in her mind and drank her coffee, then took a *chagal* from the cupboard, a canvas water container shaped like a goatskin bottle. She poured in two bottles of red wine. For a moment she thought about food, but could not be troubled with it.

She was still barefoot when she left the cottage and set out across the fields to the woods beyond, the *chagal* slung over one shoulder with the jersey. The rough ground did not trouble her feet. She had walked unshod through mountains and desert from childhood to puberty.

Two hours later she halted for a few minutes by a bluff on a high green hill, not to rest, but to tilt the *chagal* so that the wine streamed into her mouth. The slow evaporation through the canvas under the sun's heat had made the liquid deliciously cool.

By noon she had seen only three people, two of them at a distance. The third, a farmer, had watched her out of sight suspiciously, taking her for a gipsy. By early afternoon, after six hours, she reached the end of her route, where trees overhung a brook that wound down through a wooded slope.

Now she was hungry, but again she could not be troubled to do anything about it. The grass a few paces from the brook was long and dry. She drank, put on the jersey, settled herself under a bush, and slept.

Once she half woke, smelt woodsmoke, sensed that she was no longer alone. She remembered the marked map she had left in the cottage, and a little touch of gladness warmed her as she sank down into sleep again.

The sun was still warm when she woke and sat up. Ten paces away Willie Garvin lay on his back beside the heaped and still glowing ashes of a fire. She reached down the *chagal* from the branch where she had hung it and went to sit beside him.

''Allo, Princess.'

'Hallo, Willie love. I'm starving.'

He sat up and parted the heaped ashes with a stick. In a hollow scooped beneath them lay two balls of blackened clay, as big as melons. 'I got a couple of 'edge'ogs,' he said, and took out a knife.

'You're spoiling me.' She meant it. Hedgehog, the *hotchi-*

witchi of the gipsies, was a very good dish. They were rolled in the balls of clay now, and had been under the hot ashes for two hours. When the clay was broken open, the spines and skin would peel off with it. The meat was tender, the flavour superb.

Willie worked deftly. He had collected and washed some leaves of great burnet. These had the pleasant smell and taste of cucumber, and were to wrap the pieces of meat for eating.

It was a curious fact that if you gave Willie a larder full of food, an array of kitchen equipment and a modern cooker, he would produce an unrecognisable mess. But turn him loose in the woods with nothing, and he would contrive an appetising meal.

They ate in comfortable silence. 'That feels better,' she said at last, and passed him the *chagal*. 'Are you on foot, Willie?'

He shook his head. 'I only got to the cottage this afternoon. Saw the map an' drove 'ere. The car's twenty minutes away.'

She got up and went to wash her hands in the brook, then came back and stood looking down at him with wry humour. 'So we got jilted then.'

He nodded. 'Shook me a bit. I was all set to go respectable.' He paused. 'I think.'

'Me too. I was going to be made an honest woman of.' She sat down again, frowning. 'Well, I hadn't really decided. But if anyone was going to decide, I expected it to be me. That's natural, isn't it? I mean, I'm a vain bitch and I've never been given the old heave-ho before.'

She took the cigarette Willie had lit for her. 'The thing was, poor Steve got in such a tangle I found I was trying to help him out in the end. Everything he said kept sounding funny.' She suppressed a giggle, and looked surprised at herself. 'That's better. My wounded pride seems to be healing.'

'What did 'e say?'

'Well, he was rather fraught and very embarrassed but very determined. He said he loved me and so on, but he found

284

my way of life too exacting. He'd actually died six times while I was fighting Wenczel; and when he found I wasn't on the Skywagon after take-off, his brain fell down through his neck into his stomach. He said I wasn't just a woman, but an environment, a very harrowing environment, unfortunately. He knew the same sort of thing was bound to happen again, because I was incurably trouble-prone. And he simply couldn't face it any more.'

Again a little spasm of laughter touched her as she remembered. 'He was all pale and serious, but it sounded so funny. At least, I can see it was funny now.' Her voice took on something of Collier's intonation. 'He said that he was by nature a fragile spirit, ill-equipped for the no doubt stimulating exercise of walking hand in hand with the Grim Reaper and jumping clear just before he swung his scythe—don't you *dare* laugh, Willie!'

'Sorry, Princess. I could just 'ear Steve saying it.'

'Yes, I know. Well you can laugh a little bit. Anyway, the end of it was that he and Dinah had got together with a view to marriage, as they say. He loved her, in a different kind of way, and thought they'd suit each other very well, and hoped I didn't feel he was too much of a bastard. Now it's your turn. What did Dinah say?'

'Much the same. She cried a bit, so I 'ad to make it easy. Main thing was, she said I didn't need her. Not really *need* her. You know. And a girl has to be needed, she said. So that was it.'

'And what did you say?'

'I said she'd broken my 'eart and destroyed all my male confidence. That I'd probably end up in a monastery. That I'd never 'ave the nerve to get another girl, and the best I could expect was to throw a faint outside Holloway Gaol and 'ope one of the women police would try the kiss of life on me.' Willie sighed and squinted up at the sun. 'Come to think of it, she and Steve got pretty close during that time in Mus. They kind of saw each other through it.'

285

'Yes. The funny thing is, I told her to lean on Steve so he'd feel needed.'

'I told 'im to lean on Dinah for the same reason.'

'Ah, well.'

They were silent for a little while. It was an amiable silence, unshadowed by discontent. At last Modesty said, 'I've got a date in Panama sometime, but I don't feel like it just now. Too hot at this time of year.' She looked at him. 'Have you got any plans?'

'Nothing special.' He brooded. 'Suppose I opened a boutique? That's the thing now.'

She shook her head, smiling. 'Too many dollies. You'd only get yourself into a load of girl-trouble.'

'That's out, then. I'm not in the mood.' He pondered for a moment or two. 'We could go and dig up the treasure. If we gave it to the nation I reckon they'd make us both Life Peers.'

'It's a thought.' Her eyes were alight with laughter. 'But some other time, Willie.' She stubbed out her cigarette. 'What was that loot like? I remember you telling me you were driving out to bury it, but I couldn't be bothered even to look at the damn stuff before you drove off.'

'I wasn't much interested meself at the time,' he said soberly, 'and I only opened one crate. But it really took your breath away.' He sat up straight and began to fumble in his pocket. 'That reminds me. You dropped about eight thousand quid paying off Skeet Lowry, so I reckoned we ought to cover that.'

He held out his hand to her. On the palm glowed two huge and magnificent rubies, awesome in their beauty.

'My God . . .' she breathed, and was silent for long minutes as she held and studied the superb gems.

'That's all I took,' Willie said. 'One three-'undredth of the Garamantes jewels. Just to cover expenses.'

She looked up. 'But I already covered Skeet's pay-off.'

'Covered it?'

'Yes. I sold short on Presteign Holdings two days before we signed him off. Just over fifty thousand. They dropped twenty-five percent on news of his death. That left just enough after tax to pay Skeet and break even.'

Willie stared, then began to laugh. 'Just enough. No charge for labour. We must be slipping. What about the rubies?'

She handed them back to him. 'Set them in a pair of silver napkin rings and we'll give them to Dinah and Steve for a wedding present.'

'It'll be different, that's for sure.' He put the gems carelessly in his pocket. 'Got any plans yourself, Princess?'

'Plenty,' she said positively. 'I'm going to——' She broke off and looked at him uncertainly. 'Look, have you got a dolly lined up to help mend your broken heart?'

'No dolly.'

'Or plans for same?'

'No. Honest, Princess.'

'Then come on a shopping spree with me. I've had enough sweat and toil for a bit, so I'm going to have one hell of a spend in London, Paris and Rome. I'm going to buy some fabulous clothes. I'm going to walk into the top fashion houses with that pearl necklace you gave me, and I'm going to say, "Right, just show me something to stand up to *that*!" I'm going to have manicures and pedicures and hair-do's, and I'll probably have a daily bath in Guerlain's very latest perfume.'

She saw his face crease in a happy smile. Few men enjoyed fashion shows or female shopping. Willie Garvin revelled in both. The setting of a fashion show, the beanpole models parading along the catwalk in sometimes unbelievable clothes, the background music, and above all the extraordinary jargon of the commentary—this was a combination he found utterly hilarious.

'And here is Deirdre,' he murmured reverently, 'wearing a cute little fireman's helmet in shrimp straw, and the newest thing in wild silk bloomers of burnt sludge.'

He also enjoyed being present when Modesty was buying

clothes. She liked him to be there, because he had excellent taste and a remarkably good eye for style and colour. But when the mood took him he could cause chaos, pretending to be her husband and a temperamental French film director, her lover and an eccentric English nobleman; and, on one occasion, a bodyguard supplied by the Mafia.

'You'll have to behave yourself,' Modesty said. 'I'll never forget that poor little man in Paris bursting into tears and swallowing a pin.'

'I went out and got 'im six rounds of cottonwool sandwiches,' Willie said with mild protest. 'That's what you're supposed to eat if you swallow a pin.'

'You don't have to have mustard on them.' She knelt up, arching her back and stretching like a cat. The tensions which had driven her out on the long day's walk had dissolved and were gone. She felt good now. 'Let's be going, Willie love.'

He stood up, kicked earth over the ashes of the fire, then held out his hand and helped her to her feet.

She said, 'When we've had enough of the bright lights, we'll go to Tangier. It's lovely at the villa there around this time of year. We can just swim and laze.'

'I'll like that, Princess.' He picked up the empty *chagal* with his free hand, and together they began to walk down the hill beside the winding brook.